THE ABNORMALS

THE
ABNORMALS

BOOK
ONE

ISABELLE SORRELLS

First paperback edition 2021

Book cover design by Lance Buckley

ISBN: 978-1-7366928-0-6

Published by Amazon Direct Publishing

The adventure of a lifetime waits just beyond the horizon.
All you have to do is go there.

ONE

lex doesn't live what you would call a "normal" life. Up until he was ten years old he had been living in Jacksonville, where he had friends, a life, and a loving family. That was as close to a normal life he'd ever had. But one day, a month before his tenth birthday, his family changed. The people he lived with for nearly a decade underwent a transformation over the span of just a few days.

Parents that used to love him and treat him like the son he was started to treat him like an annoyance, a burden, a stranger they couldn't get rid of. He wasn't the only one who suffered. His family's friends were pushed away, and his parents lost their jobs. Everything he used to know fell apart before his eyes. Nothing made his parents happy anymore, they were never satisfied. By the time he was eleven his family was moving from town to town, state to state, never staying in one place long enough to put down roots. It hasn't changed since. So when Alex's father said the plan was to stay in Orolson for a while, Alex's normal response would be to roll his eyes and try to guess where they would end up next, placing bets with himself for how long they would last.

Orolson is the second greatest city in Florida, the first being Orlando, of course. Placed right on the east coast, it is a town thriving on the sea, attracting thousands of tourists year-round. This is what Alex considered himself now. He's never a resident, forever the tourist. Only staying in a place for as long as a tourist would. There and gone, never knowing anyone but those he lived with, never having a connection. It was a lonely existence, and Alex prayed to God every time they moved that his life would change. Perhaps that's why he didn't have his normal response this time. He had an unfamiliar feeling that his prayers had been answered, and that scared him.

"Alex, mom said you need to go to school now," Jessica said from the other side of the door.

"Okay, I'll go in a second," Alex called back, rolling his eyes. He pulled his arms into the sleeves of his black leather jacket, and just as he reached for the doorknob his eyes drifted over to the sheathed sword that rested against the wall. Memories threatened to pull him into a reverie, memories of a better time and a better place, but Alex didn't let them. He knew it would do no good to dwell on the past. Alex shook his thoughts away and grabbed the sword from its resting place, hiding it in his closet. Alex glanced at the few unpacked boxes that were filled with his belongings before turning back toward his bedroom door.

Alex's mother and father were yelling at him now, their shouts echoing through the walls of the house. Alex grabbed his backpack and ran out the door before his mother could scold him for taking forever to wake up.

By the time Alex got to his new school, it was still early and the teachers were still getting prepared for their classes. Not a single kid was in sight. One teacher in the parking lot ran out of his car with his arms full of papers toward the building, tripped over the door, and dropped all of the papers in his arms. He had brown hair and blue eyes and dorky brown glasses. He was dressed in a wrinkled brown suit and a striped tie. One elbow on his suit had a lighter patch of brown while the other had a darker brown patch. Alex ran over to the teacher and started to help pick up his papers from the pile scattered across the floor.

"Thank you very much, sir. I guess I wasn't paying attention to where I was going," the teacher hurriedly apologized as he quickly gathered the papers into a messy pile. Alex and the teacher finished picking up the papers and stood up. That's when the teacher got a good look at the person who helped him pick up his papers.

"You're not an adult...are you a student?" The teacher asked as he adjusted his glasses.

"Yes," Alex replied. "Is there a problem?"

"Uh...no. It's...really early for you to be at school isn't it?"

"Maybe. It's my first day and my mother didn't give me much information about the school. I just decided to come when my old school usually starts."

"What grade will you be entering?"

"Eighth."

"Hm."

The teacher cocked his head and stared for a moment, as if he was analyzing him. Suddenly his gaze shot toward the clock on the wall and he gasped. "Well, my name is Mr. Pandemonium. It was a pleasure meeting you, Alex. Thank you for your help, but I really must be going. The kids will be here in a few minutes, but I hope you have a great time here at Winston High!" The teacher shouted and waved as he ran down the hall and out of sight.

Alex cocked an eyebrow as he recalled his moments with the teacher. When did he tell him his name? Alex straightened his backpack and looked up at the clock that rested against the wall just above his head. Only a few more minutes before the kids would come pilling through those large metal doors. Alex didn't want to run out of time to explore so he took off in search of his locker.

He found it in one of the courtyards along five more rows of lockers. The courtyard was a large square area outside in the open. A roof hung over a concrete sidewalk in front of the lockers. Beyond the concrete was a small grass field. In the middle of the grass field were a few tables for people to eat lunch or hang out. The school had a blue theme to it with a lot of large windows that allowed sunlight to seep in and flood the school in bright light. The building was much larger than any other school Alex had gone to. There were five floors above ground and he had no idea how many underground levels there were. Everything around him looked almost brand new. Although it was a public school, no one would be surprised to find it was an exclusive private school. Without all of the students to occupy the halls, it seemed almost ghostly.

Alex slipped his headphones on to block out the uncomfortable and eerie silence of the empty building. He didn't have much time to explore the top and bottom floors before he heard the first bell ring and then heard thousands of screaming voices and pounding footsteps over his music.

Alex began walking in search of his homeroom but he didn't get too far until he found a group of older kids picking on a younger one. One of the older boys was leaning up against a locker with the other, younger boy's back up against it. He was cornering the younger one while the other boys were surrounding the two against the locker with a few spaces in between everyone in the surrounding circle.

Alex started to walk past them until his plans changed when the boy cornering the one against the locker lifted his fist. The boy with his fist raised began to laugh in a mocking fashion. The boy was about to throw the punch until Alex leapt in front of him and caught his fist in his hand with a grim expression.

3

"The strong are supposed to protect the weak, you know? Not beat them up," said Alex.

The boy stopped laughing and stared at his fist still clasped in Alex's hand, stunned. The younger boy took one look at the boy with his fist in Alex's hand before running away. Once the younger one disappeared around the corner, Alex let go of the boy's fist and shoved his hands in his jean pockets, resuming his walk toward his homeroom.

Meanwhile behind Alex, the older boy stood still with his fist hanging aimlessly in the air, waiting for a target that would never come. His eyes were opened wide, staring at his fist. His friends stood behind him motionless, as if they were stuck in time.

TWO

When Alex walked through his homeroom door, he was the fifth person to arrive. He walked over to the desk in the back corner closest to the windows, sat down, and stared out the window, waiting for the second bell to ring and the class to start. Alex watched in the reflection of the window as a group of four kids gathered around a desk in the middle of the room continued to talk about who knows what. One of the girls in the group glanced at Alex for a few seconds, and he quickly looked away. Alex could hear them but couldn't understand them because the room was getting so loud he could barely even hear his own music.

He had been trying so hard to focus on the music in his ears and tune out the noise in the room he didn't notice when the room went quiet. When he finally did realize it, he quickly ripped his headphones off.

"Good morning, everyone! I'm sorry I'm late. I had to run to the printer to retrieve a few things. Now, let's get started with attendance," Mrs. Greenberg announced.

Alex looked around the room for the first time and noticed it was a mix of purple and gray with posters and quotes from mathematicians, such as, "Pure mathematics is, in its way, poetry of logical ideas," by Albert Einstein, and, "All human evil comes from a single cause, man's inability to sit in a room," by Blaise Pascal.

Mrs. Greenberg called out Alex's name and Alex snapped his attention back to the teacher.

"Alex Schaffer?"

"Here," Alex replied.

"Oh, are you the new student?"

"That's right, ma'am," Alex said calmly.

A few kids snickered at how Alex addressed the teacher.

"Well, welcome to Winston! I hope you learn to fit in just fine." The teacher ignored the laughing students with a proud smile. The teens talked while Mrs. Greenberg finished work at her desk until it was time to say the pledge of allegiance. The class soon spun out of control. Even though some kids were simply sitting around and talking, other kids were running around the room and throwing paper airplanes and spitballs while pounding on desks and chanting.

After the announcements, Mrs. Greenberg stood up and started to teach the class algebra. When the bell finally rang, Alex grabbed his backpack and walked out the door, down the hall toward the stairs.

He was walking down the steps when suddenly loud and quick footsteps started pounding closer and closer. Out of the corner of his eye, he saw two boys behind him speed down the stairs laughing.

The boy in the lead had light, short brown hair in a classic cut and icy blue eyes. He was taller than Alex by more than a few inches and wore a blue short-sleeve shirt with the words—"I wish common sense was more common"—printed across. The boy behind him had short, wavy blond hair and jade green eyes. He wore a plain bright green hoodie underneath a dark green jean jacket and ripped jeans. Before the one in front could react, the one behind let out a loud yelp and tumbled down the steps head-first.

Mark and David walked out of the classroom with Brooke and Nicole at their heels, discussing the previous lesson.

"Hey guys, we'll see you at lunch, all right?" asked Brooke as they stopped before having to go their separate ways.

"Yeah! See you then!" David waved as Brooke and Nicole walked off down another hallway.

"I'll race you to our next class," said Mark as a sly smile formed on his lips.

"Yeah right, like you can beat me," replied David.

"See you there!" Mark exclaimed as he took off full speed toward the stairs.

Mark bounded down the steps with David close behind.

"Wait up! You're going way too fast!" David cried out as his foot tripped and he started tumbling head-first down the steps.

Just before he could hit the steps and tumble down, Alex leapt in front of him and caught him. He sat David down on the steps and asked if he was all right. David didn't say anything, only breathed heavily. Alex asked him again if he was all right.

"Yeah…. I'm fine. Thanks," David finally managed to say.

Mark had stopped running and was looking back at David and the strange kid that rescued him with his mouth agape.

"How…? Did you do that?" asked Mark.

"Do what?" Alex replied.

"Catch him like that! I didn't even see you move!" Mark said.

"You were just too busy running down the steps to pay attention to your surroundings," Alex told him.

Mark stared at Alex wide eyed. Alex turned back to David.

"Are you sure you're okay?" Alex asked. His tone was flat but his eyes betrayed his concern. Alex knew this kid from somewhere. He recognized his face. But from where?

"Are you in Mrs. Greenberg's math class first period?" Alex asked.

"Uh… yeah…. we both are," Mark answered.

"Well anyway, tie your shoe before you get up again," Alex said to David before continuing to walk down the stairs without another word.

Mark stared at the mysterious boy who had saved David. The boy wore a black leather jacket over a dark blue T-shirt. He had short, dark-brown, almost-black hair. He wore navy blue jeans and white and black Converse that went up to his ankles. The fabric of his shoes was dirty and torn as if he ran around all day to no end. His eyes were a mixed hazel color and slight bags could just barely be noticed under them. Around his neck rested a pair of old headphones that connected to a small Walkman attached to his belt. *Strange*, Mark thought, *I've never seen one of those before. I thought everyone used the new stuff nowadays.*

As Alex stepped down the rest of the stairs, he recalled seeing the two boys from his first-period class. They were among the group that had arrived before him. Alex strode into his second-period class and found a seat next to the door. As the bell rang, Alex sat down and Mr. Sherlock stood up and began talking.

After Mr. Sherlock gave the class a lecture on the Battle of Marathon and the bell rang, Alex was heading to english with Mrs. Antonio on the third floor for two periods. It took Alex a while to find his classroom, but he managed to find it before the bell rang. Her room was unusually colorful with books all over and covers of books pinned against the walls and windows.

For two whole periods, Mrs. Antonio talked about the author's purpose and text structure. She was probably one of the most boring teachers Alex had ever met. She had black hair and albino eyes, and she was wearing a white shirt and a gray pencil skirt. But there was something about Mrs. Antonio that separated her from the rest. Mrs. Antonio was expressionless. She never portrayed any emotion, and her facial expression barely changed. Her personality and looks certainly didn't match her classroom.

Finally, after four long periods of class, it was time for lunch. Alex went back to his locker and put his backpack inside. He brought nothing but his headphones to a loud and cramped cafeteria. Alex went outside to get away from the chaos and reclined on one of the hills in the school's large yard. He pulled his headphones over his ears and turned on his music, staring up at the sky. After a while, Alex heard footsteps and voices over his music. Alex sat up and found the two boys that he saw running down the stairs earlier standing over him along with the two girls who were talking with them during first period.

The first girl had long, wavy strawberry-blonde hair and sapphire eyes. She wore a gray sweater with a white shirt underneath. Her jeans were ripped, and she wore light brown military boots. Under her arm, she held a textbook. Her hands were stained with splotches of black. Alex assumed it was oil. The taller one wore a gray, red, and yellow V-neck Minnesota t-shirt and jorts. Her jet-black hair was tied up in a high ponytail, and her eyes were a mix of green and brown. She threw a baseball up and down in her right hand.

"Hey. My name is Marcus, but you can call me Mark," said the boy in the blue shirt by way of introduction. "You saved my friend earlier, and I just wanted to thank you. This is David in the green, the one you saved. Brooklyn in the grey, but you can call her Brooke, and Nicole in the Minnesota shirt. What's your name?"

"It's Alex."

"Are you new here?" Mark asked.

"Yeah, the teacher said that during first period," Alex replied.

"Nice headphones," said David.

"Thanks? Is there a purpose for this visit or… just what do you want?" Alex demanded. He felt this situation was getting a bit more than awkward and he wanted more than anything to leave it.

"Well…we just wanted to say thanks for catching David earlier. He could have gotten hurt if it weren't for you," explained Mark.

"You're welcome. But you shouldn't be running down the stairs in the first place," Alex replied, standing up.

The four stood awkwardly and glanced around them anxiously at the other teenagers loitering around the yard. He was slightly confused for a moment until he looked around. A bunch of kids scattered in groups were staring at the group and giggling.

"Oh, so that's what this is. A joke," Alex muttered to himself. He should have been angry. Furious even. But he was calm as he brushed by David and Nicole and walked off.

"Have a good day!" Alex called bitterly.

Alex pulled his headphones over his ears and clicked the cassette player on. He kept walking. Not turning back.

"Hold up! Alex!" Mark called after him.

Mark wanted to go and see what was wrong, but his feet wouldn't move. It felt as if his feet were rooted to the ground. All he could do was watch Alex walk away.

Alex walked over to his locker and grabbed his backpack. He slammed the locker shut and made for his next class. He arrived before the period was done, so he sat outside the door waiting for the bell to ring.

The bell rang and kids from the next grade up started pouring out of Mr. Smith's classroom. None of them noticed the kid sitting on the floor next to the door, lost in his music. Once everyone was out of the classroom, Alex went inside and sat in the corner next to the window. The rest of that day dragged on, barely managing to drag Alex along with it.

He found himself relieved that he would be ending the day with art. He wasn't the most gifted artist, but he enjoyed it all the same. Alex stepped inside to see his teacher greeting the students. Alex could see easels and tables with clay on them and colored pencils and acrylic paint and pastels and so many other materials scattered all over the room. This was the first class he's been in that didn't have a bunch of seats in straight rows. Instead, there were a bunch of tables covered in paint from projects with permanent materials. Alex looked out the window to see a few kids playing outside and one of the janitors mowing the yard. Alex went over and found a seat next to the closet near to the door and watched as kids started piling in. Four more students in particular walked in.

Mark looked around the classroom for an empty table seat and saw Alex. His eyes grew wide as the two made eye contact. Alex looked away. Mark sighed, and he and his friends walked to an empty table in the middle of the room.

When the day was finally over, Alex rushed out the door and started for home, eager to get away before Mark or his friends could meet up with him. He didn't resent them. He just wasn't very fond of drama.

THREE

Alex was by the parking lot as he heard someone behind him call his name.

"Alex! Alex, wait up!"

Alex turned around just in time to see Mark, David, Brooke, and Nicole run up to him and double over, gasping for breath.

"Here to make fun of the new kid again?" Alex asked calmly.

"What? We aren't making fun of you," David gasped in between breaths.

"Then what do you call that stunt you pulled during lunch?" Alex asked.

"Um, introductions?" Mark said as he sat down on the grass.

"Look," interrupted Nicole. "We got off on a wrong start. Let's re-try this, shall we?"

"Fine by me," Alex said with a sigh.

"Awesome!" said David. "So. Where are you going?"

"Home. Where else?" Alex asked. "These people get comfortable way too quickly," Alex mumbled to himself.

"Well…," Mark turned and looked at everyone and they all nodded their heads.

"What?" Alex asked skeptically.

"You should come hang out with us! It'll be fun!" David smiled broadly.

Alex thought for a minute and during that time no one spoke. They all held their breath for his answer.

"Sure. It's not like I have anything better to do," Alex said thinking that they probably wouldn't leave him alone so he might as well cooperate with them.

The group of four started walking and Alex followed them, wondering where they were leading him. As they walked, Alex got lost in thought. His father wouldn't take it kindly if he heard Alex was hanging out with other kids. But he didn't have to know, did he? If he was late, he could just say he had gotten lost as an excuse. New town. Different roads. It is definitely a possibility.

David interrupted Alex's thoughts.

"We're here," David said.

Alex looked up from the ground and around the place they had led him to: a park next to the beach along the ocean surrounded by trees with a few picnic tables in the grass.

Alex and the others put their backpacks over on one of the picnic tables and went to sit on some of the swings.

"So, do you guys have a dock for cargo ships going out to sea here?" Alex asked.

"Sure do! We'll have to take you some time!" David said as he swung.

"Since you just moved here, we can take you around town and help you get familiar with the area," Mark offered.

"We can introduce you to our city. You up for it?" asked Nicole

"I'm sure I'd be bored out of my mind if I didn't anyways," Alex smirked.

The four of them talked together about school and other things until twilight when they all had to go home. They all walked home together until Alex was the last one walking, since his house was the farthest away. He couldn't believe it. He actually had friends.

Alex reached out to open the door, but his hand froze on the handle. No, he can't have friends. He'd just be in the way. What were his parents going to think? He hadn't done his chores and the sun was already setting. Maybe he could sneak in his window and act as if he had been in his room the whole time. No, that wouldn't work. Before he could think about anything else, the door flew open.

"Alex! Where have you been?"

There, stood his father in the door. He was furious.

"There are chores to be done! Why were you out so late? You should have been home six hours ago!"

"I'm sorry. It won't happen again, I promise," Alex lied. "I got lost."

"I don't want to hear it! Get to work on your chores!"

"Yes, father," Alex said.

Alex finished his chores then trudged up the stairs. He pulled his jacket off and flung it on the floor. He flopped down on his bed and looked at the alarm clock on the floor. In bright red letters it read, "11:30." Alex pulled his headphones over his ears and stared at the ceiling, going over the past day's events. His chores had taken much longer than he had expected and he was exhausted. It wasn't long before Alex fell fast asleep.

FOUR

'*Beep...beep...beep...*'– Alex woke with a start, realizing that it was morning and he had accidentally fallen asleep. Alex jumped out of bed and smacked the button on top of his cracked alarm clock, eager to make the annoying sound stop, and quickly dressed himself. He pulled his jacket on, covering the fresh bruises on his arms, and grabbed his backpack before running downstairs and out the door while his father yelled something after him. Something, he did not hear.

Bruises were a fact of Alex's life. No matter how hard Alex tried he could never please his father. Alex's performance and behavior at home were often met with anger—and violence. His father ordered Alex daily to do a long list of time-consuming and exhausting chores, from military-style cleaning of the premises to house repairs and maintenance that would typically require a paid contractor. It didn't matter whether Alex did a good job or not. His father, often drunk on beer and other forms of alcohol, would insult and sneer at Alex, taunting him and frequently grabbing him or pushing him to the point of Alex becoming bloody and bruised. All the while, Alex's mother and sister would sit back and watch the show with a wicked grin of satisfaction plastered across their faces, only ever stepping in to throw another insult or a slap across the face.

Alex was already around the corner by the time his father finished yelling. Alex continued running until he saw the towering walls of the school ahead of him. He was early...again. Alex stepped in through the door to find a vast, deserted school. Instead of going to his locker or his classes, Alex decided to check out the underground levels. He only had time to check out the first underground floor, but he did find out that all the extracurricular activities took place down there and that some of the janitors' offices and supply rooms were there.

Alex looked at the clock. Only five more minutes until the bell rang. Alex went up the stairs to ground level to find Mark, David, Nicole, and Brooke coming around the corner. Brooke spotted Alex first.

"Oh hey, Alex!" she shouted.

"Hey!" Alex shouted back.

They walked up to him and David asked, "How long have you been here?"

"About twenty minutes. Why?"

"Why are you at school so early?" asked Mark.

"Why not?" Alex asked.

"Never mind. Do you want to walk with us to first period?" asked Nicole.

Alex nodded.

The group had decided to meet up during lunch and talk about their plans for after school. The rest of that morning went by like a blur, and before Alex knew it, it was time for lunch. Alex walked up to the hill where the five of them first met and lay down, staring at the clouds, waiting for the rest of them to arrive. They arrived minutes later. Alex's ears perked up beneath his headphones at the sound of their footsteps approaching. He waited until they all sat down on the grass around him until he finally pulled his headphones off and acknowledged them.

"So, what's the destination for today, hmm?" Alex asked.

"The docks. You were curious about it before so we thought it was a good idea to take you there first," said Brooke.

"While we're there we are going to take you to this great place called the Shack," Nicole added.

"What's the Shack?" Alex asked, furrowing his brow.

"It's only the best ice cream place ever!" Nicole threw her hands up in the air to exaggerate her point.

Alex lay back down to look at the clouds as his friends pulled out their lunches. Mark watched Alex before joining him on the grass.

The others soon joined Mark and Alex, watching the clouds change and move into different shapes until the bell rang and it was time to go to their next class.

The rest of that afternoon went by slowly like a snail trying to get across a continent. So when the final bell rang, Alex was the first one out the door. He walked up to one of the empty bike racks and leaned against them, waiting for everyone else to get out. While he was waiting, he looked up and saw someone on the roof. Alex squinted to try and see what the person was doing until he realized someone else was there as well. What Alex saw made his heart skip a beat in fright. As he stared up at the roof, he witnessed two figures, one of them pushing the other off the roof.

"Come on. Please, Steven! Why are you doing this?" Jim asked frantically as he walked backwards, desperately trying to get away from Steven. What was his friend doing?

"Really? You have to ask? A wimp like you doesn't belong in this world," Steven slowly cracked a smile. For a fraction of a second, his eyes flashed as though a bright fire burned within them, before turning back to normal.

Jim jumped and fell to the ground out of fright.

Suddenly, Steven stopped and threw his head back, laughing maniacally. Jim started to crawl backwards until his back hit something. Jim turned around to find the edge of the roof behind him. His eyes widened as he slowly turned around to see Steven standing right in front of him still laughing. What was going on? This wasn't Steven! The Steven he knew never acted this way! They were best friends!

"You. Are. Dead!" Steven whispered in his ear evilly before grabbing Jim by the shirt and lifting him up, over the side of the roof.

Alex dropped his backpack and ran inside the building. He dashed past Mark and the others but didn't have time to stop and explain. He continued to run up the stairs toward the roof, desperate to get there before it was too late.

"Where are you going?" Mark called after Alex but he didn't stop.

"Let's follow him. It looked like something was wrong," David suggested.

They began to run after him. They had gotten up three floors and were just about to reach the top when they all stopped in their tracks. A blood-curdling scream pierced the air. Alex pushed onward. He reached the fourth floor and slammed open the door to the roof. A strong cold wind greeted him. To his right, at the very edge of the roof, a boy hung over the side in another boy's strong grip, struggling uselessly against his offender.

Steven turned his head to the side slightly and his pupils traveled to the corner of his eyes. Behind him, he could see a kid in a leather jacket burst from the roof door. Alex. His smile grew wider at the success of his bait. Jim stared at him with wide eyes, filled with fear and confusion. *Why does Steven seem happier now that someone has come to the rescue?* Jim thought. *Unless, they aren't here to rescue me.* Jim began to squirm relentlessly in his best friend's grip. Since when had Steven gotten so strong? He looked down beneath his dangling feet. He could see thousands of teens pouring out of the school doors and scattered about the field, all oblivious to what was happening above their heads.

Steven wasn't aware of what he was doing to his best friend. He and Jim had just gone up to the roof to finish a project. It was his idea too, or at least, he thought it was his idea. He had no way of knowing that it was someone else's. He didn't know he was going to be dragged into a cruel plan to lure another into a test. He began to loosen his grip on his best friend, all the while unaware of his actions.

Alex dashed forward, he was only a few feet away. His eyes widened in horror as he saw the grip around the poor victim's neck loosen. He flung out his arm in an attempt to grab the kid before he let go, but, he was too late. The boy let go of the other, sending him to a perilous death.

At the same time, Alex slammed the heel of his palm against Steven's shoulder angrily. Steven was sent sprawling across the roof from the force of the blow. In one swift movement Alex leaned over the side and latched onto Jim's hand before he could fall any further. He immediately began to pull the boy up, both of them latching onto each other tightly. Alex jerked Jim up and over the side of the roof, sending them both flying backwards onto the hard concrete.

Alex quickly stood up in search for Steven but found him to be nowhere in sight. Alex glanced at the door in case he had gone that way, only to find his friends standing there, open-mouthed and wide-eyed. Alex turned back to the boy and held out his hand for him. Jim hesitantly took it and Alex helped him to his feet. The boy had tousled dark brown hair with blonde highlights. He wore a blue sweater over a white T-shirt and jeans. The knees of his jeans were torn and speckled with dirt from the roof. His hands had small scratches that bled slightly. He was taller than Alex by a few inches with a slightly more agile appearance.

"Are you hurt?" Alex asked as Jim dusted himself off.

Jim looked up at Alex to respond but found that no words would come out. Instead, a small squeak broke through before he was thrown into a coughing fit. When he was finished he brought his shaking hands up to his throat. Around his neck were fresh bruises shaped like a hand.

"I'll take you to the nurse," Alex said. "Can you walk?"

The boy nodded. Alex led Jim over to the door of the roof. His friends had recovered and rushed to Alex's side.

David and Brooke walked down the steps in front of Jim, and Mark and Nicole walked behind him while Alex walked next to him. When they finally arrived, they escorted Jim to one of the spare beds and watched as the nurse handed him a bottle of water. After she extracted his name from him, she left to retrieve bandages for his hands.

"Who was that?" Alex asked Jim after he took another sip of his water.

"That's my best friend, Steven. I don't know why he was trying to kill me. We were just going to finish an assignment. He began to act strange. It wasn't him. He has always been a kind person. It was almost as if someone was controlling him, he didn't know what he was doing. Steven would never do something like that!" Jim ranted. "Now that I think about it, he did have a strange collar around his neck that I've never seen before," he mumbled.

"Did he have any reason to do that to you?" Nicole asked. She was leaning against the wall next to the door, and everyone looked up at her as she spoke.

"No!" Jim shouted at her but his voice cracked. "Did you hear what I just said? It wasn't him! He's my friend! He would never do that to anyone!"

Before they could ask any more questions, the nurse walked through the door with disinfectant and bandages. They all shut their mouths as she entered, unsure if they should tell anyone. Jim quickly covered the bruises on his neck with the collar of his shirt. The nurse began to tend to his hands as the five of them walked out. Alex turned toward Jim to say one final goodbye. Jim looked up at him and mouthed the words, *don't tell anyone*. Alex nodded to his request before turning and leaving the room.

When they finally made their way back out of the building's huge double doors and onto the streets, almost everyone had left. The only ones left were a few groups of kids skateboarding on the steps and curb. They made their way to the bike rack where Alex dropped his backpack. All of the bikes that had been chained to the bars before were gone.

"Do you really think Jim was telling the truth?" Brooke asked as Alex scooped his bag off the ground. "Or do you think he was too shocked by his friend's betrayal to believe the reality that was playing out before him?"

"The more important question is where did Steven go?" Nicole asked.

"Did you see him leave the roof?" Mark asked.

"No. He was just... gone," Alex replied.

They all stood in silence, lost in thought. Where had Steven gone? Did he fall over the edge? Did he run when they weren't looking? Did he find another way out? Was he really aware of what he was doing and did he truly have the intention to kill his best friend? These were the thoughts that swam around in their heads.

"Well, it doesn't matter anymore. Jim is safe and Steven is gosh knows where," David blurted suddenly. His voice was bright and cheerful. He wrapped his arms around Alex and Nicole's shoulders and looked to each of his friends. "Now I don't like silence very much, as you all know. What do ya say we head over to the docks?"

They laughed briskly before falling into another uncomfortable silence. Alex followed them as they made their way out of the parking lot and into the street.

FIVE

lex followed them down a wooden boardwalk at the very edge of the water. It was littered with fisherman shops and separate decks that jutted out into the water like little peninsulas. Small boats and yachts were tied to cleats along the sides of the dock. Farther down the docks were much bigger boats; freighters, large fishing boats, and cargo ships. A few stores down they came across a small wooden shack with the words, *The Ice Cream Shack* written across the top in white letters outlined with red. A triple scoop of pink, white, and brown ice cream was melting on the *C* of *Cream*. A small family was departing as they walked up to the window.

After they paid for their ice cream they walked over to a strip of the port that was farther from the freighters and bigger boats and separate from all the canoes and smaller boats. No one used it because the waves were too rough and the freighters were on the other side of the port. The only reason the dock was still there was because no one thought it was worth their time to knock it down, according to Nicole.

"Here, let's sit on the edge." Nicole pointed toward the end of the dock.

Once they finished their ice cream, they placed their garbage on the wooden planks, sitting and staring off in the distance in silence.

"Thanks for bringing me here," said Alex.

"No problem. But there's still one more thing we need to do," said Mark as he stood up and began walking toward Alex. A mischievous smile slowly crawled across his face.

"Oh yeah?" Alex asked, cocking an eyebrow and standing up to meet Mark. He was slightly worried by his friend's comment and expression but hid his concerns. "What's that?"

"This!" Mark shouted as he lunged at Alex. Alex's eyes widened as his mind went over endless scenarios. Mark grabbed Alex by the arms and threw the both of them off the dock into the ocean. The others followed after them, jumping off the dock and laughing. Alex floated there in the water's depths for a while, looking above at the water's surface and at the kicking feet of his friends and the bubbles forming around them. The evening light shone through the surface and lit up the bubbles their constant movement created. Alex burst up to the surface to join them.

"Alex! You scared us! We thought you drowned! Don't do that!" Brooke slapped her hand against Alex's shoulder angrily.

"Why were you scared? I was just down there for a few minutes!" Alex protested, rubbing the spot on his shoulder where Brooke had slapped him. She was much stronger than she looked.

"Because we're your friends! We're supposed to be scared when you suddenly disappear beneath the water!" said Mark.

"We? Are... friends?" Alex asked slowly, as if processing the information. He really wanted them to be his friends, but he wasn't sure if they felt the same way.

"We are, aren't we?" David asked.

"Yeah," Alex replied quietly. "I guess we are."

They splashed around in the water for hours until the sun began to lower. They all walked home soaking from head to toe, leaving the pavement dark and damp in their wake. The house was asleep by the time Alex arrived home late that night. He quickly and quietly dashed up the steps and into his room, changing out of his drenched clothes into dry ones. He immediately got to work on his chores, not wanting to wake up to his father's screaming voice the next morning.

When Alex finished his chores, he took his jacket into the bathroom to dry. He rubbed a towel on the fabric, but he was unable to remove all of the water. He grabbed his sister's hair dryer, which worked to some degree. By the time he finished drying the jacket and towel, and taken a shower, he only had five minutes before he had to get up for school. Where had all the time gone? He was walking down the hallway with his jacket in hand, when he was startled.

"Alex! What are you doing home so late?"

His dad was awake. How could he have been so careless? He should've known better than to make so much noise. His father stepped out of the doorway of his bedroom into the hallway where Alex was standing.

"I'm sorry, Father, I was out with friends and it got late—."

"Friends? Friends!" Alex's father cut him off. "You don't have time for friends!"

"Look. I'm sorry, but I got my chores done and it's been a long day. Can I just go to bed?" Alex pleaded. "For the five minutes I have left?" Alex mumbled the last part.

"Don't you dare talk back to me!" Mr. Shaffer raised his arm above his head and paused in mid-air before dropping it at full speed, directly in line with its target.

Beep. Beep. Beep.

The alarm in Alex's bedroom interrupted him before he could slap Alex. They both looked from one another to the suspended hand and the alarm clock. Alex's father dropped his hand to his side and sighed. *Saved by the bell,* Alex thought.

"Tsk. Go turn that blasted alarm off. We are not done here!" Mr. Shaffer growled as he walked back to his room and slammed the door.

Alex returned to the bathroom once he was dressed again and splashed his face with water. He was so tired. The bags that were usually under his eyes from exhaustion were darker. Alex had to turn his music up all the way to keep himself from collapsing onto the sidewalk from lack of sleep. Alex arrived with only ten minutes to spare. He dragged himself across the parking lot and plopped himself down beneath a tree, closing his eyes. Maybe he could catch a little sleep before school started.

After Alex sat down, he felt a hand slowly creep onto his shoulder. His shoulders tensed as he jumped up and spun around to find his friends standing behind the tree, staring at him with startled expressions.

"Oh, hey. It's just you," Alex sighed and allowed his shoulders to slump.

"Yeah, just us. Why is your music so loud? I could hear your music at the other end of the parking lot!" Mark said sarcastically.

"Seriously, though, you're going to go deaf one of these days and you won't be able to listen to music at all anymore," Brooke warned.

"If I was going to go deaf that would have happened a long time ago," Alex replied. "Come on, the other kids will be here soon."

"What do we have for ninth period today?" David asked no one in particular.

"What do you mean?" Alex asked.

"Since you have ninth period with us every day we'll have a different class for ninth period. On Mondays we have art. Today we'll have home ec. with Mrs. Finch," Nicole explained.

"You'll have to take me with you because I have no idea where that is," Alex replied.

"We kinda figured," Mark smirked.

The rest of the school day went by fast though Alex was struggling to keep himself awake. He was doing fine up until last period because all the teacher did was talk about diseases and what can and can't kill you. Since she didn't give the class anything to do and did nothing but talk, Alex fell fast asleep. Next thing he knew he woke up to a loud snapping sound of a ruler against a table and the teacher glaring daggers at him.

"Do you think what I'm teaching is boring Mr. Shaffer? Do you think you are too good for my class, Mr. Shaffer? If so, the door is over there," yelled Mrs. Finch as she pointed toward the door with the end of her ruler.

"No, ma'am, I do not, and I'd rather stay in this class if you don't mind, ma'am," Alex replied, sitting up as straight in his seat as he could, resulting in a few giggles from the kids around him.

"Thank you. Now please pay attention. I don't want to have to talk to you again!" Mrs. Finch snapped as she walked back to the front of the classroom.

"Hey, Mark," David whispered into Mark's ear after the teacher continued the lesson, never taking his eyes off their barely conscious friend. "What do you think is wrong with Alex? He seems out of it today!"

"I don't know," Mark whispered back. "He fell asleep in some of our morning classes too! Maybe we kept him up too late last night."

After the bell rang, Alex forgot to wait for the others and made his way outside without them. His foot barely hit the last step before his head began to spin.

"Are you all right Alex? You look tired," said a voice behind him. Alex turned around lazily to find Nicole and the others standing at the top step.

"Yeah, I'm fine. I didn't get the chance to go to bed last night, and I went to bed really late the other night," Alex replied.

"Do you want to just go home? We don't have to go out today," David suggested.

"Yeah, I'm sorry. I'm really tired," Alex sighed.

"See you tomorrow then?" Mark asked.

"See you tomorrow," Alex mumbled before pulling his headphones over his ears.

"It's too bad. I really wanted to take him to that place today," David grumbled.

"It's strange though, isn't it? We left the port right at sundown. What was he doing for the rest of the night that kept him from sleep?" asked Brooke.

"I think he does it a lot. Whatever it is. He always has circles under his eyes," David pointed out. "Video games maybe?"

"I don't know. He doesn't seem the type to play video games. But then again it's not really any of our business," replied Nicole.

"Let's just head home for the day. I've got to make more lunches for the family this week," Mark said before they all went their separate directions for home.

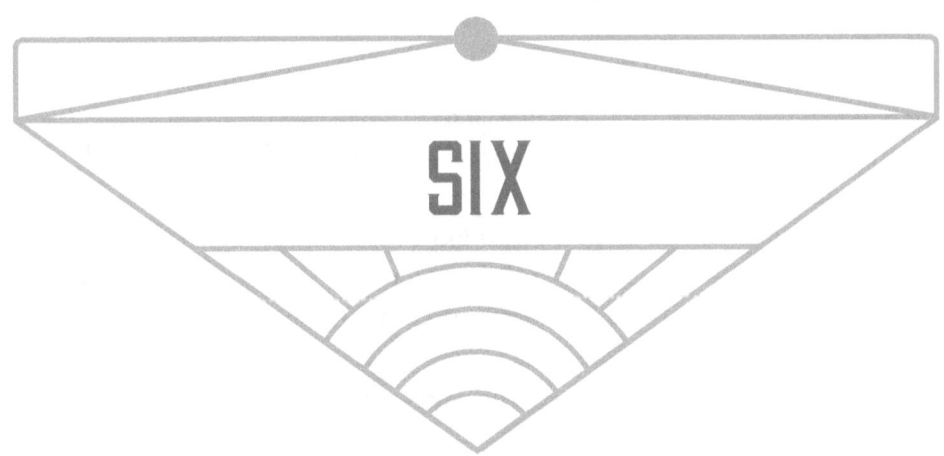

SIX

Being tired and not sleeping well for the last two days was not the only reason Alex was so weak for the past day. He was usually able to go a long time without sleep, but he also hadn't eaten in four days so that added to the sleepless nights, unless one counted an ice cream cone as a meal.

Alex walked into his house to find it empty. He wandered into the kitchen and found a note on the refrigerator.

It read, "Alex, we have gone on a camping trip with your sister and will be back in two weeks, Monday night. Do your chores. From, Mother."

Alex tossed the note into the garbage and began scouring the cupboards for food. After he ate, he found some food for his lunch the next day and tossed it into a paper bag. Once that was finished, Alex slowly trudged up the stairs and flopped onto his bed, not moving for the rest of the night.

When Alex got to school the next morning, he found the others waiting for him by the entrance. They all let out a breath of relief after seeing the circles under their friend's eyes completely disappeared and his complexion much less pale.

"Good morning, Alex. Are you feeling better?" Mark asked.

"Yeah, I feel great. And refreshed after going to bed so early," Alex said.

"So we can go out today?" asked Brooke.

"Yeah. Where do you wanna go?" Alex asked.

"We. Are. Going to…DUN, DUN, DUN! The boardwalk! There's this awesome miniature amusement park over there on the end of it that is so much fun!" David answered quickly before taking another bite of a breakfast bar.

"But we might be there for a while. Usually when we go it lasts late into the night if that's okay with you," added Mark.

"That's good," Alex said. "My family went camping and won't be back until next Monday."

"Wait, why'd your family go on a camping trip without you?" asked Mark.

"Not a fan of camping," Alex lied, waving off the question. He actually had never gone camping so he had no idea if he liked it or not.

Later that day, during lunch Alex went up on the usual hill and ate his meal, waiting for the others to come join him.

"Wow! You really are hungry!" Brooke laughed from behind Alex.

"Can you guys stop sneaking up on me?" Alex asked, biting the last bit of his sandwich.

"What would be the fun in that?" Mark asked as he sat down in front of Alex along with the others.

"What's over there?" Alex changed the subject, nodding questioningly toward a big patch of trees so thick that it went past the school's boundaries and throughout town.

"That's just the woods," said Nicole. "We aren't allowed in there. There are a lot of wild animals and since it's so thick you can barely see more than a few feet ahead of you."

When Alex went outside after school that day while waiting for his friends, his gaze drifted over to the woods, wondering what made the woods so thick and imagining what other things could be in there besides wild animals.

As Alex gazed, his friends came out of the doors deep in conversation. Mark stopped contributing to the conversation when he caught Alex staring at the woods in a daze, oblivious to the world around him. In a panic, Mark jogged down the steps and waved his hands wildly in a cutting motion in front of him. Once the others realized what was going on, they rushed behind him.

"Nope! Nope, nope, nope, nope, nope! *NO! N-O!*" Mark shouted as he walked toward Alex from behind. "I know what you're thinking and *N-O.*"

"No, what?" Alex asked after he recovered from the shock of Mark's suddenly loud voice interrupting his thoughts.

"Don't even think about it!" Mark shouted.

"Think about what?" Alex asked.

"You know what I know that you know!" Mark yelled.

"Know what? For God's sake, out with it!" Alex shouted back, more than irritated at Mark's strange behavior.

"Don't go in there, you got it?" Brooke demanded.

"Okay, okay! I got it! I won't go in there. I wasn't planning on it," Alex replied, throwing his hands up in the air in defense. "Can we just go already?" Alex rolled his eyes and started walking ahead of them but stopped. "I think you should go first."

"Good idea! I don't think you know where you're going," David said as he patted Alex's back roughly.

The sun was already going down by the time the five of them got there. When they finally got to the boardwalk, Alex stopped in his tracks. He had never seen a place so full of people before. Buildings that lined the street towered over them. On the left side of the street was the beach where multiple sculptures and playgrounds stood. On the right side was a never-ending row of stores and shops and restaurants lit up with brilliant colors. In the far-off distance they could see the top half of a ferris wheel poking above the buildings along with a few rollercoaster tops. Thousands of people littered the street, going in and out of the buildings and running along the beach.

"Wow," Alex gasped.

"Yeah and we haven't even gotten to the amusement park yet!" David smiled excitedly.

The world seemed to be filled with a strange but joyous aura. A warm light coated everything it touched and warmed the hearts of anyone it touched, inviting them to come and stay there for as long as they wanted. Alex found it slightly frightening and overwhelming.

"Come on! There are a bunch of stores and other awesome places on the way that you need to see!" Nicole waved them onward as she rushed in the crowd. Although he was still unsure, Alex followed his friends deeper into the cluster of people.

"This place is so crowded that we could lose each other in an instant! If we ever get lost, meet up at the ferris wheel, got it?" Mark shouted over the roar of the crowd.

"Got it!" The teens shouted in unison.

"Come on! I have the perfect place where we can start!" Mark shouted.

They followed Mark until he slowed to a stop in front of a comics shop. He opened the door and Alex went inside to find the store filled with boxes and shelves filled with comics. Along the shelves, lights on strings were strung that lit up the shelf in yellow light and more of the same string was draped across the ceiling. Above the shelves were signs taped to the wall with superheroes and their names on the wall. Below them were sections of that superhero.

"Alex, come here!" David called from the other end of the store.

Alex looked over to see David standing by a shelf that said 'Captain America.'

"Check these out. Jim Lee did Captain America for a while. He's an amazing artist."

David showed Alex a comic that said 'Captain America Lives Again' but Alex didn't have enough time to look through it before Mark called him over to check out a Batman comic. Mark ended up getting a bag full of comics, and David left with a few Captain America.

After they left the store, it was David's turn to choose the next place they were going to go.

They ended up at an arcade and played tons of games including laser tag and Pac-man. Afterwards, it was Brooke's turn to choose.

Brooke led them to a little shop where she picked an image of some sort and the artists would spray-paint it onto a hat or shirt or some other type of clothing. Brooke picked a purple hat with her name sprayed on it like graffiti.

When it was time for Nicole to choose they went to a sports shop and she purchased a soccer ball, saying that they'd find out what it was for when the time came.

Finally, it was Alex's turn to choose. Mark and the others were all making suggestions but, none of them sounded interesting. Alex was about to ask them to choose for him but then he saw it.

"Over here!" Alex called as he took off into another store.

"Yo! You have to wait for us! Alex!" David called as they chased after him.

He broke out in a sprint and dashed out of the middle of the crowd and to a bookstore called Boardwalk Books. Alex walked in to find the store filled with books from top to bottom with so many books that you could barely get around the store without running into a bookshelf or knocking a stack of books down.

Nicole walked in, followed by the others to find Alex sitting against a bookshelf reading an action adventure called Sorrowline with a few more books piled up next to him.

"Wow… you are fast," Mark gasped.

Alex didn't respond.

"Earth to Alex! Hello? Anyone home?" David asked as he waved his hand into Alex's face.

"Huh? What did you say?" Alex placed a finger in the book and looked up at his friends. "Sorry, I didn't hear you."

"If you like that book so much why don't you get it?" David asked.

"I am. Along with these other books: *Ferals, The Last Thing I Remember, Leven Thumps and The Gateway To Foo, and Fahrenheit 451*," Alex replied.

"Wow… that's a lot!" Mark said.

"Says the guy who left the comic store with a bag full of comics!" David pointed out.

"So did you!" Mark countered.

"Yes, but I'm not picking on Alex for getting only four books, am I?" David asked teasingly.

"Touché," Mark replied.

"Come on! Go pay so we can go to the main event!" David urged, pulling Alex up from the ground.

"Main event?" Alex asked as he walked to the counter to pay.

"Amusement park!" Brooke exclaimed, grabbing Alex by the arm and pulling him out into the boardwalk. They all started running and before long Alex lost them in the crowd. Now that it was later at night, more people started to show up making the streets more jam-packed. Alex headed for the ferris wheel in order to meet up with them again, in hopes that they would be there.

Alex finally came up to a big bundle of tents and buildings of what he assumed was the amusement park. Alex looked around and found the others leaning up against the side of a building just outside the park, trying to catch their breath.

"I lost you a while back. Sorry about that," Alex called as he ran up to them.

"Oh. We thought you were behind us the whole time," said Mark.

"We are glad you are with us now," Nicole said. "Now, let's go!" Nicole grabbed Alex's arm and dragged him into the park.

Once they got inside, the amusement park seemed bigger than it looked from the outside. In front of them was a big crane with some seats attached that would bring the riders swinging about wildly through the air. To their right was a fantastic roller coaster and to their left was a waterslide. Beyond those they could see the lights of countless other attractions. Since it was dark, the amusement park was ten times better because all of the lights were as bright as could be.

"All right, guys, listen up!" said Mark. "Let's all pick a ride of our own before we do the ferris wheel."

"Let's just go already! I'm dying of excitement!" said David. "I'll choose first! To the Spider, everyone!" David cried as he took off running.

The Spider was a big pole going straight up and splitting into twenty different seats that would spin its riders around while bobbing them up and down. The group sat in one seat, since each seat held five, and started moving. At first the ride started slowly while moving up slowly and then all of a sudden it stopped.

In the large bench that held the five on with a single metal bar, Alex was on one end while Nicole was on the other. Mark was sitting next to Alex, while David was sitting next to him with Brooke sitting between David and Nicole.

Alex looked down and found that they were only a fourth of the way up and still had quite a ways to go. All of a sudden with no warning whatsoever the ride started moving at full speed up and around, spinning in circles toward the top. People in the other benches were screaming their heads off.

When the ride ended, Mark, Brooke, David, and Nicole were practically falling over each other they were so dizzy. Alex helped walk them each to a bench where they sat down and tried to regain focus.

"Alex, aren't you going to sit down?" asked Brooke as she bent over squeezing the bridge of her nose.

"Nah. My legs were sort of crushed between Mark and the side of the bench so I'm just going to stand," Alex said.

"You're not dizzy?" asked David while laughing hysterically.

"Not too much. Are you all right?" Alex replied.

"Wow. You must be hard to break," Mark observed. "I bet we can make you dizzy or throw up by the end of the day."

"If that's the case, I'll chose next. To the rocket!" Nicole exclaimed.

"Wow, you really are unbreakable," Mark gasped after they had ridden every dizzying ride in the park.

"We all chose our rides, so let's go on the ferris wheel now!" said David impatiently.

"Okay, okay let's go!" said Nicole as she started walking toward the ferris wheel.

When it was their turn, Alex and the others climbed into a blue carriage with designs on it that resembled a circus. The carriage went up and up until it stopped three carriages before the top. The view was breathtaking.

They could see the whole boardwalk, all of its lights and all of the people. They were there for a good ten minutes before the operator brought them down.

Everyone had finally gone home and Alex was the last one left, walking alone in the darkness to his house. As he walked he heard a voice whisper through the darkness.

"Alex," the voice whispered.

Alex looked around to find a silhouette of a young man between two houses in the shadows pointing to him. Alex started to hurriedly walk away, but the silhouette stretched his hand toward Alex.

"Heed this warning. Watch your back. Many people think they know what you are capable of. In reality they can just barely see the glint of the tip of the iceberg hidden behind the fog. But they want what they think you have. What they think they can see. They will do anything to get it."

The voice paused before speaking it's final words. "We will meet again."

Before Alex could say anything, the silhouette stranger was gone. Alex stared in the empty alley, unsure of what to make of the strange occurrence. He cautiously entered the alley and walked the area. Maybe it was still there, hiding in the shadows. He sighed when he realized he was the only one there. Alex took a step toward the street, but the sound of flapping fabric up above stopped him in his tracks.

Alex tilted his head back to the roof of the house next to him. A flash of purple disappeared over the edge and onto the roof. *So I'm not alone,* Alex thought. A sly smile crawled across his face. *The mysterious stranger wasn't as careful with his getaway as he thought.* Alex spun around and searched his surroundings for a way up. A dumpster on wheels was set against the wall just where the alley met the street. A thick metal pipe disappeared into the wall before leading up to the roof, stopping ten feet from the ground.

Alex rushed over to the dumpster and gripped the top of it. With painstaking effort, Alex pushed the heavy dumpster beneath the metal pole. He climbed on top of it and reached for the pole. He still had four more feet to go before he could get a good hold on it. Alex backed up to the edge of the dumpster top and took a deep breath. Before he could talk himself out of it, he ran as fast as he could toward the wall, the plastic dumpster lid pounding beneath him. His left foot landed flat on the brick surface and he pushed as hard as he could. He swiped his hand toward the metal pole that was now growing closer.

When Alex felt the cold metal on his fingertips, he latched onto it as if his life depended on it. His feet swung below him wildly as he struggled to get a foothold.

His body swung and he collided with the wall next to him. Once he gathered himself he began to climb. Within seconds he hoisted himself onto the roof and he stood on the slanted black surface, breathing hard. He looked around him for the stranger. It didn't take him long before he saw a long purple fabric flash behind a chimney only to appear again on another roof five houses away. Whoever he was didn't look like he was in a very big hurry.

"Hey!" Alex called. The figure spun around and glanced around frantically. When he caught sight of Alex, he didn't hesitate before taking off in another direction. Alex took off after the silhouette, struggling to keep up with the stranger as he leapt from roof to roof. After they were about six blocks away from where they started, the figure disappeared into thin air.

Alex searched everywhere. Behind chimneys, inside chimneys, on the ground, in windows, in alleyways, even on all of the surrounding houses. It was nowhere to be found, whatever was.

"The heck?" Alex shouted in frustration. He plopped down onto the rough tile to catch his breath before he truly gave up and made his way home. Out of the corner of his eye Alex caught a flash of something and he turned around eagerly, hoping that maybe he hadn't lost the stranger. He was surprised when he saw a thirty year old man with a flashlight in hand come hobbling out of a window of the house he was on. The man hoisted himself onto the roof and wobbled as he stood and gained his balance. Once he was certain he wouldn't fall, he turned his attention to the boy on his roof.

"Who are you? And why the heck are you on my roof?" the man demanded.

Alex silently cursed himself. He must've been too loud.

"Nothing, sir. I'll just be on my way," Alex gestured behind him as he slowly began to sneak away.

"Oh, I don't think so! You're coming with me to the police station!" he bellowed. "Now come with me quietly. I don't want to make this harder than it has to be. I warn you, I will if I have to." The man reached out his arms toward Alex and began to creep unsteadily toward him.

"Uh…okay," Alex began to nod as he took a few more steps backwards and up the roof. "Lemme just…," Alex spun around mid-sentence and latched onto the chimney. He pushed off it and ran down the other side of the slanted roof.

"Hey! Get back here you little miscreant" the man cried out into the night. He ran up the roof, not caring to be more cautious. After barely three steps, his foot slipped on a loose tile and he skidded on his stomach down the roof. The man screamed as his feet disappeared over the edge and his waist and torso soon followed. The man latched onto the gutter and yelled for help as his palms grew sweaty.

A woman in overalls covered in white paint burst out of the house, followed by a young girl with a book in her hand and a boy with a towel around his waist and his hair soaking wet, water dripping down his body and into the grass. They all gasped in astonishment when they saw the man dangling off the roof.

"Honey! What happened?" the woman in overalls called out.

"I'll tell you later! Just get me down!" he shouted desperately.

"Okay, okay! Hang on, honey, I'm coming!" The woman rushed into the house only to come out seconds later with a ladder in her hands. She set it down beneath him and he carefully slid off onto the safety of the white-paint-splotched ladder.

Alex bounded off the roof and onto another, running as fast as his feet could carry him, desperate to get away from the angry man. Only when he was two blocks away did he finally allow himself to look back. The man was nowhere to be found. Alex smiled to himself while he made his way back to the alley he used to climb up to the roof. Alex slid down the metal pole and landed with a thunk on top of the dumpster. Once both feet were on the ground he pushed the dumpster back to its original place.

Alex wiped his sweaty forehead and sighed. He stared at the side of the house across from him and smiled before breaking out into a fit of laughter. A few minutes later he gained control of himself and headed for home.

SEVEN

When Alex woke up the next morning his muscles ached all over. He reluctantly rolled off his bed and slammed off his alarm. After he brushed his teeth Alex splashed his face with cold water and stared at his reflection in the mirror and at his ruffled and knotted hair. Only then did he realize it was a Saturday. Alex groaned. He didn't have to be up this early! Knowing he probably wouldn't be able to go back to sleep no matter how tired he was, Alex set out for a walk to soothe his mind.

His thoughts were consumed with the strange encounter with the silhouette. Because of this he was on high alert all morning. Every sound he heard he would jump. One time he was so paranoid he accidentally caused a man to fall to the ground when he bumped into him out of fear of a squirrel crossing his path.

Alex was beginning to grow tired of being so on guard. He pulled his headphones over his ears and continued walking, eager to calm his nerves. It wasn't long before Alex heard someone shout out his name over his music from behind. Just as Alex was about to turn around, someone jumped on him unexpectedly and before he could react Alex fell flat on the sidewalk.

"Ugh," Alex groaned as he saw David hovering over him, laughing.

"Sorry! I didn't think you'd fall like that!" David said, holding out his hand for Alex.

Alex grabbed David's hand and David helped Alex to his feet. He faced David and pulled his headphones off.

"Alex!" Alex and David swung their heads to see Mark and the others running up to them.

"Oh my gosh! Are you okay?" asked Brooke.

"I'm fine," Alex replied.

"That's a relief," Brooke said, looking accusingly at David.

"Hey! It's not my fault your music was too loud for you to hear anything!" David exclaimed, throwing his hands up defensively.

"Alex, you ready?" asked Mark, smiling with excitement.

"Ready for what?" Alex asked, raising an eyebrow.

"Exploring the city! Oh! We didn't tell you. We're going to the beach!" Mark grabbed Alex's shoulder and pulled him next to him.

"This town has everything, doesn't it?" Alex asked sarcastically.

"You have swim trunks right?" Mark laughed.

"Yes, I do. But you didn't answer my question." Alex narrowed his eyes suspiciously at Mark. Once again, Mark ignored the topic.

"Okay! We are ready! We just got to go to your house so you can get your stuff. How's that?"

"What?" Alex asked as his eyes traveled down to the bag in Nicole's hands. "You just have a bag full of towels."

"We're wearing our suits underneath our clothes," Nicole explained.

Now that Alex was actually paying attention he realized that David was wearing green swim trunks with a regular orange shirt with sandals and Mark was wearing blue trunks along with sandals and a regular yellow shirt. The girls were wearing flip-flops with shorts and tank tops.

"Okay. Let's go then," said David. "Where's your house?"

"It's a ways back. Come on." Alex motioned for them to follow as he started toward his house. When they finally arrived, Alex instructed them to wait outside while he retrieved his trunks. It took a while, but Alex eventually found some light blue trunks and some sandals with a long-sleeved swim shirt to cover up his scars and bruises. Alex looked around his room to look for anything else he might need when his eyes fell upon the stack of books he got at the boardwalk. Alex grabbed The Last Thing I Could Remember by Andrew Klavan and tucked it under his towel, running out the door to his awaiting friends.

"Sorry that took so long," Alex said as he slammed the door shut behind him and jogged down the steps. "It took me a while to find my trunks."

"Alex, do you really walk to school and back every day? You don't take the bus?" asked Mark.

"Of course I walk. Why wouldn't I?"

"Well… your house is pretty far from school," Brooke said, raising her eyebrows.

"It's good exercise," Alex smirked.

"If you say so," Brooke replied.

The beach was below a twenty-foot cliff with stairs embedded in the rock that led up to a small vacant parking lot. The lot was full of grass, garbage, and broken glass. A telephone pole had fallen over on the far end of the lot, crushing an old rusted-out bicycle. Rotting wood fences were lining the edge of the cliff, breaking at the stairs. Alex followed his friends as they ignored the sight around them and continued toward the gap in the fence.

When they came to the stairs, they didn't hesitate before walking down. Alex looked over at the steep stone steps that were carved into the cliff. As soon as he stepped down, he felt a rock slip beneath his feet. He leaned over the side and watched as it tumbled down and into the sand. Below him, weeds littered the sand closest to the cliff. The farther out he looked, the sand became more clear. The beach was completely deserted.

Not a single soul was to be seen. It was surprising to Alex since the temperature was so hot. He at least expected a few people to be out there. When his feet sunk in the hot sand he slipped off his sneakers and held them by the ends in his hand. He followed his friends as they walked to the clearer part of the beach and dropped their things.

"Where'd everyone go?" Alex asked.

"They're on the other side of the beach. No one really comes to this side of the beach anymore," answered Nicole.

Alex stared out at the ocean while everyone else laid down their towels and took off the clothes over their suits. As Mark and the others talked, Alex felt the overwhelming desire to escape the scorching rays of the sun and plunge into the water slowly overtake him. He dropped his things in the sand beside the others and took off toward the sparkling waters.

The cool water sent relief through his sun-baked skin. He shot up and wiped the water off his eyelids as he opened them again. He turned quickly to face his friends to find that they had not yet noticed he had already jumped in. A flash of movement caught his eye and he spun back around. Yards away, deeper into the ocean, he saw more movement, always in the same place. His curiosity overtook him and he plunged back into the water, swimming toward the movements.

Mark turned toward the water to see Alex spring above the surface many yards away, in the much deeper waters. What was he doing?

"Alex! Are you going to wait for us?" Mark called after Alex but he was unable to hear.

"What are you yelling for?" Nicole asked, stepping next to Mark. "What is he doing?" Nicole asked once she caught sight of Alex, who was now even farther away.

"I don't know. He just took off," Mark said as he shrugged.

"Well, he must have been excited to get in the water." Brooke smiled.

"Then let's join him," David said, walking into the water. "Gyah! It's cold!"

"Come on, don't be a baby. We have to catch up to him." Brooke laughed before jumping in, the others following close behind.

Alex drew closer and closer to the jerking movements that caused ripples in the water. Only when he was almost upon it did he realize what it was. A large fishing net was floating just below the surface, jerking around wildly. Alex dove underneath to inspect the net. It went all the way to the bottom of the ocean. The bottom of the net was caught on a patch of coral that held the net in place.

He searched for the source of the jerking and found it to be a small dolphin, caught in bundles of the net. Alex attempted to rip the net free in order to release the dolphin, but his efforts were fruitless. When he broke through the surface, he searched his surroundings desperately for something to aid him. A few feet below the surface was a coral-covered rock that was only a few yards away.

Alex swam toward it and latched onto it with his left hand. A jolt of pain passed through his fingers and he immediately released his grip. He broke the surface and tread water with his right hand as he inspected his left. Blood trickled down his fingertips from a fresh cut where he grabbed the rock. He disappeared beneath the surface and carefully inspected the coral-covered rock. He could feel the jagged spikes of the coral and immediately knew what he could use to free the dolphin.

Alex swam back to the net, inhaled and went back under, scraping the new broken coral against the net, slowly cutting it.

"Alex!" Mark yelled as Alex came up for another breath. "What are you doing?"

"We are really deep! And the waves are really rough out here!" Brooke pointed out.

"Come with me and I'll show you," Alex said, ignoring the four of them completely as he dove down beneath the water again.

Nicole looked at the others and shrugged before they all followed Alex into the depths. Alex continued trying to free the dolphin as the others stared in astonishment. Alex was only able to free four parts of the net before having to go up again.

"We have to help that dolphin!" David exclaimed.

"What do you think I've been doing?" Alex replied pointing toward the rock. "There should be a rock over there beneath the water. Break off the coral from it and be careful. It's really sharp. It will help to cut the net." Alex inhaled once again and dove beneath the surface.

With the others' help, Alex managed to set the dolphin free within the hour. After they watched the dolphin swim away, they swam back over to the rock to rest, standing on the very top where coral failed to grow.

"What do we do with the net?" Alex asked. "More animals could get trapped so we can't leave it there."

"We could cut it away from whatever it's attached to and bring it back to shore," Mark replied.

"It's stuck on more coral. Even if we manage to get it free, how are we planning on bringing it back without drowning or getting tangled in it?" Alex questioned.

"We'll just carry it. If one of us gets stuck, someone else can help them. That's one of the beauties of not being alone," explained Mark.

Alex and Nicole swam to the bottom of the net and began to tear away the coral as the others yanked it up from the surface. They tore the net away quickly and began to drag the net back to the shore. It was not as difficult to do as freeing it, however, for the waves continuously pushed them toward the beach, along with the net.

They all dragged the net up onto the beach and away from the water so that it wouldn't get swept away. As soon as the net was out of the way they all collapsed onto the sand, breathing heavily, staring at the sky.

"Wow. That was…" Brooke trailed off.

"Tiring," David said, finishing Brooke's sentence.

"And kind of fun, don't you think?" asked Nicole.

"Maybe a little bit," said Mark.

"I'm just glad we could free that dolphin." Alex placed his hand over his eyes to block the sun. As soon as he did so, a warm red liquid clouded his vision and he jerked his hand away in surprise. He discovered that his hand was covered in blood. He must have cut it while he was gripping and pulling at the coral. Alex sat up and walked over to where he dropped his stuff and grabbed his towel, ripping off a strip at the bottom.

"What are you doing?" Alex heard Nicole say as they all started to get up and walk over to him.

"Nothing," Alex said, quickly wrapping his hand with the cloth and wrapping the towel into a ball, hiding his hand behind his back. "What are we going to do with the net?"

"I could bring it home and my parents could take care of it," said Brooke. "I'm sure my father or I could find some use for it."

"Let's try to fold it so Brooke can carry it home easily," Nicole said.

"What do you want to do now?" asked David once they finished folding the net.

"We still have at least three hours before sun down. I'm going swimming again, how 'bout you?" asked Mark.

"Race 'ya!" cried Nicole.

Mark, David, Brooke, and Nicole all ran back into the water splashing and pushing each other on the way. Alex looked at his hand realizing he probably couldn't go back into the water without facing the risk of getting the wound infected, especially since the wound was so big and bloody. He started walking along the beach, deciding that he would go exploring while the others swam. He wasn't going to deny the fact that it was bothering him. The wound stung immensely. He winced everytime he moved his fingers.

Nicole fell into the shallow water laughing. When she finally managed to calm down, she looked around at each of her friends. What she saw puzzled her and her face contorted into confusion.

"Where's Alex?" Nicole asked.

They all stopped at her words and scanned the area for their friend.

"Did he even come into the water with us?" David asked.

"Relax, guys, he's over there on the beach," Brooke said as she pointed toward the beach where they saw Alex disappear around a large collection of rocks and boulders.

"He's probably just collecting seashells or whatever. Meanwhile…, " David trailed off before pouncing on Mark and pushing him into the salty water.

EIGHT

I still think we could just go to a place we've already been and spend the day there," David suggested for the third time. "I can't really think of anything else."

"We still have a bunch of places to go!" Brooke protested.

"Yeah, but we don't know where," Mark shrugged.

"I've got it!" Nicole suddenly shouted. "Let's take him to the soccer field. It's Sunday so it should be empty. We'll have the whole field to ourselves! I didn't get that soccer ball for nothing!"

They all nodded their heads in agreement and followed Nicole to the soccer field, which was a big field on a hill that overlooked the city. The field had no structures besides the goals and the bleachers. There was a parking lot at the bottom of the hill along with some restrooms that were locked. The parking lot was empty with not a soul in sight.

"Alex, you know how to play, right?" asked Mark.

"Yeah, but I don't know if I'm any good. It's been so long since I've played," Alex said bluntly.

"Oh, that's okay. We're just playing for fun," said Nicole. They all walked out into the field and took their positions. "We'll play one on one since we don't have enough players for a real game."

David immediately went over to the net to be the goalie while the others went to the field. They played for about half an hour before they started to hear voices coming from the bottom of the hill, growing closer. They stopped playing and looked toward the slope of the hill and listened to the voices. A large group of eighteen kids close to their age appeared from the bottom of the hill and laced their stuff on the bleachers next to theirs.

"Hey, Nicole! I thought you said no one would be here," Mark called to her across the field.

"I thought I did too!" she yelled back.

"Maybe we could play a real game now!" David yelled. "Let's ask if they want to play a game!"

"Good idea!" yelled Brooke. They all made their way over to the bleachers where the kids continued to fuss with their things. Nicole shouted introductions as she jogged over to the bleachers. When she finally reached the metal seats, she asked if they were interested in playing a game.

"Sure. We were just wondering the same thing," a girl answered as she tightened the straps on her cinch bag and turned to face them. She had long wavy blond hair and blue eyes. She wore a black and white striped T-shirt and jeans. Her sneakers were cleated, as if she expected to play soccer all the time. She had an overpowering, snarky attitude.

"Who are you?" David blurted. Brooke jabbed her elbow into his ribcage and David immediately got the message. "I'm sorry if that sounded rude."

"My name is Lily," said the girl, ignoring David's apology. "And this is Josh, Mary, Erin, Leroy, Mason, Robert, Jensen, Diana, Karrie, Jared, Bobby, Bridget, Allan, Jake, Melena, and Ian."

"Ugh! Enough with the introductions. Let's get started already! We don't need to know each other's names to play!" Josh shouted impatiently. He had muddy brown eyes and slicked-back brown hair with a few strands draped in front of his eyes that refused to stay down from the gel. He wore a black short sleeved shirt and brown pants that had splotches of dirt from the ankles to the knees. His sneakers also had cleats, as did all of the other kids in their group.

"Yeah! We came here to play!" Karrie agreed.

Giving into the two kids' whims, everyone walked out to the field and got into position. On Nicole's team were Mark, Brooke, Alex, Melena, Ian, Rosy, Jensen, Diana, Bridget, and Bobby.

On Lily's team were Karrie, Josh, Mary, Leroy, Eren, Jake, Allan, Robert, Jared, and Mason.

When everyone had taken position, they immediately started the game. That's when things started to get rough. To Nicole's team it didn't take long for them to realize that their opponents were much stronger than they looked. The ball rolled over to Alex and he began to dribble it over to the goal but it was quickly stolen.

"We really need to step up our game. We are getting destroyed out there," Mark said to the team during a break.

"What? Why? It's just a game," Alex replied.

Mark grabbed Alex and the others, pulling them away from the rest of the team. "True, but now that we got a break I can get a better look at these guys."

"Get to the point," Alex urged.

"They're from Black Forest Academy! They travel all over the world and play against dozens of teams. They are well known for being extremely aggressive. Every team they have ever played has had a minimum of five players wounded after each game. The rest of their team is back at their school is what I'm guessing because their soccer team is made up of twenty-five people."

"You're paranoid," Alex sighed. "No one's gotten hurt yet. Either that or I'm delusional."

"They wait for the moment when you least expect it! And then …they POUNCE!" David jumped onto Alex and Mark and wrapped his arms around their shoulders.

"If you guys really think so, I'll put in more effort to try to win. Although I liked it much better when we were just playing for fun," Alex sighed.

"You weren't actually trying?" David asked with a raised eyebrow.

"You weren't either, right?"

"No. We haven't even started," David wiped the sweat off his forehead with a cold water bottle in his hand.

"Okay, let's get started," Lily shouted from across the field.

When they finally resumed the game, Alex realized what Mark and David were talking about. It was almost as though each player was holding a raging monster locked up inside them and they were waiting for the right moment to let them out and destroy everything in their path. They were extraordinarily fast, swerving from left to right, bumping against opponents in their path, nearly knocking them over into the dirt.

When the ball finally came to Alex, he took one look at it and sped across the field to the goal and kicked the ball in. He did it so swiftly and with such force, no one could tell he was moving, let alone see the ball. The goalie didn't notice Alex was there. The goalie was still standing, unprepared by the time the ball hit the net.

Mason stood in a squatting position in front of the net, ready for anyone to try an attempt to get a goal through him. Mason knew, though, that none of these amateurs or anyone from his school could get past him. Not even professionals could. Ever since he had started soccer, no one had ever scored a goal in his net. That's one of the reasons he was in this school. He never expected to be so easily defeated by some rookie from some public school.

He was in the perfect position. Ready to do anything needed in order to block every attempt possible. He was ready. Yet, what was that sudden rush of air that just whipped past his head? And when did that kid Alex get here? Just a second ago, everyone was on the other side of the field. Mason's eyes slowly traveled up to meet Alex's. Mason froze out of fright from what he saw. Something about his eyes made Mason stop breathing altogether. Alex's gaze was so cold and frightening it looked as though his eyes were ice. Mason could have sworn his eyes turned a luminescent blue. But then, he must just be imagining things. Mason slowly turned his torso around to see a black and white ball spinning in the middle of the net before slowing down and dropping onto the ground, rolling a few inches away in the grass before coming to a stop.

Mason's eyes widened as his mind processed what happened. Alex turned around and walked over to David with all eyes on him. Then, as if shaking out of a trance, everyone continued to play the game, as if nothing ever happened.

"Why was everyone staring at me? Was I not supposed to score a goal?" Alex asked, confused.

"Dude. You actually scored a goal! Against Mason! That kid has never let a ball slip past him in his entire lifetime!" David shouted excitedly, clapping a proud hand on Alex's back.

Alex ignored David's remark and went back into position once again. Everything was going normally until Lily saw Alex's bandaged, bloody hand.

"Yo! What did you do to your hand?" Lily asked as she passed Alex, walking over to her position. Alex quickly averted her gaze and turned his attention to the ball that was now in play.

During the break, when his teammates discussed strategies, Mason zoned out.

"Mason! Get your head in the game, man! What's up?" Jake snapped his fingers in his friend's face.

"His eyes…—" Mason shook his head slowly, as if he was hypnotized. He refused to look at his friend. The team stopped talking and all heads turned to Mason.

"Whose eyes?" Jake asked.

"Alex's. The kid who scored a goal past me. They were so cold. They… were frightening," Mason stuttered. There was a long pause.

"Well, the eyes are windows to the soul, am I right?" Allan laughed as he swung his arm around Mason's shoulder and shook it encouragingly.

Mason turned his head to look at the other side of the field where Alex and his team discussed their next plan. What was that *thing* he saw in that kid's eyes?

"There's no need to worry about him anymore. I have a plan that could make him vulnerable. But, only if you listen," Lily whispered as the team inched into a huddle, wicked and cruel smiles spreading across their faces.

When Alex stepped back on the field to resume the game, he noticed that everyone on the opposing team had a wicked sneer on their faces as if the monsters inside them were about to catch their prey. Alex continued playing, ignoring everyone on that team and focusing on nothing but the ball ahead.

When Alex finally had the ball again, they struck. Josh sped past him and stole the ball, at the same time swiping Alex's feet out from under him. The force of the blow sent Alex toppling to the ground. Alex quickly stood up and started after Josh in an attempt to retrieve the ball. With his guard down, Lily sped past and while doing so struck his right hand. Hard.

Alex fell to his knees, clutching his hand and gritting his teeth. He looked down at his hand again. Blood was pouring out of the cut having been forced open again. Alex wandered over to his bag on the bleachers and re-bandaged the bloody hand as quickly as he could. After Alex had finished bandaging it, he quickly rushed back into the game, choosing to pass their cruel plan off as a supposed 'accident'. Although, he knew the truth.

Lily ran over to Josh grinning triumphantly.

"Critical hit!" She shouted as she threw her hand in the air and Josh slapped it.

"Ha! That looks like it hurts!" Josh laughed as he stared at their fallen opponent.

"Can't wait to see the look on his face when he gets off the ground!" Lily turned back around to watch Alex. Alex remained on the ground for a few more seconds before getting up and walking over to the bleachers. They were unable to see his face.

"Hold up. I can't see his face. What's he doing?" Josh asked.

"I don't know. I can't see his face either," Lily said. Josh and Lily watched side by side as Alex walked over to the bleachers and dug into his bag with his back turned, blocking what he was doing from the others. When he finished whatever he was doing Alex jumped down from the bleachers and walked back down from the field. That's when they saw his face. Entirely expressionless.

"What the—? He's not angry? Is he dumb or what? Does he not know what we did to him?" Lily laughed at Alex's stupidity. Alex noticed Josh and Lily staring at him. Alex looked up at them and waved with his left hand and smiled almost sarcastically before going back to the game.

"Ugh! Does he even know that was us?" Josh asked irritably.

"Oh, he knows! He knows," Lily said, sneering.

For the rest of the game Lilly and Josh never got a hold of the ball. Alex always seemed to be there whenever they were close to it and he always managed to kick it away from their grasp. Their shoes never touched the rubbery black and white ball again that day.

NINE

Monday, Alex returned to school with a healed and bandage-free hand. At the end of the day, Alex found the others conversing nervously outside. They all had anxious expressions on their faces, almost as if a bomb was going to go off unless they did something illegal. This wasn't the first time Alex had seen this. The students had been acting this way the whole day. Nervous, scared, and jumpy.

"So, where are the ghosts?" Alex asked as he walked up to them with a smirk.

"Alex! Oh my gosh! I'm so glad you're here!" Brooke let out a sigh of relief.

"I wasn't going to leave without you." Alex raised an eyebrow.

"You haven't heard?" asked David.

"Heard what?"

"Someone went into the woods because of some stupid dare. We didn't see you much this afternoon, so we thought it was you— especially the way you were looking at the woods a few days ago," replied Mark.

"Okay, so someone went into the woods. What's so wrong about that?" Alex asked before adding with a smirk, "also, just because I was looking at the woods, doesn't mean I was planning on running away and camping out there for the rest of my life."

"Rarely has anyone who has gone into those woods come out," David replied, ignoring Alex's comment. Alex was about to protest that it was only a rumor before he was interrupted when the principal began speaking through the PA system.

"Everyone listen carefully. Nina Wellington has gone against the safety regulations and ventured into the woods. We are going to send a rescue team in. Until then please stay away from the woods, go home, and school will be cancelled tomorrow.

I hope this will serve as a reminder that these rules are for your protection, and it would be wise not to go against them. Thank you for your patience and cooperation."

After the announcement, everyone followed their instructions and headed for home. Conversations centered on rumor and gossip. As his friends continued their conversation and gathered their things Alex scrutinized the woods. He watched as a large-amount of people in bullet proof vests holding guns and flashlights formed a line around the perimeter of the woods on the right side of the school.

"Why are they sending armed men in? That's a bit extravagant, don't you think?" Alex asked.

"We told you there are dangerous animals in there and we don't know what exactly 'they' are. Anyone who's been lucky enough to survive can never remember because of trauma. But each time someone survives, they end up going straight to the hospital. That, we all know for sure," Brooke said as she pulled her books out of her overfilled bag to reorganize them and make the load feel lighter.

Alex continued to stare at the woods where the search team entered until he saw something flash bright yellow in the corner of his eye. Alex whipped his head to look over on the other side of the building at the very edge of the grassy field. Flapping in the wind, on one of the trees at the very perimeter of the woods, was a bright yellow blur. Alex dropped his backpack and walked toward the woods and stopped at the tree.

Mark turned to face Alex to inform him that they were leaving. To his dismay in Alex's place, he found Alex's bookbag lying on the ground. Mark looked up and saw Alex standing at the edge of the woods opposite the rescue team. *Oh no.* Mark knew Alex too well to know what he was about to do. But Mark wouldn't let him. He wasn't about to let his friend walk to his death. Alex took a step forward. Mark dropped his backpack next to Alex's and started running. Alex wasn't going to take another step into those woods. Not while Mark had the ability to stop him. Alex was the new kid. He was ignorant of the dangers that would lead to his actions. His friends noticed the boy's absence and soon realized what was happening.

Alex could hear the others yelling for him to come back. Without looking up from the branch, Alex turned his body slightly and beckoned with his hand for them to come over.

"Alex, stop!" Mark shouted at his friend, thrusting his hand out in front of him.

Alex spun around in time for Mark to grab his collar and yank Alex to the ground.

"What do you think you are doing?" Brooke screeched.

"Are you out of your mind?" Nicole yelled, putting her hands on her hips and staring at the boy on the ground in front of her.

"You're crazy! Absolutely crazy!" said an exasperated David as he threw his hands up in the air.

"You can't go in there, Alex! You'll only get yourself hurt!" Mark warned.

"You're being way too dramatic," Alex said.

"Better that than dead!" Mark replied.

Alex said nothing as he stood up and turned back toward the tree branch. They all followed Alex's gaze toward a dirty ripped yellow ribbon tangled in a branch.

"Nina's ribbon…" David trailed off.

"So it is hers. I thought as much," Alex yanked the ribbon out of the tree. "The rescue team went the wrong way. We are just going to have to go after her ourselves."

"Not a chance! If we go in there, those woods will be our grave!" Nicole explained.

"Sounds fun!" Alex smiled.

"Not funny, Alex! We're serious!" Brooke scolded.

"I can see that. If what you say is really true, it will be Nina's grave as well. That 'rescue team' will never find her. Besides, it could be fun!" Alex turned back around and stepped onto the leaf-covered ground. "Are you coming?" he called.

Mark sighed. "Wait up! We're coming!"

The four of them quickly rushed beneath the shade of the trees after Alex. The woods around them were dark, which seemed impossible by how bright it was outside. The sky disappeared above them and a cold breeze flowed past them, causing their shoulders to shake from the change in temperature.

"Why didn't that girl just turn around when she saw how creepy this place is?" asked Brooke, gasping.

"Pride? Maybe she wanted to prove that she could complete the dare," Mark suggested.

"Or she couldn't find the way out. Look behind you," Alex pointed behind them and they all followed his gaze. What they saw behind them was not the edge of the woods against the school field. Instead, they only saw more woods.

"Where's the school?" David asked, worry clear in his voice.

"I don't know. It's so dark in here. I can't see any of you," Mark replied.

"Here. Take this," David reached in his backpack and pulled out a flashlight and handed it to Mark.

"You brought your backpack?" asked Nicole.

"Yeah, you left all your backpacks! Someone has to be prepared," David replied.

"And you just so happened to have a flashlight?" Nicole inquired sarcastically.

"I always have everything someone would need for survival. You never know when you might need it. For all you know, you could find yourself stranded in the wilderness with nothing to help you survive," David replied defensively. "Sometimes I even bring medium-sized fold-up tents. Just to be on the safe side. And the occasional sleeping bag."

"You have a problem." Nicole rolled her eyes, choosing to give up this debate, knowing full well it would be better to leave the subject as it is. The trees began to grow thicker the farther they progressed. Not soon after the trees, fog drifted to the ground, darkening the path ahead of the flashlight.

"Stay close!" Alex called.

"The flashlight isn't showing as much effect anymore. The fog is too thick." Mark swiped the flashlight across the fog around him, proving his point.

"I see something," Alex said suddenly. He ran to a jumble of thorns and pulled out a purple backpack. The fabric was tattered and was caked in mud.

"Is this hers?" Alex asked, holding it up for the others to see.

"I don't know. So many people have gotten lost in here. It might be someone else's. Check inside and see if any of the stuff in there has her name on it," Nicole said.

Alex unzipped it and looked inside with Mark shining the flashlight over his shoulder.

"Nina Wellington… Yeah. It's hers," Alex confirmed, pulling out a lunch box with her name etched across it in black marker. Alex shoved the box back into the bag and they glanced around for a possible path she could've taken.

"What is that?" asked David. The fog had begun to clear a bit and they were able to see a few more yards ahead. He nodded over to a large opening under a boulder with vines drooping down from above.

"It's a cave! Leave it alone. There might be a bear," Nicole exclaimed.

"But she could have gone in there," David argued.

"It's possible. It doesn't go in too deep." Alex began to walk toward it. He was a few feet outside of the cave when a muffled cry bounced off the walls.

"Waampfh..!" David started to scream.

49

Nicole shoved her hand over David's mouth before his scream could get any louder.

"Would you be quiet! If she's in there you'll scare her! Hello? Nina Wellington? Are you in there? We're here to get you out!" Nicole shouted into the darkness.

Silence.

"Well, that was a huge waste of not only time, but our lives as well! We are doomed!" David threw his hands up and turned around, starting to walk away.

"No," called a faint voice from inside the cave.

"What?" David asked, stopping short. His hands stayed in the air.

"No," repeated the voice.

"What do you mean 'no'?" David called, turning back around, dropping his hands.

"It's too dangerous here! There are monsters! They'll come after you. They don't want you to leave."

"Seriously? We come to help and this is what we get for thanks? I don't see any 'monsters' here do you?"

"No," the voice responded after a moment of hesitation. "That's because they only show themselves if you try to go back!"

"Please, just come out so we can talk to each other face to face! Then we can talk properly," Nicole demanded, clearly irritated.

There was a long silence until a blurred silhouette of a girl emerged from the shadows. The girl's hair was ratty and full of leaves and twigs knotted into her hair. She was wearing a muddy ripped T-shirt that looked like it could have been white but it was so soaked in muck that they could barely tell. She was also wearing black mucky shorts and only one sneaker. Her other foot was swollen around the ankle and covered in mud.

"What happened to you?" David asked in surprise.

"I fell into a large pile of mud and sprained my ankle. What? Too ugly for you?" the girl hissed.

"Is your name Nina?" David ignored her sass.

"Who else would I be? Yes, I'm Nina! You shouldn't have come in here! Your fates are sealed! You are dead. Just as I am. If not now soon enough."

"Maybe someday, but not today," Mark said, furrowing his brows.

"We'll think of something. So when did you say these 'monsters' will come?" asked David.

"They come when you go back. And you better be careful, *boy*," Nina hissed harshly. "Sarcasm won't get you far in this reality."

"Then we'll just go forward," Alex said.

"Oh! So you *can* talk," Nina said, rolling her eyes.

"You said they come when you try to go back, correct?" Alex asked.

Nina nodded.

"We'll just go forward then," Alex said as if it was common knowledge.

"We are going to die and you're making jokes?" Nina huffed.

"If you have any other ideas, I'm open to them," Alex started walking forward but Nina stopped him.

"Are we really going that way? It's full of thorns and prickers!" Nina warned.

"Yep!" Alex walked into the thorny bushes.

Finally, after hours of walking they found an opening and stepped through it, the light from the sun blinding them. They ran out and flopped down on the grass, realizing that they were out of the woods. Yes, it took them hours and they were scratched, cut, bleeding, and their clothes were torn. But they made it. The next question was, where had the woods led them too?

Alex sat up and looked around to find out where they were. They were on the other side of the field where the search team had first gone in. Alex looked over to find the entire search team sitting on the steps, tending to injured men. They all got up after they caught their breath and walked over to the principal. Once she noticed the group of kids coming out of the woods all she could do was stare at them with clenched fists and fire burning in her eyes.

"You went into the woods! To find Nina?" she growled. "Even after I specifically told everyone not to!"

"We aren't everyone," Alex said simply. The principal took a deep breath and unclenched her fists.

"How did you do it?" she asked.

"We saw her ribbon over on the other side of the school and knew the search team went the wrong way. We couldn't tell them because they already went inside," Mark replied.

"Then how did you get out? All of the men who had gone in have come back severely injured! Thank God that they came back at all."

"Well, that's easy!" Alex spoke up in a cheerily ironic voice. "We just kept going forward."

The principal ignored Alex's ridiculous reply. Rolling her eyes, she brought a walkie-talkie up to her mouth and spoke into it with an authoritative tone, narrowing her eyes at Alex when she finished. "Nurse, we have six kids here who need to be tended to. Check to make sure none of them have any concussions while you're at it."

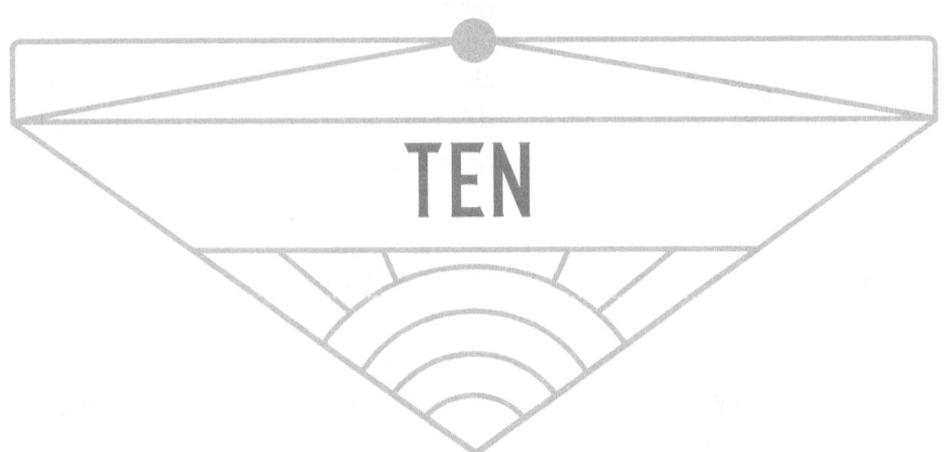

TEN

The next day the superintendent called off school for security reasons that had not been revealed, giving Alex and the others time for another day of freedom to wander around the city. They met up a few blocks away from the school to discuss what they were going to do that day. But their plans were delayed when someone was running a bit late.

"Hey, guys!" David yelled as he waved his hand back and forth to capture their attention, running up to them all the while. "Sorry I'm late. My mom had me do a boatload of chores! Where are we going to take Alex today?"

"Wait. Chores?" Alex asked, placing his hand out in front of him in order to keep them on that subject. Confusion and panic coated his voice.

"Yeah. So what?" asked David. Alex's eyes widened in surprise before he started to take off in the opposite direction at full speed.

"Where are you going?" Mark called after him. Alex didn't answer. Mark and the others started to chase after him as he ran. When Alex finally got to his destination, he flung the door open and ran toward the kitchen of his house. The others caught up to him in the kitchen and watched as Alex paced around frantically.

"Whoa! Alex what in the world has gotten into you?" Asked Mark. Alex stopped pacing and looked up at them and sighed.

"Okay... So do you remember when I decided to go home instead of hang out with you guys?" Alex asked.

"You looked like you were about to pass out from exhaustion," Nicole pointed out, crossing her arms.

"I found a note on the fridge that said my family went camping and wouldn't be back until next Monday. It also said that I needed to do my chores. And I didn't even do that!" Alex said. "I'm sorry but I can't go with you guys for today."

"We can help you if you want. We didn't have anything planned for the day anyway."

"You don't have to keep planning things," Alex replied.

"What chores do you have to do anyway?" asked David.

Alex sucked in a breath before he began. His family forced him to do all the work around the house without showing him the proper way to do it, resulting in a number of injuries and a lot of learning experience.

As Alex listed the chores, Mark allowed his mind to wander.

He surveyed the house around him. Next to the front door were stairs that led to the second floor. In front of the door was a long hallway with a table next to the wall beneath the stairs with a phone and numerous papers lying across it. Above the table, on the wall, were photos of what Mark assumed to be Alex's mother, father, and sister. On the other side of the hallway was a large opening that led to another room with a grey carpet, a couch, table, television, and fireplace.

At the end of the hallway was the kitchen. From the hallway, Mark could only see a part of the large round table and the stove. Once inside, he could see long counters on either side of the stove with cupboards lining the walls. On the right end of the kitchen was a pantry built into a wall and refrigerator. Beneath the stairwell was another door that Mark figured was the basement.

Before Mark could look around any longer, David snapped him out of his little world and brought him back to the conversation. They quickly discussed what job each was to take on before heading straight to work on the heavy load of chores Alex was to do. Alex walked with Mark to the garage to grab the ladder to do his job and found that the garage was packed to the ceiling with boxes from the move; so it took them both to fish the ladder out.

"Alex... can I ask you a question?" Mark asked as he pulled a box down.

"Shoot," said Alex as he sat another box on top of the one Mark put down. He stood back up and wrapped his hands on another box.

"Why aren't you in any of the family photos?" asked Mark, watching as Alex slid the box off the shelf.

"I'm usually the one taking them," he said, bending over to pick up another box. "My family never wanted me in the pictures anyway. Thanks for helping me remove the boxes." Alex changed the subject quickly.

Mark said nothing as Alex lifted the ladder over his head and carried it outside. Alex stood the ladder up and climbed. When he reached the top, he looked into the gutter. It was full of leaves, water, worms, and mud. It was so full of grime, he was baffled at how it could have gotten like this in a week from when he last cleaned it out.

When he had finally finished clearing out all of the grime from the gutter, Alex boosted himself up onto the roof with his feet resting on the top step of the ladder. Everyone had already finished their first chore and had moved onto their second one. Mark was doing the bathrooms, David was on the porch sweeping, Brooke was in his sister's room, and Nicole was doing the recycling. Nicole noticed Alex on the roof and waved at him before heading back to the house with the bins.

Alex grabbed the toolbox that rested at his feet and looked around at the loose tiles of the roof. He sat the toolbox at the top of the roof and grabbed a hammer and nail before hammering another nail into a nearly missing tile. The incessant pounding of the hammer echoed throughout the streets.

Alex had finished four loose patches and was about to start the fifth. He reached to the toolbox to get another nail, accidentally knocked it over, and sent it toppling onto the ladder. Alex lunged for the tool-box, attempting to grab it before it fell, but he was unable to reach it in time. Both the ladder and the toolbox crashed to the ground. The loud crash rang through the air. Alex peeked over the edge to make sure it didn't fall on anything and saw David and Nicole standing next to it while Mark and Brooke were running to see what all the commotion was.

"Sorry!" Alex called down. "Could you bring that back up?"

After all of the chores were finished, Alex and the others sat on the porch steps and ate their very late lunch.

"That only took all morning!" said David.

"Thanks. That probably would have taken me late into the night to finish," said Alex gratefully.

"No problem, as long as you help us with our chores!" David said.

"Okay," Alex replied seriously. "Just come get me next time you need to do them."

"Wait, I was just being sarcastic. You aren't kidding, are you?" David stared at Alex for an answer. When he didn't get one, he slowly cracked a smile. "Well then…"

David was cut off when Brooke smacked him on the back of the head. "He was just kidding. He doesn't need help with his chores. Thanks anyway."

There was nothing but silence as they chewed on their sandwiches.

"Do you think we could stay overnight?" asked Nicole. "A sleepover maybe? Would your parents mind?"

Alex said nothing and stared out into the street. He started thinking; his parents wouldn't be home for a number of days, so as long as they didn't make a mess of things, he should be fine, right? He had never had a sleepover before and it would be nice to be able to spend more time with his new friends as long as his parents never found out.

"If that's what you want to do," Alex said. "I'm fine with that. Like I said, my family's out on a camping trip. We just can't make a mess of things."

"We just have to go home and get some stuff," said David.

"Why don't you go do that," Alex said.

Everyone stood up and walked down the steps, with Mark and the others going different directions while Alex watched them. When they were long out of sight, Alex continued to stare at the sidewalk, his head swimming with worried thoughts. Alex had never had people his age at his house before. The whole thing made him uncomfortable. What if he messed up? What if they got annoyed with him?

Alex shook his thoughts away and jogged up the steps and into his house in search of something to make them for dinner. While he was scavenging around in the pantry, he heard the screen door swing open. Alex leaned through the doorway to the kitchen and found Mark standing in the doorway setting a backpack down on the floor.

"Hey, Mark," Alex greeted him.

"Hey. What are you doing?" asked Mark, looking at the open refrigerator and pantry.

"I'm looking for our dinner. But I can't find anything," Alex replied, walking back over to the refrigerator.

"Dinner is three hours away. We'll worry about that when the time comes." Mark smiled.

David was the next one to arrive, then Brooke and Nicole arrived together only minutes after him.

"Hey Alex, you have a TV, right?" asked Brooke.

"Yeah, it's in the living room, but I don't use it," Alex said.

"Oh, well, I brought a few movies we can watch," said Brooke. "But after dinner of course."

"About that..." Alex started.

"We'll worry about dinner later," Mark cut Alex off.

"So, what do you guys want to do before sundown?" Nicole asked.

"I know just the place," said David.

They all walked side by side until they could see the red, blue, and yellow of the park through the trees. They took off racing toward the swings. Alex jumped the last few steps and clasped onto the chains mid-flight. He pulled himself up and over the seat and plopped down onto the blue rubber. The others followed close behind. Alex swung high into the air, while it took the others a few minutes to catch up to his height.

"Whoever goes the highest wins!" shouted David. Once the others met Alex's height, he dared them to go higher. Alex swung until he was going higher than anyone had ever gone, for fear that they would go too high and fall, or the swing would go all the way on the other side of the pole. The other's eyes widened as they watched. Suddenly the swing was upside down straight in the air, high above the pole. The others barely had any time to react as they watched the scene play out before them. Alex's hands dropped from the chains and he started to fall, tumbling toward the bar beneath him.

ELEVEN

lex fell toward the bar for a few more seconds before flipping over and landing feet first onto the metal bar, swiftly and quickly regaining balance. Alex
whooped before looking down at the others, who had all jumped off by now
and were staring at him, mouths agape a few feet away from the set. Alex looked
at them, puzzled.

"Have you never done this before?" Alex asked. They shook their heads in
unison. All of them were speechless.

That's weird. Alex always thought kids did this all the time. He was surprised
they didn't do it too. When Alex was little and lived in Portland, he would sneak
out with his sister to the closest park they could find, even if it was miles away, and
a bunch of kids there taught them how to do it. That was when his relationship
with his sister was still good.

"Here! I'll show you!" Alex said. He was young when he first learned, so they
should be fine. Alex crouched down into a squatting position and grabbed one of
the chains below him. He swung his legs over and slid down the chain onto the
ground. Alex walked them through the steps on how to do it, and in no time they
were all surprised at their new accomplishment.

They couldn't balance as well as Alex could, but it was a work in progress.
They were at least able to get up onto the bar without falling, whooping and
laughing all the while. They just had to sit on the bar before they lost balance
and fell. After a few tries for practice, they all jumped up for the seventh time.
Suddenly David tottered and started to fall backwards. He couldn't even open
his mouth to scream.

Alex dashed toward David, running perfectly balanced and weightlessly on the bar. Alex reached over at the last moment and grabbed David by the collar of his shirt. He jerked David up and brought him down onto the ground to let him have flat ground to recover on.

"That… was… AWESOME!" David cried, grabbing onto Alex's sleeve as he tottered from left to right, laughing hysterically. "Just a quick question. Why is everything spinning?"

"Okay. I think that's enough for today," Alex said, grabbing onto David's shoulders to steady him.

"David! Are you all right?" Brooke exclaimed as she clambered down the chains.

David continued to laugh.

"He'll be fine. Let's just head back now. I am starving," said Nicole.

The others walked far ahead, not waiting for Alex, who was weighed down by David's arm slung over his shoulder and his feet dragging against the pavement.

"Could you at least try to walk?" Alex complained.

In response, David groaned and launched himself forward onto the ground. Once he hit the ground, he groaned again and didn't move. Alex sighed.

"You weren't even hurt! I caught you before anything could happen!" Alex explained.

David groaned again. Alex sighed again before picking David up off the ground and hoisting him onto his back. Alex noticed that the others had disappeared. Alex walked forward, having David constantly groaning in his ear and shoving his hands in his face.

When Alex had stopped walking to tend to David, Mark and the others took off running toward the house to get things ready. When Alex finally got to the house, the door was open and he trudged into the entryway. He could see the pantry half open at the end of the hallway, but he couldn't see the rest of the kitchen. The sound of pans clanging together rang through the air, and the smell of cheese wafted into his nostrils. Suddenly something jerked on his back and he tumbled forward, dropping David. Alex bent over and rubbed the back of his neck as David ran into the kitchen with his hands in the air, shouting, "I smell cheese! Whaddya make?"

Alex walked into the kitchen after David to find Mark and Nicole at the stove and Brooke buried inside the fridge. David ran over and put his arm around Mark and Nicole, peering over their shoulders.

"Oh, yeah! Homemade mac'n'cheese! My favorite!" David laughed.

"You were fine the whole time?" Alex asked.

"What can I say?" David shrugged. "I'm a good actor. Thanks for the piggyback ride by the way."

"No problem," Alex sighed as he leaned against the wall and folded his arms across his chest. "What are you making anyway?"

"Dinner. Now sit down. It's done," Mark said, pointing a wooden spoon covered in cheese toward the table.

After they finished eating dinner, they walked into the living room where they put out some sleeping bags for the night. They watched many scary movies hand-picked by David and Nicole. After about the fifth one, they all looked outside to see everything was pitch black and they could hear the chirping of crickets throughout the air.

"What time is it"? Mark asked.

Alex stood up and walked over to the kitchen to look at the clock on the stove.

"11:42!" Alex called as he walked back from the kitchen and sat down on the floor.

"It's getting late and tomorrow we go back to school. We should go to bed," Mark yawned.

"Alex, are you going to sleep in your room?" asked David.

"Nah, I'll sleep down here with you guys," Alex replied.

"Where's your sleeping bag then?" asked Mark.

"I don't need one. I'll just use the couch." Alex jumped onto the couch and put his arms behind his head. His eyes traveled down to a section on the floor where the moonlight seeped in from the window.

Hours later, Alex's gaze remained fixed on the moonlit floor, staring off into space. These people were the closest he had ever had to friends. When he was in other towns, very rarely he would get eager and make friends right off the spot, not caring to know who they were. That was a huge mistake. They always ended up being jerks in the end. Alex could only hope that this friendship of theirs would last for as long as it could. Alex walked out on the porch and sat on the steps, leaning his head against the railing.

Alex's eyes slowly opened as a slight breeze ruffled his hair and he rubbed the grogginess out of them as he struggled to remember where he was. He was still sitting on the steps; the sun shone down on his face, warming him in the morning light. Dew covered the ground and fog hovered in the air. A woman with her hair tied in a tight ponytail and a blue runner's outfit jogged past his house. Her long locks of brown hair swayed as she bounced with each step. She turned her head slightly as she caught sight of him and sent him a small wave of her hand.

Alex continued to rub his eyes with one hand while returning her wave with a lazy one of his own. He stood up and pulled open the screen door to his house. His friends were still sleeping soundly on the living room floor. He quickly bounded up the steps into his room and changed his clothes. When he finished getting himself ready for the day, he hurried into the kitchen to make breakfast for his companions.

"Mark? Hey, Mark. Are you awake?" Alex shook Mark's shoulder lightly.

"Hrn? Wah you want hmm?" Mark grumbled groggily as he swatted Alex's hand away.

"We have school today. I made breakfast. Can you help me wake the others?" Alex asked as he shook Mark awake. Mark's eyes popped open and he shot up into a sitting position. He turned toward Alex, who was crouching next to him.

"What time is it?" Mark asked worriedly.

"Not time for school, I can tell you that," Alex replied. "Don't worry, we won't be late. Breakfast is waiting in the kitchen. It's not as amazing as what you put together last night but I think it will do."

Alex stood up and patted Mark's shoulder before standing up and disappearing into the kitchen. Mark watched as Alex went and sighed as he slowly stood up. He scratched his head and fixed the twisted fabric of his shirt as he walked to David's side. David was sprawled across his sleeping bag, facing the ground. Drool dripped from the corner of his open mouth and onto the cloth bag beneath him. Not bothering to be as gentle as Alex, Mark kicked David in the side. With a snort, David lurched upward and faced Mark with an annoyed look on his face.

"What the heck was that for?" David growled.

"Breakfast in the kitchen. Wake the girls first," Mark explained briefly. "I call waking Brooke. You get Nicole."

"Seriously?" David whined. "Why me?"

"Because I think she likes you better."

David sighed and tiptoed over to Nicole. She was lying on her side with her arm tucked under her head, facing the wall. David reluctantly reached out for her shoulder, but before he could touch her a hand shot up suddenly and grabbed his wrist. David shrieked and jerked his wrist away, but the firm hand held strong. The body in front of him rolled over and he found himself staring into two eyes burning with anger.

"What do you want?" Nicole demanded. Her voice was rough with tiredness and reminded David strangely of a bear.

"Good morning?" David said in a quivering voice. "Breakfast is in the kitchen. Might want to hurry before we run out of time. We have school today."

"Oh! Breakfast!" Suddenly grizzly bear Nicole disappeared and was replaced with a cheery and bright teenage girl. Nicole released her hold on David and jumped up, hurrying into the kitchen. David let out a breath of relief and leaned back, rubbing his wrist. He hated having to wake Nicole up. She was a bomb just waiting to go off in the morning!

Once they were all awake, they made their way into the kitchen together. The round table had four plates stacked with pancakes drizzled with maple syrup and coated in a thin layer of powdered sugar. Knives and forks were set out beside the plates and glasses. Alex stood by the sink, washing out a baking pan.

"Whoa! That looks good!" David shouted as he plopped himself down in a seat, his friends following soon after.

"Maybe, it's a bit bitter. I may have put a bit too much baking flour in it," Alex called over his shoulder, grimacing a bit.

"Still, you did a good job with the appearances!" Nicole exclaimed.

"Don't let that fool you. Besides making pancakes, I can't cook or bake anything even if my life depended on it, unless you'd like burnt metal spaghetti with a touch of melted plastic spatula for dinner," Alex said as he laughed.

"I could teach you to cook a few things if you'd like. I tend to make food for my family a lot," Mark offered.

"By how good that mac'n'cheese and roasted cauliflower tasted, I would be honored." Alex turned around and leaned against the sink as he wiped the pan dry.

"If's goof!" David mumbled as he shoveled another large piece of pancake in his mouth.

"I'm glad you like it." Alex smiled broadly at the compliment, proud that his friends approved of his pancakes. It felt good to have friends, people who liked him for who he was and gave him compliments, things he didn't hear very often.

Once he finished drying the pan he picked up a plate of pancakes and ate with his friends, grimacing a bit at the indeed slightly bitter pancakes, but as he laughed with his friends he thanked God they were together, and prayed none of this would ever change.

TWELVE

A few weeks later Alex trudged up the steps of his house with a smile on his face. He had spent the day with his friends at the mall and he lost track of time, not coming back until it was late into the night. Alex walked in to find the lights on and his parents sitting at the kitchen table. The house was quiet aside from their hushed conversation. He looked around but could find no sign of Jessica. Her coat and shoes were gone from their usual place by the door, but Alex wasn't too worried. He was more concerned about getting upstairs without his parents noticing.

Alex started up the steps as quietly as possible, his heart pounding as adrenaline spiked his nerves.

"Alex, wait," his mother called.

Alex froze in his tracks and sighed. So much for that plan.

"Did you finish your chores for the day?" she asked.

"I'll do them tomorrow. I'm going to bed," Alex replied almost automatically to the familiar question. Alex waited in the silence that followed, bracing himself for his mother's predictable anger, but nothing came. He leaned over the banister and peered into the kitchen to find her stone-faced, staring at the wall behind his father's head. He couldn't help but notice the beer bottle in his father's hand. Only one this late at night? Weird. "I'll do them in the morning, don't worry. I won't forget," Alex reassured her, unsettled by her uncharacteristic response.

"Alex, please have a seat. We need to talk to you."

"Is everything okay?" Alex asked as he walked down the steps and stopped in front of the kitchen.

"Sit down," Alex's father demanded. Alex complied without complaint, sensing something wrong with this situation. Something deeply, deeply wrong.

"Where's Jessica?" Alex asked when no one spoke.

"At a friend's," his mother replied. "It's just us."

More silence. Alex was growing increasingly uncomfortable as the seconds ticked by.

"You've barely been home lately," his mother finally said. "You've been acting so strange; skipping out on responsibilities and family meals."

"I've been busy."

"Busy doing what exactly?"

"School. And I've been hanging out with my friends."

"Where have you been really?" Alex's father asked, finally looking him in the eye.

"Well, I was with my friends at the mall today…" Alex elaborated, his eyebrows furrowing in confusion.

"No! Where have you *been*?" Alex's father yelled, slapping his hand on the table with anger.

"What do you mean? Stop asking me that question! I already told you!"

"Enough with the bullcrap!" Alex's father stood abruptly, shoving his chair back into the wall. "What are you doing? Drugs?"

"God no! Why won't you ever trust me? I've been spending time with friends. That's *all* I've been doing. *Drugs*? You've *got* to be kidding me! Why would you *think* that?"

"It doesn't matter," Alex's mother exclaimed as she stood. Both of his parents were looking down at him now. "We don't want you with these "friends" of yours anymore. They are a bad influence on you. You have become negligent and are away from home too often."

Alex stood up abruptly, sending his chair tumbling backwards onto the floor. He stood a full head over his mother but his father still towered over him. "Like you've ever cared if I was home or not! If you could even call it a home! You've never given me a reason to want to be here."

"Like Hell we haven't, you ungrateful brat! You aren't even ours and we have to do everything for you! Feed you, clothe you, put a roof over your head. And for what? So you can go flouncing about the city doing God knows what! Whatever it is, you. Are. Done," his father stared him down, daring him to argue against him, but all Alex could do was stare at him, speechless.

After what seemed like an eternity, Alex could finally get the words out. "Not...yours?"

His father's expression changed in realization, cursing before setting his jaw in a tight line.

"What do you mean I'm not yours?" Alex asked in a hushed tone. He looked from his father to his mother. She was staring at her husband with a dark expression. No one spoke.

"Answer me!" Alex demanded, clenching his fists, partly in anger and partly to stop his hands from trembling.

His mother finally met his eyes, and what he saw in them made the truth all too clear.

Not *his* mother.

Alex couldn't stop the trembling anymore. He spun, tripping over his fallen chair before running up the stairs. He fell through his doorway, quickly scrambling up to slam the door shut. He slid down the wood and just tried to *breathe*. He couldn't think, he couldn't stop the trembling from taking over his body. He didn't know how long he sat there, trying to understand everything that happened. His father's words were on repeat in his mind and when their meaning finally hit him — truly hit him — one thing seemed certain — seemed right — in this mess of a night.

He had to run away.

Alex used the doorknob to pull himself to his feet and looked around his room. He pulled his wobbly desk chair under the doorknob in an attempt to buy him some time should he need it and grabbed his backpack from his bed, quickly shoving as many clothes as he could fit inside. When he was done he looked around again. What else did he need? What else? He had to be missing something.

Money. Alex dropped to his knees and lifted his mattress off the floor. Underneath lay a small wad of cash he had saved up by cleaning and mowing lawns for his neighbors or helping out kids with their homework, so that when he finally left home he would be ready for it. He never thought it would happen so soon.

He shoved the wad into his bag and zipped it up. Alex hesitated before walking over to his closet door and pulling it open. There inside lay his sword, still resting in the same place he had put it on the first day of school. Alex's fingers fumbled as he went to grab it and the thing fell to the ground with a thump. Alex cursed, heart racing as he quickly wrapped the sword against his back and tugged on a blue hoodie, with his jacket layered over. He quickly opened the window and dropped the backpack out onto the ground. Alex stood completely still, listening for the strangers' voices that had called him family for so many years and yet never treated him so.

Alex leaned against his closet door opposite his window and took a deep breath as he closed his eyes in an attempt to steady himself for what he was about to do.

Alex darted forward, running toward the open window at full speed. Alex leapt out into the cold night air. His open jacket and hoodie flapped in the wind. His arms flew above him. For a moment, time slowed and he felt as if he was flying. But that moment soon ended, and he fell toward the ground.

His feet landed on the pavement awkwardly. He fell forward. Alex tried to stop himself from falling on his face, but his trembling hands did nothing to bar his momentum. His arm bent, sending him tumbling even faster down the driveway.

Alex slammed into the metal garbage cans at the end of the driveway, sending them flying across the road. The cans crashed and clanged into the street. Alex cursed again, snatching up his bag. He had to leave now. His parents were going to find out he was gone soon, and he didn't plan on being here when they did. But where could he go that they wouldn't find him?

"Honey, make sure he doesn't try something he'll regret," Mrs. Shaffer looked up at her husband from where she had slumped into her seat. Mr. Shaffer sighed and picked up his abandoned beer, taking a long swig before he stood and pounded up the steps, his beer still gripped in his hand. He did *not* want to be sober right now.

When he got to Alex's door he clasped his hand around the knob and turned it. Or at least, he tried to. All the knob would do was jiggle. Mr. Shaffer tried again and again, but the door wouldn't budge. His anger rising, he pounded on the door until it burst open, breaking the hinges. The curtains covering the window fluttered in the fresh breeze that flowed through the open window. His son was nowhere in sight.

The beer in his hand slipped from his fingers and crashed to the floor, alcohol pouring onto the ground and seeping into the carpet. Mr. Shaffer ran down the stairs, skipping steps as he went. Alex was *not* going to get away. Mr. Shaffer jumped into his car and slammed on the gas, which sent him skidding backwards down the driveway. Flooring the accelerator once again, Mr. Shaffer sped down the road, quickly covering the distance Alex had put between them.

Alex slowed down to a brisk walk to catch his breath as well as his bearings. Which way was he supposed to go? Alex stopped completely when he realized whose house he was in front of. He should probably stop and say good-bye, right? Yes, he should at least try. He owed him that much.

Mark ran his towel through his wet hair, shaking out droplets of water when he heard a sound at his window. He looked up to see a rock hit the glass. Curious, Mark put down his towel and pushed his window open just in time for a rock to go flying past his face.

"Shoot! Sorry!" Alex called from his yard below.

"Dude! What are you doing outside my window? Its almost midnight," Mark asked as he looked Alex over. He seemed… off. Mark could see a sheen of sweat across his forehead under the streetlight, and… was he shaking? Alex shoved his hands into his pockets and glanced down the street anxiously. He had his backpack on, and it looked full. More so than usual.

"I just wanted to say good-bye before I left," Alex replied.

"Left? Where are you going?"

"I… I don't know. I just have to go. I can't stay here." Alex glanced down the street again.

"Why?"

"I can't explain right now. I'm sorry. You're a good friend Mark. Thank you," Alex looked him in the eye before glancing down the street again.

Why did he keep doing that? Was he running from something..? That's when it clicked for him. "You're running away aren't you?"

Alex started at that but his attention was quickly drawn away by some head-lights that appeared in the distance.

"I'm sorry Mark…" Alex said before taking off around the corner and out of sight. Seconds later a black suburban drove around the corner, the engine revving as it sped up. Mark watched until it was out of sight then grabbed his backpack, determined not to leave his friend to deal with whatever this was alone.

Alex took off running, unsure of where to go. His father's car wasn't far behind him, and the way the engine revved up, he's sure he'd been spotted. Knowing he wouldn't be able to outrun a car, Alex veered to the right, jumping over some bushes and dashing into someone's backyard. He tried to stay off the streets, jumping over fences and bushes and going around gardens and pools.

He could hear his father's car speeding through the streets. At one point Alex caught sight of the car on the other side of a house he was behind and he faltered, stumbling face first into a kiddie pool. A dog started barking somewhere and he took off again, now dripping wet. He passed through another yard with a motion sensor light, and was briefly blinded, crashing into a plastic slide. He pushed off again and ran out onto another street.

He stopped hearing his father's car a long time ago, but he wouldn't relax yet. A few houses down he saw a large park with a playground. Alex took off after it but stopped in his tracks when he saw his father's suburban circling the park through the trees on the other side. He cursed and looked around for someplace else to go.

He needed a destination. A place he could hide out in until he found someplace else to go. Alex looked back at the park, uncertain why he recognized it. When his eyes traveled to the swings he remembered, this was the park his friends took him to. He remembered the grand tours when they first began hanging out, and realized one of those places would get him away from this town and away from his family.

The docks. Alex took off running again, cutting through alleys and backyards, going on the streets only when he needed too. He stopped only to watch as cars went by with bated breath. When he finally got there, it was early morning, the sky a dark blue, the sun not yet above the horizon. Rows of ships stretched down the dock, and Alex ran by each one until he found a dark red cargo ship with men running to and from it. By the looks of it, they were trying to make a hasty departure.

Two men were arguing in the center of the dock. One of them was short and skinny, carrying a clipboard. His shoulders drooped and as he stood, it looked as though he struggled to hold himself up, as if his body was too heavy for his frail legs to hold. The man in front of him on the other hand was tall with broad shoulders. Alex could tell he was a man in command. Alex ducked behind one of the many crates that the men were loading onto the ship and leaned forward to listen to their conversation.

"What do you mean we still have another hour before we can leave?" the taller man groaned.

"I am terribly sorry, sir, but the delivery trucks were held up in an accident on the highway, so they were forced to take a detour that added another hour to their trip. And we still have about three-hundred more crates to load onto the ship," said the man with the clipboard.

"Well, get on with it then! We should have been gone two hours ago!"

"But sir, I saw that it's supposed to storm later on tomorrow. Won't the captain have to delay our departure for it to pass?"

"No, the storm will only be on land by the looks of it. We should be fine. Getting these shipments on schedule is what we should be focusing on. And for Pete's sake, Rick, quit calling me sir. Need I remind you that my first name is Will, not sir?" The taller man added.

"Yes, sir. Will do sir." The smaller man smiled wryly as he hurried off to help the others.

Once the two men departed, Alex dashed up the ramp onto the boat and found a hiding spot behind wooden crates covered by a sheet. Alex quickly went underneath the sheet and rested his head against the wood, finally allowing himself a shaky breath. Closing his eyes, he waited for the ship to leave.

Alex must have drifted off while he was waiting because he was startled awake from the sound of pounding footsteps and hushed voices running in his direction. Alex moved deeper into the tight little space between the ship's metal side and the crates, holding his breath and hoping that whoever was out there wouldn't notice he was there. The footsteps stopped right in front of the sheet that covered the crates he was huddled next to. They sounded rushed and confused, unsure of where to go. The sheet flew open and four figures rushed inside. It was too dark to see who they were, so Alex reached into his backpack and pulled out a flashlight he had thankfully left in his bag a few days before. Alex flicked the light on and rested the light on the four figures.

It was Nicole, David, Brooke, and Mark. They all had backpacks slung over their shoulders.

"Hey, get that out of my eyes!" cried David, throwing his arms up to shield his eyes.

"Be quiet! Do you want to get us caught?" whispered Brooke.

"Oh, right," replied David. "Sorry."

"Guys! What are you doing here?" Alex whisper-yelled.

"We're coming with you," replied Nicole. "Wherever that is."

"Yeah, where *are* we going?" asked David.

"*I'm* going anywhere but here," Alex said.

"Why? Did we upset you?" asked Brooke.

"No! No, of course not," Alex said, waving the flashlight around. "Not you. Its...complicated. How did you find me?"

"You told me you were running away, remember?" Mark asked.

"Yes, but how'd you know I was going to come here?"

"The bus terminal and train are farther out toward the main part of the city. It would have taken too long to get there. This was the closest transportation option," Mark explained.

"Phenomenal deductive-reasoning, really, but I'm not getting off this boat, so don't try to stop me," Alex said, gripping the tarp they were hiding under as if it was a tether to himself and the ship.

"We kinda figured. Why do you think we have backpacks?" asked David, pointing to his back.

"Wait, what?" Alex was interrupted when a sudden roar sounded from outside.

"What is that?" asked Nicole.

Alex lifted the tarp and peered out. The ship had left the docks and was now heading out to sea. A droplet of water slid down Alex's face, and he looked up toward the sky. Dark, heavy clouds hung on the horizon almost as if they were sitting on a shelf. Another droplet of water landed on Alex's face followed by another and another until the droplets quickly turned into downpour. Alex let go of the tarp and turned back to the others. His hair stuck to his forehead with water dripping down his face.

"It's raining," Alex remarked.

"Yeah. We can see that," Nicole laughed.

"There's going to be a storm. The ship has already left the docks. You should have never followed me here," Alex scolded.

"There's no going back now," shrugged David.

"What are your parents going to think when they realize their kids have run away? Or that they've gone *missing*? They're going to worry." Alex pointed accusingly at the four of them.

"Of course they will. But what kind of friends would we be if we let you stow away on a ship alone? Besides, won't your parents worry too?" Brooke asked.

"When we get back on land, we'll figure out a way home," Mark said when Alex didn't answer. "It's too late to go back now, so let's see where this ship will take us."

THIRTEEN

Alex woke up to a sudden jerk and a loud thud of the ship. He and his friends had fallen asleep against the crates and they were now soaked. Alex looked down to see that water had seeped through the tarp, covering the floor in a puddle of water. Alex lifted the tarp once again and looked out to see the largest rocks he's ever seen towering over the ship.

The wind roared and rain poured down on the metal deck. Alex crawled out from the tarp and hid behind some nearby crates, stretching his legs. He peered around a large wooden box. Crew members were running around frantically, trying to keep the ship from colliding with any of the rocks or being sunk by the gigantic waves. The crew members were so wrapped up in their jobs that none of them noticed the small silhouette of a boy running from behind a crate and into the covering of a tarp. Except for one.

Alex dove back under the tarp, startling everyone awake.

"What the heck? Where did you come from?" Nicole shouted.

"Outside. There is a huge storm going on and it's tearing the ship apart!" Alex shouted.

Suddenly the tarp flew open revealing Will, the bigger man that Alex had seen talking at the port not long ago. Will grabbed Alex's arm and hoisted him off the ground. More men came from behind and did the same to the others. They grabbed their bags and struggled to walk as the men were practically carrying them across, almost slipping on the wet metal of the ship's deck. Water crashed over the side of the ship and onto the deck, making it almost impossible to stand. The ship's cargo strained against the ropes in rhythm with the motion of the ship.

Will burst into the bridge where the captain struggled to hold the wheel in place. Desks were aligned all around the room, covered in multiple buttons and switches and lights. Multiple men sat at those desks and some men to the right of the captain sat radioing for help from multiple stations. Will and the other men stepped inside and held Alex and the others in front of them, facing the captain holding the teens' hands behind their backs, holding them in place. The room became quiet as they entered. A man beside the captain took the wheel as the captain spun around to face them. The captain was tall and muscular. His hair was bright red and his piercing blue eyes looked like the ocean itself reflected in them. He had a slight goatee from the lack of time to shave and sweat beaded his skin from the stress of the storm.

"What are you doing here? You should be outside! We need to get those crates secure and this ship intact!" The captain stopped when he saw the five children struggling in his crew's hands. "Children! What are children doing on my ship?" he growled.

"Captain, we found them hiding under a tarp covering a section of crates," said the man holding David in place.

"Stowaways, eh? Bring them to room 232. Gentlemen, continue your work," the captain commanded the men inside the control room as he followed the men out the door and into the hall.

The men dragged the teens down the hall and stopped in front of a door that had the numbers 232 on it. Will opened the door and held it open as the men shoved Brooke and the others into the room before shoving Alex in as well. The men then left and in walked the captain. The room was small with bare white walls and nothing but a table nailed to the floor and chairs sitting around it. At the very back of the room on the wall was a round window the size of a large plate. The storm raged on outside the window and thunder shook the metal hinges. The captain shut the door and turned to face the kids.

"So, why do I have stowaways on my ship?" he asked.

The five of them stayed silent, not making a sound.

"You know what? It doesn't matter. Do you know what I do to stowaways on this ship? I have them work. Come on then." The captain turned around and opened the door, then paused. He turned his head to face the others and suddenly his expression softened from the hard and stern one he had worn just moments before. His eyes fell on Alex as he spoke. "Don't worry. I've been in the same boat before, in a manner of speaking. You can call me Nick." And with that he turned and walked out the door, with Alex and the others following close behind. The entire walk back, one thought confused Alex the most. *"I've been in the same boat before."* What was that supposed to mean?

Nick led them back to the door that led to the dock. Outside, the deck hands scurried from left to right across the deck. Many would slip and fall, all fighting against the storm, desperately trying not to be swept overboard. Nick turned to Alex and the others. An expression of sadness and guilt washed over his face.

"I still can't believe I'm doing this. But at this rate the ship will crash either way. I am going to send you out there. I need you to try to get as many of those crates secure and attached to the deck as tightly as you can." The captain paused. "Good luck." He opened the door and after a brief moment of uncertainty, the others ran out into the rain.

Before Alex could run out, Nick grabbed his arm.

"I know you have run away from your family," Nick said.

"So? What's it to you?" Alex's eyes narrowed at the man standing before him, hiding his disbelief at how obvious he was.

"I was once a runaway as well. I know that expression all too well. I just wanted you to know, you are not the only one." Nick's face hardened into the stern expression Alex saw when he first met the captain. Alex ran out into the darkness and soon was engulfed by it.

Immediately, the sound of the crashing waves and the rain pounding against the ship's metal lining was all Alex could hear. The darkness of the night and the rain clouded Alex's vision so that he couldn't see his own hand, though it was right in front of his face. Alex continued to walk in search of his friends, but could not find them. Alex called out for them, but he couldn't even hear his own voice. Something cold and wet brushed against Alex's hand.

He felt around and realized it was the side of the ship. Suddenly, the air pressure changed and it felt as though time had stopped. A clap of thunder and flash of lightning made it all too clear. A massive wave loomed over the side of the ship. The water looked an unforgiving black in the night. Alex stared at the wave unable to move, frozen to the spot.

The wave crashed down onto the boat, washing away anything on board. Water rushed into Alex's lungs caving in on him at all sides. Alex was tossed and turned as the wave sent him sprawling off the ship and into the water. Alex hit the water like concrete. His arms and legs flailed around in utter panic, clouding all reasoning. His lungs burned, desperate for air.

Alex shot back to the surface gasping for breath. Crew members were falling in the water everywhere, along with crates and pieces of ship that had broken off. Alex looked around for the others but could see none of them. Lightning flashed incessantly, brightening up the sky for mere moments at a time. Another wave washed over Alex, and he plummeted toward the bottom. He tried to reach the surface once again, but he was pushed down farther and farther until everything went completely black.

FOURTEEN

Alex woke up to broad daylight. His eyes stung and his head pounded in the sudden light. He clutched his head as he slowly sat up to look around. As he took in his surroundings, he realized he was on a beach. Wreckage from the ship was strewn across the sand. How long had he been unconscious? Alex searched frantically for Mark or Nicole or anyone for that matter, but he could not see any sign of them. If they were there, they were beyond sight.

Alex looked down at the water that swept up his legs and then back down. From the corner of his eyes, he noticed a large rock that was the entire width of the beach, hiding the rest of it from view. With a sliver of hope, Alex stood up and made his way over to the rock. Still drenched and covered in sand, He climbed the scorching hot boulder, burning his hands in the process. When he finally made it to the top, he immediately stood up and scanned the beach on the other side.

Alex breathed a sigh of relief at the sight of them. Scattered across the beach were Mark, Nicole, and David. They were all unconscious, but Alex could tell they were alive. Alex jumped down from the massive rock and ran over to David. Alex lightly placed his hand on David's arm and started to shake him.

"David? David, wake up! Are you all right?" Alex said, shaking David awake.

"Ten more minutes," David grumbled.

Alex shook harder.

"What! What happened? Where's the fire?" David asked wearily, his words slurred.

"The boat crashed and we ended up on this beach. You're not hurt, are you?" Alex asked.

"Um, no I don't think so," David said, sitting up, becoming more aware.

"Come help me get the others," Alex called as he walked over to Nicole.

After Nicole was awake he searched frantically for Brooke, but she was nowhere to be found. He could feel panic well up inside of him as he thought of all the things that could have happened to her.

"Guys! Hey guys!" a familiar voice called. Alex looked in the direction of the voice, relief flooding through him to find Brooke walking toward them from further down the beach. Her clothes were drenched and ripped in a few places, but as far as Alex could tell, she was unhurt.

Alex returned her wave and she ran toward him. Once they met she threw her arms around him in relief, catching Alex in surprise.

"Thank God! I thought I was alone! And dead. I'm so glad to see you!" Brooke exclaimed.

"Me too," Alex said, hugging her back.

"Brooke!" Nicole yelled when she caught sight of the two, running over to them and hugging them from behind.

"Don't leave me out of this!" David laughed, running into them all and knocking them onto the sand in a laughing heap. Mark walked over to see if they were all right and David yanked him down into the sand with them. The laughter died quickly as they stared out at the sea in front of them and they sat there in silence, taking everything in, a melancholic fog settling over them.

After they had regrouped, they scoured the shoreline for their bags, which they hoped had washed up with them. Thankfully, they all managed to find their soaked bags. Some of them had torn, but they were still usable. The teens gathered their things and sat down, immediately rummaging through their bags for food. Their clothes were drenched and their bodies were coated with sand, their hair included.

"It's a good thing my backpack is waterproof," David said absentmindedly as he chewed on a granola bar.

"Does anyone know where we are?" asked Mark. Everyone stopped moving and looked at him. After a moment of silence, they all shook their heads.

"I have no idea," Brooke said.

Suddenly, David dropped the bar in his hand and his eyes widened.

"What's up, David?" Nicole asked. David didn't answer. "David?" she asked again. He kept staring. They all turned around to find a large forest stretching as far as the eye could see.

"Where did that come from?" Alex exclaimed.

"Our heads must be messed up after that storm. You would think that kind of thing would be impossible to miss," said Nicole.

"You would think," agreed David.

"No one saw that earlier?" Alex asked. He was answered by a series of shaking heads. "Freaky…"

"Maybe we would see something if we went up there in one of those trees?" asked Brooke.

Every head whipped around to look at Brooke.

"You know that's not a bad idea," said Mark.

Alex stood up and ran over to the edge of the forest. He turned to make sure his friends were following him before he jumped and grabbed the closest tree branch and hoisted himself up, quickly pulling himself higher up the tree. The rest of them followed suit. Alex pushed aside the remaining leaves and branches and looked over the canopy. There was nothing but forest and ocean that stretched for miles, showing no sign of end or civilization.

"Do you guys see anything?" Nicole shouted over the roar of the wind.

"No!" David shouted back.

Unable to see anything but trees and water, Alex started to make his way back down when a sudden movement in his peripheral vision caught his attention. Alex stopped his descent and turned toward an area farther back in the forest. Without warning, a flock of birds burst from a section of branches and up into the sky. Where the birds had fled, the trees shook, shaking off leaves and branches. Some trees broke from the sudden weight and slowly fell to the ground with a crash. As the trees fell, Alex noticed that whatever was making the trees fall was coming in his direction.

Alex climbed down from the tree quickly, trying to reach the ground in time. The others were waiting for him at the bottom. Alex turned around to face the woods and searched for any sign of what he saw in the tree. Alex could see no sign of the trees or whatever caused the commotion.

"Did you guys hear that sound?" Alex asked over his shoulder.

"What sound? We are right next to an ocean and a forest. I didn't hear anything out of the ordinary," said Brooke, peering over Alex's shoulder to see what he was looking at.

"Neither did I. Did you see something when you were up in that tree?" asked Mark.

"No. Nevermind. Just forget about it," Alex said, turning back around.

"I couldn't see any sign of civilization anywhere!" Nicole explained. "How are we supposed to get back home now?"

"Where do you think we are?" asked Mark.

"We could be on an island," replied Alex.

"An island?" replied David, his eyes widening.

"Just think about it," explained Alex. "No people, no boats, no buildings, just a beach and jungle."

"We have to find a way out of here!" said Brooke.

"Yeah, like we didn't think of that before Captain Obvious!" David snapped.

"Calm down," Mark said. "We will find a way out, so just calm down."

"What do we do now?" asked Brooke.

"We start walking," Alex replied. "There isn't really anything else we can do."

"We could stay on the beach and wait for another boat to come around. Maybe we could call out to them so they could rescue us," Nicole suggested.

"They are going to ask how we got here, and then we'll have to tell them that we were stowaways on a ship. How do you think they'll respond to that?" Mark asked.

"That is if another ship will even come around," Alex said. Everyone went silent as they digested Alex's words. Sounds of leaves rustling in the wind and waves crashing against rocks filled the air.

"Then we'll just have to make a raft," David said, breaking the silence.

"I don't think that's possible. There are really strong currents out there and to top it all off we're in salt-water. Who knows how many sharks are out there," Alex replied.

"But we could give it a shot. We have no other ideas," David replied.

Alex had stopped trying to argue and so had the others, giving into David's idea. They all scattered throughout the shore and the edge of the woods, searching for wood and vines and anything they thought would help make a raft. Alex tried to go where he saw the closest tree fall, but he could find no sign of broken branches or fallen trees. He climbed another tree and looked out. The trees that had fallen earlier weren't visible up there. He could have sworn that he saw something knock down those trees.

Alex used some of the vines they collected and wrapped them around the tree logs, securing them together as the last step to assembling their raft.

"I don't think this will work," Alex said, standing up and shaking his head after tying the last knot. "It's just a bunch of tree trunks and vines. Something that you only read about in books or see in movies. How will we know if the tree trunks won't sink with all the extra weight? How do we know they will float at all?"

"Come on, let's just try at least," said Brooke.

On the count of three, they pushed the raft into the water and jumped on, using branches as paddles. It almost seemed as if the tree trunks were going to hold, but the raft didn't get very far from the island before it started to sink.

"Guys…it's sinking," David said, panic lingering in his voice.

"Yeah, we know! Jump off! Hurry!" Nicole exclaimed.

They all jumped off and swam back to shore just in time. When they looked back, the raft they had made slammed into a rock and broke in half. A few pieces of wood remained on top of the rock while the rest drifted away with the tide.

"That was a complete waste of time," David huffed.

"At least we know for future references not to try it," Brooke sighed.

As the sun began to set, they began to set up a campfire. As Alex gave the fire room to breathe, Brooke, Mark, David, and Nicole pulled out sleeping bags from their backpacks. Alex stared at them with wide eyes.

"Why do you have sleeping bags?" Alex asked.

"We didn't know how long we'd be gone. It's better to be prepared," Nicole explained.

"Where's your sleeping bag?" asked Brooke.

"I don't have one," Alex replied sourly. "Didn't think I'd need it."

"I thought so," Mark commented. "I got you one too, don't worry."

"You guys are strangely prepared for some people who had no idea where they were going and just randomly threw a bunch of stuff together," Alex pointed out.

"What can I say? We're strange," David said, yawning.

Alex sighed and took the sleeping bag from Mark's hands. He rolled it out on the sand and crawled inside it. He hadn't realized how tired he was. He fell asleep within minutes. When the sun rose the next morning, he didn't even remember going to bed.

A black wall of water hundreds of feet high towered over Alex, ready to crash over the ship at any second. Lightning flashed, lighting up the sky before darkening again. A crash of thunder filled the air. A second flash of lightning lit up the sky, and Alex waited for the sky to darken once again but it didn't. The world remained filled with bright white light. The rain that had been falling on him before had stopped and was now floating in mid-air. Time was frozen before him.

Men and women hung over the side of the ship. Some held the side and dangled while some were suspended in the air, about to fall into the unforgiving waters below. Their expressions remained the same. Some of confusion, some of panic, and some simply of fright. Alex looked behind him to find the heavy metal door to the inside of the ship open. Just inches away from it, in a running position with his arms outstretched toward him, was Nick. His expression was completely different from the others he had seen. Alex didn't know how, but it was. A number of crew members were holding him by the shoulders and torso and pulling him to an extra life boat.

Suddenly, time resumed and rain started to fall once again and the sky went black. The crew members pulled the struggling Kick back and away. The massive wave slowly began to fall. The wave slammed into the ship, breaking it in half. People scattered everywhere. Many opened their mouths to scream only to have it filled with water. Alex braced for the impact, preparing himself for the water to crash over him and sweep him overboard along with everyone else, but it never happened. He looked up to find himself standing above it all. He looked down to see himself dragged down by the wave and disappearing into the black water. A loud scream slowly trumped the roar of the storm. Alex clamped his hands over his ears to protect them, but it didn't do much good. The scream turned into a piercing screech and became so loud it was the only thing Alex could hear.

FIFTEEN

Alex awoke with a start from the shock of the nightmare. He was surprised to find that he wasn't the first one awake, as he usually was. Sitting by the fire with a sweater on along with his sleeping bag held tightly around his body, was Mark.

"You were shivering," Mark said bluntly.

"So are you. What are you doing up?" Alex replied.

"I woke up freezing and couldn't go back to sleep," said Mark.

"How long have you been awake?" Alex asked. He felt around to make sure his sword was still next to him beneath the folds of the sleeping bag before standing up and walking over to sit next to Mark.

"I don't know, about ten minutes maybe? Not long. The sun was up when I woke up."

"It's really cold out here."

"Yeah, you looked like you were going to turn into a Popsicle!" Mark laughed.

"So do the others." Alex nodded over at the others, who were all shaking from the cold.

"They aren't shaking as much as you were though."

Alex looked around for anything that could warm them up and saw that the fire was growing dim.

"I'm going to go get more firewood."

"Do you want me to come with you? You'll be in the woods all alone."

"No, I'll be fine. I won't go too far," Alex replied, walking toward the woods.

Although the sun had already risen, the inside of the woods was dark and mysterious. Alex picked up pieces of wood and dead branches as he walked. He had already gathered a handful of wood when he heard a crack from beneath his feet and he tumbled head first down a hill.

Leaves, branches, and mud flew past him and mixed with his dark brown hair, in the process ripping his clothes. When he finally stopped falling, he had landed next to a large shallow stream made up of jagged rocks at the bottom of it. Alex heard a rumbling sound coming from above him, and he looked up just in time to see the pile of wood that had fallen out of his hands come toppling on him, knocking him into the stream.

Alex laid in the stream face up and stared at the sky that was now beginning to brighten to a dark blue through the gaps in the leaves. Alex watched as his heavy breathing faded into mist in the cold morning air. When he had finally gathered himself, he stood up and took in his surroundings. Behind him was a tree that had fallen across the stream and was leaning on the sloping side of the hill on the other side. The fallen tree made a long dark shadow that made it impossible to see what lay underneath.

"You should not have come here," a voice suddenly whispered. A shadow of a man started to form underneath the tree. Alex jumped at the voice and stumbled backwards, falling into the stream once again.

"What was…?" Alex started but stopped. Something about the voice was familiar. But he didn't know how or why. "Do I know you?" he asked. The man said nothing. "What are y…?" Then he realized where he recognized him from. "You're the one that was in between those houses back at Orolson, aren't you? You're the one I chased across the rooftops!"

"Correct," replied the voice.

Alex was stunned. He had come to the conclusion that it was just a hologram of some sort being projected through a window. But if it was a hologram how could it have ended up here?

"What are you?" Alex asked with a raised eyebrow.

"You need to be careful while on this island. There are a lot of them here. There is no escape from this island. You must figure out how to survive," the voice said, ignoring Alex's question.

"Wait, there are a lot of *who* here?" Alex was barely able to get the last word out before the shadow twisted into a circle and slowly started to decrease until it became so small Alex couldn't tell if it was still there.

Alex sighed and turned around toward the sticks and wood he gathered, which were now floating in the stream, slowly sinking. Alex groaned as he picked up a piece. It was too saturated to make a fire with so he trudged back up the hill he had fallen down. Alex was only a few feet up before his foot slipped and he fell into the stream. Alex climbed the hill again and again, but it was more of a cliff than a hill. Alex walked to the other side of the stream then turned back around to face the hill.

Alex charged at full speed up the hill and only made it a few feet more before he fell backwards. Surrendering to the reality that it was too steep to climb, Alex walked back over to the tree where the shadow once was. Conveniently enough, there was a path right behind where the shadow of the man stood. Alex sighed out of annoyance as he started to walk the path.

It only took about ten minutes to arrive back at the beach where Mark was sitting by the dimly lit fire. The others were still fast asleep in the sleeping bags. They quivered in the cold. Thankfully, the path Alex had taken to get back was littered with wood so he replaced the lost wood easily.

"What happened to you?" Mark demanded when he saw Alex's hair and clothes caked in mud and sticks.

"I was gathering wood and I took a wrong step. I fell down a hill into a stream. I'll go get washed up once I get the fire going. Are they still asleep?" Alex asked, nodding toward the others as he started to feed the fire.

"Oh yeah, they were really tired, I guess," Mark replied.

Almost as if on cue Nicole woke up followed by Brooke moments later.

"What are you doing up?" Nicole asked groggily once she composed herself enough to figure out where she was.

"And why is it so cold?" Brooke added.

"Don't worry, I'm getting the fire started again," Alex said, dodging smoke and ashes that burst out of the wood. As Nicole and Brooke huddled closer to the fire, David woke up.

"What happened to you?" David asked as soon as he saw Alex.

"Ah, I meant to ask, what *did* happen to you? You're a mess!" said Nicole.

"Ask Mark. I'm going to go clean all of this mud off," Alex called as he walked toward the ocean.

"But it must be freezing!" called Brooke.

"I'll go into the areas where the sun hits!" Alex yelled, now running. Alex ran into the shallow water and dove in as soon as it was deep enough. The water was oddly warm and it felt good against his scratched and cold skin. Alex swam out farther and farther into the ocean until he couldn't touch the ocean floor anymore.

Alex started to rub the mud and twigs out of his hair until his head was completely clean. After he was completely clean, Alex floated on his back and stared at the bright blue sky.

"Is it cold? You didn't die of hypothermia, did you?" David yelled after him, laughing.

"No! I'm still alive!" Alex called back. "It's actually really warm!"

"We're coming in then!" called Brooke.

They all ran into the water, not bothering to take off any clothes. They gasped at the temperature of the water against their freezing skin.

"It's so warm!" said Nicole as she swam next to Alex.

"It's strange," Alex said as he started to tread water.

"I wonder if there's an underwater volcano down there! That could be what's making the water so warm." said David.

"It's possible," Nicole confirmed.

"Do you want to see?" David asked with a smirk.

They all dove beneath the surface only to find that there was no underwater volcano. Alex looked at David, who had a disappointed look on his face that even Alex could see through his puffed out cheeks. David noticed Alex looking at him, and he shrugged and pointed up toward the surface, gesturing for them to go back up. Alex looked around the ocean floor one last time before swimming to the surface.

Alex and David were the only ones still below the surface, and as they swam they felt the water pressure change below them. They both looked down to see a great white shark swimming toward them with its jaws snapping open, revealing its rows of sharp white teeth and blood red gums. Alex opened his mouth in surprise and choked as water flooded in. Alex and David shot up to the surface before he could swallow too much water.

"Get back to the shore!" Alex yelled, gasping for air.

"What's going on?" asked Brooke.

"No time to explain! Just swim!" David yelled at her.

Before David could finish shouting, they all took off to the shore, each one of them paddling as fast as their limbs could carry them. As soon as they reached shallow water, they stood and dashed for the dry sand. They fell onto the beach and let the impossibly scorching sand dry their freezing bodies.

"Guys, are we going to be on this beach forever or are we going to explore? There is really no way of getting out of this place," observed David between breaths.

Alex furrowed his brow as he thought about David's comment. It was an oddly calm question. There they were, five kids stranded on an island with no other civilization in sight, and his first thought was to go explore?

"Why not? There is the possibility that there are people here. We just couldn't see them through the trees," said Mark. Alex rolled over to face the opposite direction and put his arm in between his head and the sand. His saturated shirt and jeans sagged against his skin.

SIXTEEN

They walked for what felt like hours. The sun was sinking into the horizon. They were running out of daylight and soon they would be left to the darkness. They hadn't taken a break since the beach. Alex sighed as he tilted his head up to stare at the canopy as he walked. Though he couldn't see the sun or clouds, the rustling of the leaves and light peeking through the branches were just as calming.

"We should find a place to sleep," Mark huffed, startling Alex out of his trance. "But I haven't seen any areas that we could go to."

"Do you hear that?" asked Nicole, ignoring Mark. Alex looked at Nicole curiously as she moved her hair from in front of her ears. Alex tilted his head and listened for whatever Nicole had been hearing. For a moment, all was quiet until a low howl began to fill the forest. As Alex listened, he slowly realized that the rising chorus was coming from somewhere nearby and it was way too close for comfort.

"Wolves!" cried David.

"What do we do?" asked Brooke.

"I read in a book once how to avoid wolf attacks!" Nicole said.

"Well? What do we do, then?" David asked.

"Quick! Climb the closest tree!" Nicole said, leaping up the tree next to her.

David, Mark, Brooke, and Alex all did as Nicole instructed. Alex had to run a bit farther than the others because the tree closest to him was a few feet farther away. Alex stumbled as he reached from branch to branch. Once Alex was about halfway up, he stopped and leaned against an area of the tree that was strong enough to hold him.

Alex crouched down and stared at the ground. A few minutes later, a pack of wolves trotted into the area where the teens had been standing. The wolves stopped abruptly and sniffed the ground. Alex held his breath as four wolves started to sniff at the roots of the tree he was in. After a while, they moved to the tree next to him, and Alex let out his breath all at once. The sound of his gasp was louder than he thought it would be. Alex stared down, waiting to see if the wolves had heard. They had all frozen in place, and one by one each wolf started to growl.

A loud howl broke out, and Alex was confused to realize that it hadn't come from the pack below. The howling had stopped the wolves from growling, and Alex allowed his breathing to become regular. Alex watched curiously as wolves scattered about the group started to howl, while the other half remained silent. After the howling faded, the wolves that responded sprinted out of sight while the others stayed behind. Soon the light disappeared completely, and Alex and the others were left alone, trapped among the tree branches with wolves prowling about at their feet.

"You still there?" David called into the night.

"Where else would we go?" Mark demanded.

"How are we supposed to get back down? It's pitch black and I can't see a thing! Do you know if the wolves have left yet?" asked David.

"I have no idea. We'll probably have to sleep up here tonight," Alex stated.

"Where's Nicole and Brooke?" asked Mark.

"I'm up in the tree with Brooke! I think she may have fallen asleep," answered Nicole.

"If you guys wake up, could you call out to see if any of the others are awake? I just want to have that assurance that you guys are still there," David stuttered.

"We will," replied Nicole.

Alex reached into his backpack and brought out a flashlight. He switched it on and waved the beam of light around in the darkness. Unfortunately, the beam would only reach a few feet. Alex shifted the beam over to the trunk of the tree so he could lean against it.

"Who has a flashlight?" Nicole called.

"Alex does. I can't see you because the light won't go very far. The battery is dying, I think," Alex replied as he slid down the trunk and sat on the branch.

"I can see the light but not you!" called Mark.

"Yeah, I'm sure. I'm turning it off now, to save what's left of the battery." Alex switched the light back off and slid it back into his bag. He wrapped his hand around the pommel of his sword that was still hidden beneath the folds of his jacket, resting against his back. He dozed off and before he knew it, he had fallen asleep.

Alex woke up with the odd sensation that he was being watched. It was still pitch black, and Alex moved his hand in front of his face. It had gotten so much darker that he could barely make out the shape of the tree trunk. Alex quickly reached into his backpack once again and pulled the flashlight back out. He switched the light on and swung it around frantically. Although he could see nothing, he still had the sense that something was out there. Alex snatched up his backpack and swung it over his shoulder before climbing higher up the tree.

He burst through the canopy sucking in air as though he had been underwater. The moon shone so brightly that it lit up as far as the eye can see. Alex was surprised the brightness didn't reach below the canopy, but the canopy was unusually thick. Alex tilted his head back and stared at the stars. Something caught his attention out of the corner of his eye, so he looked to the side without moving his head. In the tree beside him was a dark silhouetted figure staring up at the stars just as Alex had been. Suddenly the figure spoke, startling Alex.

"Beautiful, aren't they?" the figure asked. Alex recognized the voice as the man from the stream. "You have been doing good so far," said the man. "But no matter what your friends think tomorrow, do not go back. They'll be waiting for you there. Searching for you."

Before the man could turn into a small black ball again, Alex stopped him. "Wait! Just answer this question. Please!" Alex asked desperately.

"You may not ask who I am," said the man.

"Who is 'they'? What do you mean 'they'll be searching'?" Alex asked.

"They are the citizens of Heltiana and the creatures of the Dark," the man said simply before disappearing. Heltiana? Creatures of the Dark? What was all of that stuff supposed to mean? As the man's words bounced back and forth in his mind, Alex drifted back to sleep.

The next morning Alex woke up to his friends screaming his name.

"What is it? Is everything okay?" Alex yelled down as he climbed down to the spot he was sitting in before he had decided to climb to the top the night before. Everyone was still in the same positions they were in when they had climbed into the tree except they were all now standing up with alarmed expressions on their faces.

"Alex! You scared us! We woke up and suddenly you were gone!" said Brooke.

"I'm fine. I just went up to sleep in the canopy. It was too dark down here and the moon is so bright up there." Alex nodded up toward the top of the tree.

"I think it's safe for us to go back down now," David suggested.

"Yeah, I think we all cleared that by now. The question is, how exactly do we get down? All of the branches I used to get up here are gone! I don't know how that happened but the trunk from here down is bare," explained Nicole.

Alex looked down the trunk of the tree and noticed the same had happened with the tree he was in as well. Where had all of the other branches gone? How had he gotten up there? Alex leaned forward so he could drag his backpack off and hang it on a branch. As he reached out to hang the bag, his hand bumped into something, sending whatever it was toward his face. Sensing the movement, Alex ducked just in time to see a long and thick vine fly past him. Alex watched as the vine flew up almost right on a branch on the tree beside him before rocking back and dangling beside the branch Alex was on. That gave Alex an idea. Alex thrust his backpack over his shoulders again and gripped the vine.

"Oh, you're not really planning on doing that, are you?" asked Nicole.

Alex ignored Nicole and inched backwards onto the branch until his back was flat against the trunk. Alex took a deep breath as he counted to three in his head. On three, he ran to the end of the branch with his hands clasped around the vine. He jumped off the end of the branch and gasped as the wind hit him and he hurtled through the air.

SEVENTEEN

From where the others were standing, it looked as if Alex was going extraordinarily fast, but from Alex's view it felt as though he almost wasn't moving at all. He tilted his head and stared up at the treetops. Bright light shone through the leaves and wind whipped past his face. The entire scene was so peaceful. All he could hear was the wind rustling the leaves.

Alex jumped off and landed on another tree branch. He looked down to see if he could get down from the tree, but the problem was still the same. The trunk was bare all the way down. He looked around the forest again for more vines, and he noticed that the vines were everywhere. So much for his powers of observation. Alex made sure he was going the opposite way of the beach before grabbing onto another vine and looking back at the others, who were now behind him.

"Are you coming?" Alex called over to them. "There are vines next to you! Use them to catch up!"

"I don't know, Alex," Nicole yelled back. "What if we just head back to the beach? We could wait there! Maybe a plane or boat will see us and rescue us!" The memory of what the man said came flooding back to Alex. *"But no matter what your friends think tomorrow, do not go back. They'll be waiting for you there. Searching for you."*

"Alex?" called Mark. "You okay?"

How did the man know? Alex thought as he stared at the forest floor. How did he know they would want to go back? If that was true, what if his warning about the "monsters" was true? Not a risk Alex was willing to take.

"Yo! Alex! You're zoning out!" called David. "Earth to Alex! Hello?" Alex snapped back to reality.

"No!" he yelled back. "How would we know if there would be a boat or plane? How would we know if they would be able to see us even if there was one? And how long would it be until we ran out of food? We're going forward!"

David hesitated before grabbing onto a vine near him. The vine was farther out from the trunk than Alex's was, so David was forced to crawl out onto the branch to get to the vine. He clasped both of his hands around the vine and jerked on it a bit to make sure it could hold him. It wouldn't break.

"Whelp. Here it goes." David jumped up, swinging his legs around the vine and swinging in Alex's direction. After watching to be sure it was safe the others soon followed, and they swung through the forest like chimpanzees. They stopped at every tree that the vines led to and yet all of them had bare trunks all the way down. Though they had to swing from tree to tree for what felt like hours it was the most fun they had ever had.

"This is awesome!" Brooke exclaimed.

"It's like I'm Tarzan," David remarked.

In the distance, a few yards away stood a tree that had branches that went from the top to the very bottom like scattered steps. It was the first one that actually had branches they had come across for hours. One by one, they all swung over and climbed down the tree to the ground. Their legs had lost circulation from swinging from vine to vine, so when they touched the ground their knees buckled beneath them and turned to jelly.

Alex leaned up against the tree and used it to prop himself up. They all tried to walk, but they only made it a few steps before falling back down again. After a few tries, they finally were able to get to their feet and walk again, laughing the whole time. Out of the excitement of the moment, they all walked around the forest deeper into the island laughing and telling stories, completely forgetting their surroundings. They all jumped when a bloodcurdling scream rang out through the woods.

Alex and the others spun around to the source of the scream. Behind them, a tall purplish black creature loomed over Brooke. The creature looked to be made of smoke. It was so tall Alex couldn't even see past its knee. The strange creature was taller than the trees themselves. Brooke was frozen from shock, and her face was coated in a mix of disbelief and fear, her brows furrowed and her eyes wide. The creature raised its long leg above Brooke's head, preparing to stomp on her and coming down slowly as though it were fighting gravity.

"Brooke, move!" Alex shouted, lurching forward. She was too scared to move, and all of the others were frozen in their tracks. Out of instinct, Alex dropped his backpack and pulled his sword out of its sheath, running toward Brooke and pushing her out of the way. Alex darted to the left just in time for the humongous creature's foot to come slamming on to the forest floor. The ground trembled and everything around them jumped before falling back down. Alex circled around the monster before lunging his sword into its leg, creating a large hole with more, even darker smoke drifting out of it. The creature let out a loud yelp and fell to the ground, causing the earth to shudder.

"Come on!" Alex shouted, snatching Brooke off the ground and pulling her along as he ran. His friends shook themselves out of their frozen positions and ran after Alex and Brooke. They ran for a long time, not knowing whether the strange creature was behind them or not, not stopping until they felt they were safe. They dropped to their hands and knees next to a stream from exhaustion, panting for air.

"Since when did you have a sword?" asked Mark, panting. Alex kneeled down beside the stream.

"A while," Alex replied as he cupped his hands in the stream next to the group and started to drink. All was quiet except for the rush of the water beside them.

"That's...," started Mark.

"Awesome!" finished David. Alex choked on the water he was drinking and looked at the others.

"What else can you do besides cut monsters in half?" asked Brooke.

"I... didn't cut...him in half..," Alex replied. They all started to ask Alex multiple questions all at once, but Alex didn't seem to be listening. This certainly wasn't the type of reaction he had expected.

"Why aren't you angry?" Alex asked. Everyone shut their running mouths and stared at Alex blankly.

"Angry? Why?" Mark asked.

"I forgot to tell you I had a sword," Alex replied. "What if I tried to kill you with it or something?"

"First of all, if you were going to kill us you would have done it already. Plus, you have no reason to do so, as far as I know. Second, I know you well enough that you couldn't kill anyone. Yes, you have skill and enough courage to wound someone. But I saw you when you fought that thing. I saw the look in your eyes. You couldn't kill anyone or anything even if your life depended on it," Nicole said as the others nodded their heads. Alex looked up from his friends and noticed that the sun had started to lower in the sky.

"Let's take some time to eat before we head out again. The sun is starting to set," Alex said. Later that night, they sat in a circle around the fire to keep them warm through the night and told stories before it became too dark. Alex shrunk away from the fire and sat against a tree trunk. His eyes traveled up to the canopy.

At the very tops of the trees were gigantic colorful balls. Alex squinted his eyes to try and make out what they were. Suddenly, he realized they were fruit! Alex jumped up and quickly climbed up the trees, grabbing as much fruit as he could and stuffing it in his jacket.

"Anybody hungry? I've got dinner!" Alex called as he walked toward them with both of his hands raised and full of bunches of fruit.

"What's that?" asked Nicole.

"Fruit!" Alex replied. "Eat up!" Alex dropped the bunches of fruit onto the ground, letting some tumble away.

"Whoa! Where'd you get these?" asked David, grabbing a piece of fruit. "Wait! Did you check to see if these are poisonous?"

"I saw them in the trees! And, yes I checked if they were poisonous and before you ask, yes, I know the difference between safe and dangerous foods," Alex grabbed a fruit and bit into it. Flavor flooded into his taste buds in one single bite, and the juice splattered around his mouth as he bit down.

"These are delicious!" Brooke exclaimed, having taken one as well.

Alex walked away from the pile of fruit and sat down in an empty space of the circle the others had formed around the fire. Mark and the others continued their conversation, leaving Alex to eat his piece of fruit alone. Alex bit into it once again, and the juice splattered all over the edges of his mouth. Alex wiped his mouth on his sleeve and stared into the blazing fire.

The flames danced around and around, trapping Alex in an inescapable trance. All sounds were drowned out over the crackling and popping of burning wood. Alex stared so intently into the fire that the burning sensation that had begun to well up into his eyes hadn't even caught his attention. All of his senses had focused on the fire. Alex's fingers went numb, and the piece of fruit he had been holding tumbled to the ground with a thump.

EIGHTEEN

lex's eyes fluttered open to the all-too-familiar scene of light peeking through the trees of the canopy. Dazed, Alex stayed there and stared, confused as to where he was. What were those trees doing here? Why was it so cold? Alex sighed when he remembered. Slowly, Alex turned his head to look next to him, where the charred remains of the fire lay. A dim orange light glowed beneath the ashes.

Alex stood up and stomped onto the ashes until the orange glow disappeared and flurries of ash and smoke drifted into the air. Alex stood motionless as he watched the smoke float into the sky then mold itself with the air around him. He shuddered. Why was it so cold? Realizing he didn't have his jacket on, he scanned the area for it.

The jacket was hung on a nearby branch just a few feet away. Alex sauntered over to the tree and pulled the jacket down. When had he put this over here? More importantly, when had he taken it off? Alex didn't remember doing any of that. He pulled the jacket on and walked over to the others, who were still sound asleep. He bent over and started to wake Mark.

"Alex? Is it morning already?" Mark murmured groggily as he slowly propped himself onto his elbows. "Why is it so cold? It's still summer, isn't it?"

Alex laughed. "Yes. It is still summer. It's just cold. Get your coat on and let's wake the others. It will probably warm up soon."

Mark stood up and pulled his coat on before going around and waking up the others. Once they started walking again, Alex found himself behind everyone else. Alex watched as the teens talked and laughed, clutching their coats close to their bodies to keep warm. His breath created clouds in the crisp air. Alex watched his breath create the clouds while he walked, not paying any attention to the others.

"What are you doing?" asked Mark as he stopped to wait for Alex.

"Walking," Alex replied as he drew his attention to Mark.

"I can see that. Why are you so far behind?"

"My attention was somewhere else. I didn't even realize you were so far up." Alex looked up ahead at the others, who were now much farther away. "Come on! We should try to stay together. Race you!" Alex took off toward the threesome.

"Hey! Foul start!" Mark yelled as he ran after Alex. Before Mark could get too far, he stopped abruptly. Not hearing Mark's footsteps coming up behind him anymore, Alex turned around to see Mark leaning against a tree.

The voices of the others had also stopped, and Alex turned to see that they were also leaning against a tree. A wave of heat hit Alex, almost knocking him over. He staggered over to a tree to regain balance. His vision started to blur as the world started to spin. Alex covered his eyes and started to breath heavily through the heat. When his head finally stopped spinning, he brought his hand down to discover visible heat waves surrounding him. As the others recovered, they pulled their coats off, shoving them into their bags.

"How is it suddenly so hot?" Nicole asked, looking at David. "Just a minute ago it was freezing!"

"Don't ask me! I'm not the weatherman! I know about as much as you do," David replied, throwing his hands up.

"This place is strange. We should probably expect things like that from now on," Alex remarked, wiping sweat that had formed on his forehead. "Let's get moving."

David opened his water bottle and continued to pour water on top of his head. After hours of walking in the relentless heat, Brooke collapsed to her knees. "I'm sorry, guys. The heat just makes this whole walking thing even harder. Can we take a break?"

"It's beating us up a lot too. A break doesn't sound so bad," Nicole said.

"I'll be back. I'm going to try and see where we are." Alex grabbed onto a branch and swung himself over onto the branch above it. "I'll also see if I can find any sign of... well... you know what." Alex continued to swing himself up the tree until he burst through the leaves and into the cool fresh air. Strangely, it wasn't as hot above the trees as it was below.

"Hot down there, isn't it?" said a voice, startling Alex. Next to Alex was a dark shadow in the shape of a man.

"Have you been following us?" Alex asked.

"Yes. I have," replied the man.

"Can I ask you some things?"

"Depends on what your questions are. I may not want to answer them."

"First, where are we? What is this place?"

The man sighed, "Devil's Haven."

"Devil's what now?"

"Devil's Haven. Do not be afraid. It is simply a name the humans call it. Its real name is Alsijn. I thought you might know what I speak of if I used that name to refer to it. I was wrong. It is one of the many landforms that the citizens of Heltiana inhabit. No human has ever survived as long as you have. Honestly, I'm impressed," the man explained.

"Thanks…? Second, what is your name? I'm pretty tired of thinking of you as 'the man in the shadows.' You don't have to give me your real name, but at least give me something."

"Just call me Jack. That's my real name," Jack said in a hushed voice. Alex hadn't expected him to answer that question. Alex tried to think of something else to ask, any one of his millions of questions, but oddly, his mind was blank. So, he waited for Jack to speak, but he too remained silent. Alex turned his head to look out at the trees as an awkward silence filled the air.

"You met one of them," said Jack.

"I met one of the what?" Alex turned his head to look back at Jack.

"A creature of Heltiana. Humans may not see them unless they have seen the Alsijn moon. The Alsijn moon is different from every other for it grants those who do not originate from Heltiana the ability to see what other ordinary humans may not." The shadowed silhouette of a finger emerged from the dark figure and pointed upwards. Alex looked up at the sky where the faint gray outline of the moon rested in the clear blue sky.

"Isn't the moon just the same as anywhere?"

"No, Alsijn's moon is different from the moon from the outside world. It is coated by a barrier that surrounds this entire island. All the way beneath the water and plates beneath us. It is filled with an energy that comes from deep within this land. The creature you faced recently goes by the name Clandestine Brobdingnagian. There are many of them out there. Not even I know how many there are."

"This clanddi-whatever is the thing that attacked us?"

"Yes. Its body is nothing but pure dark energy, and the only other color on its body is its eyes. No one knows what the color of their eyes are because that creature of the dark is so tall it's almost impossible to see them. If anyone's ever seen their eyes they never lived to tell the tale. Have you heard of the saying 'the eyes are the window to the soul'?" Jack explained.

"Yeah, it's a common phrase. What about it?"

"Whatever you do, do not look into the eyes of the creatures on this island. Each different kind of creature can do something incredible with their eyes on this island and this island only."

"What other creatures are there on this island?"

"Too many to keep track of. There could be billions of them that I am not aware of. For all I know, I'm aware of barely a handful," Jack replied.

"What about humans? Are there any others here?" asked Alex.

"Good question," observed Jack. "Not exactly. Many millennia ago, Heltians lived peacefully with ordinary humans. Then history happened. Ever since then, humans are seen as enemies."

"Thanks for the warning."

"Well, to make matters worse, the ordinary Heltian looks pretty much like an ordinary human. Sure, there are countless fantastical creatures. But Heltiana and its typical residents will look like humans to the untrained eye."

Jack paused before adding, "If you have any more questions and such, you may meet me in one of these many trees. It's just more convenient. Our time together has reached its limit for today. Go. Join your friends now."

Before Alex could ask anything else, Jack was gone.

Alex sighed and continued to climb down the tree. The farther he went the hotter it got. When he finally reached the forest floor, his hair was thick with sweat.

"You were up there for so long! What did you find?" asked David. His friends were all soaked with sweat. Their hair was plastered against their skulls and their clothes clung to their bodies. Alex thought back to his conversation with Jack. Should he tell them?

"The weather up there was much cooler. I may have lost track of the time. Otherwise, the whole thing was a bust. All I found was that we ventured far enough away from the coastline that I couldn't see it any longer," Alex replied.

"Not much we can do, we should probably get going," said Mark.

"We should pick any fruit we see on the way. You never know when we will run out," suggested Nicole. As they walked, they picked any fruit they would come across and stuck it in their bags. Alex spaced out as he thought about what Jack said. Heltiana. Alsijn. Creatures of the dark. Barriers. What kind of world was this? Suddenly, Alex lost his footing and tumbled to the ground. He had been so lost in thought he had forgotten he was in a forest and tripped over a tree root.

Brooke watched as Alex walked silently with a blank stare, his eyes barely moving. She looked to her friends for an explanation but they just shrugged in reply. Brooke noticed a bundle of fruit hanging against a tree and she snatched it down. A loud thump from behind her caused her to turn around and drop the bundle of fruit. There Alex lay sprawled on the ground in a heap.

"Are you okay?" Brooke leaned forward with a stretched-out hand toward Alex. He took it and she pulled Alex off the ground.

"I'm fine. Just not paying attention," Alex replied bluntly as he gathered himself.

"You might want to start before you fall again," Brooke exchanged confused glances with Mark before moving on.

Alex continued to daydream as he walked, but his daydreaming was put to an end when he heard a branch snap deep into the woods around them. Alex stopped walking and listened for another sound like the one he heard before but heard nothing. Every once in a while he would hear a rustling sound and stop walking but only to find that nothing was there. Alex started to think he was hearing things. None of his friends took any notice of the loud sounds and continued on their way.

The sound of leaves crunching behind him haunted Alex. He got annoyed and stopped walking. Planting his feet down, he listened for the crunching, half expecting it to stop immediately. This time Alex was surprised to find that it didn't stop. The crunching sound started to grow louder and louder as Alex waited. He spun around to face the source of the sound, but nothing was there besides trees, leaves, vines, and grass.

The crunching was getting closer and closer by the second. Alex pulled his sword out of its sheath on his back. The sound of the sword being pulled out of its sheath rung out through the silent forest. Alex held his sword firmly in front of him.

"Who's there?" Alex called into the silence.

"What are you doing?" Nicole asked, startled.

"Don't tell me you don't hear that!" Alex said. "Don't talk. Just listen."

The five of them stood there motionless, staring at each other. Brooke was about to say something when she stopped.

"I'm starting to hear it," Brooke's voice cracked as she said it.

"I don't know what you people are talking about but one thing's for sure. You people have been on this island for far too long. You are starting to scare me," David quivered as he scanned the serious and determined faces of his peers. His eyes grew wide and he started backing away from the others slowly.

"David, stop! Think about what you are saying! Nobody is going crazy! Just wait for a min" Mark was cut off when a wolf jumped out from behind David. The wolf ran at David at full speed, ramming him into the ground, knocking the wind out of him.

The wolf pinned David down with its claws, with its mouth open and saliva dripping down onto David's face. The wolf's lips were curled back into a snarl, revealing large sharp and jagged teeth. David didn't bother looking at its eyes, he was too scared to bring up the courage. When he found air rushing into his lungs he didn't hesitate before screaming as loud as he could, hoping his friends would come to the rescue.

Alex threw his body at the wolf, his shoulder colliding into the wolf's shoulder blade, throwing it off of David. Alex and the wolf tumbled forward, clutching onto each other, both struggling to break free of each other's grasp. As they rolled Alex's sword fell out of his grip. As soon as they stopped moving the wolf jumped off of Alex and he struggled to get to his feet. Alex and the wolf stood motionless, staring at each other and waiting for the other to make their move. Alex's arms were scratched and his shirt was torn from where the wolf dug his claws into his arms.

That's when he saw its eyes. The outside was completely yellow except for a thin black diamond in the middle. Suddenly the wolf turned and ran the opposite direction. Alex stood there sweating and breathing hard. He heard leaves crunching behind him and spun around. There his friends stood with worried looks on their faces. Alex sighed and walked over to where he dropped his sword.

"It's gone. It ran away. I don't know where. It could come back," Alex huffed as he slid his sword back into its sheath and turned around to examine his friend's conditions. Alex's face contorted into confusion and worry. They all were fine and healthy but what troubled him was their missing companion.

"Where's David?" Alex asked. Nicole, Brooke, and Mark looked around then back at Alex and shrugged. Alex took off to where David had been pinned down. He found him leaning against a tree clutching his arm tightly in pain. A large gash ran from his shoulder cap to his forearm with blood oozing out of it and dripping slowly down his arm and off his fingertips.

"David! Oh my gosh!" Brooke's eyes widened in shock.

"I have a first-aid kit!" Mark exclaimed quickly as he rushed to pull out a box from David's bag.

Nicole helped straighten David against the tree before pouring a bottle of water over his wound to clean it. Once all of the blood had been washed off, Alex wrapped a bandage around the wound before it could bleed any more.

NINETEEN

"That sucked," David groaned as he clutched his free hand around his bad arm, nursing the wound after it was fully patched.

"No kidding," Mark scoffed. "Can you stand? That was a lot of blood."

"No. Not yet. Just give me a few minutes. That *actually* scared me," David replied with a hint of sarcasm in his voice.

"It scared all of us, mind you," Brooke scolded.

"You weren't the one who had a wolf pin you down and rip open a gash in your arm," David pointed out.

"I guess I should have believed you, Alex. I read too many comics where people lose their rockers in situations not far from this. I'm sorry I got myself hurt," David rested his head on the tree trunk behind him and stared up at the canopy.

"It's okay. It's not every day you find yourself alone on an island where everything on it could kill you. I wouldn't be surprised if we're *all* missing a few marbles after this," Alex replied as he sat on a rock nearby and began to wipe off the dirt on his sword with a cloth. "You are human after all," Alex paused before continuing. "Anyway, I should have been more on guard. It wasn't your fault."

"We should probably stay the night so David can get his strength back," Mark spoke.

Alex sheathed his sword and stood up. "I'll get wood."

"Okay see you later then," Brooke remarked.

"We'll take care of David and set up camp," Nicole added.

* * *

After nightfall everyone managed to find sleep—except for Alex. Alex's sleep seemed to run away too far for him to catch. Alex walked over to a fallen tree a few yards away from the others and sat down. Jack was there almost immediately.

"You've been waiting for me," Jack said.

"I want to know more about these 'creatures.' You kinda bailed on me when I still wanted more answers," Alex replied, ignoring Jack's comment.

"From what I know, the creatures of Heltiana make up many varieties. There are creatures or what you would call monsters, there are also animals, and even plants that are creatures of Heltiana. But you really need to watch out for the citizens of Heltiana. The ones who most resemble humans. While you would call them human because of how they look and act, they are inhuman. Some can die from only one thing and some can't even die at all. Heltiana is another world hidden to the human race. Or, a part of another world. A kingdom, you could say. We 'citizens' are technically an entire different race."

"Why are the so-called humans the most dangerous? I'd think the monsters are the most dangerous."

"They have the most power. They also know every human weakness… along with how to exploit them. They can deceive and they can conquer. Unlike any other species, they can roam freely inside the world of the humans. I am one of these citizens. And just as dangerous."

Alex jumped up from where he was sitting and backed up into a tree. "You're one of them?" Alex asked calmly.

"Yes. But I do not wish to bring any harm upon you or your friends. If I did, you never would have awoken on that beach," Jack reassured him. Alex heard the truth in Jack's words. He started to inch slowly around the trunk. "You see, I'm a bit different from everyone else," Jack said calmly. Alex leaned off the trunk and walked back over to the fallen tree and sat down. Jack stopped, confused.

"What are you doing?" Jack asked.

"You said you weren't going to hurt anyone. So, what do I have to worry about?" Alex replied.

"Would you at least want to know what I am?"

"Sure. But I can always wait if you are not ready."

Jack opened his mouth as if to say something but stopped abruptly and spun toward the slumbering teenagers. "Your friend is awake. Go. Hurry, before he sees us. Before I go, don't tell your friends about me. They are not ready. However, they will be soon." Jack disappeared into the shadows, and Alex walked back over to where his friends lay.

Jack watched Alex walk back to his friends and considered Alex peculiar. Although Jack told Alex he was part of an extremely dangerous inhuman race, Alex continued to trust him. He was very peculiar, or at least, incredibly naive.

Alex walked toward the fire to find David sitting up and staring at the sleeping bag Mark had given Alex that he never used anyway.

"David? Are you all right?" Alex asked. David spun around to the source of who had spoken to discover Alex standing behind him. David lurched in agony as pain shot through his arm and up his shoulder.

"Owww. Yeah." David clutched his arm. "Where were you?"

"I went for a walk," Alex replied. "Why are you up? It's late."

"I should ask you the same thing."

Alex walked over and sat against a tree stump near David. "Why are you suspicious? Do you not trust me?"

"What? Why wouldn't I trust you?" David asked, surprised Alex would make such an accusation, and a little suspicious.

"No reason. Just go back to sleep," Alex rested against the stump and crossed his arms across his chest, closing his eyes.

"Why don't you sleep in the sleeping bag Mark gave you?" David moved his sleeping bag closer to Alex, trying to start a conversation.

"Because it's uncomfortable."

"Alex?"

"What?" Alex sighed, opening his eyes again to look at David.

"What's that?" David pointed at a bunch of bushes behind them. His arm trembled as he pointed. Alex turned to follow his gaze. He shuddered as he saw two glowing yellow eyes peering at them through the same bushes Alex had first come out of. Alex pulled out his sword and slowly walked over to the bushes.

"What is it?" asked David.

"I don't know. Stay there." He was only a few feet away when whatever it was jumped out from the bushes and right at Alex. He leapt back just in time for the wolf to land on the spot where Alex would have been. He recognized the wolf as the one they met a few days ago.

"I guess it came back to finish the job." Alex looked out of the corner of his eye at David. David was shaking out of fright. "Don't worry, I won't let it near any of you." Alex lunged at the wolf and slashed the sword toward Its skin. The wolf dodged the attack swiftly and charged toward Alex. Alex attempted to move out of the way, but wherever he turned another tree would be waiting to block his path. So Alex went the only way he could go. He jumped up.

Everyone was dumbfounded. Alex, David, the wolf, even Jack, who was watching silently within his shadows. Alex jumped into the air with such force that he went up twenty feet in the air. The force of the jump had brought up clouds of dirt that spread about the forest floor. When Alex finally landed, he was so shocked he stumbled and fell to the ground.

The wolf was the first one to recover from the shock. The wolf immediately launched an attack, stunning everyone even more. The attack sent Alex sprawling backwards. Alex held onto the wolf so it wouldn't escape. Alex and the wolf went tumbling toward a wall of vines. Little did they know that behind that wall was a steep, rocky hill that led down to a black, murky pond. Sharp rocks jutted out from all sides that could lead to certain death if someone were to come in contact with them. At the bottom of the pond lay a bed of small sharp rocks that were deeply hidden beneath the murky waters.

They burst through the wall of vines and lurched down the jagged cliff uncontrollably. As they tumbled, it took all of Alex's energy to dodge the deadly rocks. Alex and the wolf slammed into a large rock. The force of the impact shook them out of the other's grasp and they continued to fall in separate directions, each no longer focusing on the other and only trying to avoid the rocks.

Jack watched in horror from his shadows. He itched to help but he couldn't interfere. David was awake and it wasn't time for him to know. He had to stay behind the sidelines and hope for the best. Jack winced as he watched Alex and the wolf collide into a rock that shook one another from the other's grasp. *Now's my chance*

if any! Jack thought as he shook his head and sighed. With a flick of his finger, he sent the wolf sprawling into a nearby boulder.

Alex tumbled even farther down the hill. In the corner of his eye, he caught a glimpse of the wolf colliding with another rock, then falling down the terrain. Alex dodged rock after rock, boulder after boulder. He didn't have a chance to gather himself before falling flat on to his back into the shallow pond. His head smashed against one of the rocks, causing purple sparks to appear across his vision.

Alex slowly sat up in the pool of mud and looked up. David was standing within the wall of vines and staring down with a look of horror plastered on his face. The light of the fire reflected in his eyes. Alex stood up and staggered backwards as the world started to turn. Alex shook off the dizziness and climbed back up the terrain, occasionally slipping on a rock and falling a few feet before climbing up again.

David held his good hand out toward Alex when he finally reached the top. He brushed past David, sitting down and stopping the world from spinning being the only thing on his mind, unaware of the hand outstretched to him. He walked back to where the others still lay sound asleep and staggered over to the stump he had leaned against before he fell to the ground. David stood there with his hand in the air. Still shocked from Alex's response, David shook his head, rousing himself out of his trance before walking back to the others to find Alex dozing off.

"Thanks, Alex," David said as he sat down next to Alex against the stump.

"You're welcome. Are you hurt? The wolf didn't get to you, did it?" Alex breathed as his eyelids continued to drop.

"I'm fine."

"Mmm," Alex mumbled as he began to drift off.

David didn't respond. Alex opened one eye to look at David. He had already fallen asleep. Alex let out one last sigh before allowing himself to fall into a deep sleep, the dizziness following him into the darkness.

Alex woke up to the others huddled in a circle and talking to one another. "What are... You.. doing?" Alex stuttered, his head still spinning from the night before, although marginally better.

"Morning, Alex! We thought you'd never wake up. You must've been really tired after last night," Nicole observed.

"Hmm? Oh yeah. I was really tired," Alex replied. Alex turned to David who was still sitting against the tree stump next to him. He clutched his arm as he watched the others run around playfully. "Do the others know what happened?" Alex whispered.

"Nah. I figured you wanted me to wait for you to wake up," David whispered back.

"Have you not moved all morning?"

"No. My arm was throbbing earlier. But I'm starting to feel a bit better."

"I think I saw a plant earlier that can help with that."

"Wait, what do you mean plant?"

Alex didn't have time to squeeze in the answer before the others plopped down in front of them. "Why were you so tired? You went to bed the same time as the rest of us, didn't you?" Brooke asked. Alex glanced at David, who nodded briskly in response. Alex sighed before replying.

"The wolf attacked again last night," Alex confessed. "We think it was the one from before. The one that attacked David."

They all stopped and stared at him with disbelief.

"What? It came back?" Brooke raged. "And you didn't think to wake us up?"

"Well, I'm sorry. I was too busy trying to fight it off," Alex retorted.

"It's dead now, though," David spoke up.

Brooke whirled around, "What did you just say?"

"I said, it's dead. The wolf is dead," he repeated.

"What do you mean 'it's dead'?" Nicole queried.

"The wolf wasn't killed by Alex, though. Alex and the wolf tumbled through that wall of vines." David pointed toward the vines with his good hand before continuing. "But behind the wall was a rocky slope that had sharp rocks and gigantic boulders. At the bottom was a muddy pond that was so dark you couldn't see the bottom."

"The pond was surprisingly shallow and the bottom was nothing but rocks," Alex cut in.

"They both fell. The wolf hit a rock on the way down and died. I think it broke its neck," David explained. Nicole, Mark, and Brooke stared at David. Their brains were still processing the words that had come out of David's mouth.

"Well, I'm just glad you're all right. You weren't hurt, were you?" Mark asked. Alex rubbed the lump that had formed on his head before he answered.

"No. We are both fine," Alex lied.

"What were you guys doing?" David asked as he stood up and faced the others. Alex remained seated.

"It's basically an updated game of Clue. All you need is people and a story. No additional materials," Brooke answered.

"Sounds entertaining," Alex sighed.

Brooke reached down to help Alex up but he shook his head. "Thanks, but I'm just gonna sit here for a second. We should get going in a minute though. Coyotes aren't usually alone."

"But that was a wolf," Nicole said. "Wasn't it?"

"It could be. But maybe it wasn't. I don't know. We don't want to be surprised, so we should expect the worst," Alex replied.

They nodded and walked back to their bags, hoisting them up onto their backs then continuing to walk away. Alex stood up, using the tree to keep himself steady. The others stopped and turned back around and waited as Alex grabbed his bag and made his way toward them.

TWENTY

Three nights passed and Jack had yet to show his face. Alex was waiting on the fourth night when he finally showed. Alex was sitting on a branch that hung directly over his slumbering companions. Alex hadn't expected Jack to show up in the same way he had in past nights, so when he did Alex almost fell out of the tree he had been loitering in.

"Where have you been?!" Alex shouted once he regained his balance.

"Places. I trust everything has gone accordingly since I've been gone?" Jack asked.

"Peachy. I have so many questions! Why did that wolf follow us? Why was it behaving so strange? What was that black thing that smashed into the wolf? What is going on around here?"

"You must be aware of your surroundings. This whole island is after you and your friends. You don't belong on this island. Everyone and everything can sense that."

"I don't think that answers even one of my questions," Alex complained.

"I can't give you answers to everything," Jack chuckled.

"Just one more question before you leave," Alex said quickly. "Can I expect you tomorrow?"

"Yes, you can expect me tomorrow along with all the days after. I will let you know when I will not be able to meet. You do need to sleep after all," Jack said. Alex could sense his presence disappear. Alex climbed back down and lay on the ground to get some sleep.

In the morning, everyone gathered around David as he decided he would check on his wound. Everyone was disturbingly curious as to how it looked. David stuck out his bandaged arm for Alex so he could unwrap it. As he unwrapped the bandages, the closer he got to the skin the more dried blood had seeped into the cloth. When he finally got down to the last layer of cloth, David closed his eyes. Alex unwound the cloth and they all gasped. Curious for why they all gasped, David slowly opened one eye and peeked at his arm. What he saw next caused him to also gasp. Only a bit longer than the others did.

"It's... healed?" David marveled. "It was the biggest cut I've ever seen! But there isn't even a scar! How is that possible?"

"That's the fastest healing I've ever seen!" Brooke exclaimed.

"I know I said you were human before but maybe I was wrong," Alex joked as he held out the wadded-up, bloody bandages to David. "Don't leave these anywhere. We'll wash them out once we come across water, and we'll be able to use them for something else. But don't use it and don't leave them behind until then."

"Got it." David shoved the bandages in a side pocket and zipped it. "These aren't going anywhere."

"Whelp, I guess we're heading out now!" Mark said, grabbing his backpack.

They walked for hours non stop. They were all well rested and had so much energy they believed they could go on forever. They would take a break after a few hours, but they decided they would go on throughout the night. The unusual burst of energy stunned them, but they didn't question it.

As Alex walked, he found himself constantly searching their surroundings. Every little sound or movement made him jump, but each time it turned out to be just a deer or bird. When he continued to see tall black shapes dash by his group yards away then disappear, he started to believe he was being paranoid.

By the evening of the second day, they took a vote on whether they should stay the night. The vote was four to one. Alex had felt as though he could go on forever. Sadly, the others did not agree. As soon as everyone had fallen asleep, hoping to encounter Jack again, Alex raced to the darkest tree he could find. Alex climbed hastily up the branches until he came to an area that was so dark he could just barely see two feet in front of him.

"You climbed that tree very fast, my friend," Jack said as he laughed.

"When I was walking, I saw a strange, dark shape that was following us." Alex went straight to the point.

"What do you mean?" Jack demanded. Any hint of delight in Jack's voice that Alex had heard earlier was replaced with a tremulous tone.

"The others didn't seem to see it, so I was wondering. Was that real or am I just imagining things? Or did you not see it either?"

"You saw that?"

"Yeah? Was I not supposed to?"

"No. Nevermind. I've meant to tell you something, but I wasn't able to last time we talked. I'm sure you have been wondering how I can do certain things; appear and disappear into thin air." Jack paused and Alex nodded, urging him on. Jack continued, "I am what my world calls a Contour Suzerain. I can turn into a Shadow as well as control Shadows either separately or simultaneously, bending them to my will. That is the main power or defining factor of a Contour Suzerain." Jack paused. "Now, I have a question for you."

"What's the question?" Alex asked.

"Why did you not stop last night to sleep? Why did you keep walking?" Jack asked.

"We aren't completely sure. We all just had a sudden burst of energy! Even if we did stop, we probably wouldn't have been able to sleep so we just kept going. I still feel like I could go longer but they didn't agree. I tried sleeping. No luck," Alex explained excitedly.

"That is strange."

"Enough about that. I want to know more about these so-called 'citizens.' I want to learn more about them."

"I can only inform you about a few. I am unaware of many. First, there are the Telepaths. Their powers are quite simple. They can put ideas and thoughts into their victim's head that they think are their own. This may cause the victim to do many things. Basically, they can force their victims to do their bidding without them realizing it. Once they give in, they are forced to watch helplessly as they do the Telepath's bidding.

"Then there is the Possessor. They are similar to the telepaths in many ways. Instead of putting ideas and thoughts into their victim's head, they possess the body. When the victim is possessed, they are unaware of the events that have occurred before they were possessed, during the possession, and after the possession," Jack explained. Jack looked to Alex, waiting for him to ask another question but he did not. Alex only stared blankly at the sky before shaking his head and turning back to Jack.

"They sound dangerous," was all that came out of his mouth in his astonishment. After a few minutes of the new information sinking in Alex came to a realization. "I'm going to head back down now. The sun has risen above the horizon and my friends will be up and about soon. I'll talk to you more about this later." Alex climbed down the trunk of the tree before Jack could respond.

Alex was halfway down before a shrill scream burst through the air. The scream shook Alex with fright causing him to lose his grip on the tree and he hurtled through the air. He waved his hands about wildly trying to grab for a branch, but he couldn't get a firm hold. When Alex finally hit the ground, he hit it hard. Alex landed flat on his back, his breath knocked out of him.

Alex lay still, staring up at the branches he had so desperately tried to grab. His spine ached and white dots were speckled across his vision. The feeling was different from when he had hit his head. His mouth opened and closed repeatedly gasping for air, but no matter how much he tried to suck in air it made no difference. Finally, he managed to breathe and his chest heaved up and down as he gasped. Alex closed his eyes to block out the white, but as he did branches came tumbling on top of him. Pain shot through his body, adding to the pain caused by the fall.

"Alex!" A voice shouted from somewhere above the pile of branches. Alex twisted his head to see over the pile of branches, but he was completely hidden beneath them. Almost no light shone through the needles and wood. Alex lifted his hand to move away the branches, but it wouldn't budge for it was stuck beneath all of the weight. Suddenly, light began to shine through the branches as his friends began to pull them away.

Once he was free, Mark yanked him off the ground. His eyes glistened as he stared at Alex with both surprise and fear.

"Alex! Are you okay? Are you hurt?" Mark's voice wobbled. Alex opened his mouth to answer him but no sound came out. After several tries he finally managed to say something.

"I'm fine..? Are you... all right...? What was... that... scream?" Alex choked. His voice was wheezy as he struggled to get the words out of his mouth. He took a deep breath and tried again but only a small squeak came out. Alex staggered over to his backpack where he pulled a water out. The group watched as Alex chugged it down. Once he finished, he was able to talk again.

"Is everyone okay? I heard a scream. I wasn't expecting it so I fell out of the tree," Alex coughed. Alex sat down on the ground and waited for an answer.

"That... was me," Brooke slowly raised her hand and blushed. "A spider crawled into my hair. I am so sorry."

"It's fine, as long as it wasn't anything serious. How long have you been awake?" Alex asked.

"Excuse me, a spider was about to crawl in my ear and lay hundreds of its babies in my brain. It was completely serious," Brooke huffed.

"We were all startled awake when Brooke screamed. So, not for long," Nicole answered, rolling her eyes. "By the way, why are you always in a tree? I guess It was only a matter of time before you fell out," she joked.

Alex placed his hands on his knees and began to stand, only to fall back to the ground as a sharp pain shot up his back and through his body. He moaned. Brooke grabbed his arm to steady him.

"I'm fine. Nothing's broken. Just give me a minute and we can be on our way."

"Maybe we should stay for—" David started.

"I said I'm fine. Let's just grab our things so we can go," Alex interrupted. Reluctantly, they moved away to get their bags, leaving Alex to himself for a brief moment. Taking a deep breath, Alex calmed his nerves and closed his eyes. Strangely enough, when he opened them again he felt no pain. He stood up and took a step. He felt fine. Alex walked around expecting his body to begin to ache but nothing happened.

Mark was the first one to notice Alex's recovery. Mark nudged Brooke next to him, who in turn nudged Nicole. The four stared dumbfounded at Alex as he paced back and forth showing no trace of pain or injury at all. Sensing that he had eyes on him, Alex stopped walking and shot his head up. In front of him stood four pairs of eyes staring at him attached to the faces of his puzzled friends.

"I thought you were hurt," Nicole stated.

"I told you I only needed a minute," Alex smirked although he was as confused as they were. Nicole and the others quickly shook their confusion off and continued to walk. It wasn't long before they quickly became bored having run out of stories to tell.

"Ugh! I'm bored! All we have been doing is walking for who knows how long we've been on this island," David whined. A few minutes passed and no one spoke. "I know!" David shouted. "Let's play a game!"

"We can't," Alex said bluntly. "We have to keep moving."

"Well, I know that! We can play it while we walk!" David argued. He paused to see if anyone would disagree but no one did. "All right! This'll be fun!"

"Oh really?" Nicole rolled her eyes. "What are you getting us into now?"

"Let me explain before you object to anything," David replied. "It's actually simple. Improv! Who's up for it?" They all exchanged glances before shrugging.

"Great!" David shouted as he pumped his fists. "Now who will start?"

TWENTY-ONE

The night dragged on in slow motion. Alex stared up at the leaves in the canopy. He hadn't slept a wink and sunrise was hours away. He had decided to try and sleep instead of going to see Jack, but his level of energy had said otherwise. Alex slowly stood up and walked farther away from his friends. Alex stood beneath the shadow of a tree waiting for Jack to show himself, but he never did.

Recalling their previous meetings, Alex climbed the tree, for they had mostly been above the forest floor within the trees. When Alex reached the top, a strong cold wind hit him head on. His hair swung about wildly as he brought his arm in front of his face to shield his eyes from the powerful wind. Alex propped himself against a steady branch and stared at the stars.

"Nice to see you're doing well," Jack said. Startled, Alex began to fall forward. Suddenly, a hand reached out from a shadow and caught the back of Alex's jacket, slowly pulling him back into the tree. Alex turned to see a silhouetted hand emerging back into the shadows.

"Wouldn't want you to fall. Again." Jack chuckled. "I am truly sorry about before. I was unable to reach you before you hit the ground. To tell you the truth, I am surprised you aren't dead right now."

"Thanks. You are so helpful," Alex replied sarcastically. "We have to stop meeting in trees. My friends are beginning to become suspicious. Look, I have been trying to stay as patient as I possibly can. Why must your identity remain such a secret?"

"When the time is right."

"Is that your answer to everything?"

There was no answer. Alex turned to face Jack, but he was gone. "Yo! Alex! I'm coming up!" A voice called from below. Before Alex had time to ask who it was, a head popped above the canopy and started toward him.

"Mark?" Alex asked. It was still dark so Alex was unable to make out the figure coming toward him. The figure was about Mark's height though the voice sounded more hoarse than Mark's typically did.

"Yeah, who else would I be?" Mark asked as he climbed out of the shadow and into the light of the purple moon.

"You could have been David. Or Brooke. Or Nicole," Alex pointed out.

"Well, they are all still asleep—" Mark stopped and looked toward the sky. "Whoa. Why is the moon—?" Mark stared at the moon, confused and unable to finish his sentence.

"Why is the moon purple?" Alex finished. Mark nodded, his eyes not leaving the sky. Alex opened his mouth to answer but was cut off when he heard a voice whisper in his ear.

"Not yet," Jack whispered. Alex didn't bother turning around for fear of Mark becoming suspicious.

"I don't know," Alex continued. "Anyway, how did you know I was up here?"

"I saw you leave. I tried to go back to sleep, but I couldn't so I thought I would join you. Plus, when are you *not* in a tree?" Mark righted his head and stared at Alex. Half of his face was dark and the other illuminated by the light of the moon. "Alex, can I ask you something?"

"You just did, but sure," Alex joked.

"Why did you run away?"

Alex stared at Mark, unprepared for the question.

"I think I have a right to know. Don't you think?" Mark urged.

For a moment Alex didn't speak. He didn't see this coming at all. Finally Alex spoke.

"No. No, I don't," Alex said bitterly. Mark's eyes were wide with surprise at Alex's remark.

"Okay. Fine. Don't tell me. But sooner or later I would like to know," Mark said as he turned away. Alex realized he was holding his breath and sighed.

"Sorry for the outburst. It just kind of came out."

"That's all right."

Despite those words, Alex could tell Mark was still hurt that he wouldn't tell him. It's not that he didn't want to, he just wasn't sure he was ready. There was a pause before Alex started to move.

"Should we head back?" Alex asked as he began his way down. Alex stopped and looked toward Mark for an answer. He nodded. Alex continued making his way down but stopped again. Mark didn't make any move to follow.

"Are you coming?" Alex asked.

"Where to?" asked Mark.

"I don't know, wherever the wind takes us," Alex replied with a joke at Mark's cluelessness. Mark cracked a smile and started down as well. Alex jumped from the tree and disappeared beneath the leafy canopy.

"Alex? Alex, are you okay? Where are you?" shouted Mark. Mark slid down and landed on a branch where he came face-to-face with Alex. Having scared him, Mark began to tilt backwards. Alex lurched forward and grabbed his shirt collar, and Mark hung halfway in the air. He looked at Alex and was even more surprised to find him smiling. Even laughing.

"You—...? You think this is funny?" Mark shouted, his arms flailing.

"A little," Alex stifled a laugh. "We really need to find out how to stop falling off things, though." He pulled his arm toward him, righting Mark back on the branch.

"I didn't laugh when you fell from the tree!"

"You're right, you're right. I'm sorry. But your reaction was hilarious!" Alex burst out laughing. Mark stared at Alex dumbfounded. Noticing Mark's sudden silence and strange expression, Alex stopped laughing and looked at Mark, still wiping tears from his eyes. "What?"

"You're... you're laughing," Mark stuttered.

"Yeah? Is something wrong?" His voice was odd and silvery as he spoke.

"No, it's just... it's been a while since I heard you laugh."

"Well, it's not much to laugh about lately. And the same can be said about you."

"Well, yeah it's just..," Mark trailed off and looked away.

"Are you coming or what?" Alex asked before jumping to another branch on a different tree.

"How did you do that?"

"Come on, slowpoke! You can do it too," Alex called as he jumped to a lower branch closer to the ground.

"Are you nuts? I mean, you? Yeah, sure. But me? You *are* crazy." Mark looked to the branch Alex jumped on moments before. His stomach turned to goo as he thought over what Alex was asking him to do. "What makes you think I can?"

"You're talking nonsense. You did it before you fell off that branch. Just forget about the falling-off part. These are one of those situations where you 'do' and don't 'think'," Alex called. Mark sighed when Alex disappeared beneath a branch. "Oh, but don't do that too often!" Following Alex's instructions and before he could think twice about it Mark jumped. When he hit the branch he teetered on his feet before crouching to a squatting position and grabbing the branch.

"I did it! I actually did it!"

"Yes, I can see that. Now stop gawking over it. The sun is rising and we have to get back before they wake up." Alex appeared two branches below him. Mark jumped down to Alex. They both exchanged glances before taking off and jumping from one branch to another, making their way to their friends.

"I can't believe we're doing this," Mark shouted as he leapt off another branch.

"Well, you certainly aren't dreaming," Alex smirked. Alex leapt farther and farther ahead of Mark, leaving him behind.

"I hadn't realized we went so far," said Mark once he caught up to Alex. Alex didn't answer. Mark looked down at Alex, who was now squatting with his hand against the trunk. He showed no signs of moving on. Alex's silence began to scare Mark and he started to talk.

"What's going on? Is there another wolf? Is everything okay? The others are fine, right? Wait, how would you know? You wouldn't know. Would you know? Probably not."

Alex put his fingers to his lips and Mark stopped blabbering. Minutes passed and Mark became antsy. "What are we doing?" Mark asked. Alex shot up to a standing position as a dark, tall, smoky figure appeared then disappeared behind a cluster of trees.

"Let's go," Alex's voice was sincere. He bounded from one tree to another, not waiting for Mark. Mark struggled to keep up with him and within seconds he was far behind. Alex couldn't wait for him to catch up or he would lose sight of that thing. This is probably for the best, Alex thought. If this was what Alex thought it was, Mark would better be far out of harm's way. Alex watched as the strange creature disappeared behind a tree. Alex jumped through some bushes, expecting whatever that thing was to appear, but it was gone.

Alex, now on the ground, walked back to a tree where Mark sat on a branch a few feet up.

"Man, how are you so fast?" asked Mark once Alex reached him. Alex ignored the question.

"The thing got away."

"Are you sure there was even anything at all? I didn't see anything."

Alex didn't have time to argue before a scream filled the air. Mark looked to Alex as if to ask, "what was that?" But he was already up and running through the forest.

By the time Mark had finally caught up, the creature that Alex had chased was already leaning over them all. Brooke stood frozen to the spot, and David was trying to shake her out of her trance. Nicole stood off farther away with a stick in her hand. She looked as though she were about to throw it, but she was too scared to move.

"Is that the monster that almost killed Brooke? It has a scar in the same spot you struck it." Mark pointed out a black smoky scar in the creature's side as he leapt off the branches and stood by Alex's side. Alex recognized the creature as a Clandestine Brobdingnagian thanks to his conversations with Jack.

"Go get them out of danger, I'll lure the thing away." Alex ran in between the monster and Brooke and David. Alex pushed them out of the way as the monster's hand came crashing down. With his sword out and tip pointed up, Alex braced for the impact.

"Alex!" Nicole shouted.

The Clandestine Brobdingnagian howled in pain and lifted its hand, revealing a fresh cut where Alex's sword was lodged and at the end of it, barely hanging on was Alex. Alex gripped the handle of his sword tight, for if he let go he would fall to his death. Alex watched in horror as the hand rose higher and higher into the air. Soon he was far above the trees and there was still a ways to go. Suddenly Alex felt a jolt.

He looked up in time for another jolt to cause him to fall a few inches. The sword was slowly falling out of the cut. The third jolt was the last, for it was then that his sword dislodged itself. Alex fell through a bed of leaves and continued to fall to his death. Thinking quickly, Alex lunged toward a branch and grabbed it with one hand while his other hand held tightly onto the handle of his sword.

Alex used his momentum to swing a 360 around the branch and let go, hurtling himself back toward the monster. As he flew, he swung his sword above his head. When Alex came in contact with the ferocious beast, he lodged his sword once again into its smoky exterior. With Alex's extra weight, the sword slid down its skin revealing a large black hole. Then the sword stopped sliding. The monster swiped wildly, trying to swipe Alex off him, but Alex ducked and the monster was unable to get to him.

Alex kicked and swung himself onto the edge of his sword, making him able to stand. As the monster's hand swept past him, Alex, using his sword as leverage, —jumped and landed on its wrist. Suddenly, the wrist zoomed up into the air. Alex used his sword to keep him from falling, and before he knew it he came face-to-face with the Clandestine Brobdingnagian.

That's when he saw them. Its eyes. They were a piercing fiery red with no pupils. It looked as if the monster had no soul. Alex ripped his sword out of the beast's wrist and began to run up its arm. All the while, its other arm hit and swung, desperately trying to knock Alex off. Once he was close enough, he leapt off the arm and plunged his sword into one of its fiery red eyes. The beast let out a deafening scream and fell backwards into a tree. The tree tilited, and if the monster hadn't gotten up immediately the creature would have fallen over.

Alex began to make his way toward the other eye, but the monster caught him off guard and slammed it's palm into Alex, sending him with a crash to the ground. Alex tried to get up, but the monster pinned him down with its hand. It began to push down hard, squeezing the breath out of him. Alex screamed in agony as his ribs began to cave in and air failed to travel through his lungs.

"Leave him alone!" Brooke shouted from somewhere behind him. Her voice echoed with a strong confidence, and it had so much power within its volume Alex was unable to recognize it as Brooke's. Alex tilted his head back to look at Brooke as his vision began to be consumed by darkness. His eyes widened at what he saw.

Brooke was staring intently at the trees and her arms were at her sides. Her palms were opened wide and facing the ground, outlined with a strange light purple line. David had fallen and was sitting and staring up at her in astonishment. Nicole had turned, now facing Brooke, her hands down in front of her, still gripping the stick so tightly that her knuckles were white. Mark had his back against a tree, hardly believing what was happening. Alex heard a loud crack above him, and he turned his head to look back at the monster.

Every tree surrounding him and the monster was outlined with a glowing purple, the same color that outlined Brooke's hands. The roots looked as though they were being ripped out of the ground by an invisible hand. Suddenly, the trees crashed down upon the monster. The monster let out another shriek before disappearing in a puff of smoke.

TWENTY-TWO

lex stared, completely bewildered and too shocked to move, at the felled trees where the giant monster once stood. He took in a relieved breath now that his lungs were free. Alex laid his head on the ground and relaxed, sucking in air greedily. Mark was the first to recover from the shock. Mark pushed himself off the tree he was leaning on and walked over to where David was standing, waiting for him to recover as well so he could help him off the ground. Nicole was the second to recover, standing upright, she walked over to Brooke, who had not moved from her spot. Her shoulders shook slightly, and she stared intently at the ground in front of her. Her hands were closed tightly into fists.

"Brooke? Are you all right?" asked Nicole. Brooke remained silent. She breathed heavily a few times before looking up at Nicole. Only then did she stop clenching her fists, and her breathing turned normal. After this, David recovered from the shock and pulled himself to his knees. David grabbed for Mark's hand but missed and tumbled into the dirt. Mark grabbed his hands and yanked him off the ground.

"What the?" David whispered under his breath, his eyes wide.

"Is everyone …. okay?" Brooke asked. She had regained her normal posture although her shoulders were still shaking and her mouth was parched.

"Yeah, we're all fine, but are you okay? I can't believe you did that!" replied Mark.

"I was just a little frightened, that's all. I'm still confused about what exactly happened," Brooke said, finding it easier to form words.

"Wait, where's Alex?" asked Nicole. Alex raised his hand off the ground and waved it lazily as he groaned.

"Alex! Dude, you all right?" David asked as they all ran toward the body sprawled across the ground. Alex stood up and scratched his head.

"Tip-top. Other than that fact that that monster just tried to kill me, but otherwise, tip top. Anyway, let's get going. The sun has risen, and we do not want to lose any daylight," Alex declared. "The fight with that… that… Clandestine Brobdingnagian, yeah that's it, took longer than I thought." Alex tilted his head back and sniffed the air.

"What are you doing?" asked David.

"A storm's coming," Alex replied.

"What?" asked Mark.

"A storm's coming," Alex repeated bluntly. "We should cover as much ground as we can, then find some sort of shelter. I assume you don't want to sleep in a thunderstorm?" Alex asked, grabbing his backpack and hauling it on his shoulders.

"He's right. It smells good," Nicole observed. "Fresh and… *earthly.*"

They had only gotten half a mile before the rain came down.

"We have to find shelter!" Nicole shouted over the roar of the thunder.

"I have some tents! And a few oil lamps, I think!" David shouted back. Mark, Nicole, Brooke, and Alex turned around and gave David a cold, surprised stare.

"You couldn't have told us this earlier? Oh, I don't know…when we first opened our eyes to a hot, sandy beach and not a cold, metal ship?" Mark shouted.

"Sorry! I forgot I had them. I just remembered now!" shouted David. David and the others dashed beneath a large tree and rushed to put up the tents. They were forced to work quickly as the rain grew heavy and strong, causing their final draft to not be the best tent ever built. They managed to create two tents, so that the girls could have one and the boys could have the other. Once they were safe and dry within the folds of the tent, Alex lifted up the flap for the door and peeked out. Even though it was early morning, it was as black as night outside.

"What are we going to do? It looks like we won't be going out until tomorrow at this point," Alex mused as he dropped the flap and turned back to the shadowy figures of the two boys.

"We could talk or play games until we fall asleep," suggested David. He pulled out a match out of a match-box and struck it against the side. A small flame sprung from the small stick, casting a dim light across their faces. "There isn't really much to do in this cramped tent," David said as he opened the glass door of the oil lamp and carefully dipped the flame on the candle. Once the candle was lit, he withdrew the match and closed the door once again. The tent was immediately filled with a bright light. David flicked his wrist and the match was put out.

"I guess we could do that," replied Mark. "Now that I think of it, Alex what did you call that monster again?"

"Clandestine Brobdingnagian. Why?" By the time Alex had realized what he said, it was too late to take it back.

"How did you know that's what it was called?" asked David. Alex started to wander off in thought, pondering about whether he should tell them about Jack or wait like he was told to. He didn't have enough time to decide before David snapped him out of his thoughtful gaze.

"Hello? Earth to Alex!" David shouted a little too loudly. Alex gasped and fell on his back, startled by David's shout.

"Tone it down a bit, will you? You're louder than the thunder outside," Alex said, sitting back up. "I'll tell you later." Alex looked at David and Mark. Behind them, a long shadow dashed across the yellow rubber outside. "What was that?" Alex asked quickly.

"What was what?" Mark asked, turning around and catching a glimpse of the shadow. This time it was his turn to fall backwards, except instead of gasping he screamed.

"What is wrong with you people? You are such wimps," David observed. The shadow traveled across the sides of the tent so that it was directly beside David. David jumped and quickly scrambled away, ramming into Mark, sending them both to the ground. Alex stood up and walked outside, curious of what the shadow could have been.

The heavy rain pelted against Alex's skin like millions of needles. He shivered against the freezing rain. Alex looked at the side of the tent where the shadow was, expecting to see an animal, but nothing was there. Before Alex could allow himself to be drenched any further, he jumped into the tent and wrapped himself in Mark's extra sleeping bag to warm his freezing body.

"There was nothing out there," Alex said.

"It was probably just some squirrel. Let me see." David stood up and walked outside. A minute later, David emerged from the tent flap, soaking wet and shivering. His skin was beet red, and he continued to sneeze repeatedly.

"Ah! It's freezing out there!" David sat down and curled up in his sleeping bag as Alex had done.

"I told you. You didn't have to go out there," Alex scolded.

"Looks painful," Mark laughed. "Your skin is red!" David and Mark began to laugh but were stopped cold when a bright streak of light flashed across the sky so bright they could see it through the tent, and it temporarily blinded them. Alex, Mark, and David scrambled over one another as they struggled to crawl outside. They all fell out of the tent and into the mud. Once they were out, they noticed Brooke and Nicole had also come out of their tents and were staring at the sky.

"Did you see that?" David asked, pausing to catch his breath before continuing to untangle himself from the three bodies.

"Obviously, or they wouldn't be out here," Mark stated, rolling his eyes. Suddenly, everything stopped. It seemed as if time itself had stopped and they were the only ones still moving. Even the rain stopped falling. The small droplets of rain sat still in the air, suspended by time. The bunch of tangled boys quickly scrambled to their feet to see the strange phenomenon more clearly.

"Something weird is definitely going on here," David acknowledged.

"You're just noticing that now?" Nicole asked. Alex ignored them and raised his hand. Slowly, Alex reached out and with the end of his fingertip touched a raindrop that floated in the air. At that moment, a loud boom shook the earth and then, a streak of blinding light filled the sky. When the light faded away, they looked up to see a tree in the distance come crashing down.

"Get in the tent! It's partially made of rubber so the lightning won't harm it!" shouted David. They all ran back for the tents and jumped in, landing in a dog pile.

"Hey, what are you guys doing in here?" asked Mark when he saw that the girls had jumped in the boys' tent as well.

"Sorry, it was instinct to go where everyone else goes," Brooke answered.

"You should be a leader not a follower," Alex stated. "But it's probably a good thing. We should stay together. Especially during a storm like this. But I'm tired, and I was up half the night, so good night." Alex lay on top of the sleeping bag and turned toward the door of the tent, closing his eyes.

"Are you kidding me? You're actually suggesting we sleep in this storm?" asked David.

"Yes," Alex replied. The sound of his friends' voices trailed off into silence as he drifted asleep.

Alex woke up first the next morning. He felt a strange weight against his back, and he turned his head over his shoulder. Piled up on top of one another were, his friends, sleeping soundly as close to him as they could get. Alex stood up, slowly pushing David's head off his leg, careful not to wake him. Alex listened intently for any sound indicating that the storm was still raging outside but he heard nothing.

To his surprise, Alex walked outside to see the sun shining through the thick canopy, lighting up the woods entirely. For as long as Alex had spent on this island, he had never seen the sun shine so brightly, let alone through the thick canopy.

Alex looked around him, expecting to see droplets of water dripping off the leaves and the trunks saturated with water. But there wasn't a speck of water in sight. The bark was so dried up when Alex touched it, it crumbled into his hands. Alex looked to the ground, surprised to find the dirt as dry as the desert. He knelt down and ran his hand across the dirt, only to jerk it away. It was scorching hot.

"Strange, isn't it?" said a voice from behind. Alex jumped to his feet and spun around. His hand shot up to his back toward the grip of his sword instantly. He found that the one who had spoken was a tall shadowy figure of a man, standing completely obscured in shadow.

"Oh, it's just you," Alex sighed, realizing it was Jack.

"Don't sound so disappointed," replied Jack. "Listen carefully to these instructions I am about to give you. I do not have much time. When you continue to walk, I don't want you to rest during the night. You need to keep going and be on high alert. I want you to stop when you come to a clearing, and a little to the west of that clearing will be a rocky cliff. I want you to stop there and camp there for a number of nights. Each night, I want you to take turns keeping watch. Then, we'll discuss when I am to be introduced to the others and show my face to you. I feel it is time to become involved in this all the way."

Alex stared at Jack for a moment. "Why so sudden?" But before he could answer, Alex heard a rustle from behind. Jack quickly disappeared, and Alex turned around. The tent started to rustle and move until Brooke and Nicole jumped out, followed by Mark. They all landed in the dirt, immediately jumping up and running around, wildly screaming, "snake!" Once they had calmed down, Alex asked, "What in the world are you doing? You look ridiculous!"

"Shush!" whispered Nicole. They all stared at the tent, waiting until David emerged. He was holding his arm out in front of him and a snake that was mainly brown with black specks all over it was clinging to his arm like it was a branch. David was gawking at the snake and smiling broadly while giggling.

"David. Why is the snake clinging to you?" asked Brooke cautiously.

"Look at it! Isn't it awesome? I've always loved snakes, I read about them a lot, but I've never been up so close to one before! Haha! This is so cool!" David blabbed excitedly. He continued to walk toward the group, but they stepped back. "What's wrong? Is something behind me?" David spun around in a full circle, surveying his surroundings.

"Nope, perfectly fine. Just, please, keep that snake away from us," Nicole answered in a hushed voice.

"Why? Are you scared?" asked David in a taunting voice. He stepped closer, his mouth twisting into a wicked grin. He was only a few steps away from Nicole. Nicole began to twitch as David stepped closer with the snake outstretched toward her. The snake hissed, and as it did saliva dripped out of its mouth and it slowly opened, revealing long sharp fangs. Nicole turned and ran toward a tree and hid behind it.

"Come on, David! Please put the snake down! I'm terrified of them!" shouted Nicole.

"All right! Fine." David walked over to the opposite side of the tree from Nicole and slowly squatted down to let the snake slither off his arm and into the forest.

"Guys, listen. New plan," Alex said once they had all regrouped. "When night comes around again, we aren't going to stop and make camp. I went into a tree and I saw some sort of clearing that we could probably get to in a few days or so, I'm not quite sure. It looks close. Now that we know we have some oil lamps, traveling at night won't be as hard," Alex explained, trying his best not to sound as though he was bossing them around.

"It makes sense, but why are you bringing this up all of a sudden and why through the whole night?" Nicole asked.

"We could get there sooner, and it could be a good place to spend some time re-grouping," Alex replied, shrugging.

No one objected terribly after that, so they all packed up the tents and headed off. As they marched, Alex felt an unusual gust of wind fly past him. Each time he felt a gust, he looked up at the trees or down at the ground, to see if any of the leaves or dust moved because of the strong wind. The only thing that moved was his hair, which had grown a bit long, and he was constantly brushing it out of his eyes. When night finally fell, they pulled out the lamp and continued southward.

TWENTY-THREE

During the evening of the second day, Alex could barely make out the clearing through the trees that Jack had spoken of. He broke into a sprint and ran up to the clearing to find it much bigger than he had imagined. He envisioned it as several acres wide. Instead, the clearing was a sprawling circular field of grass, encompassing the size of several athletic fields. Surrounding the field was the forest, circling it on all sides except for the west side, where a tall, rocky cliff jutted out high into the horizon.

Alex dropped his backpack where he stood and dashed up to the edge of the cliff. A strong wind hit him in the face, tossing his hair back and brushing against his face. Alex took in a deep breath and sucked in the clean and refreshing air. Beyond the cliff lay a beautiful, vast ocean stretching out into the beyond. The setting sun sat perfectly on the water, lighting up the sky with various shades of orange, yellow, pink, and purple, reflecting onto the ocean, causing it to look like the ocean was part of the sky itself. His friends joined him soon after, and by then he was sitting on the edge, staring at the ocean.

"Whoa! Now that's a sight!" David exclaimed.

"The colors are wonderful!" Brooke shouted. Her voice carried along the wind. David walked over to sit down, but his foot slipped and he fell on his behind on to the ledge. Rocks tumbled down beneath his feet and splashed into the water. Moments passed before they realized Alex had caught David from falling by throwing his arm across his torso mom-style. His eyes hadn't moved from where they were fixed on the horizon.

"Careful. That's a 160-foot drop, and at the bottom are multiple large and very sharp rocks with strong tides slamming against them. That would rip you apart," Alex explained. Once David caught his breath, the others sat down beside them and took in the view. "We are going to have to camp out here for a while. Maybe a week?"

"What? Why? What's with all of the sudden plans?" asked Brooke.

"Well, there's someone I want you to meet that's going to rendezvous with us here," Alex replied.

"How could a person possibly get here? We are trapped on this island. If people could get here, then we wouldn't still be here! We'd be at home in our cozy warm beds drinking hot chocolate and cookies, not sleeping on the ground and drinking water from whatever stream we can find or eating birds Alex slices down or fruit from trees!" Brooke yelled. She turned back around toward the ocean and clutched the rock's edge beneath them, breathing deeply and stiffening her shoulders.

"Somebody's not happy," David whispered to Mark and Alex. Alex ignored him.

He explained, "Turns out he's actually from here. He's not from the mainland. He might even help us off this island if we're lucky."

"Sorry." Brooke relaxed her shoulders and brought her arms to her side with a sigh. "When's this person supposed to show up?" she asked.

"Don't know." Alex leaned back.

"Seriously? You don't know? So we're just supposed to wait here? How do we know this person's even gonna show up?" asked Brooke.

"He'll show," Alex said. "At night we'll take turns keeping watch."

"Why are we just going to start keeping watch all of a sudden?" asked Nicole. "We didn't before."

"He doesn't trust the island," Alex replied.

"Who's he?" asked David.

"You'll see," Alex said simply. Alex stood up and walked back to where he left his backpack. He picked up the backpack and yelled to the others. "Hurry up! Where do you want to set up camp?" he called. They all stood up and jogged over to where Alex stood.

"How about the middle of this field? Facing the cliff, so we can look out and see the ocean." suggested Brooke. None of them disagreed, so they set to work. When it was finally time for everyone to sleep, Alex decided to take first watch. He paced back and forth in front of the newly made fire pit waiting for Jack. It wasn't until a full thirty minutes passed before he finally showed up.

"I apologize for being so late. I had to make sure they were all fully asleep before I could show myself," Jack explained from his Shadow.

"It's fine, I'm not impatient," Alex replied sitting down on a nearby rock. "So? What now?"

"I think it's about time your friends know who I am. But first I think you should see who I am before I reveal myself to them. How are they supposed to trust someone who they've never seen?" asked Jack.

"I trusted you. I still do," Alex pointed out. "Anyway, when are we going to introduce you to the others?"

"In two days. You are getting deeper into the island every step you take. The farther you go into the island the more of them there are." Alex was about to ask what he was talking about for the second time when Mark walked out of the tent.

"Who are you talking to?" asked Mark, rubbing his eyes.

"No one. Just me. What's up?" Alex asked.

"You've been out here for a while. I thought you might want to sleep," Mark replied. "I can take over." Alex looked back where Jack was and saw that he already left. Why was he not surprised?

"Yeah, sure." Alex walked back to the tent where David was sleeping. He lay on top of his sleeping bag and stared up at the roof of the tent watching as shadows of the trees danced around in the wind until he fell asleep.

Alex woke up to light shining through a crack in the door of the tent and non-stop laughter outside. He sat up to see that David and Mark were no longer in the tent. Alex walked outside and shielded his eyes from the bright sunlight.

"Good morning, sleepy-head!" greeted Brooke.

"You were out cold last night!" said Mark.

"G'morning." Alex ignored Mark. "What are you all doing?"

"Just talking," answered Nicole.

"When did you all wake up?" Alex asked.

"About two hours ago, I think," said David. "It would help if I had a way of telling time. Too bad my watch wasn't waterproof."

"I didn't wake you up because I didn't want to bother you," Mark told Alex.

"Thanks. Did you eat breakfast?" Alex yawned.

"Oh yeah, well, about that. We ran out," Nicole scratched her head.

"I guess it's about time. It's been a while since we gathered food. I can go look for some." Alex walked off toward the woods and waved back to the others.

"Hey! Wait! I'm coming with you!" Alex turned around to see David running after him. "It's probably best if I come with you! You know, just in case you get lost?"

"I. Don't. Get. Lost," Alex declared with mock anger. Alex and David stared at each other for what seemed like forever until Alex finally said, "Fine. You can come."

"Yeah!" David shouted while jumping in the air and pumping his fists.

"If you're coming, though, you really need to calm down. I'm too tired to deal with your excitement right now."

David immediately stopped jumping and brought his arms to his side.

"I completely understand!" David raised one of his hands and saluted.

"Uh huh." Alex nodded accusingly. When they got to the edge where the woods and the grassy field met David, turned and waved to the others.

"Come on," Alex urged, waving his hand and gesturing towards the woods. David sprinted into the woods, slowly cracking a smile.

"Don't act like you got away with anything," Alex showed his annoyance.

"Why did you want to go alone, anyway?" asked David. Alex ignored him and sped up. "Hello? Why are you so annoyed?" David desperately struggled to catch up. Alex stopped and turned to face David. His face was red from trying to keep up and he was gasping for air. Alex sighed.

"I just like my alone time. And silence," Alex turned forward and started walking again.

"Oh, I see. You could've just said that." David was still struggling to keep up with Alex and by now was jogging. "How are you so calm?"

"What do you mean?" Alex asked.

"Well… when we first met and I almost fell down the stairs, you caught me without even a flinch. And when I almost slipped off the cliff, you didn't show any sign of emotion. And when the monster thingy attacked, you weren't frozen in place by fear like the rest of us." David had started to run by now. Alex stopped again and this time turned only his head to look at him.

"Your point is?"

"My point is you are extremely calm in situations that normal people would be scared to death in!" David thrust his hands into the air waving at nothing.

"What do you mean by 'normal people'? Aren't I normal?" Alex asked a little too loudly. He began to walk again, but this time quickened his pace.

"No, it's just that…well…" David paused. "I think it's awesome!" Alex stopped dead in his tracks. This surprised David, causing him to trip over a rock and fall.

Alex reached out and grabbed the back of his shirt, suspending him with his arms hanging and with a surprised look on his face.

"What's that supposed to mean?" Alex asked, cocking his head to the side, otherwise expressionless. David shook his head snapping him out of his silence.

"See? This is exactly what I mean!" he shouted. Alex let go of David and let him stumble into a tree. Once he regained balance, he walked back over to him and grabbed onto Alex's sleeve before he could start walking.

"I'm glad we're friends, Alex," David said, his face now serious. Alex ignored him, and he continued walking, except this time he slowed his pace to a speed that David could handle. They walked in silence for a while until finally Alex said, "I guess... I am, too."

"Woah! Hey, look! Jackpot!" David pointed up toward the canopy, and Alex followed his finger to see what he was pointing at. The canopy was full of bright ripe fruit that shone brightly against the bits of sunlight seeping through the trees.

"Let's go get some food!" David ran to the nearest tree and started to climb. Alex watched as he climbed the tree until he saw the fruit. There was a broken branch just a few feet away from David, and if he were to step on it it would snap. Then his foot was on it. He couldn't pull up or go any farther or he would fall.

"David!" Alex ran up and jumped from branch to branch when David started to fall. Alex grabbed him by the arm and yanked him up into the tree before David could fall out of his reach.

"Seriously?" Alex asked.

"Heh... Thanks. That was scary. We should probably get going." David started to climb again and Alex sighed.

"Careful," Alex said. They both filled up their empty backpacks they brought along up to the brim then closed them up.

"So, how are we gonna get down? Just drop the bags, then climb down?" David held his bag of fruit out in front of him as if getting ready to drop it.

"No. That might ruin the fruit. Just sling it on your back and climb down. Don't fall this time," Alex scolded. David laughed the whole way down.

"Are you done laughing now? It wasn't even that funny."

"Sorry, It's really embarrassing. I tend to laugh when I do something stupid to hide my embarrassment. Lets just head back now." David started to walk back to the camp, and that's when Alex thought back to what he said earlier. *He was... glad? To be friends....with me?* Alex thought. *Not something I've heard in awhile.* Alex followed David, keeping a distance away from him so he wouldn't be tempted to talk to him. When they finally arrived, the others cheered.

"Yay! Our heroes!" Nicole shouted sarcastically. "I'm starving!"

David and Alex walked over, pretending they didn't hear her and dropped the bags of fruit down. Alex picked up an apple and walked over to the edge of the cliff, sat down, and stared off into the distance. He was still pondering what David had said when a memory flooded back to him.

TWENTY-FOUR

"*riends*? You want to make *friends*!" shouted Alex's father. "You don't need friends! What you need is to stay here and do your chores!"

"But can't I ever have friends?" Alex asked. "I'm so bored! All I'm doing with my life is reading and doing chores for you! Can't I have a little freedom?"

Alex watched his father pull back his hand ready to strike. Alex didn't bother trying to dodge. If he did, he knew that whatever was coming would be ten times worse if he resisted. He put his arms over his head and braced for impact. Alex could see his mother and sister standing behind his father, smiling. They were more than pleased at the events occurring that moment.

The blow was painful and strong. Alex was flung back into the wall with nowhere to run and nowhere to hide. His sword was in his room, so there was no weapon in his reach to defend himself with. Alex's father pulled out his belt and snapped it. Alex knew what was to happen next. Once, twice, three times, four. The incessant beating of his father's belt penetrated his skin, causing it to ache to the touch. Alex bit his bottom lip to keep from crying out in pain, causing him to taste blood.

Then his father yelled, "Don't ever talk back to me again! And I don't want to hear another word about *FRIENDS!*" The final blow hit him on the side of the head, then darkness. Later Alex would wake up on the floor in his room covered in blood.

Alex cringed at the memory, shaking himself back to reality, realizing that he had fallen onto his side and that he was shaking and sweating. Alex immediately sat up, wiped the sweat off his forehead, and turned toward his friends. They were all talking cheerfully and eating the newly picked fruit. They hadn't noticed a thing. Alex turned back to the ocean and watched as fish jumped out of the water only to be eaten by odd-shaped seagulls. Alex bit into the apple he was holding, then threw the core into the ocean.

"Hey, Alex what time is it?" Brooke shouted. Alex looked up at the sky and shielded his eyes from the sun.

"Somewhere around two, I think?" he shouted back. Alex was still shaken from the memory, so his voice cracked.

"Are you okay?" called Nicole.

"Just fine," Alex answered.

"You should come join us!" David shouted before turning back to the others to continue their conversation. At that moment, Alex wished he had shoved his headphones into his backpack before he jumped out of the window and ran away. Music always helped him to calm down. Alex stood up and walked back down to the tents. Retrieving his water bottle and holding it above his head, he discovered that all of the water was gone.

Quietly, Alex snuck back out of the tent and sauntered into the woods. His friends were busy talking about something else and he didn't feel like interrupting them. As he walked, he cleared his mind and focused his thoughts on one thing. Finding a stream. He didn't want any more memories seeping through the cracks of the cages he had locked them up in.

Finding a stream was taking longer than Alex expected. When he finally found one, it was so hidden he might have not found it if the sound of rushing water wasn't so loud. Alex kneeled down beside the stream and stuck his hand in it. The water was an icy cold against his fingertips. With an odd satisfaction, Alex lifted his hand out of the stream and shook the water off his hand. He unscrewed the top to his bottle and scooped it into the stream, filling it with water.

"What was that all about?" Jack asked from a nearby shadow.

"What was what?" Alex asked, standing up and screwing the top back onto his bottle. He had gotten so used to Jack's random appearances he could easily feel it whenever he appeared. Jack sighed.

"Never mind. Why didn't you tell those friends of yours you were leaving? Won't they worry?"

"If I get there in time, no, they won't. And they were busy. I didn't want to bother them." Alex stood up and turned toward Jack. "I should probably begin heading back now if I want to get there before sunset. Daylight ends quickly here. I'm sure you have noticed." Alex turned and began walking back toward the camp.

"Not yet."

Alex felt a firm hand grip his shoulder tightly. Alex twisted his head and looked at the hand. It was long, skinny, and pale but strong. Alex swung around to see who the owner was, thinking it couldn't have been Jack, for every time Alex had seen his hand it was glazed over with shadow making it impossible to see its features.

Alex staggered back in astonishment as he witnessed Jack stepping out of the shadow he was hidden in. His eyes were as blue as the afternoon sky. His hair was a light brown and slicked back like a gentleman's. A plain black top hat rested neatly atop his head. His neat gray dress pants went well with his lavender purple dress shirt, and his black dress shoes made him look like a businessman. Around his waist was a brown, square satchel. Alex did not know what was inside.

Alex might have mistaken him for a businessman if the jacket wasn't replaced with a long black cloak that went down to the soles of his feet. Inside the folds of the cloak, instead of black was a dark purple. The cloak was held together by two golden buttons on either side that rested against his collarbone and by a short golden chain that ran across the small gap, pulling the two buttons together.

Suddenly, Alex felt as though he recognized him. But from where? And from where in the world would Alex have recognized him? Alex was curious, but he decided to hide his curiosity and save his questions for later. Jack's cloak fluttered in the wind, and he held the tip of his hat down as if to greet someone.

"It's a pleasure, Alex Shaffer," Jack announced. "Or at least, officially."

That's when it hit him. He had met him for a brief moment on his first day of school.

"Mr. Pandemonium?" Alex gasped in astonishment.

"My last name, yes. Jack Pandemonium is my full name."

"Wait, it was you? You were the teacher I helped gather papers for?"

"Yes, that is true, but I don't actually teach there. Never did."

"Well, as much as I'd like to continue this conversation, I should start heading back. It took a while to get here." Alex began walking back and Jack followed. "We should start heading back if we want to make it there by sunset. And by the way, it's just Alex now."

Jack walked alongside Alex for the rest of the way. Both of them filled the trip with endless conversation, with Alex asking most of the questions. When they were a few yards away from the clearing, Jack disappeared into the night. His last words were, "See you soon."

Alex ran up behind the tents and peered around the corner. The fire had long since died out, and David, Brooke, Mark, and Nicole were all laying around in a circle fast asleep. Alex walked around the tents and over to his snoring companions.

He went around one by one, grabbing their arms and dragging them into their separate tents. When he had finished, he built up the fire again and then sat on the ground next to it, continually poking it with a stick. The fire was warm against Alex's skin and grew even warmer the more Alex threw kindling in.

TWENTY-FIVE

"So? Where did you run off to?"

Alex jumped and turned toward the sound of the one who had spoken. He was relieved to find that it was Brooke. She was standing in front of her tent with her hands folded behind her back. Her expression was gentle and her voice was soft.

"I went to go find a stream to fill my water bottle," said Alex as he held up his full water bottle to prove that his explanation was the truth.

"We were worried for a bit, you know, after we saw you sneaking away from camp. But we figured you didn't want us coming along. Am I wrong?"

"No," Alex replied. "That's pretty much it."

"We got a little anxious when a few hours passed. But we decided that we would wait and see. If you weren't back by the morning, we would go looking for you. Or at least that's what *they* decided." Brooke broke out into a wide, crooked grin. The grotesque smile curved upward from eye to eye, showing her sharp, pointed teeth. Her eyes grew as wide as they could go while her pupils shrunk to a small sliver, dancing wildly as she began to speak. This time her voice was hushed but threatening.

"How about it, Alex? Do you want to die?" Brooke's head tilted back toward the sky and she began to laugh. Quietly at first. Then gradually it grew louder and louder until it rang throughout the forest.

"Brooke? What are you doing?" Alex stood up and slowly backed away, frightened. Brooke's laugh ceased and she righted her head. Still smiling, she stared at Alex and watched as he backed away. Alex groped for his sword, but all he felt was air. Alex looked back where the handle of his sword should be strapped to his back to find nothing. Where had it gone? He didn't remember taking it off. Alex looked back at Brooke helplessly. If this really was Brooke, he couldn't hurt her, even if it meant she was going to do something horrible.

"Who are you? You're not Brooke. You can't be," Alex said hopefully. Brooke continued to laugh.

"Glad you finally noticed." Brooke launched herself at Alex, bringing her hands out from behind her back. In her hand, she held Alex's sword. Alex tried to dodge her attack only to realize his feet would no longer move. Alex willed them to run, but they remained stuck to the ground. He looked down at his feet, and his eyes widened.

Thorn-covered vines were emerging from the ground and wrapping themselves around Alex's hands and legs, swirling around his body, locking him in place. Alex watched helplessly as Brooke ran toward him with the sword outstretched and pointed at Alex. He watched in horror as the sword pierced through his stomach with a loud *squelch* and blood splattered across the ground. Brooke leaned in, pushing the sword deeper into his stomach.

She whispered in his ear, "You're dead."

Alex tried to scream but he only coughed up blood, as Brooke repeatedly screamed, "You're dead!"

Alex shot up from the ground in a panicked sweat. Was that all a dream? He grabbed his stomach where the sword had gone through. There was no wound. Alex searched the ground and his body for blood. No blood either. Realizing the sun was setting, Alex looked up as Mark, David, Nicole, and Brooke came running out of their tents.

"Is everything okay? We heard you scream!" Nicole shouted. Alex looked around at his friends, relieved it was only a dream until his eyes fell on Brooke. She was in the same position as the fake-Brooke in his dream. Her expression was calm and gentle, and her hands were neatly folded behind her back. Alex's eyes went wide as the scene of Brooke stabbing him played through his head. Alex felt for his sword and ripped it out of its sheath on his back.

"Who are you and where is Brooke?" Alex shouted at Brooke and pointed the tip of his sword at her, the blade wobbling in his grip. Brooke stepped back in surprise and dropped her hands to her side, revealing she had been holding nothing.

"What are you talking about?" asked Brooke, startled.

"You turned into a maniac and stole my sword, using it to kill me," Alex shouted. "Or… at least in my dream you did." Slowly, Alex lowered his sword and sighed, realizing how foolish he was being.

"Did vines randomly pop out of the ground and bind you to the spot?" asked David.

"Yeah, they did. How did you know that?" Alex asked, turning toward David and sheathing his sword.

"The same thing happened to me as well," David remarked. "Brooke broke out into the creepiest smile ever and she had a gun. She was just about to shoot me when I heard you scream and woke up. The worst part was that you were all standing next to her just watching and not doing anything!" David replied.

"Yeah that was like mine! But none of you guys were there and Brooke used my sword. Not a gun."

"Well, I didn't have that dream," Mark commented.

"Neither did me or Brooke," Nicole added.

"Never mind. Forget about it. Brooke, I'm sorry for lashing out at you like that. I was still caught up in my dream to realize that it was the real you," Alex apologized.

"It's fine. I would be freaked out if I had a dream like that," Brooke nodded.

"It is a warning from the Nichters," a voice suddenly echoed through the air.

"Who said that?" Mark asked the people around him. All of them shook their heads.

"I did," Jack stepped out of the cover of a Shadow and bowed, his cloak fluttering in the wind. Alex turned from Jack to his friends. They all stood frozen to the spot, slack-jawed.

"V…v…v… vampire!" David screeched, stumbling backward. "You can't have my blood!" David turned and prepared to run, but Alex grabbed him by the shirt and yanked him back. David wobbled off balance, falling at Jack's feet. David looked up at Jack's amused expression and jumped back to hide behind Alex.

"Everyone, relax. This is Jack." Alex stepped out of David's reach and stepped over to Jack's side. Alex pointed to each individual as he introduced them to Jack.

"Oh, I know. I know who all of you are," said Jack, chuckling. It wasn't until then that Alex realized Jack had been there all along. Observing them within his Shadows. *Oh that's creepy.* Alex thought.

Jack leaned forward and whispered into Alex's ear. "I didn't watch you everyday all the time. You can relax. I was only there when it seemed that you would be in trouble. Turns out you always had it under control. I do have a life, you know."

Alex scoffed as Jack stood up straight.

"You may know who we are, but we have no clue who you are," Nicole spoke up.

"All you need to know is that my name is Jack and I am your ally," Jack replied before randomly changing the subject. "Why haven't you changed your clothes this whole time? It's already been a month and a half and you haven't changed your clothes even once."

Everyone stared down at their ripped and torn clothes. Leaves and sticks caked in mud stuck to their shoes and pants, revealing infected scratches and dried blood through tears in their jeans. Their hair was knotted and dirty. How had they not noticed this before?

"But don't worry about any of that. I have just the thing." Jack smiled. Alex jerked his head up, but before he was able to ask what he was talking about Jack snapped his fingers and a white light clouded his vision. The white light only lasted for a few seconds before dying down.

"What did you just do?" Alex asked, sounding concerned.

"Look at your clothes. They look much better now," said Jack as he nodded to Alex. Alex did what Jack had instructed and found his clothes mended and clean, and his cuts healed. Alex thought back to what Jack said and remembered something he had missed.

" A month and a half?" Alex screeched. Everyone who had been studying their now clean clothes stared at Alex then at Jack. "We've been on this island for a month and a half?"

"Yes, of course. You haven't been keeping track of the days?" asked Jack.

"No, why would I? I have no way of keeping track and with everything that's been going on I haven't had much time to," Alex exclaimed.

"Well, don't worry, I have been. Now, what is this I hear about Brooke killing you? You look alive enough to me," Jack commented. Suddenly, Alex felt a jerk to the arm, and he was pulled away by Mark and Nicole.

"What are you doing?" Alex asked once they had pulled him far away from Jack.

"Alex, we just want to clarify some things right now. And to put it bluntly, we don't trust that man. Whatever he said his name was," Nicole replied.

"Don't get us wrong. We trust you completely. But we don't trust him. How do you expect us to? When he just showed up at the drop of a hat?" Mark whispered.

"His name is Jack. I don't expect you to trust him. He's a stranger. For all you know, he could be a mass murderer," Alex whispered back.

"That doesn't help," Nicole said sternly.

"It's not supposed to. I'm not asking you to trust him. I'm not even asking you to be friendly with him. What I am asking you, though, is to trust me."

"I don't expect you to trust me *either*," Jack said from behind. Alex, Mark, and Nicole all jumped and turned to the figure looming over them. "You may trust me right off the bat, or it may take a while. You may not come to trust me at all. I am not looking for your approval," Jack paused and smiled. "Now please, answer my question."

Mark and Nicole blushed as Brooke and David made their way over from where they had been standing and talking to Jack only moments ago.

"You want to know about our dream? I'm sure it was just a nightmare, but I can tell you if you'd like," David said.

"Yes, I would," Jack responded, turning to face the nearing teenagers.

"It was nothing, really. Alex and I just had a similar dream is all." David stepped in front of Jack.

"Maybe so, but I would still like to hear about it," Jack insisted. David gave in to Jack's request and told him about their strange nightmares. When David had finished, Jack nodded his head thoughtfully, going over the details of the boy's story.

"I see. If you'll excuse your friend, Alex and I need to speak alone for a moment." Jack placed his hand on Alex's back and ushered him to the silent emptiness of the cliff. "Is this true?" he asked.

"Yeah, for the most part. The only big difference is the dying part," Alex shrugged. "What's this got to do with anything?"

"This could prove my suspicions," Jack muttered.

"What 'suspicions'?"

"Well, the storm was clearly the work of a Storm Conjurer, and the dreams are clearly the work of a Prestidigitator. But what puzzles me is the fact that they seem to be working together," Jack continued to mutter under his breath.

"What's a Prestidigitator?"

"A Prestidigitator is a being who belongs to the Illusionists. They create illusions, hence the name. They have the ability to create illusions anywhere and anytime. Only the most experienced, however, may control a Nichter. While their victim is under their influence, they can force them to do anything they wish. Even kill." Jack paused. "Tell me, how did it feel when you were stabbed by your own sword? Was there blood?"

"It felt real. I thought I was awake and living the real thing until I woke up. And yes, there was blood."

"It is a good thing your friend David woke up when he did. He would have been in a much worse state if he hadn't."

"What's that supposed to mean?" Alex asked, slightly offended.

"Nothing that concerns you." Jack turned and walked back to the others with Alex at his heel.

"What? How the heck doesn't it concern me?" Alex called, but Jack didn't answer.

"Do you think we could catch some meat or something? Maybe a bird? Or a squirrel?" Nicole shouted at Alex as he walked back, holding an orange in her hand. "I seriously need some meat! After all, we have been on this island for what? A month? Month and a half? It's been too long without it."

Mark looked up from his bag at Nicole as she shouted her last words. He felt his heart pang against his ribcage and hundreds of questions flooded his mind. Home. His family. What was his family doing now? Where did they think he was? Did they miss him? When would he see them again? Would he *ever* see them again? Would he ever escape this forsaken island? Mark swallowed the lump that had formed in his throat.

Mark could tell he wasn't the only one who had felt the sudden homesickness. He looked around at his friends and noticed that they had all felt the same thing. Nicole was still holding the fruit in the air, but her eyes had traveled to the ground and she had a far off look in her eyes. David had his hand covering his eyes, and Brooke was staring at Nicole with her eyes as big as saucers. Mark swallowed again. He missed his family too much. For all he knew, he could die on this island and never see them again. Mark turned and hid within the tent so no one could notice his struggle.

"You want meat? I can have my Shadows run back to the mainland and get some if you would like." Jack said, his voice soft, and understanding. He flicked his hand as if he were motioning for something and suddenly a black thin line appeared, suspended in the air. Shadow-like creatures emerged from the line and shot toward Jack. Alex jumped back and reached for his sword in surprise but stopped when Jack only stood there, not showing any expressions of concern.

Jack smirked at Alex's reaction but kept his eyes trained on the creatures. They halted in front of Jack and he muttered commands to them. When he had finished speaking, he whisked his hand once more, and the strange creatures flew back into the thin line and disappeared. There was an astonished silence but only for a moment.

"You can go to the mainland? Take us back!" Mark blurted out. Alex suddenly came to the realization that they had all been trying to make the most of their time spent on this island and not think the worst of it. They had all been bottling up their emotions for all this time. Their emotions were only just beginning to show. And they were locking these feelings away for him. He brought them into this mess.

And I'm going to bring them out of it, Alex thought.

"Yes, I can travel to the mainland, among other things and I would gladly bring you back. Only I am not perfect and one of my flaws is the fact that I can only transport my Shadows and myself through my portals, with the exception of inanimate objects," Jack said calmly.

There was another silence except this one had disappointment lingering in the air. "I truly am sorry and would bring you back if I could, but it is simply not possible."

"That's all right. We can find another way." Nicole righted her head and she met her eyes with Jack's. Alex thought back to what Jack said, searching for a solution but he could find none. Alex straightened and asked, "do you think you could retrieve something for me?"

"Depends on what it is," Jack replied with a smile.

"My Walkman. I forgot it in my room back in Orlson."

"That, I can do." Jack waved his hand, and another black line appeared in the air and another Shadow came to his service. When it finally disappeared once again, Alex and the others were all crowded around the fire for warmth against the cold winds that had begun to drift up from the ocean.

Not a second afterwards a Shadow returned with the thin headphones connected to the small gray box. It plopped them into his lap, and Alex nodded his head gratefully at the strange creature. He slid the headphones over his ears and turned the music on. He smiled as he was greeted with the sound of a familiar song. Another pair of Shadows appeared and flew over their heads. Plates of chicken and broccoli dropped into their laps, followed by water bottles. Once their jobs were done, the Shadow creatures dissipated into the air.

"Dinner is served," announced Jack as he bowed and sat next to Alex, watching as they gulped down their new found dinner like starved dogs. When they finished, their plates disappeared from in front of them and any trace of the plates was erased.

"Where'd the plate go?" David asked, his voice muffled, his mouth preoccupied with chewing a piece of chicken.

"Don't worry, I took care of it," Jack replied.

The sun had sunk beneath the horizon completely now and the dark had taken over everything the light of the fire could not. Alex sauntered over to a rock hidden in the dark and away from the light from the flames.

"I'll take first watch," Alex said.

"Great! I'm in a good mood for sleep right now," said David as he stood up and stretched before walking into his tent, soon followed by Mark. Nicole waved to Alex before she and Brooke disappeared within the folds of the yellow rubber. When the fire grew dim and everyone was in bed, Jack walked over and stood beside Alex. In a hushed voice, Jack whispered, "I'm going to patrol the area," and with a wave of his cloak he disappeared into the Shadows.

Alex didn't bother to ask why and instead slipped his headphones over his ears and let his mind drift away into the bass that throbbed in his eardrums. Only an hour had passed before Alex was startled to see David walking out of his tent. David walked slowly onto the cliff without saying a word. Alex pulled the headphones off and set them against the rock he had been sitting on. He stood up and began to walk toward David.

"David, you can go back to sleep. I can keep watch for a little longer," Alex called after him. David didn't answer. Alex took a few steps closer.

"David, did you hear me? I said you can go back to sleep."

David continued walking, not saying a word, his eyes trained on the cliff's edge ahead. Then, Alex noticed something was off. David's eyes were closed and he was breathing as if he was still asleep. Alex remembered what Jack had said, "The experienced may also cause their victim to do anything in their sleep. Maybe even kill."

Alex sprinted forward and ran as fast as his legs could carry him to David. He was only two steps away from the edge. Two steps, one step, David was leaning over the edge threateningly, swaying back and forth until he started to lean over the rocky waters beneath him. Alex jumped at him and clasped his hand around David's arm, jerking him back. David landed on his backside hard, waking him up just in time to see Alex slip and fall off the edge and into the treacherous waters below.

TWENTY-SIX

"ALEX!" David finally came to his senses in time to see Alex slip and fall off the cliff. A small chunk of the cliff where Alex's foot had been fell off along with him. David lurched for Alex, falling to his knees with his arm outstretched for him. Maybe he could catch him in time, he thought. Alex thrust his hand forward and reached for David's hand. Alex's hand only grazed David's finger-tips before gravity overtook him and carried him farther and farther down.

David's sudden cry startled everyone awake and sent them sprawling out of their tents in a hectic panic. From deep in the woods, Jack's head jerked up as David's shout echoed through the trees. Leaping up from the ground, Jack leapt yards at a time and ran for the camp. hoping that whatever he had heard had been misconstructed as panic.

Alex watched as David grabbed blindly at the air, desperately willing for everything to be only a nightmare. Alex could smell the salty water lingering in the air, burning his nostrils. The impact of his body slamming into the freezing water sucked the air out of him, forcing him to open his mouth. The freezing water entered his gaping mouth and flooded into his lungs. The sudden rush of cold, rapid water tossed Alex around and sent him sprawling deeper into the black depths of the ocean.

In a matter of seconds, the anger of the unforgiving ocean took him over, and darkness surrounded him as he sank even deeper. Before his body gave in and his eyes shut, he caught a glimpse of a dark figure swimming toward him. Alex could just make out that it was Jack before his eyes closed and he was fully engulfed in darkness.

***

Alex's eyes fluttered open to five concerned faces hovering over him, all of them illuminated by a torch gripped tightly in Mark's hand. None of them looked more troubled than David. Alex lurched forward and leaned to the side, coughing up water. When the coughing and hacking ceased, Alex felt a sharp pain shoot from his head and down his body. Alex grimaced in pain. When he had finished recovering, he looked at Jack, who was kneeling beside him. Alex smiled.

"We really need to find a way to stop falling off things," Alex managed before he coughed again. Mark and the others all snorted at Alex's comment and stifled their laughs. Alex staggered to a standing position and steadied himself.

"Oh my gosh! You're bleeding!" Brooke shouted in surprise.

"What?" Alex asked. "No I'm not."

"Yes, you are! Look at your back!" Brooke pointed at Alex's back with a trembling finger. Alex glanced over his shoulder to see his back drenched in watery blood. There was no cut. Slowly Alex brought his hand up to his head. It wasn't his back that was bleeding, he realized. It was his head. Alex brought his hand down and stared at the blood on his fingertips.

"I'll be all right. It isn't a large cut. It's not big enough to need stitches." Alex wiped off the blood on his jeans.

"It may be just that, but we are still going to patch you up." Jack smiled with worry and waved his hand. Bandages and scissors appeared out of thin air, and Jack waved his finger in a circle. The roll of bandages unwound itself and started to wind around the large cut on Alex's head. When Jack finished, the bandages were almost completely hidden beneath his hair if not for the small chunk at the back of his head. As soon as his head was bandaged, Alex turned to David.

"David, are you all right?" Alex asked.

"Me? Why are you asking if I'm okay? You're the one who fell off the cliff!" David pointed out.

"In case you have forgotten, you were about to fall off the cliff yourself."

"I'm fine. My brain is just a bit foggy."

"Don't let your guard down just yet. It's still here," Jack interrupted.

"What's still here?" Nicole asked, both puzzled and slightly frightened at Jack's tone of voice.

"The Prestidigitator," Jack replied.

"The Prestawhatta?" asked David.

"A Prestidigitator. A citizen of Heltiana. They can create illusions and control your body. They are basically magicians. That's what caused David to do what he did. And it's still here."

"It's still here?" Nicole asked.

"Whoa! Hold up! So, I wasn't sleepwalking?" David asked. Jack looked at him and shook his head.

"Oh, good," David sighed in relief.

"The Prestidigitator sent you two a message in your dreams. What puzzles me is that their messages always come true. But today it didn't," Jack explained. Brooke, Mark, David, and Nicole all stared at Jack as though he told them he was Santa Claus. Alex was the only one who acted as though he actually knew what Jack was talking about.

A strong wind whipped past them, snuffing the light of the torch out. Alex looked up for the light of the moon, but a dark cloud covered it, leaving them in the pitch black. Thunder sounded in the distance and rain poured down.

"When did it start raining?" David shouted over the thunder.

"Storm Conjurer!" Jack shouted. The suddenly heavy rain made his words sound like a whisper. "Be ready to fight!"

"Fight? We can't fight! We've never fought in our lives!" Nicole glanced over at Alex's expectant glare. "Well, most of us haven't."

"Yes, you can! I've seen you do it! You've been fighting since the moment you stepped foot on that ship. Even if you don't think you can, I at least know Brooke can." Jack threw his arm up, brushing his cloak back. In his hand he held a dark brown leather hardcover book, thick with pages yellowed with age.

"Sorry, but I have no idea what you are talking about," Brooke said as she raised her eyebrows in confusion. "I can't fight. I have no idea how you came to that conclusion."

"Yes, you do. I don't exactly know what it is quite yet, but you certainly can do it. You used it with the Clandestine Brobdingnagian. You only need to figure out how to make that ability manifest again."

"What are you talking about? You're speaking nonsense!" Brooke shouted.

Lightning shot through the sky. In front of them the tree tops rustled in the distance. The trees that were on the edge of the clearing rustled in the wind while a behemoth of a monster stepped out. Taller than the trees, it had a long, stretched-out mouth that had rows of razor sharp teeth underneath its lips. On its sides were six rows of multiple arms and hands. It's tail was covered in black scales and spanned the entire width of the clearing and more, disappearing into the woods. It was all black except for its shining yellow eyes. The monster turned its head, and once it caught sight of the group it let out a loud roar.

"Oh my God it's Godzilla!" shouted David, pointing toward the monster.

"It does look strangely like Godzilla, doesn't it?" Nicole tilted her head and stared at it with interest.

"A monster just stepped out of the trees and *that's* what you are focusing on?" asked Mark furiously.

"Look out!" Jack shouted as he leapt aside. The monster's tail swept back and forth at them in order to knock them off their feet. "JUMP! JUST JUMP!" Jack shouted. The five of them only stood and stared at another quizzically.

"You heard him!" Alex demanded. They looked and shrugged at each other while a titanic-sized tail made its way toward them. They all bent their knees and propelled themselves off the dirt-covered ground. They leapt high into the sky and high above the trees.

Alex tumbled into a summersault and landed on the other side of the clearing. His mouth was wide open from shock. His friends had all landed in scattered positions around the clearing. David had fallen on his knees and rolled over while Nicole was crouched in a squat. Brooke and Mark were standing on their feet with their eyes trained on their shoes in surprise. David stood up and slapped his hand on his forehead, breaking out laughing.

"I must be dreaming!" he shouted hysterically. The monster let out a roar and charged at them. It's roar shook the ground, causing David to stop his hysterical fit.

"Maybe not," said David as he turned and ran the other direction and the others followed. Alex ran forward and latched onto one of the scales on the monster's tail. It thrashed its tail about wildly, shaking Alex off and sending him crashing to the ground before Alex could get a hit. Jack grabbed Alex's shirt and yanked him off the ground in time for the monster's tail to come crashing down where Alex had landed. Jack released his grip on Alex's arm and bounded up into the air.

Jack hovered in the air a few feet away from the monster's head. He held out his book in his hand and opened it. A dark purple smoke surrounded the book, and it began to lift out of his open hand. He brought his hand down and thrust his other out with his palm facing the monster. His legs were perfectly straight, and his cloak fluttered in the strong wind and rain.

He began to murmur words that Alex could not hear over the roar of the wind. He continued to murmur until Shadows were surrounding him. The Shadows lunged at Jack's command and at the monster, completely covering it. "Come on! Now's your chance!" he yelled.

Alex leapt at the monster with his sword but was soon slapped back by its tail and sent sprawling back to the ground with a thud. Alex rolled out of the path of the monster as Jack continued to throw Shadows at the beast. Brooke stood staring at the monster, scratching her head.

"I don't think I can do this! I don't know *how* I did it last time! I don't think I was even the reason it happened!" Brooke shouted.

"Hurry up and figure it out before we get eaten!" shouted David as he tumbled away from the slashing tail. "It's Jurassic Park all over again!"

"That never happened. That was just a movie! Dinosaurs are extinct, so whatever this is it isn't a dinosaur!" shouted Nicole as a lightning bolt struck the ground a few yards away from her feet.

"You're one to talk! After we watched one of those horror movies, you thought Slender Man was real for three months!" Mark laughed.

"I don't do that anymore. That was four years ago. Keep up!" Nicole shouted as she pulled Mark out of the way of a lightning bolt's path. "Be aware of your surroundings."

There was a flash of black in the corner of Alex's eye and he turned to see a man in black disappear into the woods. *Could that be the Predigistator Jack mentioned?* Alex raced after the man that disappeared into the woods. He brushed aside branches and leaves, chasing after the flash of black that moved through the trees swiftly and silently. Lightning struck a tree in front of him. Alex sped up and ran beneath the falling tree. He wasn't about to lose the strange man. Nothing was going to slow him down.

As soon as he was in the crashing tree's path, he tripped and fell. Before he could get out of the way, the large trunk came crashing on top of him.

"Timber! Ouch…that must've hurt, huh?"

Alex cursed at his stupidity and looked up from his pinned down and helpless position to see two figures looming over him. Suddenly, the rain and thunder stopped. There was only dry soundless lightning. One of the figures was a woman in her mid-twenties with smooth, brown skin and long, silvery white hair. A long white and sparkly robe with white ruffles around the neck and bottom was draped around her shoulders. The rest of her body was hidden neatly beneath the folds of her robe.

A man in his early thirties stood beside her. He was skinny and tall with short, spiked black hair. His black coat looked like that of a butler's and a red vest was placed neatly atop his white dress shirt. Both his pants and his shoes were black.

One of his hands was covered by a pure white glove. Blacked-out rectangular sunglasses obscured his eyes from view. These two looked as if they just came from some sort of charity banquet.

His skinny arm reached up and slid his glasses off and stuffed them inside his coat, revealing ice cold blue eyes. "Hello. How may we be of service?" The man asked sarcastically in a husky voice.

"Who are you?" Alex blurted, ignoring his offer for help.

"Mmm… how rude. You should learn your manners, boy," said the woman in a sing-song voice. Alex scowled.

"Fine. Fine. Since you asked, my name is Jaheim, a Prestidigitator. This is Winona, a Conjurer," the man gestured to him and the woman. The woman knelt down on one knee and put a hand up to Alex's face and brushed it gently.

"Now what are you, boy? You seem extraordinarily young." Alex pulled his face away from her gloved hand and grunted. Her hand too, had a white glove over it but instead both of her hands were gloved and at the end of them were more fluffy white ruffles.

"Refusing to talk? That's just fine. We'll leave you here while we go play with those friends of yours." The woman smirked as she stepped over the tree and walked back toward the campsite. As soon as Jaheim and Winona were gone, rain and sound returned. Alex turned himself over and, with great effort, rolled the tree off him and began running.

Alex thrust his hands in front of him and shoved the last of the branches away before tumbling onto the mud-covered ground, face-first. Alex looked up to see all of his friends trapped inside a cage that looked as though it were made of lightning. Jack was still busy fighting the monster with his Shadows. Beads of sweat had formed on his forehead and he was gritting his teeth. Winona and Jaheim were standing in front of the cage and talking to their prisoners.

Alex couldn't make out what they were saying over the roar of the thunder. He ran toward them and sliced his sword through them. Both of their bodies dissipated into thin air.

"What the—?" Alex stuttered in surprise.

"I'm surprised you fell for that," Jaheim laughed. Alex spun around to find Winona and Jaheim standing behind him.

"That was a typical illusion trick. It was a low-level one, too. I'm surprised you didn't recognize it as an illusion immediately. Don't they teach you that in school?" Jaheim commented.

"Oh, give the boy a break. He is young," Winona scolded. "But that isn't an excuse for us not to hurt you." Winona's smile was cold and bitter as she started to slowly pull out her hand from under her cloak. "Now what should it be, Jaheim? Quick or slow death?"

"I think a slow one as punishment for his ill manners shall do."

"I agree. But one thing I don't know is what the cause of death will be," she said as Winona and Jaheim slowly started to walk toward Alex. Light poured from Jaheim's hands while the sky rumbled and flashed with lightning.

"I've been meaning to ask, what's with the bandage around the head?" Jaheim pointed a finger at Alex's head. "Oh wait! I remember now!" Jaheim laughed.

"Don't play games with me. Why are you here?" Alex demanded.

"No reason. We are only doing our job," Winona replied calmly.

"And what's that?" Alex asked.

"None of your business," Jaheim answered in a sickly sweet voice.

"Why does everyone keep saying that?" Alex rolled his eyes.

Jaheim and Winona both lunged at Alex to attack. Alex fell to the ground and rolled to the side and out of the way. They chased him around the grassy field at full speed. Alex raced up the tail of the monster with Winona and Jaheim at his heels. Alex stabbed the monster and jumped off just in time for its tail to come flying up and hit the exact spot where Winona and Jaheim had been. Jack hovered in the air staring at the monster while Alex waited on the ground. When the tail finally came down Winona and Jaheim were nowhere to be found.

"Where'd they go?" Alex asked as the monster dissipated. "Did they leave?"

"Not quite," a voice whispered from behind. Before Alex could turn around, a skinny arm wrapped around his neck and another arm forced Alex's hand to drop his sword. Alex latched his hands onto the arm gasping, trying to loosen it but it only got tighter.

"This will all be over soon. Oh, but don't worry we'll still keep that promise about the slow death," said Jaheim from behind. Alex's vision blurred as he watched Winona walk toward him with a lightning bolt crackling and sparking in her hand.

TWENTY-SEVEN

"I wonder how a bolt of lightning straight through the chest feels."

"I'm sure it's quite painful."

"Probably is," Winona said with a smirk. A scream pierced the air. "'What is this?" she shouted. Alex felt the grip around his neck loosen until Jaheim's arm fully released Alex's neck. Alex doubled over coughing and looked up to see what had caused them to stop.

Jaheim and Winona were covered in rose vines sprouting up from the earth. There was a strange green glow outlining the vines. The thorns scraped against their skin, revealing bright red blood pouring out of fresh cuts. Alex looked back at his friends to see David's hand outstretched toward the vines. The same green light on the vines emanated from the palm of his hand.

When Alex looked back, Winona and Jaheim were gone. The rain stopped, and thunder and lightning no longer filled the air. The clouds that covered the moon retreated and the light of the purple moon shone once again. The vines slithered back into the ground like snakes and the ground closed up where the vines had previously emerged. Alex stood up and walked back to his friends where they were standing in a scorched square in the grass where the cage had been.

"Are you okay?" Alex choked. A red mark had formed on his neck on the spot he was strangled. Mark was cradling his left arm while Nicole was limping. "What happened?"

"We got burned," replied Mark.

"I should have stuff for that in my bag," said Alex as he turned his attention to Jack, who was drifting to the ground. "Why didn't you come back down and help us? The monster dissipated long before they left."

"I apologize. I don't know what happened. I believe Jaheim placed a barrier around you to prevent me from coming to your aid. I was unable to reach the ground," said Jack as he took off his hat and twirled it. As it spun, it slowly began to shrink. In an instant it was gone.

"How'd you know his name? He never told you what his name was," said Alex skeptically. "Or at least, you weren't here for him to reveal it."

"I know him from previous encounters. But I was wrong. Apparently Brooke wasn't the only one who has an 'ability'. David has one as well." Jack placed a hand on Alex's shoulder and scanned the teens surrounding him. "And he might not be the only one."

"What do you mean he might not be the only one? What are you talking about?" Alex asked, shrugging his hand off and turning to face him.

"I need to run a few experiments, don't worry they are harmless. It may be some well needed exercise." Jack smiled.

"Whoa whoa whoa. I'm not going to be someone's lab rat," David said hurriedly.

"It's nothing too extravagant. I merely wish to find out if any of you have powers of your own. If so, how powerful and to what extent? What type of powers do you have? Why do you have them? Sadly, I most likely will not discover all of this information all at once. After all, you are all only human, so if you even do have powers it will take much longer than one simple experiment to force them out. Anyway, we will start that all tomorrow. Today, you must rest. We have fought long and hard, and it will be a waste to start experiments so soon."

"What do you mean by today? It's still night-time," noted Mark.

Jack nodded off at the cliff without a word. Everyone turned to follow his gaze. Off on the horizon, the sun had just begun to rise. They all stared in awe at the amazing sunrise for a few minutes before turning back to one another.

"Mark, Nicole. Can you stay out for a bit so I can fix up your burns?" Alex asked.

Mark and Nicole nodded and followed Alex to the smoldering makeshift fire pit.

"We'll see you later. We're going to bed," David called as he and Brooke retreated into each other's tents. Alex bent over one of their bags to retrieve disinfectant and other items needed to tend to his friends. As he pulled out the supplies, he caught Jack sneaking off into the outskirts of the forest.

"Where are you going?" Alex called after him. Jack turned around at Alex's voice.

"I am going to scout the area, become familiar with it so I can plan for the experiments tomorrow. Goodbye!" Jack quickly turned and disappeared beneath the leaves and branches of the forest.

Alex sighed and turned toward his wounded friends. "How did you burn yourselves? I don't recall them throwing fire at you," Alex asked as he mended their wounds.

"When that woman trapped us in that weird cage, we tried to get out by force and somehow this happened," Nicole explained. She gestured toward their wounds as if they would explain all of the unanswered questions.

"That's because those bars were made of lightning bolts. How did you not get that?" Alex asked as he wrapped the bandages around Mark's arm tightly.

"It was her idea. She said she needed help," Mark grimaced as Alex finished.

"Thanks. That red mark around your neck still hasn't gone away. Exactly how hard did he squeeze your neck?" asked Nicole.

"Hard enough," Alex said bluntly as he shoved the bandages into the bag. "Something is bugging, me though."

"What is it?" Nicole asked.

"That was a bit too easy, don't you think?" Alex asked. "Trap them with thorn-covered vines and suddenly, Poof! They're gone? They seemed extremely powerful. It doesn't make sense."

"I see your point. Maybe we just caught them off guard? They didn't expect it? I don't know but at least they're gone now," Mark said. "Let's go and get some rest now. Who knows what Jack has in store for us tomorrow." They walked back to their tents, and Alex threw the bag in, not bothering to try to avoid hitting David.

The heavy bag smacked David in the head and he grabbed blindly at it. Once his fingertips found the canvas, he latched onto it and tossed it on the other side of the tent before curling deeper beneath his blankets.

"See you tomorrow," said Nicole with a laugh as she walked into her own tent.

The next day Alex felt a cold presence hovering over him, and he opened his eyes. He found one of Jack's Shadows hovering over the trio at the top of the tent. The cold eyes stared back at Alex as he made eye contact. Once Alex's sluggish brain processed what he was staring at, he bolted upright, and the Shadow disappeared out of the tent. Mark and David were both sitting up, and they looked at each other with questioning and confused expressions. Before they could say a word, they heard a scream from the girls' tent. They were all out in time to see Brooke and

Nicole run out of their tent with another Shadow close behind. The two Shadows took off toward the cliff before disappearing.

"I apologize for the rude awakening," said Jack as he tipped his hat in greeting. "Time to see what you can do. Alex, please leave your sword in the tent." Alex looked Jack in the eyes without blinking.

"I never part with it," Alex said, his voice hoarse.

"That's a lie. You were without it all the time back on the mainland." Jack gestured with his eyes from the sword to the tent before meeting Alex's gaze sternly. Alex sighed in annoyance from how much Jack knew and unstrapped the buckle that held the sheath against his back. Alex tossed the sword inside the tent. It felt strange to be without his sword. After all that had happened, he felt completely naked without it.

"So, I had my Shadows examine all of you. I am still unable to figure out what your main abilities are or if you even have any. That sort of area is not in my expertise. However, I do know that you all share one main power. It is very common among the citizens of Equelibreiangeria, so it was quite easy for me to locate," Jack explained. Jack took a step toward Brooke and leaned in, staring into her eyes as if he was sizing her up.

"What are these abilities we all have?" asked Brooke, leaning away from Jack awkwardly. Jack stood upright again.

"Oh, I'm not telling you," Jack smiled wickedly.

"Why not?" asked David.

"Because you need to figure out what they are for yourselves," said Jack. He turned around, hiding his smile. "And I know just how to do that."

Suddenly, three Shadows shot out from behind them and knocked Mark, Nicole, and Alex to the ground, pinning them to the dirt and grass.

"What was that for?" Nicole shouted angrily.

"Your abilities manifested when your friends were in danger," Jack said casually as he slowly walked away.

"This is not going to help!" shouted Brooke.

"We'll see."

Six more Shadows appeared and started to charge after them before Jack disappeared.

"Come on! We have to try to get those Shadows off them before the other Shadows reach us!" Brooke told David. Mark, Nicole, and Alex thrashed about wildly in an attempt to escape the Shadows' cold and firm grip, but the Shadows only closed in on them the more they moved. That's when Alex came up with a quick solution.

"Stop moving!" Alex shouted. "Just relax!" David and Nicole stopped moving at Alex's commands. Gradually, the shadows stopped moving and began to loosen until they dissipated into the air. A few seconds later, they came back diving for them again. They scrambled to their feet and took off running into the trees.

"Split up!" Alex shouted. Mark and Alex ran off in one direction, while the others ran off into the other. Five of the Shadows went after David, Brooke, and Nicole, while four of them went after Mark and Alex. They didn't have to run for long before something sent them tumbling back through the air and sprawling to the ground.

"What was that?" asked Mark.

"I don't know," said Alex, He stood up and reached out his hand. The air rippled at his fingertips before something sent him flying backwards.

"It's called a force field," a voice echoed.

"What was that?" exclaimed Mark, suddenly up and in a fighting stance. "You really don't recognize my voice? Wow... I'm disappointed, Mark. That's a force field made of all of my Shadows connected together reflecting light in such a way that you only see a mirror image. And that force field circles the entire outside ten-mile radius of the campsite. Can't escape now!"

"It's Jack! Run!" Alex urged. "He exists in the Shadows. Climb up that tree and get to the top. Hopefully the sun will block out any Shadows close by."

Alex and Mark ran to a nearby tree and began climbing as fast as they could. Alex bounded up the tree in seconds. He looked down to Mark, who wasn't too far behind, but was far enough. The Shadows started to fly up the tree right behind him.

"Hurry up! They are right behind you!" Alex shouted. Mark looked down as a Shadow swept by him. The Shadow flew up in between Mark and the tree trunk, startling him. With his surprise his grip loosened and he slipped off the branches, falling through the branches. Alex jumped after Mark and grabbed his arm.

He flipped himself upward and tried to grab onto one of the passing branches but the Shadows grabbed them and brought them high above the canopy. Then, they let go. Alex and Mark continued to fall seventy feet. Alex swung himself and Mark around so that Alex would be the first to hit the ground. If they were going to fall, Alex would take all of the impact. Mark had his eyes closed and his arms up over his face protectively. Alex closed his eyes as they plummeted to the ground.

Alex felt the air whipping past his face until it stopped for a second. Alex opened his eyes to see that he hadn't gotten past the canopy and was still high up in the air. The Shadows ripped Mark out of his hands and then let go again. Alex tried to grab him, but he was too far away. Alex ripped through the canopy. Branches and leaves hit them on the way down, causing him to lose focus. The world became nothing but a brown, green, and blue blur. Alex watched as the ground came closer and closer.

Alex pulled his arms over his head to brace for impact like Mark had but the impact never came. Slowly, Alex pulled his arms back down to see the ground had stopped zooming toward him. He was upside down, feet facing the sky and head facing the earth, only a few inches above the ground. Alex looked up to see if the Shadows had caught him by the ankles, but they were nowhere to be found.

In front of him, Mark was lying, back toward the ground in mid-air with his face still covered by his arms and his eyes still squeezed shut.

"Mark?" Alex watched as Mark slowly brought his arms down and he opened his eyes.

"Are we dead?" Mark asked.

"Nope, not that I know of. I have no idea what just happened."

"We are still in theeeeeeahhh!" Mark was cut mid-sentence when he shot up into the air. "Whaaaaa!" he screamed. Mark stopped right before his head could come in contact with a tree branch.

"How did you get u—?" Alex shot up into the air without warning before he could finish. "What the—?" Alex stopped next to Mark.

"Well, look what we have here!" Jack stepped out of a Shadow on a trunk. "So… both of you can fly? Interesting," Jack grinned.

"Are you doing this?" Mark demanded.

"Nope. You're doing all of this on your own."

"We can't possibly be doing this. How would we be able to? We don't have powers!"

"When you think about going up, you go up. When you think about stopping you stop. That's how you stopped yourselves from hitting the ground. It really is that simple."

"I wasn't thinking about stopping when we were falling," Alex claimed.

"But that was what you really wanted, wasn't it?" Asked Jack. "Think about flying."

"Why?"

"Just do it."

Alex rolled his eyes doubtfully and thought about flying above the canopy. Alex darted up toward the canopy and Mark followed.

"This is defying the laws of gravity!" Mark shouted with glee. Alex, still unable to believe that he was causing himself to fly, continued to fly, refusing to stop. He only stopped when Mark screamed at him to wait for him.

"Don't go so high." Mark struggled to catch up. Jack followed.

"I'll have to have my Shadows check the others and see if they can fly as well," said Jack as he opened his hand and pointed to a patch of trees and simply murmured the word, 'go.' Three Shadows flew up from the other direction before zooming off where Jack was pointing. A few seconds later, the Shadows were flying up above the trees carrying Nicole, David, and Brooke by their ankles. They were all screaming their lungs out.

The Shadows stopped directly across from Alex and Mark a mile away. They looked at the duo in shock when they spotted them floating in the air with no Shadows around them to support them. Before they could ask, the Shadows holding them in the air dissipated and they started to fall.

"We have to help them!" Mark shot toward his shocked falling friends in hopes of aiding them. Jack grabbed his shoulder and dragged him back.

"Hey! What was that for?" Mark shouted.

"You can't get them. This is the only way to see if any other powers will manifest."

They waited to see if they would begin to fly. They didn't pass through the canopy. But they didn't stop either.

"Think about flying!" Alex cupped his hands over his mouth and yelled.

"What? Are you insane?" David shouted back. His voice was wobbly, wavering in and out of volume, filled to the brim in panic. They were getting closer to the treetops.

"Just do it!" Alex shouted. They shut their eyes and covered their heads. Just before they could disappear beneath the canopy, they all stopped falling and started to float.

"Think of flying upward!" shouted Mark. They flew upward.

"Whoa! What is going on?" Brooke exclaimed in amazement. Mark and Alex flew uncontrollably over to them. They wobbled and dipped and swerved, struggling to fly in a straight path. From Nicole's point of view, they looked like babies who were learning how to walk for the first time. Apparently, flying up and down was much easier than flying straight.

"How is this possible?" asked Nicole. Before Alex could answer, his head suddenly felt light and dizzy. Alex's eyes rolled into the back of his head and he, along with Mark, began to plummet. Before they could disappear beneath the leaves, Jack flew down and caught them.

"Are you guys okay?" called Brooke from up above.

"I don't know. I'm really dizzy, though," Mark said.

With one hand, Mark clung onto Jack's arm and with the other he covered his eyes as the world around him spun. Jack slowly descended to the ground, careful to not drop the teens. David and the girls followed close behind.

"Um...I think I'm starting to feel a bit dizzy too," said David as he fell, soon after, the girls followed. Jack shot out his hand and three Shadows zoomed over and caught the three, setting them softly on the ground.

"You had this ability manifest itself only recently. You have no idea how to use it and I'm surprised you held up for so long. You did good for your first time," Jack complimented. "Don't worry. It will become easier with practice, and soon you will think of flying as something as normal as walking. However, one problem everyone faces is that it's tiring and it tends to exhaust you. Don't use it more than you need to. If you use it too much, you won't be able to fly for a while. But a quick period of rest should fix that."

"That's great and all but what's with chasing us around with those Shadows? Or that barrier thingy keeping us in? Oh, and, why did you try to kill us?" Nicole ranted, throwing her hands up in the air. Jack held up his index finger to stop her from continuing.

"Ah, yes tried, not succeeded."

"That's besides the point! We could be dead right now if it wasn't for our 'powers manifesting' or whatever you called it."

"Precisely. I had to create a near-death situation to force them to manifest. You aren't dead, are you? Even if your powers didn't save you, I coated the forest floor with a specific transparent substance that would feel as though you were jumping on a mattress if you were to fall on it."

"Oh..." Nicole stared blankly at him, astonished, but not quite over her anger.

"Now we know you can all fly. I will be happy to teach you how to control that ability of yours. We will be able to see how fast you can go and how high you can go before you run out of oxygen. After all, I had to go through the same experience."

"When do you start teaching us?" asked Brooke.

"Now."

"We just got chased around the woods by Shadows and dropped hundreds of feet in the air and almost died. You want us to start now?" David complained. "Alex! How do you feel about all of this? You haven't said a word!" David turned to Alex who was standing silently with his arms crossed over his chest.

"There's no time better to learn than the present," Alex replied, shrugging his shoulders.

"Great! We are all gonna die!" David shouted, throwing his hands in the air. "I give up!"

"Did you not hear what I said to Nicole? I'll keep my Shadows in check. But don't blame me if I slip and the Shadows send you to your death," Jack smirked. "But that won't come until later. Right now, I'm gonna teach you to fly properly. It really is simple. It might not even take more than a day. But then again you did learn about all of this recently and they only manifested a number of minutes ago. This might take longer than I thought. We will have to see!

"Tell yourself to fly," Jack clapped his hands together in order to gather their attention. Doing as Jack had instructed, they began to chant in an awkward tone, "Fly! Fly! Let's go! Fly!" But nothing happened. Jack laughed at their ignorance.

"Sorry, it seems I might have to be a bit more specific. Just think of flying. Think of what you felt earlier when you were up in the air. Think of the danger of falling, but don't be afraid of that danger. Don't let yourselves be bound by the chains of gravity. Think of being free."

Alex closed his eyes and repeated Jack's words in his head. He imagined the chains keeping him down on the earth. He willed to fly. Slowly, the chains cracked and broke. Alex opened his eyes to see his feet were no longer on the ground, but looming over the treetops. He hadn't realized he had gone up so far. Alex looked up from his feet to see his friends hovering in the air in a circle with Jack in the middle.

"Like I said. It isn't that hard. But now that you have the flying thing down I need to know what your air capacity is," Jack observed.

"How are we supposed to figure that out?" David asked with an eyebrow raised.

"You fly up, of course. The whole flying thing, it's simple really."

"Yes, you keep saying that. So, you want us to just go up?" Brooke tilted her head back to look up at the clouds.

"When do we stop?" asked Nicole.

"When you can't breathe anymore," Jack replied.

"Do you want us to all go up at the same time?" Mark asked.

"Only when you think you're ready," Jack nodded. Alex didn't wait for any more conversation. He had all the instruction he needed. Alex shot up toward the clouds, eager to get away.

"Hey, Alex! Wait for us!" shouted Mark as he and the others shot up after him. Alex didn't wait for them. He flew as far as he could. The smell of the fresh and clean air. The sound of it whizzing past him. It was glorious. Alex hit the clouds and zipped through them, sending a puffy white trail in his wake.

He refused to stop, despite the glare of the sun reflecting off the clouds, burning his eyes. Long past the highest cloud, the sky turned a dark blue, indicating he was getting closer to space. Realizing his friends were no longer with him, he stopped and looked down. They were nowhere to be seen. With a moment of hesitation, Alex decided to continue and didn't stop until the air grew thin and he was gasping for oxygen. He moved down a bit so that he could breathe easier, finally stopping where the edge of the mesosphere met with the thermosphere.

Alex floated there in the air and stared up at the stars. They were so much bigger there than down on the ground. Alex lost his mind in the wonder of it all as he stared at the white bright lights that twinkled throughout the vast blackness of space. When he finally realized he had places to be, he shot down into the clouds reluctantly, the passage of time lost to him.

TWENTY-EIGHT

When Alex reached the troposphere, he found Jack and the others waiting for him. Jack watched Alex with crossed arms and a smile plastered across his face.

"And here he comes! It's not like we were waiting for him or anything," said Nicole with a hint of sarcasm.

"How far did you go?" asked Jack, ignoring Nicole's comment.

"Sorry I took so long. I had to stop where the mesosphere meets the thermosphere," Alex answered apologetically, his eyes bright with excitement, "*if* I remember those terms correctly."

"It's a good thing you didn't go any higher, or the Space Crawlers would have gotten hold of you," Jack chuckled, his smile broadening.

"What are Space Crawlers?" asked Mark.

"It is nothing but a fairytale our parents tell us as children, mostly to keep us from going up too far," said Jack as he waved off the question.

"Can you tell us the story? I love stories!" Brooke clasped her hands together, and all heads turned to her with questioning expressions.

"What? I do." Brooke placed her hands back at her sides.

"I would love to tell you the story." Jack looked around at the eager faces. Excitement of the memories of past stories glinted in his eyes. "As the story goes, Space Crawlers are horrendous creatures, for they have no conscience. These creatures originated from humanity and Equelibreiangeria. Space Crawlers are formed whenever a terrible deed is done or a terrible thought is created in one's mind. The strongest and the most powerful among this species are human souls themselves.

161

"They are the remnants of a human's soul when they die a gruesome death. It is a terrible fate to have. When they are born, they are equal to that of a monster, but if they continue to evolve they may regain their bodies from their previous lives. These creatures are doomed to the loneliness of space. The Space Crawlers have a growing hatred for anything and everything that lives and breathes on Earth. They would attempt to destroy this planet itself if it wasn't for their inability to get past the thermosphere. They certainly have the power to. Can you recall the Apollo 13 mission?"

"It's the one that failed, right?" asked David. "We learned about it in science last year."

"It was aborted after a rupture of the service module oxygen tank," Brooke said matter-of-factly.

"That's right. Do you know what caused that rupture?" asked Jack.

"I don't remember if they told us that part," said David as he rubbed the back of his neck and looked to Brooke for answers, who in turn shrugged her shoulders and shook her head.

"Some conspiracy theorists believe it was the Space Crawlers who had attacked the oxygen tank with the intent to kill the astronauts inside, but they were stopped before they could get to the point where the oxygen ran out completely. The stories of the Space Crawlers are told everywhere in Equelibreiangeria; in Heltiana, and…,," Jack trailed off and seethed for a moment, as if recalling a bad memory. It was brief, but long enough for most of them to pick up on it.

"And…? What?," asked Nicole, ignoring his moment of anger.

"Apologies, I lost my train of thought," Jack explained. "They were described as extraordinarily powerful and enormously feared creatures. As a kid, this story frightened me to the bone. But as you can see I am not a storyteller."

"I don't know about that. I am somewhat frightened." Mark shrugged. His hands were shaking and clammy with sweat. *When did that happen?* Mark thought. Mark opened and closed his fists before wiping them against his pants.

"Well, good." Jack looked at Mark's hands, pleased with the effects of his story.

"Why can't they get past the thermosphere?" Alex asked.

"No idea, again, they are just things made to keep kids from flying too far and dying in space. That happened more than enough times to make parents come up with these fictitious creatures. There are quite a few more story-like versions, much like your Little Red Riding Hood, but I'll attempt at telling one another time. Now!" Jack clapped his hands together and everyone jumped at the sudden outburst. "Only two more lessons before we call it a day. And if we can get them both in today, we might not have to do them again. First, we will test speed. Then, we will handle actually flying with control."

"Speed? Do we have a limit to how fast we can go?" asked Nicole.

"That's what I want to see. Then we will have just a small race to see how fast you are compared to each other."

"Are you planning on timing us? With what?" Mark gestured toward the air. As if to answer his question, a handful of Shadows appeared from behind Jack and burst through the air. The Shadows swirled around them and then scattered all over the sky. After a few minutes of this, they all conjoined together and formed a massive timer in the air, the numbers made out of gaps in the large blob of shadow where the sky peeked through to the other side..

"With that." Jack nodded toward the timer without looking at it.

"Okay. That'll work, I guess," Mark replied, staring at the purplish black timer in the sky with a bewildered expression on his face.

"Don't worry, this will only be some friendly competition. Brooke, why don't you go first? Show us how fast you can go."

Brooke sighed, "why do I have to be first? ugh." She took off flying. Brooke stopped at a finish line Jack formed with his Shadows that he said was exactly six miles away. Jack mumbled something before shouting, "Good job! Nine minutes and seven seconds!" Brooke flew back and looked scornfully at Jack for making her go first.

"I'll go next." David thrust his hand in the air. Jack nodded at David and he took his place. Jack shouted 'go!' and he flew.

"Congratulations! Six seconds faster than Brooke!" Jack shouted. David came back with a triumphant grin. Brooke crossed her arms across her chest and glared.

"My turn. I'll get a better score than either of you two," declared Nicole as she took off. When she came back, Jack announced her score.

"Eight minutes and fifty-nine seconds."

"Ha! In your faces!" Nicole put her left hand on her hip and with her right hand, jabbed her pointer finger into David's chest. David scowled. When Nicole turned away, David nodded to Brooke and they both chuckled before bumping the backs of their fists together. Alex wondered what plan they could possibly be forming.

"During the race, we will beat you to the finish line!" Brooke exclaimed. Nicole turned and began to banter with the two with a competitive smirk.

"Mark, you're up!" Jack ignored the bickering trio and continued. Mark took off on Jack's command.

"Now, what do we have here? You have the same score as our competitive friend, Nicole! Eight minutes and fifty-nine seconds!" Nicole eyed Mark as he made his way back.

"I'm going to be the one to beat that time. Just watch!" Mark flew past her and hovered next to Jack.

"Highly unlikely!"

"You'll see!" Mark replied.

"Yeah, we'll see!" Nicole rolled her eyes at Mark's stubbornness.

"Alex, you—" Jack was cut off when Alex zoomed past him and took off toward the finish line. Alex adored flying. He was living the impossible in an impossible world. For all he knew, he was just dreaming. If anyone else had this opportunity, they would have done the same. Well, his friends weren't doing what he was doing, but if they were him… Alex burst into a broad smile and laughed aloud with excitement.

The ability for humans to fly was beyond all comprehension. It was against the laws of physics. He hadn't even flown for more than a day, but he still felt a strange welcoming feeling while he soared through the air. He felt freedom that he had never felt before. He was no longer bound by his adoptive parents' laws and expectations or even the rules of gravity. He felt home. He was finally free!

Alex caught sight of a large, dark, and smoky finish line just ahead of him, floating in the air. Alex felt an adrenaline rush as he shot toward it. Not bothering to stop, Alex placed his feet on the shadowy finish line and used it to push himself off. The large banner made of Shadows dissipated beneath his feet as he took off.

When Alex came in sight with Jack and the others, he tried to slow down but his body refused to listen and he barreled on. Knowing that stopping was useless, Alex swerved around Jack and flew into a tree trunk face-first. That certainly helped him stop. Alex slid down the trunk a ways before falling through the air a few feet. When Alex finally found his way back to Jack, everyone was laughing their heads off. Even Jack was struggling to stifle his laughter.

"Seven minutes is your time!" Jack avoided Alex's eyes for fear if they made contact he would officially lose it.

"You beat my time?" David managed to pull himself together for a few mere seconds before bursting into uncontrollable laughter once more. Watching his friends struggle to form words caused even Alex to laugh a bit.

"Okay, let's just do the race. Mark is ready to eat my dust now," said Nicole as she took in a fresh breath of air and calmed her laughter. Mark straightened at this and locked eyes with her.

"The only thing I'll be tasting is that finish line."

"You won't be tasting anything if you don't get ready," said Jack, gesturing impatiently in front of him. The five of them hovered in a line and readied themselves for the next few words.

"Ready! Set! Go!"

Alex took off as fast as he could fly at Jack's words. When he reached the newly formed finish line. he turned to see how far behind his friends were. They had barely left the starting line. Alex watched, puzzled, noticing that they were barely moving at all. They looked as though they were moving in slow motion.

Alex's ears perked up to a sudden rustling noise coming from the trees below. Alex looked down to catch a glimpse of movement within a bunch of branches. He looked back at his friends before diving down beneath the tree cover. As soon as he passed beneath the thick leaves, all light was cut off and the world went black. Why was it so dark down here? Alex's thoughts were disrupted when a voice broke through the silence and echoed through the darkness.

"Dark, isn't it?" The strange voice began to laugh.

"Who are you?" Alex called out into the darkness. The owner of the voice ignored him and continued laughing. Then a thought occurred to him.

"Why'd you make it so dark?" Alex asked. The voice stopped laughing. "Do I know you?"

"Yes, you do! We only met just a few days ago! Sadly Winona is not here with me today, but I just came here to retrieve a little information!" Alex strained his ears to try to pinpoint where the voice was coming from but the voice ricocheted off invisible walls. "How did you meet the Contour Suzerain?"

"What Contour Suzerain?" Alex asked, slightly confused for a moment. "You mean Jack?"

"Yes! Jack! How do you know him? Are you family? What do you know about him? Tell me now!" The voice demanded.

"Why should I tell you? What do you plan on doing with him once you obtain this information?" Alex asked.

"I ask the questions here! Not you!"

"You're out of luck, buddy. I'm not telling you anything."

Suddenly something hit him in the stomach and Alex lurched forward. He gasped at the sudden impact and began to fall until a hand grabbed his jacket, catching him in mid-air. The voice whispered in his ear, "You will regret this, Alex. I can't wait for the day when I will destroy your frail body." The voice paused as if mulling over what it should say next. "Don't tell your friends about this little rendezvous between you and me or I won't hesitate to kill them immediately."

The owner of the voice let go of his jacket and Alex dropped. He began to panic, but his panic ceased as he realized it would do him no good. Alex took a deep breath and shot up through the canopy. The blinding light penetrated the darkness that had clouded his vision moments before, causing him to lose his balance.

"Alex! Where in the world did you go?" Nicole shouted. Alex opened his mouth to explain but quickly shut it. The voice's words came back to him. "*I won't hesitate to kill them immediately.*" What if the strange voice was telling the truth? Alex wasn't planning on risking it.

"I wasn't anywhere. The sun was starting to get to me so I went below the trees for some shade." Alex quickly covered up the true events with an excuse.

"It's not that hot." Mark looked at Alex with an eyebrow raised.

"Anyway, who won?" Alex asked in an effort to change the topic.

"You, of course! You got here before we even got a foot away from the starting line! But Nicole came in second, I came in third, Brooke came in fourth, and David came in last," Mark looked at David and smiled wickedly.

"I only came in last because Brooke pushed me and I almost fell! You're lucky I caught myself before I fell to my *death*!" David shouted in Brooke's face.

"You aren't dead, are you? I thought so!" Brooke replied.

"You all did great. And you will each get faster the more you fly."

Alex lurched forward, startled. Alex turned to see Jack standing behind him.

"Don't do that," Alex sighed.

"Now that we have that settled, everyone! Down to the canopy!" Jack pointed down to the trees and nodded to Alex in apology. Nicole and the others went head-first and flew beneath the canopy. Before Alex could disappear with them, Jack grabbed his shoulder and held him back.

"The sun wasn't really getting to you, was it?" he asked skeptically. Alex refused to look Jack in the eye for fear that his eyes would betray his secret.

"Yeah. It was getting really hot," Alex said as he shrugged Jack's hand off. He turned around and faced Jack, shrugged, smiled, and before Jack could say anything else he dropped toward the tree-tops. Alex allowed himself to fall freely through the leaves and brush. As he fell, he whizzed past his hovering companions. They all leapt back in surprise as a dark figure flew past them. Alex grabbed a nearby branch and swung himself back up so that he would hover next to them.

"You scared us!" Nicole shouted.

"Sorry." Alex shrugged his shoulders and smiled. Jack appeared next to them and went right to business.

"The canopy has been coated with another force field. Your job is to find a rip in the force field and get up into the sky." Jack pointed above them. They all looked up to see a bright purple fluorescent wall stretching throughout the sky, coating the forest with the same light.

"Oh, this will be easy then," Brooke stated egotistically.

"But, that's not all. My Shadows are going to chase you. If they get you, they will automatically transport you to a secret base. You have an hour to do this. Good luck."

"Wait, wait, wait. Hold on for a second. How does this have anything to do with maneuvering?" David asked.

"I'll be waiting." Jack ignored David and disappeared. In his place, a handful of Shadows hovered in the air. There were so many it was difficult to count.

"Scatter!" Mark shouted, taking off. The group scattered in different directions as the Shadows flew after them. Alex shot down as several Shadows chased him from behind. He swerved in and out of trees in an attempt to shake them off his tail but they refused to fall. Alex shot up again only to run into Nicole.

They didn't have any time to formulate a plan before the Shadows that had been chasing them grouped together and continued to gain on them. They cast glances at one another before flying side by side, away from the Shadows. They bounded off trees and under branches, flying as fast as they could manage.

Alex glanced back to the Shadows behind them. He furrowed his brow in confusion at the sight he saw. He could have sworn there had been more Shadows chasing them. Where had they all gone? Alex turned his head in time for a tree to pop in front of him. Alex swerved around the tree only to have more Shadows appear and slam him against the other side. Then, everything went black.

TWENTY-NINE

Alex opened his eyes to an upside-down world. He squinted and rubbed the backs of his hands against his eyelids. The trees around him were hanging from mid-air with the tops facing a strange purple fluorescent ground. An upside-down blue bird flew past him a few feet away. Alex grew dizzy as he felt blood rushing to his head. Suddenly, Alex realized the world wasn't upside-down, he was!

Alex looked up at his feet. His legs were clenched around a branch, on the verge of slipping. He quickly pulled himself upright onto the branch and looked around. The Shadows who had caught hold of him earlier were nowhere to be found. A scream pierced the air behind him and he spun around. Nicole was above him swerving in a figure eight around two trees, trying to shake off multiple Shadows.

One of the Shadows didn't maneuver as well as the others and flew into a branch and consequently, dissipated. The scene that had just played out before him gave Alex an idea. He stood up on the branch and flew toward the Shadows. They quickly noticed he was behind them and half of them flew after him while the other half stayed on Nicole.

Alex flew violently at trees and branches, missing them by a hair. He swung his head around to see if his plan was working. Only a handful of Shadows were left. Alex watched in the corner of his eye as Shadows ran into the branches. When all of the Shadows that had been chasing him dissipated, Alex flew back to where he left Nicole.

The Shadows had overcome her and were surrounding her. A bright purple light much like the light radiating from the force field keeping them inside burst from the mass of Shadows. Alex lunged forward at the black ball and covered his eyes with his forearms to protect them from the light. Just as the light died down, Alex went through. He stopped flying and uncovered his eyes when he had yet to come in contact with anything solid. He turned to find the large ball of Shadows, along with Nicole, gone.

With Shadows no longer following him, Alex flew around the forest in search for his friends. He hoped at least one of them found the secret base Jack spoke of. Nicole had to be there. A loud alarm rang throughout the forest, followed by Jack's booming voice.

"Half an hour!" Jack's voice boomed.

Alex raced around the forest until he reached the end of the enclosure where it came in contact with the ground. There was no sign of Brooke, David, or Mark.

"Mark! Brooke! Anyone there?" Alex cupped his hands and shouted at the top of his lungs. There was no answer. Alex composed himself and hovered in the air, completely still. He closed his eyes and strained his ears, blocking out the sound of his breathing and his heart. All was quiet. Alex listened as the sounds of the forest drifted up to him. He pushed the noises aside and listened for something, anything, else. A few minutes passed and Alex sighed in irritation. Then, he heard it. The faint whisper of a familiar voice.

Alex flew silently but quickly through the forest as he followed the sound of the voice. The voice grew louder and louder until it sounded as if the source was directly under him. Alex looked down to a big black square elevating off the forest floor. He slowly descended feet-first toward the square, his jacket flapping in the wind. The closer he neared the square the more he could make out what it was. A cage.

When Alex realized what it was, he flew over to a tree opposite of it and squatted down on a branch to see what was inside. Inside the cage were Brooke, Mark, David, and Nicole. Mark was pacing around the cage, while David sat cross-legged on the ground, poking at the dirt with a stick. Brooke was leaning her head on one knee while the other was stretched out, and Nicole was doing a handstand out of boredom.

Alex scanned the area for any nearby Shadows before jumping down and walking over to the cage.

"Alex!" Mark exclaimed in surprise as he saw Alex walking toward them.

"Where are the other Shadows?" Alex asked.

"They flew off," Nicole replied as she dropped her feet and returned to a standing position.

"I'm going to get you out. What is this cage made out of?" Alex placed his hands on the bars.

"We think it's made out of the Shadows," Brooke tipped her head up toward the roof of the cage.

"Can you cut it open or something?" asked David.

"I don't think so."

"Can you try?"

Alex sighed. "I can give it a shot. But I don't think this will work. It's just too easy." Alex unsheathed his sword as his friends backed up to the far end of the cage. Alex positioned his body and swung his sword hard into the solid bars. The bars swirled into smoky clouds at the points Alex hit before re-forming themselves.

"I thought so," Alex commented, sheathing his sword once again.

"Alex, watch out!" Brooke suddenly shouted and pointed behind him. Alex spun around in time for multiple Shadows to barrel into him and send him crashing to the ground. He grimaced and stood up again only to be knocked back down. The Shadows began piling themselves on top of him in a heap. *They're trying to lock me in the cage the same way they locked the others up.*

Alex shot through the dog pile of Shadows and shot up toward the sky. Four groups of Shadows flew after Alex at increasing speed. He dropped as two groups collided with another and disappeared. More masses of Shadows soon took their place. Forming another idea, Alex flew and hovered directly on top of the black square roof of the cage. He stopped hovering and let gravity take over his body, dropping to the roof of the cage. As he fell, he turned so he was facing the Shadows and his back was to the cage.

The Shadows were close behind. Alex fell rapidly and with every second he fell, the closer he neared the ground. The Shadows soon covered the distance between each other and they were on top of him in no time. Alex flew out once he was only an inch from the cage roof and came in contact with the ground. Alex skidded to a stop, all the while creating a trail of dirt leading from the cage to where he lay.

The remaining Shadows were unable to pull up in time and hit the top of the cage with a thud. The Shadows along with the cage disappeared. Alex stood up and brushed off dirt on his pants as his friends rushed over.

"Nice one! Now we need to get out of here!" Mark patted Alex's shoulder. Alex looked Mark in the eye and pointed up toward the field.

"Already got that covered," Alex smirked. Up above was a hole in the shape of a square right above where the cage was.

"I saw it as I fell," Alex said.

"Why hadn't we seen that before?" David asked.

"Probably because you're blind," laughed Brooke.

"You were there with me!" David shouted. Brooke laughed even harder. Alex jumped high into the air and began to fly up toward the gaping hole in the purple enclosure. The others soon followed and they were all flying side by side. Alex kept his eyes trained on the gaping hole and smiled. But his smile didn't last long. The hole began to close and shrink smaller and smaller. Alex gasped as a voice boomed through the trees.

"One minute!" Jack's voice gave them a jump scare.

"Hurry! Before it closes!" Brooke shot up into the hole and held it open with her body wedged in between. The force of the field was stronger than Brooke thought and it continued to close in on her, only slower. Beads of sweat formed on Brooke's forehead as she gritted her teeth.

"Now!" she shouted. One by one, David, Nicole, Mark, and Alex zoomed through the rapidly closing opening. As Alex shot through, he grabbed the back of Brooke's shirt and yanked her through. Brooke did somersaults in the air before she finally regained her balance.

"You looked like a balloon!" David laughed.

"If it weren't for me, you would be stuck down there right now. I wouldn't laugh," Brooke huffed, crossing her arms in frustration. David stopped laughing and placed his hand on her arm.

"You're right. Thank you," David said. A hint of sarcasm lingered in his voice.

"Yes, thank you, Brooke. You did well," said Jack as he hovered above their heads and clapped his hands together.

"You aren't even surprising anymore," Alex complained.

"It really is too bad you couldn't complete this task any sooner. And to make it worse all but one of you were captured." Jack looked down on them with accusing eyes.

"We still made it, though! We still completed it on time!" Nicole pointed out.

"Yes, but that wasn't exactly the goal."

"Then what was?"

"Efficiency. Even though you all made it out in time you were still caught. I could have easily commanded my Shadows to destroy you on the spot. When you face similar situations like this, other people won't be so sympathetic. Do you understand?" Refusing to answer Jack's question, they all bowed their heads in defeat. As Alex bowed his head, he caught a strange movement in the corner of his eye. Alex spun around in alarm and scanned the trees but saw nothing. He turned back around and was surprised to find that no one had noticed his actions or the odd movement.

"Is that all for today?" Alex asked.

"Yes, it is," Jack replied.

"When you are all done moping, you can meet me back down at camp." Alex turned to go but was stopped by Nicole.

"Of course, you don't feel guilty, you didn't get captured."

Alex stopped cold in his tracks. He turned and faced Nicole. "No, I didn't, but I failed anyway. We are friends, and we are a team. We should have been working together, and I failed you. I shouldn't have let you get captured. That was on me, and I'm sorry. Next time, we will work together. I promise you, this won't happen again," Alex said hoarsely.

Before they could respond, Alex dove beneath the trees, desperate for a moment to breathe. They were all tired and stressed and missing their families. And it's not like they are chased by flying Shadows everyday. He felt guilty. He let his friends down, leaving them trapped with no way out. Again. He made a promise to himself, no matter what happened, he would get them through this. He would get them out and he would get them home.

Alex flew back to the cliff, leaving his friends hovering in the air. Alex landed on the very edge of the cliff and looked down at the water below. He may have almost drowned in it before, but now it didn't seem so frightening. A flash of black dashed across the surface of the water before disappearing beneath the cliff.

Alex hesitated as his body loomed over the edge. The feeling of gravity over-taking him and sending him into the depths sent a shiver through his spine. He jumped when the dark figure appeared once again. Alex considered jumping down when he realized he had something that he didn't have last time. He could fly! He could lower himself down just as easily as coming up. Before he could think about the subject any longer, he leaned over the edge and allowed gravity to take over once again.

Half way down, Alex took off and returned to the surface of the water, hovering over it. Alex reached down to feel the freezing cold water but was shocked to find it oddly warm. He looked at the large jagged rocks that stuck out from the ocean. The waves were not crashing up against them, for there were no waves at all. The ocean remained patiently still.

"Alex! Where are you?" Brooke called from the field, interrupting Alex's thoughts. Alex flew up and stopped just under the edge of the cliff, hidden from sight. He looked out at the field where he witnessed his friends running around, frantically searching for him. When all of their backs were turned, Alex shot up and over to the woods. From there he walked out onto the tall grass of the field.

"What? You guys are so loud!" Alex scratched his head and squinted his eyes, attempting to put on an act that they would all believe he had come out of the woods.

"There you are! We didn't know where you went!" David said.

"Sorry ab—" Alex was cut off when a sudden realization hit him. His eyes lit up with excitement with what he was about to say. "We can leave!" Alex shouted. His friends all stopped and swung their heads to look at him. Even Jack.

"What'd you say?" Mark asked.

"We can leave this island!" Alex repeated. "We can fly! If we can fly long enough, we might be able to reach the mainland!"

"If only it was that simple." Jack's eyes traveled to the ground sadly. "There is another force field much like the one I created that closes this island off to outsiders."

"Oh, really? Then how are we here? If there was a force field, we wouldn't be here right now!" David stared at Jack, waiting for an answer.

"Occasionally a rip in the force field will occur allowing anything to enter. This rip only stays open for a short time before closing again and moving to a different location around the island. You just happened to pass through that rip." Jack raised his eyes and looked at Alex.

"When will the next rip occur?" Alex asked.

"The next two months or so. Why?"

"We haven't lost hope yet! We just have to get to the next location of the next rip occurrence and pass through!"

"That is a wonderful plan but there is another problem," Jack said and then paused. "I have no idea when the next rip will occur. The only one who knows is on the other side of the island in Borthenaheim!" Alex glanced at his friends' faces. Their eyes were filled with disappointment once again. Alex was beginning to dislike that look. Yes, he had wanted to run away, but even he didn't want to be on this island anymore.

"Then let's go find them! Who are they?" Alex replied. Jack looked at Alex, surprised with his sudden optimism. Jack struggled to find the words to explain.

"He's an old man… and an old friend of mine. I don't know how he will react to you guys… but he trusts me," Jack paused as if mulling over his own words.

173

"Yes… yes, this could work!" Jack began to pace back and forth while formulating a plan aloud. "It will be a long journey since this island is so big and it will take even longer because of all of the citizens here. But you can fly now so it might not take as long as I thought," Jack trailed off, going through the math in his head for how long the journey might take.

"This will work! We leave in an hour!" Jack suddenly shouted, startling everyone.

"An hour? I thought we were going to stay here for a while," Alex said.

"The faster we get out of here and on the road the sooner we will arrive. Leave your bags and supplies here. You will not be needing them. Now go get yourselves prepared. This journey will not be a short one nor an easy one."

THIRTY

"Are you sure we should have left all of our stuff?" Brooke asked as they soared through the dusk sky. "We were lucky enough to have been stranded on this island with it all and are we just going to abandon it? What if we need some of it later on?"

"How many times must I explain this?" Jack insisted. Annoyance tainted his voice. "Those supplies would only be extra and unnecessary weight. We have everything we need. My Shadows can both retrieve and provide any food you might need, among other things."

Brooke sighed and turned to the sky ahead of her. The sun had sunk below the horizon and the colors of day had faded to a dull gray. Clouds covered the sky. The world around them grew silent. The only sound was the whirr of the wind whipping past them. Purple light seeped through the clouds, granting the world the smallest bit of light.

Alex looked at Jack, who flew silently beside him. His face was hidden from the purple light and obscured within the darkness. Brooke, Mark, and Nicole flew in silence just the same. Alex watched through the corner of his eye as David opened his mouth in an attempt to break the awkward silence only to close it and look the other way.

Alex allowed himself to drift away in his thoughts, but no matter what he thought about his mind always wandered back to one specific topic. What was that black blur that he had been seeing lately? Was it following him? Why were the others unable to see it? Could Jack see it too? Was he just pretending he couldn't? Or was Alex the only one? He was worried; what if it was there to hurt them? After all the things he's seen on that island, it wouldn't be impossible. If it was good, why was it following them around, not showing itself? Alex pondered all of the possibilities of the black thing he constantly saw following him. Only when a loud crash rung through the air did Alex stop thinking about it.

"What was that?" David shouted in alarm.

"I'm sure it was just a tree falling," Mark said, waving the matter off.

"That is not the sound trees make when they fall," Jack pointed out. Alex ignored them as they continued to fight over what a tree sounds like when it falls and scanned the trees for the source to no avail. Another, much more quiet crash sounded though his friends did not notice it because they were too busy arguing. Alex looked up as he realized where the sound was coming from. A pure white light painted the black sky as a streak of lightning shot down from the clouds. Alex watched in horror as the bolt came down. In seconds, it would collide with its target and send them burning to a crisp. Alex lunged forward with his arms outstretched toward the target. Jack turned his head in time to see Alex's horror-stricken face and a white streak barrel down on him. The impact sent him flying back into Nicole, the air knocked out of him.

The white bolt hit hard. But strangely enough it didn't feel like electricity. Brooke plummeted toward the earth, the speed disorienting, turning the world around her into a blur. At first she was confused. Why was she falling? But it didn't take her long to remember. She saw the lightning bolt come down. She had tried to push Jack out of the way, but apparently Alex already had that covered. Alex managed to get Jack out of the way, but not her.

Her shoulder ached and she reached up to grab it. Her body refused to cooperate. With more effort than it should have been, she turned her head to her shoulder, expecting her shirt to be ripped and her skin scorched. The gray fabric of her soft sweater fluttered against her shoulder in the wind, and her skin was still the same tan color it had always been. Brooke willed her body to fly, but her muscles refused to move. Was she going to fall to her death?

Alex looked down at the body plummeting toward the earth. Before Jack could catch his breath, Alex dove down. More cracks sounded through the air followed by more bolts that shot through the sky. Alex weaved and ducked and swerved as he avoided the blows. He wasn't about to let Brooke fall. Alex grabbed her arm and hoisted her limp body in his arms. She was still breathing and she looked at him with bewildered but relieved eyes. Alex flew upward but struggled to fly with the extra weight. Flying may be easy but he was still new to the whole thing.

Alex struggled to avoid the bolts but managed most of the way. He was only a few feet away from his friends when the bolt came down. It hit him square through the chest, sending him sprawling backward. The sudden light before his eyes blinded him. When he finally regained his sight, Brooke was falling alongside him only a few yards away. Alex urged his body upward, straining against the pain. He flew at her once again and scooped her out of the air. Brooke pushed away from Alex and gave him a reassuring nod, the entire left side of her face twitching. She would be okay.

"Where'd this storm come from?!" Brooke yelled over the sound of the dry thunder.

"Don't ask me!" Alex shouted back.

"Maybe you should ask me." A voice vibrated through the air around them like static.

Alex looked up to a white figure drifting down toward them. He realized who it was almost immediately. Winona lifted her hand and a lightning bolt formed in her palm. She quickly raised her arm and thrust the bolt like a javelin. Alex and Brooke shoved their arms above their heads in defense. When the impact never came, they opened their eyes to find Jack hovering in front of them with his arms spread out. His hands glowed and a dark purple shield hung in the air in front of them. David, Nicole, and Mark quickly flew behind the protective barrier.

"Oh, come now, Jack. Don't take out all of the fun!" Winona lowered so she was directly across from them. "Jack, you know those bolts aren't all that dangerous. They are merely numbing bolts! You know that!" Winona glanced from the bolt in her hand then back to Jack. "I am quite perplexed, though," said Winona as she dropped into the trees and disappeared.

"Where did she go?" Nicole asked.

"I don't know. But I do know that she is *not* gone." Jack turned his wrists in a circular motion. The barrier in front of him began to expand in a circle around them, forming into a ball.

"You should listen to him. He is a very intelligent man," Winona whispered. They spun around as the barrier began to close over their feet. Another bolt formed in her hand and she hurled it at the barrier. The barrier glazed over with a surge of energy after it was hit before coming to a halt. The purple barrier began to lower again. Jack dropped his hands and turned back with the others.

"I must say I am quite impressed," said Winona as she leaned closer into the group of kids. "Those bolts were not deadly, but they should have still numbed your muscles for a while, as our friend Brooke here experienced. But you didn't seem to be affected for more than a second." Winona turned and glared at Alex.

"What is your goal, Winona?" Jack snapped.

"What? I can't talk with my fellow Contour Suzerain?" Winona shook her head in question and sighed. "Well, my new-found partner sends his regards, Alex. He certainly enjoyed your last meeting."

Before Alex could ask what she was talking about, lightning flashed through the clouds. Alex glanced up at the clouds before returning his eyes to the Conjurer. Her head tilted toward the sky to watch the lightning, but her gloved hand was raised and pointed directly at Alex. Her head snapped back and stared in the direction her finger was pointed. Her eyes glowed white, and small sparks sizzled in the corners.

"You may have been able to withstand one numbing bolt. But what about more?" As if on cue, lightning shot from the clouds and with the bolts forming around Alex, trapping him in a lightning cage, a larger version of the one his friends had been trapped in during their last encounter. "What do you think, Alex?" Winona cocked her head and more lighting shot down.

"Brace yourself!" Jack shouted as he lunged at Winona. Alex did as he was told and hugged his legs against his chest and buried his face in his knees, squeezing his eyes shut. The light from the bolts grew brighter against Alex's eyelids and he squeezed his knees tighter. He could just barely hear the screams of his friends through the sound of dry thunder, crackling around him.

As if to answer his prayers, the light died down and the crackling stopped. Alex cautiously brought his legs back down and his hands to his sides. He looked over to Jack's hands clasped against Winona's in a desperate struggle. In less than an instant, she regained her composure and focused her sights on something bigger.

"All right! Maybe you *can* withstand that many numbing bolts!" Winona shouted through gritted teeth. "But I don't think your friends can!" Winona snapped her head away from Alex and focused on the others. Lighting shot from the sky as it had done to Alex. Jack broke away from his struggle with Winona and lunged back toward the coming lightning. He was too late. The bolts surrounded the group and encased them in white. Alex spun around to face Winona once again but she was gone.

Alex watched as the lightning cage faded and revealed his friends suspended in air. Around them acting like a protective barrier was a dark purple sphere. Alex looked back at Jack, who had his arm outstretched for the group, who in turn nodded to answer Alex's anticipated question before it could escape his lips. Alex sighed in relief and flew to his friends as the barrier lowered.

"Is everyone all right?" Alex asked.

"We are fine, thanks to Jack, but what about you?" Brooke asked. Concern flashed across her eyes. The twitching had gone down, now reserved to her left eye and eyebrow. She placed her hand on her face in an attempt to stop it.

"I-I think I'm okay," Alex said uncertainly, looking down at himself as if he didn't know his own body.

Brooke gave him an uncertain and worried look that Alex returned with an equally confused glance before Jack flew over to the group and urged them to move onward.

"Please hurry. We must leave this area. It is no longer safe," Jack said. As he spoke, his eyes constantly drifted up toward the sky. "I fear that Winona has left us with a departing gift."

The sky rumbled as a strong gust of wind swept past them, and the air became frigid. Alex zipped his jacket as his companions rubbed their arms against the sudden cold. Without a word, they began to fly once again.

THIRTY-ONE

Winona's hurried footsteps echoed through the dark corridor. The occasional torch fastened to the wall provided the only light. Shadows of patient soldiers danced against the wall where the light from the fire met with the black. The vaulted ceiling rose high into the air, and at the very end of the long hallway loomed two large double doors that soared impossible lengths above. In front of the door were two soldiers who held their spears high.

Winona stopped in front of the guards and glared at them in disgust.

"I demand an audience with his highness!" Winona announced.

"Papers, please." The first soldier held out his hand and grabbed the air, gesturing for her to hand them over.

"This is a matter of urgency! I must speak to his highness at once!" she exclaimed.

"Papers, please," the soldier repeated patiently.

"Allow me through!" Winona growled.

"Why are you here, Conjurer?" echoed a voice through the corridor. "You are causing a *much*-uncalled-for *ruckus*."

Winona spun on her heel to a silhouette standing behind her, hidden within the dark. The figure stepped out and into the light of the fire, revealing a young man in what appeared to be his early twenties. His black hair was slicked back and his ruby red eyes sparkled. His white dress shirt was covered by a gray vest that matched his black dress pants. His looks reminded her of Jaheim's.

"I will speak with him and you will not prevent me from doing so!" Winona thrust her hand out and with the flick of her wrist sent the soldiers crashing into the wall with a breeze. With another gust of wind, she thrust open the large, heavy doors. Winona began walking toward the doors. A force field of wind surrounded her and shoved into the wall anyone who attempted to stop her.

The room was spacious and dark. Unlike the corridor, there were no torches or fire to light up the room. An eerie blue light illuminated from a single line that circled around a throne before her. The throne was empty, beside it was a dark figure of a man whose back was to her. Winona took a few more steps before dropping to one knee. Following close behind her was the man she had encountered in the hall. The man stopped next to her and bowed before his lord apologetically.

"Sire! I deeply apologize for this woman's actions," he said. The man glared at Winona through the corner of his eye and she in turn scowled at him. "She shall take her leave immediately." Before the man could say anything else, he was cut off when the dark figure held up a hand. "But sire-" The figure's head turned so that half of his face was visible. The shadows contorted his features so that they were unrecognizable. Without another word, the man bowed once more then took his leave, shutting the doors behind him.

"Your report?" The figure's voice bounced off the walls of the room.

"He has not yet been captured."

"How many companions does he have?"

Winona thought for a moment before answering.

"Five. They all have the ability of flight, but none of them seems to have any other abilities. One of them may be able to manipulate nature, but he seems unsure of how to control himself. He is not a threat. His companions are none other than teenagers, sire."

The figure turned and even though he was covered in darkness she could almost see the grin forming on his face. "This could be used in our favor."

"Sire?"

"Yes. It may be easier to capture him than I imagined. We may be able to use his companions to our advantage. I want this done right. Winona, you and Jaheim must not fail me. Otherwise, I will be forced to send *others*."

"Understood," Winona said. She stood and turned toward the door but was stopped when the man interrupted her.

"One more thing. I hope you were not so weak as to allow them a chance to escape defeat." The figure's voice was deep and threatening and slow.

Winona chuckled out of amusement. "You think of me as someone who could lose a battle so easily? I may have fled from their presence, but I have left them a gift that I *know* they will enjoy."

With that, she walked out of the room, past the unconscious soldiers who had tried and failed to stop her. She pushed the doors open once more and strutted out, determined to finish what she had started.

THIRTY-TWO

The group dove beneath the canopy in an attempt to escape the harsh winds. Though the wind was not as strong below the safety of the trees, it seemed to grow stronger by the second, and each of them struggled to fly against the strength of it.

As Alex flew, wind and dirt seeped into his eyes. He rubbed his eyes to force the dirt out but every time he got his eyes clear of dirt a new gust of wind would force more in. His eyes grew red and irritated, and soon he found himself struggling to see. When he finally managed to see again, a dirt storm swarmed around him and he was left to the mercy of the wind. He could no longer see or hear. He moved to fly forward, but the wind held him back. He tried desperately to regain control, to no avail.

A thought occurred to him that caused his heart to skip a beat. Where were the others? Alex fought against the wind and peered through the storm. Not even their silhouettes were to be seen. Alex opened his mouth to call out for them, but his voice was lost. Amid his panic, the force of the wind shoved him into the trunk of a tree. The roar of the wind was drowned out by silence as his vision was clouded black.

In what seemed like a few seconds, Alex's eyes fluttered open but struggled to keep from closing. Alex frowned in confusion as he realized that he was still floating. He remembered he had lost consciousness, so shouldn't he have been lost to gravity by now? His vision was still blurred, but he was able to hear the muffled sounds of the wind and thunder. Alex brought his hands almost effortlessly to his eyes, expecting to struggle against the wind. He rubbed the last of the dirt out of his eyes, and his vision was suddenly clear.

He examined his surroundings to find all of his friends floating unconscious around him and surrounding them all, himself included, was a purple luminescent square. Alex shot into an upright position to discover he was not flying. Something was forcing him to float. But what?

A grunt from behind him caused him to spin around. Jack was facing the luminescent wall of the strange square that encased them. With his arms spread wide, Jack's hands were outlined in the same light purple of the square. A few beads of sweat formed on his forehead and slipped down his cheeks. He grunted through his gritted teeth from the effort. Alex forced his body to fly across the distance between the two.

"Jack? Where are we? What's going on?" Alex asked once he was directly behind him.

"Oh good, you are finally awake. How are the others?" Jack ignored Alex's question.

"They are still unconscious, but you didn't answer my question. How long was I down for?"

"We are in the middle of the storm Winona created. I am attempting to shield us, but it is excruciatingly difficult. We have to get to permanent shelter, but through all this wind and dirt I can just barely make out my own hand. And you were not under for long. Maybe ten minutes or so." Jack winced as a strong wind struck the wall in front of them; it was quickly followed by two more gusts. A large crack began to form within the luminescent glass. "This is causing to much strain for my magic."

A crackling sound rang out through the small enclosed square as a piece from the wall broke off and fell into the dirt storm.

"If only we could—" Alex's mouth snapped shut as a sharp pain ran through his head. His eyes went wide in astonishment as the world became almost colorless except for the light blue line outlining each object. Alex looked at the black outlined shape of Jack's concerned face in utter confusion. Though he looked concerned, he did not move from his position.

"Alex? Is everything all right?" Jack asked.

Alex only managed a nod as he turned back to the wall ahead. His head began to throb and he squeezed an eye shut from the pain. That's when he noticed the strange outlines he could see beyond the wall. He mostly saw trees, but as he focused he realized that just ahead of them was a mountain. Eroded just inside of it was a cave.

"We need to go," Alex muttered, not taking his eyes off the cave.

"I know that, but where?" Jack asked as he watched the top of Alex's head through the corner of his eyes.

"You said we needed to find shelter, right? There is a mountain just ahead of us and in that mountain is a cave. We can find shelter there until the storm ends."

"How would you know that? I can't see a thing."

"I'm not really sure. I can see it but I can't. It's just black outlined in a bright light blue. It's not far, it's only about a mile away. We can make it if we fly fast and without stopping." Alex continued to stare at the outline of the opening. Defined outlines of leaves and dirt crossed between his vision and his head throbbed harder. Each speck of dirt and everything else around him was clear, visible, and well defined. Every animal, every gust of wind, every leaf, every stick was in his sight. Nothing could pass him without being noticed. The sight before him wavered and he lurched in pain. Alex shut his eyes and turned away, pinching the bridge of his nose to stop the horrible migraine. Jack turned his head to look at Alex with a raised eyebrow.

"What's wrong?" Jack asked.

"Nothing. I'm fine. But we should get to that cave," said Alex as he opened his eyes and sighed, relieved that the world was back to normal—in color at least. The storm continued to rage. The throbbing in his head had receded, but a small tug still remained.

"I'll send a Shadow out to check," declared Jack as he turned back to the wall and flicked his eyes up and forward. At his command, a Shadow flew out from the folds of his cloak and into the wall. The wall around the Shadow rippled as it forced itself through and disappeared.

Alex jumped in surprise as the Shadow returned. The Shadow floated in front of Jack for a moment before dissipating. An expression of surprise and wonderment flashed across Jack's face, but only for a moment before he controlled himself. Jack turned back to Alex with a controlled, and relief filled expression.

"So there it is. In order to get there we will have to fly without the force field. I have used too much of my strength, so I am incapable of moving us all while holding up the defenses," said Jack calmly, as if he had less strain from when he was struggling to hold the shield moments before. "Please, go wake your friends. You do not have much time."

Alex did as he was told and after a few tries, managed to wake his unconscious companions. After everything was explained, they all stood ready, preparing themselves for Jack to drop the barrier.

"I will clear a path by creating two walls that will hold the storm at bay, but I can only do this for four to five minutes at most. If you do not make it to the cave by then, you will have to figure out how to get there through the storm. If you are separated, do not panic and focus on getting to that cave. Am I understood?" Jack explained.

The teens nodded in response.

"All right. Be ready and good luck." With one final nod Jack dropped his arms and time slowed to a crawl. Jack's arms slowly disappeared within his cloak as it fell around him and hid his entire body. The line of teenagers all leaned their upper bodies forward. Their hair whipped around against the wind and dirt flew in front of them. In an instant the wind stopped and the dirt fell. Immediately they could see the tree trunks scattered in front of them lit up by the moonlight. To their sides, up above, and behind them four giant walls that glowed a light purplish-pink blocked the storm from them. A few leaves fluttered past them and to the ground from the sudden silence.

Time sped up as they lunged forward and took off into the night. They swerved and ducked and dodged trees and branches as they flew as fast as they could to the cave. It wasn't very far away, but with everything they had to get through it would take longer than it would in open space. They were halfway there when a loud boom echoed through the air, soon followed by a long ear-splitting crack.

Without thinking, they stopped and looked around. Above them the barrier cracked and the crack bagan to grow and stretch across the distance that they covered with greater speed than theirs.

"Hurry up! We have to get there before the barrier breaks! We are almost there!" Jack shouted over the cracking sound.

They took off once again, desperate to get there before the tip of the growing crack reached them. No matter how far or how fast they flew, the crack gained on them by the second. They all sighed in relief when they caught sight of the cave. Their feet had barely grazed the rock floor outside of the cave when a boom sounded and broken shards of sparkling luminescent shield fell from the sky.

The force of the blow sent them tumbling into the darkness of the cave. Alex immediately stood up and spun around. He watched as the shards of broken shield floated down, the moon light reflecting off them and creating millions of purple sparkles in the sky. It was beautiful. Almost calming.

The calm soon ended when the sparkles were swept up into the storm as it burrowed through the air, bringing sticks, leaves, and dirt along with it. Alex turned and backed into the safety of the cave as a light purple wall shot up from the ground and blocked the storm from entering the cave. The sudden end of the storm caused an eerie silence to fill the black open space. That silence ended when a faint crackling sound from behind him caused Alex to spin around.

Two more cracks followed before a light burst forth and flooded the cave. Alex shielded his eyes from the sudden light. Once he was used to the light, he lowered his arms to see Mark and Jack squatting in front of a fire. Jack sat beside Mark and watched him as Mark poked the fire with a stick. Alex sighed and took in his surroundings now that the light allowed him to discern a few yards ahead of him.

The walls of the cave were damp. The low ceiling barely gave Jack enough room to stand. The rocks that jutted out from the ceiling were only inches above his head. An occasional rock stump stuck out from the rough and bumpy floor. Nicole leaned with her arms crossed and her eyes closed against a tall rock that reached from the floor to the ceiling. Darkness remained where the light ended. Only a few shadows could be seen. Sitting next to her, criss-crossed on the ground, was Brooke who stared intently into the growing flames. David was climbing the rock wall but continued to slip and fall as unstable rocks collapsed beneath his feet.

Out of the corner of Alex's eye, a flash of black leaped from one rock to another before disappearing. Startled, Alex spun around but, as he expected, nothing was visible.

"What's up?" Mark looked up and raised his brow in curiosity as he watched Alex spin around and look deeper into the cave. After a moment of silence, Alex spoke.

"Nothing. Just a trick of the light." Alex shrugged it off and sat across from Mark to warm himself with the fire.

"What did you see?" Mark asked. Alex's head shot up from the ground and his eyes widened. Could Mark have seen it too? No, he couldn't have. His expression told him so. Grunts from the other side of the cave filled the air as David fell once again. Jack looked from Mark to Alex before standing up and walking over to David, who continually climbed the wall only to fall and try again.

"David, what are you doing? Please stop you are going to hurt yourself," Jack's voice trailed off as he walked farther away.

"Did *you* see anything?" Alex asked casually, regaining his composure.

"No, I didn't but—"

"Then you have your answer," Alex snapped. Mark threw his hands up in defense.

"Okay! I was just wondering." Mark picked up the stick and began to poke the fire again. Alex turned his head away and stared at the ground awkwardly. That's when he remembered his headphones. Alex looked down to check to see if they were still there. Sure enough, they were still resting against his collarbone. He had completely forgotten that he had brought them. He may have had to leave the rest of his things back at the cliff, but he didn't care about any of that.

When he lived in California, he had found his headphones in a dumpster. They were dirty at first but after he cleaned them they were good as new. They were old and only played music from a cassette, but he took what he could get. He only had a few cassettes anyway. Before he found the device, he had never heard music. So of course he thought this discovery was better than sliced bread.

Alex turned on the music and closed his eyes as all sound was drowned out and he was carried away into the world of music. Alex laid back onto the cold hard ground and chuckled.

"You know what would be even better right now?" Alex muttered. Mark looked at him questioningly. "Hot chocolate," Alex laughed. Mark smiled in agreement.

"You know what else would be good?" Mark asked as he settled down.

"What?"

"A warm bed."

THIRTY-THREE

Alex awoke to darkness. His music still pounded in his ears. He sat up and turned his music off before sliding his headphones around his neck. *The fire must have gone out.* Alex listened for the howl of the wind, but he only heard the faint drip of water falling onto the cold stone floor.

"David? Brooke? Anyone awake?" Alex called into the darkness. His voice echoed deep into the cave and he shivered. When he didn't get an answer, he concluded that they must have been asleep. Alex felt around in his pockets for anything that might help him start a fire. He pulled out a piece of gum, a paper clip, a crumpled piece of paper, an eraser, and a battery. Alex kept the battery, paper, and piece of gum and shoved the rest of the contents back into his pocket. He unfolded the gum wrapper and plopped the gum into his mouth. He ripped off a strip of the foil and wrapped the ends around the ends of the battery. As soon as a spark was started he put it on the paper, placing it in the makeshift fire pit.

His friends were scattered about the floor around the fire and sleeping soundly. Even Jack was sleeping, and he never slept. Alex stood and stretched his back. As he stretched, he watched the shadows dance against the light of the fire on the ceiling. Alex stretched farther back, expecting to see the faint purple luminescent wall, blocking off the outside. What he saw caused him to gasp. Caught off guard, he lost his balance and fell. He immediately scrambled to his feet and stared in shock at the scene before him.

The opening to the outside was no longer there and in its place was another passageway that led farther into the black oblivion of the cave. Alex looked behind him to see if he was merely looking in the wrong direction. Unfortunately, he was not. The only entrance to the outside was gone.

"I should've known this would happen."

Before Alex could turn to whoever had spoken, a hand rested on his shoulder. Alex turned to look at the hand and slowly observed Jack's irritated expression. Jack didn't bother to look at Alex and instead kept his irritated gaze locked on the black emptiness ahead of them.

"Finding refuge so easily in that storm, I should have realized there would be a catch," Jack shook his head in annoyance.

"What are you talking about?" Alex looked to Jack, confused.

"We are after all in one of the states of Heltiana. You never know what will happen in these kinds of places." Jack ignored Alex's question and continued to ramble on. Alex sighed and gave up trying to get more information out of him—information that made sense at least. "We will just have to go forward. If we are lucky enough, we might find another opening. Go wake the others. We should go as soon as we can."

"Go where? There isn't an entrance anymore," Alex said as he gestured around them.

"We go forward. It is our only way of getting out of here. Unless you'd like to stay?" Jack raised an eyebrow at Alex and smirked. Alex shook his head and turned to wake his slumbering friends. They certainly were used to sleeping in, he noticed; they were always a struggle to wake up. And nearly two months on an island did nothing to break them of that habit.

Jack snapped his fingers and a bright ball of purple light appeared in the air. The bright light illuminated the rock around them, showing them the way out. Alex snuffed out the fire and with Jack in the lead walked into the black oblivion. The ball of light floated high in the air, only inches from Jack's side. As they walked, the ball moved with them. It stayed the same distance away from Jack, never coming any closer or straying any farther.

They walked in silence, their footsteps echoing off the cold damp walls. The rock path began to slant slightly. They took no notice of it until they were forced to grab onto the walls for fear they might slip and fall.

"Is the ground getting steeper? I feel like I'm going to fall!" Brooke exclaimed as she clung to the wall,

"This path must lead underground. Just be careful and mind where you step. It will only get steeper. If you keep your hands on the wall, you will be fine," Jack explained. As if to prove him wrong, the ground beneath them became slippery and their feet came out from under them. Their hands scraped against the rocks in the wall as they tried desperately to pull themselves back up, to no avail.

Jack's concentration faltered and the ball of light disappeared. They crashed onto the ground and continued to slide down into the dark abyss. Their screams bounced off the wall as they tumbled down and they clamped their eyes shut in fear. The trip down was short. The rock path they had walked on moments before transitioned into sand and they stopped falling, landing in a heaping pile of tangled limbs.

They waited, refusing to move. No one dared to open their eyes. Alex rolled off his friends, expecting to fall onto the cold hard surface of rock. To his surprise he didn't. Instead he fell on a soft flat surface. Out of curiosity, he opened one eye to a tan, crumbling floor. Sand! Alex opened the other eye and stood up. His hair was messy and filled with sand, and his clothes didn't look much different. He looked as if he had undergone a wrestling match at the beach.

Alex brushed the sand off his clothes. He then realized he could see, and not because of Jack's light trick. Alex looked up and his mouth flew open in awe. They had stumbled into a large cavern that stretched farther than two football fields. The ceiling and walls were rock while the ground was sand. Rocks and stalagmites jutted out from the ceiling and hung loosely. Ahead of him was a lake that stretched from one end of the cavern to the other. Boulders were scattered throughout the lake. On the other side was another opening with a staircase where light seeped in. The lake cast an eerie light blue. The water was as calm as glass.

Alex scanned the area for any way to go around the lake but the only way to get to the opening was to go across. His friends soon joined him in his awestruck amazement. Jack walked up to them and took in a deep breath.

"Amazing, isn't it?" Jack asked. All the bunch of kids could do was nod. "But we have to get across. That looks like the only way out."

After a moment they managed to gather themselves, and they began to search for a way across.

"Wait a second! Can't we just fly over?" Nicole asked.

"No. I recognize this cavern from somewhere. I don't know where, but I do. I have a feeling we shouldn't use our powers here," said Jack as he shook his head. Reluctantly, Nicole went back to work, in search of something to aid them in their escape.

"Hey! I think I found something!" David shouted from behind a boulder. Jack, Mark, and Alex rushed over while Nicole and Brooke continued to search. Behind the boulder was a boat with two paddles inside. The wood around the edge was banged up and the paint was nearly gone, but the sides remained intact.

"Just our luck! It doesn't even seem to have any holes in it!" Mark pointed out. "Hey guys! We found a boat!" Mark shouted over to the girls and they ran over. With everyone's help they managed to haul the boat over the sandy beach and into the strange blue water. Water rippled around the boat. Beneath the boat the water turned black and, like paint, seeped beyond the boat before disappearing. Alex looked to the others for an explanation but no one seemed to notice.

Alex opened his mouth to ask Jack, but he was cut off when he was pushed into the boat and they began to row farther out into the lake. Jack and Nicole manned the paddles, while Brooke, Mark, and David sat behind them, awaiting their turn. Alex sat at the stern and peered over the edge, watching the clear luminescent water. Although it may have been the clearest water he had ever seen, he was still unable to see the bottom.

Alex's eyes traveled to the water surrounding the paddles and watched as it turned pitch black with every contact before disappearing and returning to its original clear blue state. Alex's brow furrowed in confusion and concern. Something wasn't right. Alex's head shot up from the water as he felt the air pressure change.

"Alex? Is something wrong?" Brooke asked as they switched positions.

"Whatever you do, don't stop rowing," said Alex as he waved Brooke off and sniffed the air. Something definitely wasn't right. Alex looked back at the water and out of the corner of his eye, the water rippled and turned black behind them. Alex spun around to see waves beginning to form from the beach and come closer. As the waves neared them, even more began to form. Through it all, his companions didn't seem to take notice, for the strange phenomenon was too far away for them to see.

A gust of wind whipped past them, ruffling the sand out of their hair. Wind? There shouldn't have been any wind. They were in a cave! That's when all of the puzzles inside Alex's head clicked and fear filled his eyes. Alex whipped his head back to the others.

"Go faster! We need to get out of here! Now!" Alex shouted. The sudden urgency in his voice startled them and they stopped rowing. "What did I tell you? Don't stop rowing!" Brooke and David immediately began to row again at Alex's command.

"What's wrong?" Jack asked. Alex grabbed his arm and pulled him to the back. Alex pointed toward the beach they had left, and Jack followed his gaze. When he saw it, his expression stayed the same but Alex could see the concern in his eyes.

Jack turned around and stood in the boat. The boat rocked and Alex grabbed onto the edge to keep from falling.

"What are you doing? You're going to tip the boat!" Nicole snapped. Jack ignored her and tilted his head to stare at the ceiling. Jack squinted his eyes and watched to see if he could detect movement. After a moment one of the stalagmites above them wobbled slightly. It looked as though its sole purpose was to fall.

Jack sat down, his eyes full of understanding. Jack waved Brooke and David out of their seats and gestured to Alex.

"Come. Help me move this boat. We have to get moving as fast as we can," Jack said as he pointed to the empty seat next to him and the paddle. Alex sat down and began to row the boat. With both of them paddling, they managed to go faster than the others had.

"What is going on? Why are you guys acting so on edge?" David asked. He and the others were still clueless.

"This cavern is a death trap for any unlucky travelers. Any who have stumbled into this place are doomed. They are so awestruck with the beauty of it they would never come to the conclusion that this place would be their grave. Look down at the water," said Jack as he paused to catch his breath and allowed them time to look down. "You can't see the bottom but it's clear. No one knows how deep it goes but one thing is for sure. All of the missing unfortunate souls that have come here are now lost in that infinite abyss."

Suddenly the cavern shook and the water wasn't as glass-like anymore. Fierce wind barreled through, and above them the rocks that hung loosely from the ceiling came cascading down. The sharp stalagmites pounded into the water, causing tsunamis to form.

"Ah, forget it!" Jack jumped up and turned toward the back of the boat. Jack thrust his hands forward and multiple Shadows shot out and latched onto the back of the boat. "Everyone hold on! Things are about to get bumpy." The Shadows shot forward and the boat took off. They were only a few yards away when waves crashed down on the back end of the boat, washing away the Shadows with the light that illuminated from it. The wave sent the boat flying, and they all landed on the rocky surface just outside of the staircase.

"Run! Up the staircase!" Jack shouted. The six of them scrambled to their feet and dashed up the steps. The steps went a long way, but they could see at the very end the bright yellow light of the afternoon sun.

The water behind them began to rise, and before they knew it the water was climbing the stairs only a few steps behind them. Suddenly a scream filled the air and they stopped to turn behind them. At the very back of the line, David lay sprawled across the stairs. A large hand formed out of water was clamped firmly around his leg. David barely had enough time to make eye contact with them before the hand dragged him into the water and to his doom.

THIRTY-FOUR

David stole one last look at his friends' horror-filled expressions before the water yanked him into the lake. He sucked in air just before his head disappeared beneath the surface. His arms trailed above and behind him as he was dragged farther and farther down. His eyes widened as the water formed in front of him once again, into a gigantic bald head. The head opened its mouth and seemed to scream. A rush of water flew past him, causing his torso to tilt backwards, his vision blurred. He was dazed into helplessness.

When he finally righted himself, the head was gone but the hand continued to drag him under at an even faster pace. He looked up and watched as the surface stretched farther away from his reach. The water above exploded multiple times as he saw five figures jump into the water. He recognized who it was immediately and turned his attention to the situation at hand. He had to get out of there before he drowned. He could feel his lungs begin to burn but he held fast. David swung wildly at the watery fist but it did nothing to help him. Was he really going to die here?

Before they could think, the five of them were diving into the water and to the rescue. Oddly enough, the water was warm and welcoming. But they weren't going to be fooled by the water's calm. They held their breath as they plunged deeper into the clear water. In seconds, they spotted the speeding shape of a hand dragging David deeper into the water. David was swiping aimlessly at the hand that continued to drag him under as he struggled to hold his breath.

If they kept going at this pace, they would never reach David in time. Alex lunged forward and swam as fast as he could, finding it much easier to maneuver in the water if his muscles were relaxed. His friends noticed Alex's ease and did the same as he had.

Once they caught up to David and the hand, they latched onto David's arms and began to pull him out. The hand pulled back in an effort to keep its hold on David, turning it into a game of tug-of-war. Brooke held up a hand and began to count down from five with her fingers. When she reached one, they all pulled at the same time and the hand released David.

The six of them flew backwards and were flung to the surface. They quickly swam to the stairs and dashed as fast as they could to the top. Each of them refused to look behind them or stop running.

The bright yellow light blinded them as they charged through the opening into the heat of the afternoon sun. They landed in the soft green grass, out of breath. A cool breeze soared past them, causing their wet bodies to shiver. Alex's chest heaved up and down as he sucked in the fresh air. Suddenly David began to laugh and after a few seconds everyone else joined in. They didn't know why and they didn't need to. They had gotten out and they were safe. For the moment.

Alex lay there completely still, allowing the summer sun to soak up the water from his wet clothes. He sat up and looked at Jack who sat across from him with his elbow resting on his knee and his head tilted up, staring at the clouds in a peaceful and relaxed manner.

"Why didn't you let us fly? We could have gotten out much faster if we had. We might have even avoided that whole incident if we did," Alex pointed out.

"I understand why you think that but that would have had the opposite effect," said Jack as his light brown hair whipped around in the wind, coming out of its usual slicked-back hair-do. "That cavern runs on the energy of power anything or anyone tries to use. If you tried to fly, the water would have just become stronger. I was stupid and reckless and used my shadow power. That hand formed because I used it. The cavern grew stronger because of me. But we still managed to make it out of there." Jack righted his head and looked to Alex for a response.

"You did it to get us out of there and you did. It'll just suck for anyone else who stumbles on that place. Should we block off those stairs?" Alex asked.

"No. If we do that, we have to block off the other entrance. In order to do that, we'd have to go back in. We were lucky enough to escape from that place," noted Jack with a small and warm smile before returning his gaze to the clouds. Unfortunately, the peace that had come onto them did not last long.

A loud roar burst through the air, shaking the trees. The group jumped to their feet. Startled, they searched their surroundings. One thought raced through their heads. They were foolish to let their guard down for even a second. The clearing they had fallen in was small and closed off. On one side of the clearing was the mountain that they had escaped from. On all of the other sides was never-ending forest. In front of them, the trees shook and they positioned themselves, ready for whatever it was to emerge from the branches and attack.

A black shape whizzed past the trees before disappearing. Alex looked to the others, sure that they had to see at least that, but they did not. The trees parted and a black figure stepped out, covered in the shadow of the canopy. Everyone stood still and silent, waiting for the figure to show itself. The figure began to growl and everyone tensed. Except for Alex.

He didn't know why but the sound of the growl caused him to relax. For some odd reason he even found it calming. Why was he finding comfort in this? Whatever that thing was it had to be something dangerous. But why did he feel as if that wasn't true? A wave of dizziness shot over him and he clutched his head. Alex looked up and just before his vision went black, he caught a glimpse of silver within the shadowed figure.

Everything was black. There was nothing but silence. He was alone. He was afraid. Alex opened his mouth to call out but his voice was lost to him. Where was everyone? A white light appeared in the darkness far away. Alex began to walk toward it, but something grabbed him and jerked him backwards. He tried to move his feet, but they were stuck to the ground. The light grew smaller until it was nothing but a tiny speck. Then it was gone.

He wanted to leave. It's not like he hated being alone. It was the place itself. The air was thick and suffocating, like smoke. Gravity pushed down on him, crushing his lungs. He couldn't breathe. Alex fell to his knees and clutched his chest. Then, as quickly as it had come, all of the pain vanished. In the darkness a silhouetted figure emerged. Alex stood as the figure walked toward him, stopping right in front of him. Understanding, Alex bowed his head and closed his eyes as the world around him spun and the darkness vanished.

Alex opened his eyes to the real world once again. His friends were still standing at the ready, waiting for the figure in the shadows to make its move. Everything was just as it was before, as if none of it had happened. Alex's vision was still blurry and the wave of nausea had not passed, so he was unable to see and hear clearly. Alex turned back to the shadowed figure, but it was no longer there. Alex sighed and walked over to Jack. "It's gone. What do you want to do now?" Alex's tone was impatient but unusually calm. Jack turned back to where the shadowed figure once stood to find an empty space.

"That's strange. It was sitting in a shadow for pete's sake! Why couldn't I tell what it was?" Jack asked rhetorically, throwing his hands in the air. Jack looked at the questioning faces around him, sighed, and visibly relaxed, but everyone could tell that, underneath, he was still on edge. Jack stopped moving and looked around as though he had only just realized something.

"What's wrong?" David asked.

"I think I know where we are!" Excitement shot through his eyes as the cogs in his brain began to turn again. "We are close! That mountain just saved us weeks of travel!"

"What are you going on about?" Nicole asked as she walked over from where she had been caught standing when the strange figure appeared.

"If I am right, there should be a town not more than an hour flight from here—three if we were to walk," Jack explained. "There is no time to waste. I understand you are all tired; we will find some rooms when we get there. You aren't all so tired that you are unable to fly, am I correct?"

They all nodded in response.

"Wonderful." Before anyone could ask when they would leave, Jack shot into the sky. They jumped off the ground and into the air after Jack.

The air felt blissful against their skin as they flew. They hadn't tasted the calm air since Winona showed up. It felt as though it had been an eternity, though it had only been two days. Alex's hair whipped against his face and he brushed it back. The wind was cold against his damp body.

In front of Alex, Jack stopped short, and behind him, everyone else did too.

"What's wrong?" Nicole asked. Jack spun around to face them and stared at their clothes.

"Your clothes," Jack said bluntly.

"What about 'em?" David crossed his arms and stared at Jack expectantly.

"They are still wet?" Jack asked, raising an eyebrow.

"Yeah, they're a little wet but we'll live," Brooke said as she held out the bottom of her shirt and it sagged.

"Maybe but you could still get a fever. If danger were to come knocking at our door you would not be ready to face it if you are sick with a fever," said Jack as he brought his hand up and pointed at the group. Above them a flat, dark, purple square formed and slowly began to lower. They all looked up in surprise when they felt the strange presence and watched as it lowered onto their heads. As it lowered onto them, they all shuddered as they felt it drop through them. As it dropped, they felt the water disintegrate and disappear.

When the square passed through their feet and dissipated, their clothes were completely dry and even a bit soft. Alex reached up and ran his hand through his dry hair. Alex looked back at Jack to say his thanks but he was already flying farther away in the sky. Alex sped forward, slowing down once he was at Jack's side. His friends followed and once they were all caught up they were flying in one straight line, side by side.

Alex turned his head and stared at Jack until he realized he was staring at him. When Jack met Alex's gaze, Alex offered a smile of gratitude before turning back toward the horizon.

Jack's eyes caught on something in the distance, his face lighting up and he sped on. Alex struggled to keep up with the speeding adult, confused as to why he was so excited. Then Alex saw why. Just ahead of them was a town. Jack nose dived into the forest below and they followed. Once they were beneath the branches, they discovered Jack was nowhere to be seen. They spun around but he was no longer in the air. David looked down and found him walking in the direction of the town on the forest floor.

"Down there!" David pointed down at Jack and they flew down to him. Alex landed on the ground a few feet behind Jack. He stood and waited for him to stop walking but he didn't stop. Alex ran up behind him and tugged his sleeve. His friends hovered over them as they walked.

"Why not try waiting for us, huh?" David asked. David floated on his back with his hands behind his head, merely inches from Jack's head. When Jack didn't answer, David flipped upside down and met Jack's gaze. Jack stopped mid-step and stared at David in surprise as if he had forgotten he was there.

"I apologize. I seem to have spaced out for a moment. I was lost in thought," Jack said as he bowed his head apologetically.

"Okay?" Brooke raised her eyebrow but shrugged it off. "Anyway, are we going to that city we saw on the way here?"

"First of all it's a town not a city. Second of all yes, we are. You no longer have to fly. Please walk," said Jack as he gestured with his hand to the ground.

"What if I don't want to?" The corner of Brooke's mouth rose in a smirk, her tone coated with defiance. Jack raised a stern eyebrow at Brooke which said it all. Brooke reluctantly floated back to the ground, followed by the others.

"When we step into that town, none of you will speak. I will do the talking. You will follow me and you will not stray. Do not fly or use any other powers unless there is a dire need for you to do so. One wrong move could cost us our lives," said Jack as glared at them, hinting that they needed to etch this into their brains and not forget.

"Why is it so important that we do these things?" Mark asked.

"You are currently in one of the more populated areas of Heltiana's Devil's Haven. If anyone were to find actual humans here?" Jack paused as if mulling over his options. Jack let out a troubled sigh before finishing. "It would mean death. If not, worse."

"What could be worse than death?" David asked. Jack's head whipped around to face him. His eyes were wide and his hands twitched.

"You have no idea," Jack answered sternly before walking farther on. The five of them exchanged both confused and worried glances before following. No one dared to say another word.

Jack stopped abruptly, and everyone lifted their head from the ground to see what had caused him to stop walking. In front of them just beyond some bushes and trees was a hill. The green grassy hill sloped down and at the very bottom was a town. Roads scattered everywhere across the flat landscape surrounding it and connected with the town in random openings that transitioned into cobbled streets. The sound of bustling life drifted up the hill with the cool breeze. Brooke dashed out of the forest and looked down onto the blissful town.

"It looks like it's right out of a fantasy!" Brooke shouted in excitement. Jack began to walk past her and down the hill but stopped and turned back to face her and the other teens standing beside her.

"Remember what I told you in the forest and do not forget it," Jack said.

Alex ran down and stopped when he was beside Jack.

"Don't worry. We won't," said Alex as he looked to his friends for support. They all nodded their heads in agreement.

"Really, we won't," Mark said reassuringly. Jack visibly relaxed and smiled at them.

"Thank you." Jack's voice was warm as he said those two words of gratitude. They all began to walk down the hill without another word. They were all thrilled to be in the midst of civilization once again.

THIRTY-FIVE

Alex's shoes clicked as his heels hit the cobblestone pavement. The streets bustled with life. People ran in and out of stores with grocery bags in their hands. A woman tugged two crying children across the street in front of them. A group of drunk men poured out onto the sidewalk from a local bar in a hysterical fit. In an alley, a group of teens danced to a boombox. Everything almost looked normal. Almost.

An odd yellow light flew around the teens that were dancing in the alley as they performed fantastical feats with their dance moves. Everyone around them was dressed oddly. Not like they would dress on the mainland. Ahead of them, two women in cloaks ran out of a building, pulled out swords, and began to fight. One woman's sword was knocked from her hands, and she shot out her hand toward it, not looking the slightest bit worried. To Alex's surprise, the sword sprang from the ground and flew into her hands.

Brooke tugged Alex's sleeve and pointed wordlessly. Alex followed her finger to a man and woman standing on a stage. Their hair was jet black and their eyes were a peculiar bright orange. The man was half-naked except for a pair of black pants with flames running up the sides. Two gold cufflinks were latched onto his wrists. He was barefoot. The woman wore the same pants and a black leather jacket over a white T-shirt. Stacked gold bracelets dangled from her arms and two gold rings hung from her ears. She was barefoot. They looked like twins.

The man and woman faced the crowd and raised their arms toward the sky. They held their palms flat, and balls of fire appeared inches above their hands. The balls began to spin slowly at first, then faster. As the balls spun, they floated up into the air and formed a square. Lines emerged from the four balls, connecting them all. There was silence as the square turned slowly. In an instant, fire leapt from the square and expanded.

A tornado of fire formed and reached high into the sky. The sky above blackened with smoke and ash fell. Suddenly, as if it never happened, the sky returned to the same cool blue and the tornado of fire shrunk into the hands of the man and woman. The duo closed their eyes and concentrated. The small tornado of fire exploded and red-orange sparks flew into the sky. The man and woman faced the crowd and bowed. The crowd burst into applause.

Jack stood behind Alex and watched in amusement at the agape teenagers. He placed a hand on Alex's shoulder and Alex looked up in surprise. Jack nodded toward the street ahead, indicating that they needed to keep going. The group managed to snap themselves out their trances, and they walked on, away from the gathered crowd.

Jenna and her brother straightened and looked at the crowd with a smirk. They had captured their audience once again with their spectacular performance. Jenna turned to her brother, more than happy with the day's results. Jensen looked at her with a mischievous and expectant smile and Jenna cocked her head in confusion. Jensen pointed behind him at the street below with his thumb toward a particular group of people that were walking away from the crowd.

There were six of them. One was a tall man with a top-hat and flowing cloak. The others were young teenagers.

Jenna looked back to her brother, her expression changed to that of her brother's. They both knew what each other was thinking before the other said a word. This day was just getting better and better!

More and more people poured out onto the streets as the sun descended into the horizon and darkness washed over the sky. Street lamps and lanterns flicked on, lighting up the dark cobbled street. Tents full of food and trinkets lined the streets, attracting joyous customers. Performers stood on stages, pedestals, or boxes and performed their magic. Some created stories and images with a strange magical substance or water and fire, others flew around the sky, all the while performing tricks.

Jack turned onto another, less populated street and walked up the steps of a two-story building. Alex, Mark, Brooke, Nicole, and David were close at his heels. Jack stepped inside. They stepped into a small square room with three old couches placed sloppily around a broken table to their right in front of the wide window. The fabric of the couches was ripped and the color was fading. The wood of the table was splintered and one of the legs had broken in half but was repaired with duct tape.

The wallpaper on the walls was ripped and falling off and the wood floor was sticking up in places under the shabby dull carpet. Doors lined the walls with numbers on each that were barely attached. At the very end of the room were some stairs and right beside them was a desk with a flickering lamp. Two legs were propped up on the desk, the owner's face hidden in the folds of a giant newspaper.

The door closed behind Brooke with a loud thump. The person at the desk didn't move. Jack walked across the room and stopped in front of the desk. The person didn't look up. Jack cleared his throat to gather the person's attention. The person didn't even flinch. Jack cleared his throat again and the person behind the newspaper flipped the page.

"What do you want?" a gruff voice from behind the newspaper asked impatiently.

"I'd like a room. The biggest one you have, please," said Jack. He remained calm and pulled his hand out of his cloak, which was balled into a fist, a string sticking out between his fingers. Jack placed his hand on the table and set a small brown bag on the desk. The bag made a clicking sound as it came in contact with the hard wood surface. The man closed his newspaper and folded it up, setting it on the end of the desk.

The man's bare chest revealed his large muscular build. He had long brown hair and a long brown beard that covered half of his chest. On his wrists were black cufflinks with sharp silver spikes. On his left hand he wore a black fingerless glove while his right hand was bare. In his right hand he held a large cigar. A scar ran down his closed right eye and traveled down his face, stopping just above his mouth. His eyes glowed red with hatred and annoyance. His appearance gave off an intimidating and frightening aura.

The man took one look at Jack, then at the pouch he placed on the counter. The man slowly stood from his seat, looming over Jack. Jack did not back down or look the least bit shaken. The man slanted his eyes as he glared at the slim man before him. Jack glared at him in turn and after a few minutes the man returned his gaze to the small brown leather pouch. The man opened the pouch and poured out the contents on the desk. Gold coins scattered across the desk.

The man stared at the contents without a sound for what seemed like an eternity. He grunted and looked behind Jack at the five teenagers huddled together in silence. He grunted again and scooped the coins back into the pouch. The man tossed the bag up and down in his hand as he turned and placed it into a safe. When he turned around, a skeleton key attached to a piece of leather dangled from his fingertips. Jack held out his hand and the man dropped the key into his palm.

"Upstairs," the man grunted and nodded toward the old grand staircase next to him. Jack clasped his hand around the key and spun around. He nodded to the stairs and the teens followed him as he walked toward it. Alex shivered as he felt the gaze of the strange man follow him up the stairs.

The wooden steps creaked beneath their feet as they climbed the stairs. The top of the stairs led to a long hallway with doors on each side. The second floor was just as bad as the first floor. The wood floor was rotting, the walls were cracked, and the wallpaper was peeled off. Jack turned down one end of the hall and walked until he was at the very end. He turned to a door with the number forty-six on it. The four hung upside down and the metal was dented. Jack slipped the key in and turned it. The door slid open, barely hanging on to its hinges.

Jack stepped in and held the door open as everyone else followed. He shut the door behind them and walked over to a wobbly table against the wall. Jack set the key down, then inspected the drawers and contents of the table. David felt for the light switch and flipped it. The room remained dark. The only light came from the street outside. The room was long. On the other end of the room was a window that faced the more populated side of the street. A single tattered curtain hung in front of it. There were four twin beds against one wall with a small rotting table in between each. Next to the window was an old red cushioned chair, the color fading to a gray. Beside the table where Jack stood was a wooden rocking chair. The walls were cracked and water dripped from a damp patch in the ceiling.

Alex walked over to the window and looked out at the festival below. Brooke and Nicole walked over to some beds and flopped on them with a sigh. Mark and David exchanged glances before running and flopping onto the other remaining beds. Once Jack finished inspecting the room he turned and sat in the wooden rocking chair beside the table.

"What are we going to do about the sleeping situation?" Mark asked. "There are only four beds and there are six of us."

"I'm fine with this chair," Alex replied as he pointed to the chair behind him, not taking his eyes from the window.

"I will be content with this rocking chair. It is actually quite comfortable," Jack said as he rocked back and forth.

"Well that settles it then," Brooke sighed. "I haven't been in a bed for so long! It feels so nice! Even if it's not a hilton!"

"Jack, what's going on down there?" Alex asked as he watched the performers through the window.

"It's technically a festival, but they do it every night. It will last a very long time. Until very late in the morning. Of course all of the children retire before then. The adults do whatever they want. And the teens loiter around and watch the performances. After all, we do not need much sleep. Yes, we still need it but not as much as you humans do."

"Is it all right if I go walk around for a while? I won't talk to anyone," Mark asked, bolting up into a sitting position.

"I'll go with you," Alex said, turning around.

"When you come back, just knock on the door and I will let you in. That is if you are the only two going?" Jack looked to David, Brooke, and Nicole expectantly but they were all fast asleep. "Which you are. Stay together. Don't trust anyone but yourselves."

"This'll be sweet!" Mark beamed and pumped his fists in the air in a silent cheer. Alex turned and walked toward the door. Mark hopped off the bed and followed.

"Be aware of your surroundings," Jack called after them as the door closed behind them. Jack leaned back in his chair and chuckled to himself. What was he worrying about? It was just a festival after all. What could go wrong?

Alex and Mark turned and made their way down the staircase. The steps creaked beneath their feet loudly. When they reached the bottom the man at the desk looked up at them and grunted before returning back to his newspaper. Alex and Mark acknowledged the man before hurrying out into the street.

Mark and Alex turned the corner side by side onto the more lively and populated street and walked through the crowd, observing the tents and performers and activities. As they passed the alley of teenagers, their music drifted into their ears. It was unlike any music they had ever heard. "Whoa! Check it out!" Mark shouted over the loud music and grabbed Alex's arm. Mark pulled Alex through the crowd, shoving people out of the way. He finally stopped behind a large group of people gathered in front of a stage. The crowd was loud, roaring and cheering things that Alex could not determine.

A man with slicked-back dirty-blond hair and blue eyes stood on the stage. He was young and fit and wore a white pirate's coat that went down just below his knees. Beneath the coat was a dark blue long-sleeve shirt. Along with his jacket, he wore white pants, and around his waist was an empty sheath. In his right hand, he held a blood-coated sword. He sheathed it and nodded to another man in a blue T-shirt. The man nodded back and bent down toward a motionless body sprawled across the stage. The man carried the body off the stage and handed it to what looked like nurses, a handful of men and women in matching jackets with the same labels printed across the arm and chest, who then took the body, placed it on the ground, and placed their hands over it. A bright yellow light emanated from their hands, and the body began to stir.

The body stood up and pushed the nurses away. Alex couldn't see who it was but he could see the dark outline of the man. His body was large and muscular and he was extremely tall. The man spun around and stuck out his index finger at the man on the stage.

"Curse you! I will get my revenge!" the dark-outlined man bellowed. The man in the blue T-shirt laughed and bent down, scooping up a sword. The man tossed the sword to the dark outline.

"Yeah, okay! Keep walking," the man in the blue T-shirt nodded to the street. With a grunt, the outlined figure disappeared into the crowd. "Now! Who wants to see if they can defeat the great swordsman?" The man threw his hands out to the crowd. "Any volunteers?" A hand shot up from the crowd and the man beamed. "You, sir! Do you have your own sword or is one to be provided?"

"I have my own," a gravelly voice spoke up.

"Alrighty then! Please step up! Do not worry if you are injured! We have healers at the ready!" The man in the blue T-shirt stepped off the stage as another stepped on. Alex's eyes widened in surprise. It was the same desk clerk from their inn!

"Let's get on with this then," the man from the inn said as he laughed loudly. The swordsman merely smirked and pulled out his sword. The swordsman was sure to be the one to lose against that beast of a man. To the crowd's astonishment not even a minute passed before the man from the inn fell from his feet and crashed onto the ground in a heap. Alex's eyes widened as the nurses climbed onto the stage and began to heal the horrifyingly still man.

"We should go," Alex whispered into Mark's ear as he began to turn away. Alex grabbed his arm and tugged Mark away from the crowd.

"You there! Boy in the blue sweatshirt!" the man in the blue T-shirt called. Alex and Mark froze in place. Slowly, they both turned back around. "Yes, you! Come here! Let's see if you can defeat the great swordsman!" Alex clenched his jaw and glared at the man. Mark looked from Alex to the man in horror.

"I'm sorry but my friend would not like to participate in your charades. We really must be going," said Alex as he stepped backward. In a few seconds, he would give the signal and he and Mark would book it. Alex's back came in contact with something hard. He turned to find two men staring down at him, smiling. The men walked past him and picked Mark up by the arms and carried him toward the stage. Mark kicked and struggled but he couldn't break from the men's grip. He turned his head over his shoulder to Alex for help. Alex's fists were clenched and he refused to move. The two men set Mark down on the stage and walked away. The man in the blue T-shirt handed Mark a sword.

"Do your best, kid! Oh, and remember, you can't leave the stage until you are injured! Or you defeat the swordsman! There is no surrendering in this game!" The man laughed before jumping off the stage to watch from the ground. The swordsman looked to the man in the blue and cocked his eyebrows as if to say, *really? You want me to fight this kid?* The man in the blue gave him a wink and a thumbs up. The swordsman rolled his eyes and started to slowly pull his sword out of its sheath.

Mark watched in horror as the sword slipped out of the sheath and the swordsman held it high in the night sky. The purple moonlight glinted off the edge of the sword. Mark's whole body shivered in fear. He had never used a sword in his life! If this was a fist fight it would be an entirely different story. But this wasn't a fist-fight. It was a sword fight. The sword shook in his sweaty palms as Mark closed his eyes and braced for the impact.

"Enough!" Alex shouted. Everyone stopped and all eyes turned toward him. Alex walked to the stage and reached for his back. Alex pulled the sword halfway out of its sheath and let the metal glint in the moonlight before sheathing it once again. "Leave him be. Let me fight in his stead."

The man in the blue T-shirt looked at Alex as if seeing him for the first time then nodded to the two men. The men walked toward Alex and grabbed his arms.

They carried him up to the stage and set him down. Alex stood directly in front of Mark. Mark's shoulders slumped and he stared wide-eyed at Alex. Before they could exchange another word, the two men plucked Mark from the stage and placed him on the ground. The man ripped the sword out of Mark's hands and placed it in his belt. Mark took one last look at Alex before running through the crowd and out of sight.

THIRTY-SIX

Mark dashed through the crowd, pushing people out of the way. Once he was free from the sardine can-like crowd, he rounded a corner onto a less populated street. He ran until he found the familiar two-story building and flew open the door. The man was at the desk once again, but Mark ignored him as he dashed up the steps and down the hall. Once he reached the door at the end of the hall, he began to pound on it furiously.

"Jack! Jack! Open up!" Mark shouted into the door. In a few seconds, the knob turned and the door opened. Jack was standing in the middle of the doorway.

"We are not the only ones staying here, mind you," Jack hissed. Jack's eyebrows rose in confusion as he finally noticed the sweating and shaking boy standing before him. Then he realized it was only *one* boy. Not *two*.

"Where is Alex?" Jack's voice rose in alarm. Mark panted heavily and strained to get words out. Jack gritted his teeth and turned around. He waved his hand in front of the door and the room shimmered purple before dying out. "Let's go!" Jack spun back around and shut the door behind them, locking it. Jack stormed down the hallway and Mark ran to keep up.

"What'd you do?" Mark asked.

"I placed a protection spell over them since I wouldn't be there to protect them myself," Jack answered. Jack and Mark rushed down the stairs to find the man from the desk waiting for them.

"You'd better hurry," the man at the desk said. "That boy is fighting the swordsman. Who knows what he'll do to him."

Jack sped past him, breaking into a run. Mark did the same, following close behind him.

"It's just around the corner and up the street a little ways! We'll be there in no time!" Mark called to Jack over the shouts of the crowd.

Alex watched as Mark disappeared into the crowd before returning his gaze to the swordsman. What had he gotten himself into now? The swordsman bowed slightly.

"I will enjoy this. You seem to be a skilled swordsman. At least, more skilled than anyone else I have fought tonight. Sadly, I will have to fight you before you may grow even more experienced," the swordsman said with a chuckle. Before Alex could see it coming, he lunged forward and knocked Alex to the ground.

Alex fell on his back and the swordsman brought down the sword into the stage, just inches from Alex's head. The swordsman leaned into Alex's ear and whispered, "It really is a shame, isn't it?" Alex gritted his teeth and rolled to the side, shoving the swordsman off him. The swordsman flew back and landed on his toes. Alex sprung to his feet to face him. The swordsman bolted forward and jabbed his sword at Alex. Blow after blow, Alex dodged every single one. The swordsman's smile faded. He was growing impatient.

"I am growing tired of playing cat and mouse, *boy*," the swordsman sneered. "Fight back!" Caught off guard and cornered, Alex had nowhere to run. The swordsman brought down his sword with the aim to kill. A wicked sneer was plastered on his face. With only one choice left, Alex unsheathed his sword and brought it up to block the man's sword. The two swords came in contact. The crowd around them went wild. The swordsman did not back down.

The swordsman put more of his weight on his sword and Alex struggled to keep his sword away from him. Alex caught a glimpse of sorrow flash across the swordsman's face but he continued to push harder. Alex removed his left hand from the handle of his sword and placed it on the flat edge of the blade. His shoulders threatened to collapse at any second. Alex gritted his teeth and gathered all of his strength. He spun his blade so that the sharp edge was now against the other sword and pushed.

Jack and Mark stopped running once they reached the crowd surrounding the stage. The crowd had grown since Mark had first been there. But then again, no one had ever lasted as long in a battle against the swordsman as Alex had, according to the spectators around him. Ahead of them Alex was leaning against the railing of the stage, struggling to keep the swordsman from slicing him in half.

The swordsman's sword cracked and, all at once, broke in half. The swordsman fell backwards and the top half of his sword flew into the air. The broken blade landed in a dark alley with a loud *clink*. The swordsman stared in bewilderment at the bottom half of his sword. Never in his lifetime had his sword ever *broke.*

"Alex! We're here!" Mark cupped his hands over his mouth and shouted. Alex looked over the crowd in surprise until his eyes fell over the boy waving his arms wildly in the air and the man in a top hat and cloak looking at him with startled eyes. *Mark and Jack.*

The swordsman glanced from his broken sword to the boy before him who had broken it. The boy was distracted, searching the crowd. The swordsman saw his chance and took it without hesitation. In one swift movement he was across the stage and looming over the boy.

Alex barely had enough time to move out of the way before his sword came crashing down. The end of the blade scraped against Alex's cheek and he stumbled backwards. Alex brought his hand up to his face and felt the blood oozing out of the cut. The swordsman spun around and ran at Alex again. He flipped the end of the blade so that the pommel of the handle was facing him. He brought the sword down and Alex attempted to dodge again.

Alex was fast, but not fast enough. The pommel of the handle hit hard against Alex's spine and he sprawled forward onto the stage. The swordsman ran toward him again, prepared to finish this game. Alex looked up as the swordsman jumped into the air and began to fall back toward the earth, with the sharp end of the blade pointing down. His trench coat fluttered in the wind and his broken sword glinted in the purple moonlight. Something about him changed. The way he moved became more dangerous and less forgiving. Lunacy glinted in his eyes.

A bright purple light filled their vision. When their sight finally cleared, Alex found a dark purple force field surrounding him. He looked up to find Jack floating above him with his arm outstretched to the swordsman.

"That is quite enough swordsman! You and I both know that he is but a child!" Jack shouted. Anger and a deep hatred lurked within his voice. The swordsman did nothing but laugh. Jack floated back to the stage and the barrier around Alex lowered. Jack and the swordsman glared at each other. For the first time, Alex noticed something that he hadn't seen before. Around the swordsman's neck was a leather collar. In the middle of the collar was a red jewel.

Alex caught a glare of red in the corner of his eye and he turned to face the crowd. After some searching, he found the man in the blue t-shirt standing in the very back. In his hand he held a larger version of the stone on the swordsman's neck. He held it close to his mouth, smiling evilly. The man began to speak onto the red jewel and it flashed a brighter red as he spoke. The swordsman began to speak.

"Move, outsider. I must finish him," the swordsman shouted. His grip tightened on the broken sword, preparing to fight. All at once Alex understood the situation. Jack opened his mouth to speak but before any words could escape a breeze rushed by him.

Alex flew past Jack with his sword at the ready. Alex kicked the broken sword out of the swordsman's hand and brought down his own. The swordsman was shocked but couldn't gather himself in time to dodge the boy.

In one single swift motion, Alex brought his sword down and cut the collar around the swordsman's neck. The leather ring fell to the ground and the red jewel shattered into a million tiny pieces. Alex landed behind the swordsman in a crouch and stood, turning around and sheathing his sword. The swordsman fell to the ground, unconscious.

Alex did not hesitate for a second. He leapt off the stage and flew at the man in the blue T-shirt holding the strange jewel. The man stumbled backwards and fell but quickly stood and dashed into an alley. Alex followed.

The alley was dark but Alex could just barely make out the outline of the man. Alex landed on the ground and walked toward him. Once he reached him he grabbed the collar of the man's shirt and pulled him close. The man's right hand was hidden behind his back. Alex grabbed the man's hand and pulled the jewel from his grasp.

"How were you controlling him? With this? Why?" Alex held the red stone close to the man's face. The man leaned back from Alex's hand. He didn't look the least bit threatened. A smug smile crawled across his face.

"Talk!" Alex shouted into the man's face. Alex clamped his hand tighter around the large stone. Fury burned in his eyes.

"You are quite the interrogator. But I will not comply," the man laughed. Suddenly, the man's body began to dissipate into smoke. The man's shirt seeped out of Alex's grip. Where a man once stood, floated a blue and gray figure made of smoke. The man continued to laugh as the smoke drifted above the alley and into the night sky.

Alex growled and tightened his grasp on the jewel. His hand tightened until his knuckles turned white. Finally, the stone collapsed under the pressure and the jewel crumpled to a sparkling red powder. Alex stared wide-eyed at what he had just done as the powder poured through his hands onto the ground. Shaking his head, Alex dropped the remaining red dust and stormed out of the alley.

Alex ran back to the stage and jumped up. Jack was staring wordlessly at the swordsman, still motionless on the stage. Alex bent over and picked the swordsman up, draping him across his shoulders.

"Could you grab his sword? Or at least the bottom half of it anyway," Alex said as he nodded toward the broken sword lying on the stage. Jack nodded and picked it up. He walked to the edge of the stage and floated down to the pavement. The crowd had lessened, leaving only a few groups standing and staring in astonishment. Mark stepped forward and followed Alex as he walked back down the unpopulated street.

Jack went ahead of Alex and opened the door to the two-story building. Alex walked through and offered a nod of thanks before walking to the shabby couches surrounding the broken table. Alex laid the unconscious swordsman on the couch and stretched his back. The man at the desk stood up from his seat and marched over to the trio.

"Are you insane?" the man fumed. "How dare you bring this lunatic into my inn!"

"Sir, you don't understand. This man was being controlled!" Alex positioned himself in between the man and the couch.

"Oh yeah? With what? Where's your proof?" the man asked skeptically.

"Right here," said Alex as he fished the leather collar out of his pocket and held it up to the man. The man's eyes widened at the sight of it. He snatched the collar from Alex's hand and inspected it, his curiosity growing. He glanced up at Alex and sighed, handing the collar back to Alex.

"You should have a professional check that out. Stuff like that is dangerous," declared the man softly. He turned away and sat back down at his desk. Without another word, he unfolded his newspaper and went back to his reading. After a moment, Alex handed Jack the collar and walked to the door.

"Where do you think you're going?" Jack asked.

"To get the other half of his sword back. Watch him?" With a final nod, Alex opened the door and stepped back outside and into the warm night air. Jack looked from Mark to the collar in his hand.

"What just happened?" Mark asked. "Weren't you just trying to save Alex from this guy? Why are we taking care of him?"

"I haven't a clue," Jack answered. Jack sat down on the table across from the unconscious swordsman. He smiled to himself. Maybe there was more to Alex than he had thought.

THIRTY-SEVEN

lex turned the corner onto the crowded street and began his search for the sword remneant. For thirty minutes, he scoured the area and came up empty. He looked carefully on the ground around the stage where they had fought, around the nearby booths and performers, on the stage itself. He didn't remember seeing the sword fragment land, but he recalled hearing a clang when it landed. It sounded as though it landed someplace with walls and definitely outside. Alex's eyes traveled up into the starry night sky.

He didn't have to think too long before he realized where it had fallen. *An alley!*

Alex ran to the empty stage and jumped up. Alex stood in the same spot he was in when he cut the sword in half, right up against the railing. The sword had flown toward the right, Alex remembered. There were two alleyways in that direction. Alex jumped down and walked toward the one closest to the stage. He came up empty.

Alex walked to the second alleyway. He was a few inches from the alley entrance when he heard voices. Alex slammed his back against the wall and peeked around the corner. It was dark, but he could barely make out the shapes of five teenagers. He figured they were around sixteen and seventeen. They were deep in inaudible, whispered conversation. Alex strained to hear what they were saying.

"What is it… going to have a blast…where'd… from… sharp… broken… sword?" The words were vague, and he only caught a few of them but the last word caught his attention. Alex dared to lean forward and peered deeper into the dark. In the middle of the alley was a patch of light from a nearby lamp, but the group was on the other side of it, hidden deep within the dark.

"Let's hold onto it!" said one of the figures in an excited and shrill voice.

"What are you so excited for? Why would we want to keep this thing?" Another figure bent down for a second before standing up again. In his hand was a long thin piece of metal with a sharpened point on one end while the other was broken and jagged.

"We could mend it and turn it into something! Maybe turn it into a dagger of some sort?" the one with the shrill voice replied. The figure holding the sword turned his head slightly and whispered to the others before tossing the broken blade to the ground.

"Hey! We know you're there! You can come out now," the figure shouted as he turned around and faced Alex. He had been discovered. With a sigh Alex stepped around the corner and into the shadows of the alley.

"Who are you and why were you watching us?" the figure demanded. Alex didn't answer.

"He asked you a question, I suggest you answer him!" the one with the shrill voice interrupted. Alex sighed again.

"Look, this is all just a misunderstanding. You see, that sword, I was looking for it. It's mine." Alex took a few steps forward and gestured toward the blade lying on the ground. The group of teens took a step back behind the broken sword. The figure who had dropped the sword looked down at it and then at Alex with a smirk.

"What's so special about this, huh?" he asked gruffly. He shoved the sword with his foot. "It's broken. It's useless. Just move on."

"I *need* it," Alex said as he took another step forward. This time the group of hidden figures did not step back.

"You don't need it. It's broken," the figure insisted.

"Yes, actually, I do," Alex said as he stepped forward again.

"Okay, dude just chill! It's just a hunk of junk now! Why would you need this kind of thing? It's *useless*."

Alex stopped walking toward them. The tips of his sneakers were barely touching the strip of light in the middle of the alley.

"You're wrong," Alex said.

"Excuse me?" the figure asked. He stepped into the light. The teen's hair was a bright red and squashed beneath a blue beanie. His shirt was white, and a black sweatshirt hung loosely around his waist, just above his jeans. He was taller than Alex by a few inches. *5'7 maybe?* A frown was displayed across his face and his eyebrow twitched in annoyance.

"I said you are wrong," Alex repeated. "Just because something is broken does not mean it is useless. It can be mended, and if it can't, it can be made useful in some way or another." Alex stepped forward into the light and smiled. "Although, I can't say the same for you."

The boy before him shuddered and stepped back. Alex followed him with his eyes as he moved. The boy nodded to the alleyway entrance and the group of teens took off running. After they had gone, Alex relaxed his shoulders and the muscles in his face. *I can't believe that worked. Trying to be intimidating is difficult.* Alex ran a hand through his hair and looked up at the large purple moon.

Alex rubbed his eyes and brought his attention to the broken blade before him. He picked it up and turned to the crowded street.

Jack sat by the window, watching as people walked by. Mark had fallen asleep on the sofa long ago. The swordsman remained unconscious. Jack turned to the man on the sofa as he stirred. The swordsman rolled to the side and brought his hands up to his face, covering it. He groaned. The man shot to his feet and looked around the room. His eyes fell on the man sitting by the window.

"Who are you?" he asked in a guarded tone.

"Jack Pandemonium, at your service." Jack merely tipped his hat in greeting.

"Where am I?" the swordsman asked.

"An inn. There is no need to be so on guard," Jack said as he nodded to the sofa. The Swordsman hesitantly took a seat. He reached for the pommel of his sword to find nothing but air. He looked to his sheath in surprise. Where was his sword? The swordsman glared at Jack. Jack smiled and pointed gingerly toward the table between them. Upon it lay the first half of his sword.

The first… half? The swordsman's eyes widened. Where in the world was the other half of his sword?

"What happened to my *sword*?" The swordsman demanded angrily. Jack held up his hand.

"I wouldn't do that if I were you," Jack said calmly.

"Do what? I wake up in some strange place with a stranger and my sword broken. Not to mention the other half completely gone!" the swordsman raised his voice. Jack pointed to Mark, still sleeping soundlessly on the other sofa.

"Please, there are children sleeping. You wouldn't want to wake him up." Jack paused before returning his gaze to the swordsman. "Don't get all high and mighty. I am not too happy with *you* either."

"What could I have possibly done to upset *you*?" The swordsman rolled his eyes sarcastically.

"You almost killed an inexperienced child! And for *what*? *Entertainment!*" Jack growled, his composure almost gone. The swordsman's eyes traveled in shock to the boy sleeping on the sofa.

"No, not him."

"Then who?"

"His name is Alex. Now for the life of me, I cannot understand why in the world he thought it was a good idea to help you even after you tried to kill him! That boy can be perfectly insane at times," said Jack as he shook his head in puzzlement.

"He did what...? Wait... I tried to kill him? For entertainment?" The swordsman's voice rose in alarm. Jack nodded and raised an eyebrow quizcally at him. Why did this man sound so surprised by his actions? The swordsman placed his elbows on his knees and buried his head in his hands.

"I don't believe it. He finally got to me. After all these years!" The swordsman shook his head violently inside his palms. "Oh no," His head suddenly shot up from his hands, his eyes wide with horror. "How long has he had me for? What else could I have done?" The swordsman shot up and began pacing around the room. Jack stood up and watched as he paced, confused. Jack took a step toward him and placed a hand on his shoulder, ushering him back to the sofa. He sat down and Jack sat across from him on the table's edge.

The sudden creak of a door diverted their attention. The door creaked shut and Alex walked into the room. He stopped short when he caught sight of the now-conscious Swordsman. In his hand was a long thin object wrapped tightly in cloth. When he finally recovered from the shock, he walked over and sat beside Jack, across from the swordsman.

"You're awake. How are you feeling?" Alex asked.

"I'm fine, thank you," the swordsman replied.

"My name is Alex." Alex stuck out his hand. The swordsman stared at his hand disbelievingly. If this was the boy Jack was talking about, why was he acting so open and unguarded around him? The Swordsman looked to Jack and raised his eyebrow. Jack nodded. After a moment of hesitation he finally took hold of the boy's hand.

"Hello, Alex. My name is Alan. Alan Moore," the swordsman said as he shook Alex's hand. Alex caught a glimpse of the broken bottom half of the sword on the table behind him.

"That reminds me!" Alex picked up the long piece of cloth that had been resting on his lap and held it out to the swordsman. "Here's the other piece of your sword, Mr. Moore."

Alan grabbed the cloth and began to unwrap it vigorously. When it was finally unwound, a sharp end of a sword lay before him. Alan grabbed for the bottom half and held the two pieces out before him.

"I'm sorry your sword broke. But, you see, I had to defend myself," Alex said as he scratched the back of his head.

"Show me your sword!" Alan snapped. Alex flinched and, without thinking, unsheathed his sword. The swordsman reached for it but Alex shot up and backed away quickly. When he realized that he had taken out his sword, he sheathed it at once.

"Do you think you can fix it?" Alex asked. Alan stared at the boy for a moment before relaxing.

"That is a fine sword you have there. Never have I ever encountered anything that has been able to penetrate my sword. I apologize. I was simply surprised. But there is no need to worry. I can fix it easily." Alan stood up and placed the two halves of his sword together. There was a bright blinding light and in an instant the sword was repaired. The swordsman licked a fresh cut that had appeared on his hand from pushing the sword together. Slowly the spit seeped into his wound and the cut shrank until it was gone.

"Cut down that light, would ya'?" said Mark as he sat up from the sofa and squinted his eyes with his hand above them.

"Ah, Mark. Have you finally decided to wake up?" Jack asked playfully.

"Not by choice. Won't you let a poor growing teenage boy get his sleep?" Mark groaned.

"I apologize for the rude awakening," said Alan, smiling warmly. Mark looked at the Swordsman as if seeing him for the first time. After a moment of allowing Alan's presence to sink in, Mark's eyes widened with realization.

"Holy—!" Mark brought his legs up to the sofa, stood, and jumped behind it. Alex walked over and bent down over the side of the couch, whispering, "Mark, cut it out. It's fine. Even if he was going to try and kill us, you think hiding behind this couch will do any good?"

Mark reached up and grabbed Alex's collar before yanking him down with him, and Alex let out a loud yelp as he fell.

"What's he doing here?" Mark demanded.

"He's not a threat. I don't think what he did was on purpose," Alex whispered.

"Oh really? Then, what you're saying is, he didn't want to try to kill us? It looked like he was ready to do his worst without even a shred of guilt!" Mark whispered back.

"I have a theory."

"You do, huh?"

"Yeah. I think he was being controlled."

Mark was taken aback. "You sure you haven't read too many sci-fi books, Alex?"

"At first I noticed a strange collar around his neck with a strange red jewel. Then I saw the guy in the blue shirt in the back of the crowd with a larger version of the same jewel in his hand. It had the same blinking light as the collar. Whenever he talked to the stone, the swordsman would talk simultaneously. I chased the guy into an alley. I was just bluffing but I accused him of controlling him. He didn't deny it. In a way, he admitted to it." Alex stopped talking and let the fresh information sink in. Mark sighed and nodded.

"All right. Sounds legitimate enough," Mark nodded. Mark and Alex stood and cleared their throats awkwardly as they walked back around the couch.

"Have you calmed down?" Jack asked.

"Enough to look at him directly, yes," Mark glared at the swordsman.

"My name is Alan Moore. And you are?" Alan smiled again and reached out a hand. Mark continued to glare.

"Marcus." Mark didn't take the man's hand. "Call me Mark. I don't tend to go by my full name very much."

"It's a pleasure," Alan said as he kept his hand raised. Finally Mark sighed and shook his hand. "Now, I understand you say I tried to kill you? Is this true?" Alan's eyebrows furrowed in worry.

"Yeah, it is. By any chance do you think you were being controlled?" Alex went straight to the point, not bothering to delay the subject any longer.

"Well, it depends if there was a col—"

"A collar around your neck?" Alex cut him off. Jack reached into his cloak and pulled out the collar. Alan snatched the collar out of Jack's hand and inspected it. His shoulders slowly tensed.

"I am going to need to speak to Jack. Alone," Alan said.

"Of course," Jack nodded. Alex looked up at them and felt that they were both aware of something that he was not aware of. "Alex," Jack said as he turned to Alex and Mark. "Why don't you take Mark up to the room and get some rest? Alan and I will be heading out for a while. We shall be back before morning." Jack slanted his eyes and waited for Alex to respond.

Something about his gaze told Alex he didn't have much of a choice. He would have protested even though he knew he couldn't win, but he didn't. He was too tired to argue. Alex nodded and muttered "goodnight" to the two men before following Mark up the staircase and into their room.

Nicole, Brooke, and David all lay fast asleep when the door creaked shut behind the two boys. Mark grunted and flopped on his bed, not bothering to get under the warmth of the blankets. Alex walked over to the chair by the window and sat down. He whispered "goodnight" to Mark but there was no response. He was already fast asleep.

Alex curled up into a ball in the corner of the chair and rested his head against the cushion on the back. He stared out the window at the bright lights and the crowds filling the cobbled streets. In a matter of minutes he was drifting off to sleep.

THIRTY-EIGHT

ack and Alan watched the two boys walk up the stairs before departing. They walked out the door without a word. This silence between them continued as they walked down the populated street and up the steps to a small building. Saloon doors hung in front of them. Light and cheerful voices poured out from the windows. The smell of liquor lingered in the air.

Jack stepped through the doors and entered a large room lit by chandeliers and candles. Tables were scattered around the room and in the very back was a long bar. Stocked on shelves behind the bar were a multitude of wine bottles and cases of beer, the counter lined with beer taps. Cabinets beneath the shelves held glasses and bottles. Groups of men and women crowded the room. Multiple bartenders manned the bar and waiters walked from table to table. People engaged in deep conversation and laughed loudly when others told jokes, even if they weren't funny. A group of men gathered around a pool table in a corner. The night was still young.

Jack took off his hat and placed it on a coat rack before leading Alan to a table next to the door beside a large window. Jack and Alan took their seats.

"I believe it is safe to assume you know of my concerns," Alan said as he leaned forward and placed his hands in front of him on the table.

"Your assumptions are correct," Jack confirmed.

A waiter dressed in a black vest and a white napkin slung over his arm walked up to them and offered to get them a drink. Alan ordered a beer and Jack did the same. The two men remained silent until the waiter returned with their beverages. The glasses were a foot tall with a handle sticking out from the side of the wide glasses and were overflowing with white bubbles. Only then did they continue their conversation.

"I'm going to get straight to the point, Swordsman," said Jack as he frowned and glared at Alan. "I do not care for the Domesticators and do not plan on affiliating myself with anything that is involved with the matter. No matter which side they are on. Tell me Swordsman, who are you? What is your *real* name?"

Alan didn't look the least bit surprised at Jack's outburst. "I had hoped we would be able to get along without any problems. I am not against you. I have told you my true name. I have not lied the entire time we have been together. Please, let's be civilized." Alan returned Jack's gaze and sighed, knowing that Jack would not give up without proper answers.

"There is no need to be alarmed. I am a member of Resolton. I honestly never expected to cross paths with you," Alan admitted.

"So what are you doing here on Alsjin?" Jack asked, leaning back into his chair and crossing his legs.

"I was acting as a spy a number of months ago. I was careless, and somehow the head of the Domesticators caught some interest in my skills. I believe you can map out the rest. I plan to leave before dawn. There are things I must do before the next ship to the mainland leaves."

"Do you know where it will be leaving from?" Jack asked.

"Yes. In the next city over," said Alan, gesturing behind him with his thumb. "In the town of Borthenahiem."

"We are traveling there as well. I was actually looking for information on when the next rip would occur. I didn't think it would happen there."

"Speaking of, I know who those children are, Jack," Alan said. He leaned forward across the table and grabbed his beer and drank half of it without a gasp for breath. He set the glass down on the table loudly and grinned triumphantly. Jack waited patiently as Alan wiped his mouth with a napkin. Jack's glass of beer remained untouched. "There is no reason for you to hide that fact from me. Keep those children by your side as much as you can. You do not want the wrong people to discover them. Humans do not belong here. It is best that you go to them."

Alan nodded to the door. Jack stared at him for a moment then stood up. He picked up his untouched glass of beer and downed it in one gulp. He slammed the glass down onto the table and wiped his mouth with the back of his hand. With a swish of his cape he turned and began to walk away.

"Oh, and Jack?" Alan called.

Jack raised an eyebrow and turned toward the Swordsman.

"Do me a favor, will you?"

"What is it?"

"Don't get caught."

With that final exchange of words, Jack turned and snatched his hat off the coat rack, placed it on his head and walked out the saloon doors.

THIRTY-NINE

Alex rubbed his eyes from drowsiness. *When did I fall asleep?* He looked out the window at the bright blue sky. *What time is it?* Alex returned his gaze to the room. Jack sat hunched over in the wooden rocking chair with his arms crossed over his chest, breathing heavily. *When had he gotten back?* Everyone else lay asleep in their beds. Alex stood, stretched, and yawned.

He froze in place when he caught a glimpse of black from underneath the wedge of the door. When the black disappeared, Alex walked over to the door silently, peering through the keyhole. The lights in the hall were on. He caught another glimpse of black down the hall a ways. It disappeared again. Without a sound, Alex opened the door and crept into the hall, slowly shutting the door behind him once he was out. Down the hall, a black shadow the shape of a cat walked down the stairs.

Alex dashed to the edge of the stairs and looked down. The shadow turned behind the banister and into the lobby. He took a step down onto the stairs and paused. He turned and stared at the door to his room. *Should I stay?* Alex thought for a moment. *Nah, I'll be back before they wake up.* Alex tiptoed down the stairs and halted. Slowly, he peeked above the banister at the sleeping man at the desk.

He released a gasp of air that he hadn't realized he was holding. The shadow of the cat walked into the door and disappeared in a cloud of smoke. Confused, Alex raised an eyebrow and dashed for the door, swinging it open. The bell above jingled, but the man behind the desk did not stir. Down the street, the shadow of the cat turned the block. *How is it so fast?*

Alex sprinted into the broad daylight and around the corner. The shadow disappeared into an alley. Annoyed, he ran into the dark alley. Two familiar silver eyes peered at him through the shadow. *Where have I seen those before?* Alex walked slowly into the darkness after the eyes. The silver eyes slowly began to shrink away, deeper into the dark. Alex lunged forward before the eyes could get away, as his head felt the rude shock of collision with the brick wall.

Alex staggered backwards and clutched his head. He searched the darkness once more but the eyes had gone. He walked onto the street and scanned the area. Neither the eyes or the shadow could be seen. Alex sighed and rubbed the drowsiness out of his eyes, leaning against the brick wall. *What am I doing?* He thought. *I just woke up. I'm probably daydreaming. Even if I'm not, I'm chasing a cat! I shouldn't have left in the first place.*

Alex walked back to the inn and trudged up the stairs, not bothering to be silent. The man at the desk grunted when he was startled awake. Alex reached for the doorknob to the room and turned it. The door wouldn't budge. *I forgot. Jack locks it from the inside.* Anyone inside could get out, but no one could get in. Alex knocked on the door and in seconds Jack was at the door.

"How'd you get out here?" he asked, surprised.

"I opened the door and walked out," Alex answered flatly.

"Why are you out here, is what I meant to say."

"I was looking for the bathroom."

"And? Did you find it?"

"Yes."

Alex brushed past Jack and plopped down on the chair. His mind wandered back toward the strange black shadow. *Yes, I may have been hallucinating, but why did it seem so familiar? Those eyes, too.* Alex slumped in the chair and crossed his arms, still half-asleep and unable to think clearly. Jack shut the door and faced Alex.

"Please wake the others. We leave immediately," Jack said.

Alex didn't respond.

"Alex."

"Hm? Sorry, I was thinking." Alex sat up and uncrossed his arms, facing Jack. "Did you say something?"

"Would you please wake your friends? Once they are awake, we will head out of town and on to the next," Jack said as he nodded to the sleeping teenagers. Alex nodded and stood. He shook Mark awake and helped wake the others. As soon as everyone was up, Jack ushered them into the lobby.

Jack stopped by the desk and talked with the man while they all waited on the couches around the table. When Jack had finished, he rushed them outside.

"Are we not going to see Alan before we go?" Alex asked Jack. Having heard Alan's name sparked Mark's attention and he quickly joined the conversation.

"No. He knows we are leaving. We have overstayed our welcome, and it is best that we get to our destination," Jack replied. He did not look down at Alex as he answered, keeping his gaze straight ahead and alert.

"Will we see him again?" Mark asked.

"It is possible. He is also looking to travel to the mainland. But there are so many boats and ships traveling there that it is impossible to know if he will be boarding the same ship we do until the voyage begins and the ship leaves port." Jack looked around anxiously as he spoke. His voice was lowered so only they could hear.

"Hey, is everything all right? You seem to be on guard for some reason," Alex pointed out.

"Not for 'some reason'! Keep in mind, you are humans on Heltiana's land! I am afraid someone could have become aware of your presence." Jack stopped abruptly and turned to David, Brooke, and Nicole who were falling behind in the crowd. "Brooke! Nicole! David! Do not lag behind! Keep up!" Jack shouted over the crowd.

Alex, Jack, and Mark waited for the three to catch up before moving on. Jack raised his voice to a normal volume so that the other three could hear as well.

"We will be out of this town and onto the road again. There are only a few blocks between us and the edge of town. The journey from then on should only be two days on foot," Jack said.

"Oh, so it should only be one day's travel if we fly!" David said excitedly.

"No. We will not be flying. That road is traveled frequently because it is in between the two towns. I do not want to raise much suspicion. Those who fly tend to be in a hurry. It takes too much energy. We will look suspicious and most likely be stopped and asked who we are and what our business is. It is too risky. Be careful. Soon, flying will begin to be tiring if you do it too much and eventually you may not be able to do it at all for a while."

"If we stop being able to fly, will we not be able to fly again?" Nicole asked, alarmed.

"A few days of rest should enable you to fly once again. Much faster for a while, too," said Jack as he stole a glance at Nicole and smiled. "So much faster."

The group of teenagers fell silent with their questions as they mulled this over. Jack chuckled to himself and walked on. Ahead of them, yards away, they could see a large arch hanging over the street, connected to two buildings. Beyond that, no more buildings or streets could be seen.

Jenna leaned against the wall in an alley, coated in shadow, resting. Her brother sat beside her, chewing on an apple. She felt a slap on her leg. Startled, she jumped, and looked down scornfully at her brother.

"What in the world was that for?" she growled.

"Look," Jensen pointed to the crowd at a man surrounded by young teenagers. He wore a top hat and cloak. Jenna recognized him immediately. She smiled wickedly. *We haven't lost them completely*, she told herself.

"When do you want to make our move?" Jensen asked.

"Not now. I know where they are going. We will finish our act here and meet them there. In four days, we will go," Jenna replied. "I've always wondered what it felt like to kill a human."

FORTY

hortly after leaving the town, they came across more forest. David complained, but Jack reassured him there would be no more forest once they got to Borthenaheim. Once they left the last town and were on the road again, Alex took notice of Jack's slowly growing comfort the more distance that was put in between them and the town. Alex had asked what about the town bothered him so much, but Jack refused to tell him.

They traveled on a well-worn wide dirt path in the middle of the forest. As they walked they passed many strangers. Some were in cars or wagons or went on foot. Most were merchants or traders or businessmen. Occasionally, they would see people seemingly traveling for personal purposes, as they were.

Before they knew it, night had fallen and they were forced to retire. Jack instructed them to find a place a distance away from the road in order to sleep. Everyone seemed to find trouble sleeping, but eventually they managed to doze off. Even Jack slept. Unlike his companions, Alex found himself wide awake. Not an ounce of drowsiness lingered in his eyes.

For a while, he lay back against a tree and stared at the stars, twinkling brightly. He lay like that for the night, restless. Dawn finally came, and he hadn't slept a wink. Yet he still seemed to have enough energy to last the day.

"Man, why is it so hot out today?" David asked, fanning himself with his shirt collar.

"Now that I think about it, it's gotten so much hotter in just a few hours," said Mark as he shielded his eyes from the sun as he stared up into the blue sky. Nicole pulled her hair in a ponytail. Beads of sweat had formed on the back of her neck.

"We'll be fine. Just a little heat won't kill you," Nicole said.

"I can see heat waves!" Brooke shouted as she pointed in front of her. Everyone squinted in the direction she was pointing in an effort to see what she had.

"This sudden heat is only a sign that we are closer to Borthenaheim. The area around Borthenaheim is much hotter than the rest of the island. The reason is unknown. Borthnaheim is much cooler than the areas around it. To this day, I still find it strange. It is right next to the ocean. That is why there are boats and ships docked there," Jack explained.

"Ah, water," David sighed dreamily. "That sounds so good right about now. My throat is as dry as the desert!"

Alex stretched his arms to the sky and yawned, walking behind the others silently. Though, even he had to admit it was hotter than he was accustomed to. Suddenly, a black blur passed in front of him, and a strong wind knocked him off his feet. Alex looked beside him, to the forest, where the strange black blur seemed to go. The forest on that side was shrouded in darkness.

Jack and the others turned to see what all the commotion was and gasped when they saw what Alex was staring at. A figure formed within the darkness and began to emerge. What they saw made all of their hearts stop. The figure loomed high above them, its slick black fur shimmering in the sunlight, erie silver eyes shining brightly, and sharp claws digging into the soft earth. The beast that stood before them was a tall black silver-eyed lion— twenty times larger than any other ordinary lion.

The lion opened its large mouth, revealing long sharp teeth, and let out a roar that filled the valley and beyond. Birds flew from the trees and animals scattered, seeking protection. When the lion's roar died down all was silent, and the air was still.

"Alex! Get over here! Now!" Jack shouted.

Alex remained where he was, frozen to the spot. But not with fear. He didn't understand why, but he wasn't afraid of this beast. He felt as if this ferocious lion was familiar.

Jack lunged forward and stood protectively in front of Alex.

"What is that thing?" Nicole asked nervously.

"A Mienthian," Jack said as he breathed unconsciously.

"A what?" Brooke asked.

"Stay back. It's dangerous! Alex get up!" Jack demanded. "We don't know what this thing is capable of."

Alex stood, but he did not move.

"Go!" Jack repeated, nodding to the others.

Alex stared at the lion. The lion stared back. David rushed over and tugged on Alex's arm.

"Dude! C'mon! We have to go." David tugged harder.

Alex shrugged him off and brushed past Jack. Everyone stared in silence and bewilderment as Alex walked to the lion. He stopped when he was barely inches away from its face. The lion bowed his head and dug his claws into the ground. Jack began to run forward but stopped when Alex reached out his hand and let it hang in the air. Then, he began to pet the lion's head slowly.

The lion purred and nudged his head into Alex's shoulder. Alex jumped but continued to stroke it. He remembered where he knew this lion from. The lion was the one that had been following him around and showed up in Alex's dream.

"It's fine," Alex said. "He isn't going to harm us."

The lion laid on the ground and allowed Alex to stoke him some more. Alex turned and faced Jack.

"He's on our side," Alex said.

"How can you be so sure?" Brooke asked.

"Yeah, it's an animal! How can you prove that it's not going to bite our heads off?" David asked. Alex smiled.

"I can't. You are just going to have to trust me," Alex said as he gestured to the lion.

Mark sighed and after a hesitant step walked over and placed a shaking hand on the lion's smooth black fur. Alex was taken aback at first. He didn't expect that quick of a reaction. Mark clamped his eyes shut and waited for the beast to bite his hand off. He waited but he didn't feel anything. Slowly, he opened his eyes to see the lion's eyes were closed and it was purring softly.

As it purred, Mark could feel vibrations through his palm. The lion's fur was soft. Mark laughed nervously and stroked its fur. The lion nudged him with its head and Mark stepped backwards. He laughed nervously and relaxed, petting the smooth fur more calmly. Nicole and Brooke soon followed along with a hesitant and trembling David.

Jack recovered and joined them.

"Just be careful," Jack said.

"Whoa! He's so cold!" David exclaimed, throwing himself into the lion's fur. "Ah… It feels so good! I thought I was going to melt!" Everyone threw themselves onto the lion and sunk into its fur. They all sighed contentedly from the relief of the heat.

"We should get going. If we wait any longer we will have to spend another night," Jack explained.

"Aw… just a couple more minutes?" Brooke whined.

"It's so cold!" Nicole said.

"I'm sorry to drag you away but we have to get into town. It will be much cooler there," Jack said as he started walking, not waiting for any of them to catch up. Reluctantly, they pulled away from the lion and hurried to catch up. Alex stood for a minute and watched them walk before turning to the lion.

"I have to go. Maybe we'll meet again?" Alex turned and ran to the others as they walked away. He had just met the lion, but he felt as if his heart ached from the idea of leaving him. He was a bit farther back from the others just as before. He didn't get far before something nudged him in the back.

He spun around to the lion looming over him. Alex turned and ignored him, walking away. The lion followed, and again, he felt a nudge but he brushed it off and walked on. The lion nudged harder and Alex spun around. The lion rubbed his head against Alex's chest and Alex laughed. Without warning, the lion scooped it's head against Alex's stomach and jerked upward. Alex was sent head-first into the lion's fur and onto his back.

The lion took off and Alex nearly fell off it's long back. Alex clung onto the lion's mane and pulled himself upright. The lion ran unexpectedly fast and Alex bounced up and down, almost as if he were galloping on a horse. He watched as his friends' backs grew closer. He was going to run into them!

"Whoa! Stop! Hold on! Wait!" Alex shouted, but it was no use. The lion kept running. "Look out!" Alex shouted at his friends.

They all turned just in time to see a large black lion leap over them with a boy barely clinging onto its back. Alex gripped the lion's fur tighter as it leapt into the air, barely hanging on. When the lion hit the ground again, it bounded a few more steps before turning to face the astonished group of teenagers and more than amused man in a cloak and top hat.

Jack was laughing hysterically, tears falling from his eyes. Alex had never seen Jack laugh like that before. The four teenagers soon joined him.

"Hey…" Alex trailed off. He was still breathing hard from the constant bouncing and screaming.

"Hay is for horses," Nicole laughed.

"I don't see the humor in this!" Alex shouted. They laughed even harder. "You try riding on the back of a running lion! It isn't exactly easy!" Alex slid off and, as if answering his request, the lion bounded forward and swept the five of them onto his back, running forward. They weren't laughing so hard then.

The lion skidded to a stop. They all slid off and plopped themselves onto the ground in a heap. Jack had much more control over himself than the others. While they were scrambling to get their balance, Jack was standing and brushing dirt off his shirt.

"Now, as much fun as this was we really must be going," said Jack as he held his hands out toward Brooke and David, who was sitting down, waiting for the dizziness that had built up to fade. They both took Jack's hands and staggered to their feet.

Once everyone had gathered themselves Jack ushered them onward. The lion watched as they went for only a second before bounding after Alex. The lion stopped running and began to walk beside Alex. They had walked a few miles before Jack finally noticed the silent lion trailing next to Alex.

"Alex. We can't take that lion with us," Jack said, moving next to Alex so they could walk and talk at the same time without having to yell.

"Why not?" Alex asked.

"It's a lion. We can't bring it into a town! Not to mention it's a Mienthian! We aren't trying to bring attention to ourselves! In fact we are trying to avoid it!" Jack explained.

"What's so special about Mienthians anyway?" Alex asked.

"Mienthians are a very powerful and extremely dangerous species that was believed to be extinct five millennia ago! This lion should not be here!"

"How do you know this lion is one of them?"

"I've studied them in books for quite some time. This lion, according to the books at least, is one of the most powerful of them all. It's said that they didn't belong to any kingdom, world, whatever you wish to call it. They belonged to no one."

"Why'd they go extinct?" Alex grabbed the lion's mane as they walked.

"They were hunted," Jack sighed sadly.

"*Hunted?*" Alex exclaimed. "Why?"

"They were dangerous. Out of control. And they wouldn't join anyone's side. There was also a belief that if you killed one and wore their pelt you could gain some of their power. Many tried and failed but those who succeeded were respected and seen as someone powerful. No one would go against them. No one."

"Did their pelts give them more power?"

"From what I've seen? Not by a long shot. The worst part was, we know next to nothing about them. Only that they were powerful and how to identify them. We had no idea what kind of power they possessed. Only that it was power not to be trifled with. My point is, we can't bring a Mienthian into an overpopulated town with people just craving for more power."

Alex looked down at the ground and watched his feet hit the dirt road. His palm holding the lions fur began to grow cold and Alex jerked his hand away. He looked up at the large lion and watched as black smoke swirled around it. Alex jumped back and stared in astonishment as the lion continued to walk. As the lion walked, the smoke swirled and the lion began to shrink. Alex rubbed his eyes and looked again. Sure enough, the lion continued to shrink.

The lion gradually became smaller and smaller. The smoke finally disappeared and the lion stopped shrinking. In the lion's place stood a small black cat with silver eyes. Alex walked up to the cat and crouched down. The cat walked up to Alex and walked around him, nudging him with its head all the while.

"Is that... the lion?" Brooke asked.

"Yeah... I think so," Alex gasped, unsure of himself. He reached out his hands to the small cat and it walked into his hands. He looked into the cat's silver eyes and, automatically, he knew.

"Yeah, it's him," Alex said confidently. He held out his arm, and the cat walked up it and onto his shoulders. Alex stood and faced Jack. "So? Do you think he can come to town with us now?" He asked.

Jack stared at the small black cat resting on Alex's shoulders. "That... was amazing. I had no idea Mienthians could do that. But yes, we can bring him. Speaking of which, we have stopped too many times for this cat. No more breaks. If we keep going, we should make it there just before sun-down."

FORTY-ONE

After many hours of walking, the teenagers and Jack found that the forest ended and another hill lay before them. The heat tickled their necks and sweat beaded on their skin. David pulled off his hoodie and jacket and tied the sleeves around his waist. Brooke rolled her jeans into cuffs and Nicole tightened her ponytail. Mark wiped sweat from his forehead and did the same with his hoodie as David had done to his.

"I'm melting! This heat will be the death of me! When I'm melted, gather my liquidy remains into a bucket and bring me to my parents for me, will ya?" David fell to his knees dramatically and clutched his chest with one hand while groping at the sky with the other. "Cherry! Is that you?"

"Who's Cherry?" Nicole laughed.

"My dog. She died when I was seven," said David as he paused and gasped for breath. "Oh! It really is her! She's calling for me! Goodbye, my friends! It was a pleasure knowing you all!" David fell onto his hands and took one last breath before falling flat on his face in the grass.

"Oh no! We don't have a bucket to put his melted remains in! Oh well, I guess we'll just have to leave him here. Too bad. He won't be able to see his parents after all," Brooke called behind her as everyone walked past the motionless "melted" body of David. Hearing her words, David shot up and scrambled to his feet. The five of them were already far away from him, farther up the hill.

"Whoa! Wait up! I'm not actually dead!" David ran after them.

"Oh, you weren't?" Nicole asked when David caught up with them.

"I never would have guessed!" Brooke added.

"It's just that you were such a good actor!" Alex chimed in.

"You made me think you were really dead!" Mark said sarcastically.

"How much further do we have to go?" David whined, ignoring their remarks. "The sun is setting for pete's sake!"

"As a matter of fact, not far. Once we get up this hill, we should…," Jack began to explain. Their heads rose above the top of the hill and a cool breeze greeted them. They froze in place once their feet met the top and their eyes widened in awe from the scene before them.

The hill sloped into a valley. To their left was a grand, vast ocean that sparkled in the setting sun. Docks and boats outlined the coastline and, not far from there, was a city. It was so big they couldn't see the other side of it. The dirt road that led up the hill trailed down and through the city. Freighters were being loaded at the docks, and a boat drove around farther out, towing a young man on skis. The sun sank below the horizon, and the sky turned into a dark shade of blue.

"So much better. If we didn't get out of there soon, I would've…," said David as he sagged his shoulders and took in a big gulp of air.

"Melted?" They said in unison.

"Yeah, how'd you know?" David asked.

When they all gathered themselves, they walked down the hill and down the rest of the dirt road and into the city. Jack didn't allow them time to look around. Even if he did, it was too dark to see anything. He quickly ushered the group deep into the city and into a tall hotel. It wasn't much different from the other one. The only difference was that it had an elevator and many more floors. He stopped by the front desk and exchanged a few words before snatching something from the desk clerk's hand and directing them into the elevator. Once the dented and rusting metal doors closed in front of them, Brooke placed her hands on her hips and asked, "So, what's our room number?"

"Our what?" Jack asked, meeting her gaze.

"Our room number! Like, what floor are we on?"

"You'll see when we get there," Jack said, disapproving of her sass. Brooke sighed and turned her attention to another resource to find the information she wanted. The elevator buttons. One button in particular was lit up in yellow. The black print was fading and peeling away, but she could just barely make out the number 13.

"Thirteen!" Brooke screeched. "We are going to the thirteenth floor?"

"That is correct," Jack smiled. "Amazing what the powers of observation can do for you."

"But why?" she asked.

"You aren't superstitious, are you?" David jumped in on the conversation and nudged Brooke's arm with his elbow.

"I've read a lot of stories and seen a lot of videos. Let's just leave it at that," said Brooke as she jerked her arm, shoving David off. A faint *ding* rang through the elevator as it came to a stop and the doors creaked open. The hallway lights were all off except for one at the very end of the hall that flickered on and off. In front of them was a long window that covered the entire wall from ceiling to floor. A dead plant was set in front of it, and two wooden chairs faced each other against opposite walls.

"Honestly, why do you keep picking the dreary hotels and inns?" Brooke asked.

"It's safer," Jack said before stepping out of the elevator and turning down the hallway with the flickering light. He stopped at a door a little ways down and stood in front of it, struggling with a stubborn lock.

"What does he mean by that?" David whispered to Brooke. Nicole stepped in between them and wrapped her arms around their shoulders.

"Whatcha talking about?" Nicole said loudly. Mark stood beside Alex, exchanging a worried glance as they waited for Jack to open the door. When the door finally opened, Jack turned to them, smiled wryly, and said, "The lock is old and cheap."

The room was in better shape than the other, but the setup looked almost exactly the same. The only difference was the large window that covered the back wall. They all rushed over and stared at the many lights of the city. Alex looked up at the night sky and sighed.

"I never did like the city," Alex grumbled as he stroked the large black cat's fur.

"What? Why?" Nicole asked, shooting him a look.

"You can't see the stars," Alex said as he pointed at the plain black sky.

"I've noticed you look at the stars a lot. Are you into astronomy?" Mark asked.

"Ha! Not a chance. I just think the stars look cool," Alex laughed. "What are you into?"

"Me?" Mark backed up and flopped on a bed. "I want to be a chef! Or a baker! I always find myself cooking or baking for my family. I love the feeling that you get when someone enjoys the food you've made!"

Alex sat down against the window and watched as each of his friends went to bed. Jack stood by the door and placed his finger on the door's splintering wood. A purple light shot from his fingertip and covered the entire room before shimmering for a slight second and disappearing. When he was done, he sat down against the wall and listened to their conversation.

"I want to be an FBI agent!" Nicole said.

"I'm going to be an engineer," Brooke said. "What about you, David?" David had remained silent during their conversation and remained silent for a moment before speaking.

"I'm torn between two jobs, so I don't really know," David blushed and looked away.

"Well, what are they?" Mark asked. After a moment, David whispered in response.

"A comic book artist," said David as he averted Mark's gaze.

"And? You said there was two," Brooke pointed out.

"An actor. I want to be an actor," David exclaimed quickly, burying his head in his hands in embarrassment.

"An actor?" Nicole asked flatly.

"You don't have to say it like that!" David groaned.

"Why are you embarrassed about it?" Mark asked.

"You've seen my acting! You know how bad at it I am!" David flopped on his back and stared at the ceiling.

"When you aren't goofing around you can be pretty good," Brooke said.

"What about you, Alex?" David asked, changing the subject. He looked over at Alex, who was sitting on the floor next to the window with the black cat in his lap, purring softly.

"I don't know," Alex replied. "I've never really given it much thought."

"You'll figure something out eventually," Brooke encouraged him. The five of them continued their conversation and moved from one topic to another. As the night dragged on, their conversation trailed off into silence and they nodded off to sleep.

When they woke up the next morning, Jack brought the five teenagers into the city. This city was much cleaner than any other city they had ever seen. Although there were some tall buildings, there weren't any tall enough to be considered skyscrapers. Many people were in the streets, including unsupervised children and teenagers their own age. Magic surrounded everything on every corner.

They walked for blocks until they came to a small shop on a crowded street. They stepped inside to find shelves stacked from top to bottom in books and maps and scrolls. The shop was dimly lit by candle-light. A brighter light emanated from deep within the building. David leaned forward and poked Alex in the side.

"Look, Alex! Books," David teased.

"Yeah, I can see that," said Alex as he shrugged him off.

Jack walked through the middle bookshelf and deeper into the store. Not a single person was in sight. In the very back of the store was a red curtain that draped over the back wall. Jack pushed it aside and stepped through; the others followed. Inside was a small room filled with burning candles. Bookshelves lined the walls and papers and scrolls and maps littered the floor. In the very middle of the room was a desk with a large book laid out on top of papers covered in ink. On the corner of the desk was a silver ball that floated motionless in the air.

A man sat behind the desk leafing through the pages of the book, unaware of their presence. The man mumbled to himself and turned around. He ran his fingers along the bookshelf until his finger landed on one title. He slid the book off the shelf and slammed it on top of the other one. A cloud of dust filled the room.

Jack cleared his throat into a clamped fist in an effort to get the man's attention. The man did not hear him and continued to leaf through the second book. Jack cleared his throat once again, this time louder. The man looked up, surprised, then threw his arms out in greeting once he saw who had entered his shop. It was only then that Alex got a good look at him.

The man was as tall as Jack with gray hair saturated with ink. He wore a pair of thin gold-colored glasses with magnifying pieces that moved up and down. He wore a dark gray shirt with sleeves rolled up to his forearms, revealing unyielding muscular arms. His hands were covered in ink-stained brown leather gloves; Ink-stained overalls hung loosely from his shoulders. He wore light-brown work boots. A jubilant spark overcame the dullness of his old gray eyes.

The man lifted up the magnifying part of his spectacles and walked around the table. He walked up to Jack with a broad smile and clamped his hands on Jack's shoulders. Jack smiled back and they both hugged one another, patting each other's backs merrily. When they finally let go of one another, they were laughing.

"Jack Pandemonium! It's good to see you, old friend! Where in the world have you been?" The man laughed cheerfully.

"Everywhere and nowhere! A lot has happened since the last time we've met!" Jack replied. "What have you done to your hair?"

"Oh this?" The man reached up and ran a hand through his hair. "A bucket of ink fell off the shelf and my head happened to be in its path!"

"Yes, the ink but what about the color? Your hair is gray, my old friend!"

"Jack, I am of old age. Though my dying day still has yet to come!"

"You may be old in body, but your soul is as youthful as ever! Now, there are some people I'd like you to meet," Jack exclaimed, turning the man around to face the five teenagers. "Darrien, these are Alex, Brooke, David, Nicole, and Mark."

Darrien's eyes widened at the sight of them and the corner of his mouth rose up in a smirk. "How long has it been? I didn't think it was that long since we had seen each other! I never thought of you as one to have children!" Darrien exclaimed.

"No! Of course not! These aren't my children! Have you lost your mind?" Jack shouted.

"Haha! Yes, of course I am aware that these are not your own. I am only joking," Darrien laughed haughtily. "So, whose are they, then?"

"That is one of the things I have come here for," Jack sighed. "They are human!"

Darrien's eyes widened and the color drained from his face. He glanced back at the five of them, then back to Jack. "Humans? This far in the island! That is unheard of! Completely impossible! What are they doing here?"

"They crashed here after a storm. I need to get them back to the mainland as soon as possible."

"We need to speak about this matter privately," said Darrien as he rushed into the main part of his shop and closed all of the curtains and blew out all the candles. He locked the door and hurried back to the other side of the curtain. He sat down at his desk and folded his hands in front of him.

"I trust you will keep this under wraps?" Jack asked.

"Of course. I trust you have good reason to be taking care of these humans," Darrien said as he watched suspiciously from the corner of his eye as Alex and the others got comfortable, fully aware they were going to be there a while. "Please, tell me how they were able to survive the island. Humans have never even made it past the beach! Which side of the island have they come from?"

"Far south. I began to assist them further along their journey, though. A good portion of their success was made on their own," Jack replied.

"Far south? You've nearly made it halfway across the island! This is incredible!" Darrien glanced at the teenagers warily. Jack sensed Darrien's discomfort and brought his attention to the group.

"Why don't you head out to one of the restaurants and get yourselves some lunch? Darrien and I will stay here and catch up on things," Jack told them. "Meet back here when you are done."

"We don't have any money," David pointed out.

"Here. Take this. This should be enough," Jack said as he took a small brown drawstring bag out of his cloak and held it out. Mark took the money and placed it in his pocket. The five of them turned to leave but were stopped when Darrien called out to them.

"There is a decent restaurant that is also cheap by the beach. I highly recommend it," Darrien called.

"Thanks! We'll look for it!" Nicole called back as they walked out the door.

"So, how are we going to get to the beach?" David asked once they were outside.

"Follow the scent of the ocean," Alex said.

"I can't smell anything right now. We aren't hound dogs you know," Brooke said as she tapped the side of her nose.

"I can smell it. Just follow me." Alex sniffed the air then began walking. To their surprise, they weren't very far from the beach at all. After two blocks of walking, the others began to smell the salt water drift into their nostrils. The cobbled streets soon turned to sand, and they entered a calmer and less dense part of the city. The buildings were smaller, including the kinds of houses they were familiar with. Some buildings stood above the sand on beams while others were floating. Floating steps led up to porches for the floating ones, while wooden steps were connected to the ones on stilts. People of all ages populated the sandy streets. At the very end of one street was a park where a large group of teenagers and children played baseball.

They finally found the restaurant that Darrien had recommended. It rested stilts and its back side facing the sea. On the front porch were tables with umbrellas without poles that hung in the air. The restaurant didn't seem especially busy, for there were not many people out on the porch. White double doors hung open, inviting customers inside.

They climbed the steps to the restaurant and walked through the doors. The inside was lit by a chandelier. Small black tables were scattered about the room and a long counter was covered in sweets and drinks. A woman stood at a podium next to the door, gathering menus. She wore a pink short-sleeved shirt and black pants. A black apron hung around her waist and a white towel was hung against it. Inside the pockets of the apron were a notepad, a pen, and straws. Her hair was tied up in a tight ponytail. She looked as if she were a senior in high school.

"May I help you?" the young woman asked.

"Can we have a table, please?" Alex asked.

"Of course. How many?" the hostess asked.

"Five," Brooke spoke up.

"Please follow me." The woman took a stack of menus out of the pile on the podium and began to walk to the back of the restaurant. In the back was another set of doors that led to a porch that overlooked the sea. Connected to the porch was a wide wooden staircase that led to the beach. The woman guided them outside and sat them at a table before leaving.

Soon after the hostess left, another woman came and took their order. When they finished eating, they sat back and let the cool breeze drift up from the ocean and cool their heads from the summer heat.

The small black cat left its perch on Alex's shoulders and curled itself up in his lap. The cat was always cold to the touch. Alex began to stroke its fur and the cat purred happily in thanks.

"What are you going to name him?" Mark asked.

"Name who?" Alex asked.

"The cat. What are you going to name the cat?" Nicole said.

"I don't know. I'm still thinking," Alex explained. Alex stared at the cat in his lap as the others talked. What was he going to call him? He needed a name. Wait… what if he already had a name? The cat looked up at him with its bright silver eyes as if it knew what Alex was thinking. The cat's eyes flashed brightly for a moment and, unknown to Alex, his own eyes did as well. At that moment, somehow, Alex knew what the cat's name would be.

"Argent," Alex said.

"What?" Brooke asked.

"His name is Argent," Alex repeated.

"Well, now at least we know what to call him," Mark remarked.

The server who took their order walked over to them and stuck out her hand.

"That will be five ngoen, please," the woman stated.

David leaned over and whispered to Mark, "What does she mean by that?"

"I think she means money," said Mark as he leaned to the side and dug around in his pocket. He pulled out the small brown drawstring bag Jack had given him. He pulled out five coins from the bag and handed it to the woman. She took the coins and held her hand out once more. Mark looked at it and arched an eyebrow in confusion. What else was he supposed to do? Then it occurred to him. He pulled out five more coins and put them in her palm. The woman smiled, nodded gratefully, and tucked the extra coins into her apron.

"Have a nice day!" the woman called over her shoulder as she walked away.

"What should we do next? I'm sure Jack wouldn't mind if we stayed out a bit longer," said David as the corner of his mouth rose in a mischievous smirk.

"How about the beach?" Brooke offered.

"Yes! Let's go!" Nicole exclaimed. They all nodded in agreement and pushed back their chairs, making their way down the steps.

FORTY-TWO

Jack and Darrien watched behind the curtains and listened for the sound of the door opening and closing. As soon as they were sure the teens had gone, the pair got straight to the point.

"Are you mad? How could you bring humans to Alsijn? Sheltering humans will get you killed!" Darrien shouted.

"Yes, I understand that! But I am not the one that brought them here in the first place! I am only assisting in getting them out of here and back to where they belong!" Jack countered.

"And where is that exactly?"

"The mainland. Their families. Their homes."

Their yelling ceased after Jack's words. A brief silence passed between them.

"How are you going to manage that?" Darrien finally asked. "You can't send them through your portals or…"

"I know," Jack snapped. "We'll board the first passenger ship that leaves."

"I can help with that."

"Something is bothering me, though."

"And that is?"

"They are humans…"

"Good! That should bother you!"

"I didn't finish. They are humans and yet they have the ability to fly. I have seen evidence that they also have many other abilities, powers, magic, whatever you wish to call it. I have seen it and I can sense it. All that I've seen and sensed, however, feels like merely the tip of the iceberg." Jack waited for his words to sink in.

"That is concerning," Darrien nodded. "And you say that they survived some chunk of the island without your assistance?"

"This is true," said Jack as he looked to the floor and sighed. "You do understand that we may have to tell them about our history. They are not like their own kind. They will have to learn it for both the kingdom's sake, and theirs."

Darrien ran a gloved hand through his gray ink-stained hair and chuckled. "You always were a troublesome boy."

"Who said I ever stopped?"

Alex's bare feet sank in the scorching sand. Argent walked beside him as the others ran ahead. Children were scattered about the beach, running up and down the sand and swimming into the depths of the ocean. A man in a boat moved his glowing hands up and down as fish bathed in the same glow left the sea and flopped into his boat.

"Come one, come all! Into the sea!" Brooke shouted as she ran toward the water.

"But we don't have any extra clothes!" David told her.

"Who cares?" Nicole grabbed his arm and dragged him into the water. As David and Nicole ran past Alex and Mark, David squirmed out of Nicole's grip and latched himself onto Mark's and Alex's wrists, dragging them behind him.

The warm water splashed against their faces, and they threw their arms up instinctively to protect their eyes from the sprays. Alex found it difficult to swim with a giant sword on his back along with a leather jacket weighing him down, but he didn't find it safe to part with it in this strange world. Afraid he might damage them, he placed his sword and sheath on the beach anyway, along with his jacket. It was funny, Alex thought. No matter what happened to them, the storm, the shark, the cavern, the cliff, they always found themselves running into the water as though they had no cares in the world.

They splashed and wrestled and swam and played. Before they knew it, the sun had begun to sink into the horizon once again. They reluctantly made their way out of the water and scooped up their shoes from the sand, which were guarded by a sleeping cat that was not particularly fond of water. The five walked back to the shop completely drenched and barefoot, carrying their shoes and socks.

Argent refused to rest upon Alex's soaking shoulders. Instead, he strutted by his side, avoiding any falling drops of water.

Jack and Darrien laughed loudly as they recalled a fond memory. They quieted down once they heard the door open and laughing from the front of the shop. Jack tilted back in his chair and pulled back the curtain separating the shop from the room he was in.

"We are back here!" Jack called, fully aware of who had entered the shop.

"We can't come in any farther than this! We will just wait until you are done!" Nicole called from the door.

"Yeah, we're still wet!" David said with a laugh.

Darrien and Jack exchanged a confused glance before standing up and making their way through the shelves and stacks of scrolls to the front of the shop. When they rounded the last shelf, they stood staring at the soaked teens before them.

"Why in the world are you drenched in water?" Jack asked, slightly raising his voice.

"We hung out at the beach. No big deal. We'll dry sooner or later," said Brooke as she rolled her eyes.

"Do you want to get sick? Because in clothes like that, that is what will happen. I don't want to have to be looking after five sick human teenagers. I already have enough on my plate," Jack said as he scolded them and waved a glowing hand in front of them. A dark purple smoky cloud formed above them and lowered onto them, drying their clothes in the process. Darrien leaned against a shelf and smiled, watching the exchange before him. Once they were dry, Darrien walked up behind Jack and whispered in his ear.

"You sure they aren't your kids?" Darrien chuckled as Jack growled and opened his mouth to protest. "All righty then!" Darrien clapped his hands together before Jack could speak. "It has gotten awfully late! You had your fun, but I really must kick you out!"

Jack pushed them out of the shop and waved goodbye as Darrien locked the door behind them. He stood in front of the window and watched as they turned the corner and out of sight. He sighed and turned back to his shop, immediately setting to work. He had some tickets to retrieve.

"What's his job?" Mark asked as they walked along the now-dark street back to the hotel. "I figured he just ran a bookstore, but when I saw the back room I wasn't quite so sure."

"He's a cartographer," Jack told him. "I told you about him a while ago. He's the friend I said we had to go visit. The books in that store are all based on travel and maps and past cartographers and so on. Darrien and I go quite a ways back. He is a good man."

The exhausted group remained silent as the elevator moved upward. All were eager to return to their beds, except for one. Everyone had fallen asleep only moments after their arrival. Alex, however, was not at all tired and found himself lying awake and bored. Finally giving up, Alex came to the conclusion that he would not be sleeping that night. Since they were in the city, he could not see the stars so he had nothing to occupy himself with.

Alex quietly stood and stealthily moved past a sleeping Jack. Argent perked his head up at the sudden movement and meowed at Alex. Alex turned to the small black cat curled up by the window. He moved his finger up to his lips and the cat ceased the noise. He turned back around and began walking to the door. As he walked, his foot collided with the dresser and he yelped in pain. The dresser wobbled against the wall, and Alex thrust his hands forward to steady it.

"Where do you think you are going?" Jack whispered. Alex looked up at Jack in surprise. He was hoping to take his leave going unnoticed.

"I'm sorry to wake you," Alex apologized. "I'm heading out."

"Why do you feel the need to leave?" Jack asked.

"I couldn't sleep. I'm going to look for a bookstore. I won't be gone all night," Alex replied.

Jack nodded and crossed his arms over his chest, closing his eyes. Alex whispered his thanks and proceeded to make his way to the door. As he reached for the handle, he felt something soft brush past his legs. Alex looked down to see Argent rubbing his leg. The feline jumped up onto Alex's shoulders, and Alex snuck out the door, closing it softly behind him.

Alex pulled his headphones over his ears as he walked down the busy city street. People walked back and forth, all in their own hurry and keeping to themselves. Alex occasionally saw kids of different ages walking or hanging out in groups, but mostly he was the only one of his age out on the street. He scanned the buildings as he went by, in search of a bookstore.

Finally, he found one on the opposite side of the street. Once there was a break in traffic, Alex made his way across. The shop was a six story building. Above the doorway was a sign that read, "The Timekeeper's Books." Alex stepped inside and was welcomed by a warm, bright light.

In a circular room with a high ceiling— so high, in fact, that Alex couldn't see the top. It was strange, bigger inside than outside. The walls were lined with books and bookshelves that rose high in the air. They were the tallest Alex had ever seen. Ladders with wheels leaned against the bookshelves that allowed the customers to reach higher. A cloud lingered above him and prevented him from seeing any farther above, obscuring the ceiling and more floors. The books extended both below and above the clouds. A staircase spiraled around the room and led up to small platforms next to the books. The platforms then moved around so that every book was within arm's reach. Candles floated in the air, surrounded by gold light, lighting up the room. Not a single shadow was to be seen. People roamed the shop and perused the books. Next to Alex was a long, smooth wooden checkout counter. Five candles floated, spaced out, only inches from the wooden surface. A man, two women, and a boy around the age of eight sat behind the counter.

The boy was perched on a stool; he sat, hunched over, absorbed in a book. The kid wore brown pants with the cuffs rolled up to his calves and a black hoodie with the sleeves pushed up above his elbows. The hood was pulled up over his head, obscuring his face from view. The man standing beside him looked to be about fifty with a strong build, gray hair and equally gray eyes. He wore a green vest over a white T-shirt and brown pants. His shoes were made of brown leather and shone slightly beneath the candle-light. On the other side of the boy, farther down the counter, was a plump woman with gray hair and gray eyes. Her black glasses rested on her nose and a chain connected them to her pink floral-patterned shirt. Her long wavy tan skirt matched perfectly with her tan flats. Lastly, was the slim woman at the end. This gray-eyed woman looked about thirty. Her long brown hair was pinned up in a bun, and she wore a long black sweater and gray pants. Black high heels were the same shade of black as her sweater. As the man busily flipped through files, the two women were taking care of the customers that were standing in line, ready to buy their books of choice.

Alex closed his mouth, which, he discovered, had been open in astonishment. He walked into an aisle between shelves and began to look at the spines of books. When he got to the ladder at the end of the aisle, he climbed it and began to pull himself across the shelf, reading the spines as he went. He picked one up and read the red cover. The title was written in some other language that he couldn't understand. Alex moved to put the book back but stopped when he saw the title again. This time it was written in English. That was weird. Alex pulled the book back and read the cover: "Understanding a Dragon." The letters looped and swirled in fine gold print. Below the title was a gold silhouette of a dragon curled into a ball. Alex turned his head and looked at Argent questioningly.

"You can turn into a cat and a lion. Can you turn into a dragon, too?" Alex asked the small black cat. Argent picked his head up off of his paws and meowed before setting his head back down and closing his eyes. "I'll take that as a no then," said Alex as he slid the book back onto the shelf and paused.

"If magic exists and you exist, does that mean dragons exist too?" Alex muttered under his breath. That shed a whole new light on things. What else is real that he thought for so long was a lie? Alex began to climb down the ladder but stopped halfway when he heard a grunt and a crash below him. He looked down to see the boy sprawled across the floor, covered in books.

Alex climbed down the rest of the rails and ran quickly to the boy's aid. He immediately began to gather up the books scattered about the floor into a neat pile as the boy, seemingly unharmed, did the same. They continued to do this in silence until the job was done. That was when Alex was able to get a good look at the kid. His face was covered from the hood pulled over his head, so Alex was unable to make out the boy's face or hair. But what he hadn't noticed before was that the youngster was barefoot. The skin on his feet was rough and dirty from repeated exposure to the hard ground.

"Are you all right?" Alex asked as he handed a stack of books to the boy.

"Thanks for the help," the boy muttered as he took the books and walked off. Alex watched as he walked to the end of the aisle and placed one of the books in an empty slot before moving on. Alex jogged after the kid and caught up with him.

"So… what'cha doin'?" Alex asked as he followed the boy.

"Putting books away. What's it look like?" the boy asked.

"Oh. Right. Having fun?"

"Before I met you? Yeah. I was."

The boy turned and walked to the other side of the aisle. Alex ignored his remark and continued to follow him.

"So, how old are you?"

"I'm eight."

"You seem much more mature for your age. My name is—"

"Alex. I know."

Alex stared wide-eyed at the boy. How did he know his name?

"You mean you've been talking to me this whole time and you didn't know?" The boy asked, turning slightly toward Alex but making sure to keep his face covered.

"Know what?"

"Never mind," said the young sales clerk as he made his way to the shelves connected to the walls, ignoring Alex as he walked. Or at least, showing as little attention to him as possible.

"Well, since you already know my name, I think it's only appropriate that I know yours." Alex crossed his arms and stood behind the boy as he waited for him to put the last book in the stack on the shelf.

"Etha—" The boy froze in place as he realized what he was doing. He clenched his fist and spun around. He whipped his hood off, revealing a boy with dull gray eyes and raven black hair. "How am I talking to you?" The boy whispered harshly. Alex cocked his head innocently as a mischievous smirk spread across his face.

"First, you open your mouth and your brain coordinates your stomach muscles, voice box, lungs, lips, tongue, teeth, and your nose to create any noise, words, or speech. This then allows others to understand any message you wish to convey to them. Sometimes you even engage in meaningful conversation! It really is magic!" Alex explained sarcastically.

The boy growled in response and stormed off. Alex quickly followed.

"Hey! I didn't really catch your name," Alex said to him once he caught up to the agitated child.

"Are you going to leave me alone at all?" the boy complained.

"Probably not, no," said Alex with a chuckle.

"It's Ethan."

"It's a pleasure to meet you, Ethan." Alex darted in front of the boy and stuck his hand out. Ethan stared at Alex's hand with wide eyes. Reluctantly, he took Alex's hand and shook it slowly.

"Are you usually this annoying?"

"Actually, no. Not usually."

"That's good to know," said Ethan as he let go of Alex's grip and stared at him suspiciously. Alex dropped the playful attitude when he noticed the distrust in the boy's eyes.

"What's up?" Alex asked.

"You know what I am, don't you? So why are you talking to me?" Ethan asked. Venom coated his voice.

"Because I can. Can't I? Or are you some super-important prince that I need to stay away from for security reasons?"

"No. I'm not," Ethan sighed as if some great burden was upon his shoulders.

"Then what are you so worried about?"

"I'm a—"

"Ethan! What are you doing?" A voice shouted from the end of the aisle. Alex and Ethan both turned to see the man from the front desk running at them. His face was coated with concern. When he finally caught up to the two boys, he seemed to notice Alex for the first time. His whole expression changed to that of menace when he saw Alex.

"What are you doing to my grandson?" The man jabbed a strong finger into Alex's chest, forcing him to back up a step. The stranger continued to step forward, pushing Alex back. Alex threw his hands up in the air to show he meant no harm when his back came in contact with a shelf.

"Are you harassing him? What are you doing?" the man repeated.

"Sir, I am very sorry if I did anything wrong, but I was unaware of it. Can I ask what I might have done? I am not here to cause any trouble," Alex said firmly, not breaking eye contact with the frustrated man.

The man's eyes widened at Alex's reaction but quickly narrowed. There was a strong resemblance between the man and Ethan, especially their eyes. The encounter between Alex and the grandfather caught the boy's attention. Ethan cleared his throat and walked up to his grandfather.

"Relax. He didn't mean any harm," Ethan said. Immediately, the man relaxed and his expression softened. But his eyes remained fixed on Alex. Alex leaned off the shelf and began to pick up the few books that had fallen. Ethan and the man watched as Alex gathered the books and exchanged confused glances.

"So is anyone going to tell me what's going on?" Alex asked once all of the books were gathered.

"My name is Mr. Epoch. My question for you is, why were you talking to Ethan?" Mr. Epoch asked.

"Again, with this question! Can't a kid just talk to someone without anyone jumping to conclusions?" Alex threw his hands up in the air in annoyance.

"I don't think he knows what we are," Ethan whispered in Mr. Epoch's ear.

"It's strange. Most anyone can sense what we are immediately," Mr. Epoch whispered back.

"What don't I know?" Alex asked, having heard their poorly hidden exchange of words. Mr. Epoch straightened and sternly looked Alex in the eye.

"We are Pardictors," Mr. Epoch said. Alex stared back at them in confusion.

"What is that supposed to mean?" Alex asked.

"You… don't know what a Pardictor is?" Ethan asked. Ethan and Mr. Epoch stared at Alex in astonishment.

"Should I?" Alex asked. "Why are you people so bewildered over this?"

"I am terribly sorry for my irrational actions. They were false but I assure you, they were appropriate. May I ask what you are? What is your race? I like to ask people before seeing myself," Mr. Epoch added.

"What do you mean by what am I?" Alex asked.

"What species are you?" Ethan translated.

"Um… I'm human," Alex said hesitantly. "Aren't you human?"

Mr. Epoch and Ethan stepped back in shock. Their eyes were wide and mouths agape as they stared at Alex in disbelief.

"Dear God! A human! On Alsjin! It's not possible!" Mr. Epoch cried.

"Can someone fill me in?" Alex nearly shouted.

Mr. Epoch grabbed Alex and Ethan by the arm and pulled them into a huddle.

"You must speak of this to no one! Do not tell anyone you are human! You are lucky you have come across us before you told anyone else. If the wrong person finds out what you are, you will be put in grave danger!" Mr. Epoch explained. "Ethan! Never speak of this encounter! Ever! Do you understand me?"

"Yes, sir!" Alex and Ethan replied in unison.

"Wait!" Alex cried in sudden realization. "What time is it?"

"5:30 in the morning. The sun should be rising soon." Mr. Epoch looked at his watch and read the time. "Why?"

"I've got to go!" Alex took off down the aisle. When he reached the end, he turned. "Can I come back later today?" Alex called.

"Of course!" Mr. Epoch called back after a moment of hesitation. Alex smiled and waved before turning back around and running out the door. Where had the time gone?

Ethan turned toward his grandfather. "Will you really let him come back?" he asked. "Even if he's a human?"

"Why, of course! I wouldn't get much business if I didn't let people in just because they were different now, would I?" Mr. Epoch smiled at his grandson.

"No. No, you wouldn't," Ethan replied as he smiled before turning and walking back among the shelves.

FORTY-THREE

Alex dashed around the corner and up the sidewalk to the hotel. He was just outside the door when he slammed face-first into an unsuspecting stranger. He and the unsuspecting stranger toppled backward and onto the concrete pavement. Alex slammed his hands out in front of him and just barely caught himself in time. A small jolt coursed through his wrists, but he shook it off as he quickly moved to help the stranger. He held out his hand to the stranger, who was lying face-down on the ground.

"I am so sorry! Are you all right?" Alex asked with worry and guilt in his voice. He received a groan in response. The stranger's hand swiped Alex's away as he slowly stood up. Alex could barely make out his features for he wore a robe that covered his entire body, including his head. Alex caught a flash of a mix of orange, red, and yellow beneath the hood as the man growled.

The man looked up at Alex for the first time and gasped before rushing down the steps and farther down the sidewalk. Beneath the man's robe were two bare feet. *Seriously? Does anyone wear shoes anymore?* Alex watched as the cloaked man disappeared down the street before turning back to the doors. In front of the doors beneath the overhang stood Jack, Nicole, Brooke, David, and Mark.

"I see you've been making new friends," Nicole smirked.

"How long have you guys been standing there?" Alex asked.

"Only long enough to see that guy push past you. Man, he had an attitude. He even growled!" Brooke laughed.

"I don't blame him. I was the one who knocked him over," said Alex, defending the stranger.

"Why'd you do that?" Mark asked.

"I was rushing! I had to get back before you guys left!" Alex replied.

"All right, well, I'm famished! Let's please just go already!" David threw his hands out and gestured to the steps dramatically. The group walked down the steps and Alex followed next to Jack.

"I thought you said you wouldn't be gone all night," Jack said to Alex.

"Yeah, I lost track of time. I really didn't realize how late it had gotten. By the time I had realized it, the sun was just about to rise," Alex replied.

"I trust you found what you were looking for?" Jack asked skeptically. "That is, if you actually went?"

"Of course I did! In fact the bookstore I found was absolutely spectacular! It was humongous! There were so many books! Actually, I was planning on going back later today."

"What is the name of this 'spectacular' bookstore?"

"Timekeeper's Books."

Jack's eyes widened at the mention of that name, but he quickly composed himself before too much of his surprise could show. Although Alex caught it all, he chose not to ask about his reaction.

Jensen groaned as the pain flowed through his nose after coming in contact with the concrete slab. He heard the voice of a boy offer to help him up. Out of the corner of his eye he could see the boy's hand outstretched toward him. Jensen slapped it away and quickly stood. He growled at the boy for knocking him over— let alone talk to him.

He trusted his features were hidden as he looked down at the teenage boy who was almost as tall as he was. He gasped when he realized who it was. He was one of *them*. Jensen brushed past him and quickly hurried down the steps to get away from him before his cover was blown.

As soon as he was far enough away, Jensen ducked into an abandoned alley. He held out his palm and a small wall of fire formed. Seconds later his sister, Jenna, appeared within the fiery wall. This technique reminded him of holograms the Resolton frequently used. Of course, theirs had many flaws. Their holograms could be easily hacked, or "wire-taped," as they called it, and broken. He wasn't familiar with the latest technology. Jensen lowered his hood. His black hair fell in front of his slightly glowing orange eyes, but he didn't bother brushing it away. His eyes glowed when he was excited, especially when he gained coveted information.

"What did you learn? Where are they?" his sister asked from the fire wall. Her eyes began to glow slightly once she saw him. She always knew exactly why his eyes glowed. Her eyes did the same, after all, although, not always for the same reason.

"They're staying at the Hilonton Hotel. I probably wouldn't know they were if I hadn't run into one on my way out. Or more like he ran into me."

"He didn't see you, did he?" Jenna asked. "You didn't blow our cover?"

"No! Of course not. He didn't see me," Jensen replied angrily. Did his sister take him for a fool? He wasn't an amateur. He knew how to handle things. He'd been in this business for ten years, after all!

"Relax! I was only asking. Otherwise good work."

"When do we plan on making our move?"

"Jobs like these take time and patience. Lots and lots of patience."

"I'm aware."

"I know you are. Now we find who they are associating themselves with. See how much they care about these people. Get under their skin. Once they are so blinded by the need for vengeance, then and only then, do we strike," said Jenna with an evil smile.

"We might want to wait a bit longer. If we wish to get under the humans' skin, we will have to wait for them to grow close to others. They don't know anyone. Even if it's only one of them that grows close to someone."

"That might happen sooner than we thought. I followed the boy last night. He seems to be on the verge of a relationship with those Pardictors," Jensen replied. Jenna scrunched her nose up in disgust. "As to why them, I have no idea."

"We will have to talk more about this later. I'm heading your way." Jensen clamped his fist shut, putting out the small fiery image of his sister. He pulled his hood back over his head before walking out of the alley and onto the crowded city streets.

"So, I'll see you guys later?" Alex asked as they stepped out of the diner.

"Where are you going?" Nicole asked with a hint of attitude in her voice.

"A bookstore," Alex replied simply.

"Meet us up for lunch at the place we ate yesterday. We're going to go exploring the city ourselves," Mark said.

"Nicole and I thought we saw an arcade someplace and wanted to go check that out," David explained.

"I'm going to go look for some autoshop or something. I want to see if I can figure out how the cars work here. That might help me make some sense of things. Plus, it'd be nice to be with something familiar in this strange world," Brooke said.

"You like cars?" Alex asked, unaware that was something Brooke was into.

"You didn't know that? My dad repairs cars for a living. I help him out from time to time and he sometimes lets me drive them," said Brooke with her head held high.

"Aren't you too young to even have a permit?"

"The cops in our town know me pretty well. I am very responsible. They don't mind it as long as I am obeying the laws."

"That's not the only thing they know about her," said David as he elbowed her in the arm.

"Shut up! That was a one-time thing!" Brooke hissed. Her proud demeanor was replaced with embarrassment.

"Really? One time?" Nicole dragged her words accusatively. "More like one time too many."

"Thirteen to be exact," David said matter-of-factly.

"Who's counting?" Brooke snapped.

"I am," David said as he smirked.

"What are you talking about?" Alex asked, utterly confused.

"I am quite confused myself," Jack said, having been listening to the conversation with growing interest.

"Brooke makes all sorts of inventions at her house with spare parts or things she finds in random places. Much of it is from the junkyard. Let's just say more than a few have gone AWOL," Mark chimed in.

"Oh yeah? And where do you plan on going?" Brooke scoffed, her cheeks flushed to a hot pink.

"Nowhere. I want to inquire how the cooks were able to make the consumme so clear. I've been trying for a number of months now and still have yet to figure it out," said Mark as he pointed with his thumb toward the diner behind them.

"What's consomme?" David asked.

"It's a type of clear soup made from chicken broth. It's very hard to make as the process to make it requires very complicated procedures, and it needs to be perfectly clear in the end. If it isn't, you know you failed," Mark explained. "I also want to know why they have such an exotic menu for a diner. They have things like seafood paella, som tam, chilli crab, arepas, bunny chow, pastel de nata, rendang, baked alaska, cassoulet, these are all meals from around the world. Why and how is this diner making them?" Mark ranted, listing various foods off his fingers.

"You have fun with that," Nicole said sarcastically.

"What? I really will!" Mark exclaimed.

"Mark, have fun. I have to go!" Alex said as he began to walk off.

"Good luck, Mark," Brooke called as she dashed down the road and waved goodbye. David and Nicole took off to find the arcade, and Jack headed to his cartographer friend, leaving Mark standing alone in front of the diner. Mark watched as his friends went their separate ways before turning and walking back through the diner doors.

Mark had only been in the diner for half an hour more before he found himself on his way again. He had walked up to one of the waitresses behind the front counter and had complimented the diner on its peculiar but delicious cuisine. He had asked her why the menu was the way it was, and she replied quickly, spouting off an intricate and spellbinding story that Mark knew was merely a marketing tactic, with little to no truth in it.

Mark patiently waited as the waitress finished her story and forced out a few amazed remarks before he asked her if he could speak to any of the cooks. Her attitude changed then, from happy and eager to draw in more customers, to defensive and skeptical. No matter how hard he tried, in the end, Mark had left the diner as ignorant as he was when he first walked in.

Brooke walked four blocks before she came across an autoshop. It was a short blue building with cracked walls and chipped paint. The sign at the top was rusted out and the letters had peeled away. The front of the building was made up of three wide garage doors that were all open, revealing a number of cars being worked on inside.

One particular car caught her attention. An old blue 1973 Chevrolet Nova with two stripes on the hood was lifted on one side while a man in blue overalls and a white oil-stained shirt continued to attach a tire to the car. The car was a beauty, and oddly enough, normal. Freshly polished and waxed; the sun glinted off the shining metal surface.

The man leaned back on the ground and cursed, wiping away sweat that had formed on his forehead. Brooke walked toward the man and tapped on his shoulder. The repairman jumped, clearly startled, and arched his neck to see who had tapped his shoulder.

"What seems to be the issue?" she asked.

"I can't seem to get this tire to stay on," the man growled. He shrugged her hand off his shoulder and turned back to the tire. "What can I help you with?"

"Oh nothing, I just noticed you were having some trouble there so I wanted to see what I could do to help," Brooke said with a shrug.

"*You?*" The man scoffed. "What could *you* possibly do to help?"

"Excuse me?" Brooke was taken aback by this man's rude response.

"I don't think I need help from a teenager. Go get an education," the man retorted before placing a wrench on a nut and pulling down. Brooke crossed her arms across her chest in annoyance. What did her age have to do with anything? Brooke smirked as she unfolded her arms. She made her way to the other side of the car. The man ignored her as she bent down and out of sight. When she stood back up again, she stood in front of the man and leaned on the side of the car. Brooke opened her palm and let a small metal bolt fall onto the floor with a clink. The man picked up the small bolt and looked to the teenage girl for an explanation. Brooke smiled knowingly.

"Would you look at that?" Brooke stood up straight and strode confidently out of the shop, leaving a baffled and defeated man behind her.

David and Nicole hurried through the large glass doors of the arcade. Both were extremely excited. They couldn't recall how long it had been since they had gone to an arcade. Game consoles and game boxes were lined up in rows. Other, more active and manual games were scattered between the rows and on the walls. David and Nicole immediately took off in separate directions, each finding game after game to engross themselves in.

Two hours passed before they saw each other again. David had found a large crowd gathered around one particular game, and in that crowd he found Nicole. She was staring up at the game with wide eyes. David hadn't bothered to see what game it was. He was too focused on getting Nicole's attention. She finally looked down at him when he began to shake her arm.

"Check it out!" Nicole nodded toward the game. For the first time, David got a good look at it. It was one of those Dance Dance Revolution games. The platform had variously colored tiles that lit up with arrows on them. A screen in front of the platform showed two columns with arrows that matched the ones on the platform. When the specific arrows reached a line at the top, the player would have to hit the same arrow with their foot on the platform. There were thousands of different levels and the farther up you went, the harder it got.

At the moment, two teenage boys were competing viciously at one of the harder levels. That was one of the reasons the crowd had formed. The other reason was that one of the boys seemed indestructible. He wore a dark blue baseball cap and a black shirt. A grey hoodie was wrapped around his waist and he wore tan shorts. His shoes were torn up and dirty. His feet moved so fast they were almost a blur. He had short blonde hair and muddy brown eyes. The boy in the blue laughed aloud as the kid next to him failed and his screen flashed red. The boy that failed jumped off the platform and a few other teenagers clapped him on the back, cheering him up.

"Who's next?" The boy shouted across the crowd. You could tell that he knew he would win against anyone who dared try. The crowd burst to life as people pushed and pulled their way through the crowd and over to the platform, desperate to show their skill.

David heard Nicole growl next to him and he snapped his head to look at her. She was glaring at the boy on the platform as she pulled her slick black hair into a ponytail. David's eyes widened knowingly. He knew exactly what was going to happen next.

"I'm going in," Nicole growled, not taking her gaze off the boy. She was determined to wipe that egotistical grin right off his face.

"Beat him to a pulp!" David gave her an encouraging push and she stormed forward. Nicole always was a great dancer. He was a good dancer too, but he was not ashamed to admit she was better. Much better. He had no doubt that she was going to win.

"I'm next!" Nicole shouted, shooting her hand up into the air. She was a bit tall for her age and had a very loud voice when she wanted it to be, so everyone noticed her immediately. The crowd went quiet as she made her way to the platform. The boy in front of her smiled more widely, if that was possible.

"Hello, challenger! My name is Nathan! I am pleased to make your acquaintance!" The boy stuck out his hand. Nicole took his hand and shook it, gripping it more than needed. She glared at him and told him the message that she wanted to convey. Only three words were needed.

"You're going down."

Alex stepped through the open doors of the bookstore. It was much busier than the night before. People littered the entire store, searching the shelves for books. Someone bumped against Alex's shoulder and Alex quickly turned to face them. A man in a blue cap and light blue jean jacket stumbled forward next to Alex. In his hands he held a large stack of boxes that towered above his head. A few of the boxes at the top tumbled off but were stopped in mid-air when a yellow substance surrounded them.

"Watch it, kid. I almost dropped these because of you," the man grumbled as he walked farther into the store. Ethan and his family were gathered at the front desk, unboxing thousands of books out of the bountiful supply of deliveries the delivery man had recently finished bringing into the store.

Alex rushed up to them and stopped next to the man he ran into.

"That's the last of 'em," the man said before turning to leave. When he saw Alex, he scoffed and dipped his cap in front of his eyes before departing.

"What'd you do to that guy?" Ethan asked from across the counter.

"I stood in front of the doors for too long and he bumped into me. He almost dropped some boxes, but he caught them just fine," Alex explained. "Where'd all of these books come from? Don't you have enough?"

"No, thankfully, reading is popular in this city. We got this new shipment from the west side of the island, and there is a lot of work ahead of us. We have to unpack, put them in our database, and shelve them," Ethan replied.

Mr. Epoch caught sight of Alex's arrival and walked around the long desk from the computer and placed his hand on Alex's back in greeting.

"Good morning, lad," Mr. Epoch said.

"Good morning, Mr. Epoch," Alex replied. "You seem really busy. I only left a few hours ago."

"Yes, but while you are here we could use your help. Please, come. Ethan, you too."

Ethan placed a hand on the desk and leaped over the top of it, landing at Alex's side. Mr. Epoch walked over to the farther end of the long desk where tall stacks of books covered the surface. He reached up and took a five-foot-tall stack of books and split it in half. He handed one to Alex and one to Ethan. They both huffed under the sudden weight of the stack.

"I need you two to shelve these books. They are already put into the system. We will take care of the unpacking and recording all of the other books, but we need you to put them away. Now shoo," Mr. Epoch said as he placed his hands on the two speechless boys' backs and pushed them into the endless maze of bookshelves, Argent walking between them.

Once they were inside, they exchanged glances with one another before setting to work, both on one side of the hallway. They placed the pile of books on the floor and grabbed a smaller stack from their piles. The small black cat prowled about the shelves as they worked. Ethan asked what breed it was, but Alex quickly dodged the question. Alex had taken care of four full stacks of books himself before he came across another book that belonged to a series that they already had. He had to find the series. When he finally found the series, it was at the top shelf of the bookcase. The ladder was all the way at the other end and was being used.

Alex waited patiently until the person was done and quickly retrieved the ladder. He dragged it across the case over to where he needed it. He put the book away and put a few others away that needed to go in the same area. A slight rattle shook the rungs of the ladder and Alex looked down, surprised.

"Relax, it's just me," Ethan said from beneath him as he slid a book into its slot.

"You scared me," Alex sighed as he continued his work.

"Yes, I saw," Ethan replied.

Silence stretched between them before Alex asked him another question.

"What else do you do?" Alex asked.

"What do you mean?" Ethan looked up at Alex curiously.

"When you aren't in the store where do you go? Do you go out into the city and hang out with friends?"

"You're the only friend I have. I've never been outside for fun. There's also that problem with being a Pardictor. We aren't exactly welcome among everyone else," Ethan bowed his head and put away his last book before climbing back down the ladder. Alex quickly followed.

"What's being a Pardictor got to do with it?" Alex asked.

"Never mind. It's too much to explain," said Ethan, who then walked to the pile of books and bent down to pick one up. Alex stood in front of him defiantly.

"I don't care. I want to know."

Ethan sighed, defeated.

"Fine. Pardictors can see the past and the present. If we touch someone, we can see their past and very rarely multiple possible futures. But since the future is never set for sure, it's only one of infinite possibilities. People don't want us to see what goes on in their lives. We're rare as it is; they still think of us as filthy trash. There's no use trying to hide our true abilities either." Ethan paused, and looked up. Alex's confusion read clear on his face, so Ethan continued. "All Pardictors have dull gray eyes, so we are easily recognized. Everyone thinks that Pardictors can only see pasts and possible futures if we touch another person, so they avoid us as if we were diseased. But it doesn't matter, we could see it all without even coming close to someone if we really wanted to. However, no one knows that, and I'd like to keep it that way."

Alex shook his head to that. "Don't worry I won't. That's all so terrible… But I can almost understand their fear." Alex leaned against the bookcase and crossed his arms solemnly.

"We can't be trusted. I can't change that. No matter how much I would like to," Ethan shrugged. "It doesn't help that there have been more than a few Pardictors in the past who have used their powers for less than good things."

"Well I trust you," Alex assured him. "Tell you what, my friends and I will take you out of here! Before we leave, we'll take you to the beach or something. It'll be fun. We can get you sunglasses or something."

"I look forward to that. But there's something strange about you, Alex. I've tried to see your past before. I'm sorry, but I can't help it," Ethan confessed.

"What did you see?" Alex asked, leaning off the shelves, suddenly alarmed. His family had done so many things to him, many of which he didn't want others to know about, especially this… kid. No matter how mature he may seem.

"Nothing. That's the strange part. I can't see anything. Your past, even possible futures are blocked off."

"That's a relief," Alex said with a sigh as he relaxed his tense shoulders.

"What's a relief?" Ethan asked.

"Nothing. Don't worry about it." Alex waved him off. "Do you know what time it is?"

"2:10. Why? Got another hot date?"

"Oh crap! I have to go! I have to meet my friends for lunch!" Alex took off down the aisle but stopped halfway. "One day I'll bring my friends and we'll take you for the time of your life! I promise you that!" With that, he took off down the aisle and out of the store.

Alex was the second to arrive after Mark so they sat at an outside table to wait for their friends. Jack was next to arrive with Brooke seconds behind him. Ten minutes passed, and still there was no sign of Nicole or David. After another five minutes, they were tired of waiting and made their way over to the arcade.

When they arrived, they found a large crowd of people in the very back of the building. Almost every customer had migrated in that general area. Some people were on the ground cheering while others stood on chairs or sat on top of the games, struggling to see something. Some people even floated in the air. They found David sitting on top of a Pacman game. Alex walked over to him and tapped him on the knee. David jumped at the sudden contact and tore his gaze away from whatever was in front of him.

"Don't scare me like that!" David scolded them although he was smiling. "What's up, guys? Get bored and come to join us?"

"No," Alex said as he pulled up his sleeve and pointed at his bare wrist. "Someone hasn't been keeping track of the time."

"What do you mean?" David looked up at a clock on the wall in the back of the store to discover it was 2:30. "Now, would you look at that! I could have sworn we were here for only twenty minutes!"

"Well, you were wrong. Where's Nicole?" Brooke asked.

"Over there!" David looked up and pointed toward the center of the crowd excitedly. "She's been trying to defeat this dude that's presumably" unbeatable". She's held up against him the longest out of anyone who's tried, though. She's ripping up that platform, man!"

Alex, Brooke, Jack, and Mark all turned their heads to follow David's finger. They could just barely make out the screen of a Dance Dance Revolution game over the crowd. Alex climbed up the game next to David and sat on the top of it in order to get a better view. Then he saw Nicole and another, taller boy dancing furiously next to one another.

Nicole was sweating like crazy. Her shirt was soaked and her hair was plastered against her forehead. The boy next to her was also sweating, but he did not look like he was straining himself as much as she was. You could tell she was getting tired but she was amazing! In astonishment and pride, they watched their amazingly talented friend.

Minutes passed that soon turned to an hour. After a quick break, another went by. Alex could see her muscles lagging and her movements slowing. She had managed to keep going for so long, it seemed impossible.

"Come on, Nicole, you can do it!" Alex shouted. It didn't help. Only a minute later, Nicole collapsed to her knees in exhaustion. Her platform flashed red and Nathan was announced the winner. Nicole dragged her aching body off the platform and over to her waiting friends. A few strangers complimented her and she muttered her thanks.

"Oh my gosh! You were amazing! I didn't know you could dance like that!" Brooke shouted.

"Yeah, it's amazing how long you were able to keep going like that!" Mark exclaimed.

"I didn't beat him, though." Nicole kicked the game Alex was on angrily.

David jumped down from the arcade game and grasped Nicole's shoulders. He spun her around and pointed at Nathan, who was now leaning against the red bar and panting heavily, wiping sweat from his forehead and fanning himself with his shirt collar.

"Do you see him?" David asked, smiling broadly. Nicole nodded. "You may not have won, but you still put up a fight. You saw how he was winning within five minutes against all the other players without breaking a sweat. Yet, you managed to go for hours without stopping while making him actually work hard. You may not have beat him but you did give him a challenge."

Nicole stared at David. "That was quite the speech there, David," she laughed.

"Sorry. I got excited," said David as he stepped away from her and rubbed the back of his neck bashfully.

"I'll have you know that speech of yours worked well. Thanks, David," Nicole squeezed David's shoulder and smiled in thanks. David smiled back at her. Nicole's eyes widened and she stared out at the glass doors and the night air outside for a second before returning her attention back to her friends.

"It's night-time?" Nicole shouted. "That's impossible! How long have I been dancing?" Nicole furrowed her brows in shock.

"About five hours," Jack said.

"Yeah. You were very determined to beat that boy. Iit also means you've kept us from lunch. Can we go eat now?" Mark spoke up.

"I'm sorry, I didn't know how long it'd been. I could use some fresh air. Let's go," said Nicole and they followed her out the door.

A cool night breeze greeted them as they walked out. Nicole was grateful for the cool air against her sweating body. They had only made it past one block before they heard someone shouting.

"Hey! Hey, you! Wait up, will ya?" A voice called behind them. They all turned to see Nathan, the boy Nicole had danced against, running up to them. When he caught up to them, he had a smile spread across his face. "Thanks for waiting," he said.

"What's wrong?" Nicole asked.

"Nothing. I just wanted to say, you weren't all that bad! I've never met anyone who could hold their own against me for so long. I mean, you wouldn't have beaten me anyway. I've been dancing like that since I could fly. I just wanted to tell you that. Great job," Nathan explained.

"You weren't so bad yourself," Nicole smirked. Nathan chuckled a bit at that.

Alex stood next to Jack and could feel him tense. Alex looked up at him to see him looking warily off to their left, out into the street.

"Well I ought to get back," said Nathan. He began to turn around but another voice off to the side caught their attention.

"Get into the alley. Now," a hoarse voice commanded. A figure stepped out of the shadows of the street and into the light of a street lamp. They wore a black hoodie with the hood over their face completely. Their hand was outstretched toward them and it glowed an eerie yellow.

FORTY-FOUR

"Who are you?" Nathan asked. He didn't sound the slightest bit scared.

"I said, get into the alley! All of you! NOW!" As the figure shouted the last word, a bright yellow spark flew out of his fingertips and collided with the street lamp. The glass and bulb broke, shattering all over the pavement. Jack nodded silently to them and they all backed into the alley slowly.

"Are we being mugged?" David whispered.

Mark couldn't suppress a nervous laugh. He doubted this person wanted their money. And if he did, he chose some incredibly broke people to mug.

"Stop laughing! Hurry up!" The figure followed them in, keeping his glowing hand trained on them all the while. Once they were between the two buildings and away from the streets the figure lowered his hood with his free hand, revealing the same boy Nathan had battled and defeated before Nicole came into the picture.

"Bryan?" Nathan asked, having recognized the boy. "What are you doing?"

"You humiliated me in front of my friends! I was supposed to win! But I didn't and now they left me. I have no one now!" Bryan shouted.

"Those are some really sucky friends you have there," Nathan said calmly.

"It doesn't matter anymore. Because you are going to pay!" Bryan brought up his other hand, and it turned into an electrifying yellow too. His palms were facing them and he smiled wickedly. Alex and his friends' eyes widened in surprise. "Maybe they'll come back if they find out I finally beat you!"

"Man, you really think that? They won't come back. They will be too busy running away from a killer," Nathan slowly began to walk toward Bryan.

"Shut up! You don't know anything!" Bryan snapped his wrists so that his fingertips were pointed at Nathan. Electricity from his hands shot out at Nathan. Alex leapt into action; he ran into Nathan and knocked him onto the ground before the electricity could hit him.

"Ahhhhhh! Leave us alone! This is between *us*! Stay out of this!" Bryan screamed in frustration and shot another bolt of electricity at Mark and the others. There was nothing they could do. It was too fast. They braced for the impact. But instead of hitting them it formed a barrier around them, locking them in a thin electric cage.

Jack immediately melted into a Shadow and slid beneath the ring of electricity. His "'-Shadow-" self crawled against the wall of the alley and behind Bryan. The teen didn't notice. But Alex did. He stood up in front of Nathan and stared at Bryan.

"You can't kill anyone and you know it," Alex said calmly.

"Shut up! Yes I can!" Bryan fired another bolt but it landed on the ground, more than a few feet from its target. His body was shaking.

"You can't. You could have killed them with one strike. One strike would be all it took and they'd fry," Alex gestured to his trapped friends. "Instead, you chose to spare their lives and merely trap them," said Alex. Alex moved aside so Bryan could see Nathan, lying on the ground. "You don't want to kill this kid. You can walk away, Bryan. This whole incident will have never happened."

Bryan continued to shake but his expression hardened. He looked from Alex to Nathan and then back to the electric cage. He broke out into an evil smile once again. "I'll prove you wrong," Bryan pointed his hand toward the cage and began to curl his fingers inward. Simultaneously, the cage around the others began to close in on them. Dangerous electric sparks licked at their skin.

They all leapt off the ground. Ignoring Jack's warning for them not to fly, they flew up. There was an opening at the very top of the tall cage. Bryan cursed and jerked his hand. Slowly, the opening at the top began to close. They all pushed up as fast as they could go and flew out just as the cage closed in on itself. A loud boom rang through the alley as one final bolt of electricity disappeared, and the only trace left behind was a large, round scorch mark embedded into the pavement.

Bryan moved to shoot them again, but when he was distracted, the Shadow form of Jack formed behind the teen, looming over him. He barely had enough time to turn around before he was engulfed in shadow.

The alley was silent. Only the sound of distant music and chatter of people echoed in the distance. The silence was finally broken when Bryan's limp body tumbled out of the Shadow and onto the ground. Jack formed into his normal, solid self and stood inches away from the boy.

"Is he dead?" David asked, breaking the silence. His voice cracked.

"No. He is only unconscious and will remain so for a number of hours," Jack replied. He turned to Nathan. "I suggest you leave before he wakes."

"Is he… normal?" Nathan asked.

"What do you mean by 'normal'?" Brooke asked.

Nathan stood up and walked over to the unconscious body. The teen's chest slowly rose up and down as he breathed. Nathan bent over him and pulled his shirt collar down, revealing his neck. He then moved on to both of his wrists and ankles. When he was done, he stood up and sighed.

"What did you just do?" Mark asked.

"I know it's cruel to think this, but I was hoping the Domesticators have gotten him. Then that would mean he at least had no idea what he was doing. Sadly, he did know. And he was fully prepared to do it," Nathan explained.

"What are the 'Domesticators'?" Alex asked.

Nathan stared at Alex in shock. "Did you seriously just ask me that?"

Alex nodded.

"The Domesticators is some kind of organization. They have found a way to control others with some collar and jewels and have been stealing away people from the city for God knows what. That's really all I know about them. But for some reason we haven't had many attacks lately. Personally, I think they've moved on," Nathan whispered the last part. He bent down and picked Bryan up, placing his arm over his shoulder, and stood up. He turned and began to walk out of the alley. "But you didn't hear that from me!"

"Where are you going with him?" Mark called.

"This kid won't remember what happened when he wakes up! Maybe he'll find better friends in me than he did in those other jerks!" Nathan turned the corner and disappeared.

Alex stared at the corner where he watched him go, deep in thought. What Nathan described sounded an awful lot like what happened with Alan Moore. Alex looked over to Mark, who seemed to be thinking the same thing.

"You know. I don't think I'm very hungry anymore," Brooke thought aloud.

"Let's just go back to the hotel. I'm tired from dancing so much," Nicole added.

They all agreed and made their way out of the alley.

"Are we just going to let him take Bryan? Won't he try to go after Nathan again?" Mark asked.

"Yes, we will," Jack replied. "He won't remember anything from the past day so he won't try to go after Nathan again. At least he shouldn't," Jack smirked at Mark. "Unless the same things happen again, which is not impossible. Nathan will have to fend for himself on his own. However, I doubt he ever needed our help in the first place."

"What do you mean?" Nicole asked.

"Nathan was much stronger than that kid. If it comes to it, Nathan can take care of himself," Jack explained.

A week passed. There wasn't as much danger as there had been in the woods, though. Their week had even been fun. Alex had spent most of his days either holed up in the bookstore or out doing something with his friends. Jack helped Darrien out in his store, and everyone else, when they weren't doing something together, wandered the town in search of something to cure their boredom—which wasn't very hard. It was now Sunday evening and they all sat at a cheap but crowded restaurant, eating their dinner. Across the street, two hooded figures leaned against the brick wall of a building, discussing plans, keeping their eyes trained on the restaurant in front of them.

"They haven't grown very close to anyone in particular," Jensen reported to his sister. "But one of them, the boy with the sword, seems to have grown much closer to those Pardictors in the past week. That will be useful to us, I believe. Especially since the boy is at the very emotional state in adolescence."

"Yes. I see how that may be useful," Jenna replied. "I too have come across a discovery. Upon following the cloaked one, I have found that he has an extremely close relationship with the cartographer. I can already see a plan forming. A flawless one too. We'll capture those humans before they even find out what is going on."

Jenna and her brother stared at the doors to the restaurant as six figures stepped out. They patiently watched as they walked out onto the street.

"Tomorrow night, then?" Jenna asked her brother. Their eyes were locked on the figures.

"Tomorrow," Jensen replied. A flame began to grow at their feet and slowly engulf their bodies. When the tip of their heads disappeared beneath the flames, the fire extinguished. The fire and the two hooded figures vanished.

The six of them stepped out of the restaurant, laughing their heads off from another of David's jokes. They were surprisingly funny. They all knew David was funny, but they didn't know he could be funny on purpose! Alex's laughter soon died when he felt a warm presence surrounding him. It wasn't a good warm feeling either. His friends were unaware Alex had stopped and continued down the street.

Alex scanned the crowd until his eyes fell on two cloaked figures leaning against the building directly across the street. They seemed to be the source of this strange presence he was feeling. Alex began to make his way toward the figures. The crowd in front of him grew thicker and he struggled to make his way across. Alex tripped over another's foot and he fell to the ground. Through the thousands of feet padding against the street he could just barely make out a faint orange and yellow glow. He quickly pushed himself to his feet and ran to the safety of the building.

When he made it through the crowd, he found himself standing where the figures had stood. At least, where they should have been. Alex searched the crowd for the cloaked figures but saw no sign of them. He sighed. Maybe he was just being paranoid. It was awfully strange that nothing dangerous happened at all that week, but then again, maybe he was just overthinking things.

"Alex! Are you coming? What's up?" Brooke called from the corner on the other side of the street.

"Nothing! I'm coming! Thought I saw something!" Alex called back to her and waved before jogging to her side.

FORTY-FIVE

They all sat in a circle in the back of Darrien's store, surrounding his desk. It was eleven o'clock at night, outside was pitch black. Jack leaned up against the wall, his arms folded across his chest, standing behind Darrien, who was sitting at his desk and straightening some papers. Alex sat against a bookshelf on the ground with his legs stretched out. David sat on top of a stack of books with Mark leaning against the shelf next to him. Nicole sat backward in a spare chair and Brooke sat criss-crossed, diagonal from her, with Argent pleasantly purring in her lap.

"So… why are we here again?" David asked. "So late at night, I mean," he added.

The room quieted as they waited for someone to answer. Darrien finished adjusting the pile of papers and placed his elbows on the desk. He clasped his hands together and leaned on his fist for a moment before speaking.

"Jack and I believe it is time for you to learn a little history," Darrien said through his closed fist.

"History of what?" Nicole asked.

"History of this world hidden among the world of men. At first we thought it all to be too dangerous of a risk to take. You are humans after all, and you will be going back to your world. Children, no less. We can't have you spilling any information to humans," Darrien replied.

"We may be young, but we all know how to keep a secret," said Mark. He looked to each of his friends and they all nodded in agreement.

"Good. If you didn't, we would have to wipe your memory completely. But neither of us have that kind of skill, so then we would be forced to kill you," Jack cut in bluntly.

"Indeed. However, you seem to have powers of your own, so that won't be needed. That is the main reason why we have decided to tell you this. Now bear with me because this may take a while. We may not cover everything tonight. And please, keep all questions and comments to yourself." Darrien paused and waited for anyone to oppose his words, but no one spoke.

Darrien continued, "There is a separate world that we call Equelibreiangeria. A handful—I know. This is the world we live in, although it is not separate from yours. For the most part. Heltiana is one of the largest kingdoms in this world. The other is called Lenonium. Lenonium and Heltiana have been enemies since the moment they were formed. Exact opposites. Long ago, we had many wars. As time progressed and countries and governments were formed, humanity grew larger in numbers, with scientific discoveries being made in rapid succession. We learned to keep away from each other. Citizens of these kingdoms have had clashes where they fought long battles, but always in secret. Although we manage to stop ourselves from creating wars, we still seem to despise eachother to the very core and find other ways to overcome the other.

"You see, mankind bases everything on science. They have to understand everything. If they can't make sense out of it, they think it is evil and do their best to rid the world of it. Or, they try to use it. No matter the costs, no matter who they hurt. So, many millennia ago, these kingdoms decided to come together for the first and last time in history. They worked together to destroy any evidence of their existence. They wiped memories, burned books. When they were done, nothing was left. Then, they scattered about the world and into entirely different dimensions, in order to create new lives for themselves. Only a small percent remain on Earth. But to you, that small percent may seem like the whole of our kind."

"How many of you are left on Earth?" Brooke asked, her voice thick with skepticism.

"Roughly three hundred million. But that is only five percent of the whole. We live much longer than humans do. But we have not lost connection with the others. There are gateways and rifts in the universe we dwell in that lead to others of our kind. I'm not planning on getting into the whole science and magic of it all," Darrien replied with a wave of his hand.

"While our people are hidden away in islands unknown to mankind and landforms that we have kept from their knowledge, we also live among them. Many of us hide among them to gather information or to create new lives. Many prefer the lives of Heltiana because life is so much easier. Dangerous, but easy. Hiding away is but a small price to pay," Jack added.

"Yes, and while there are many people among Equelibreuangeria there are also creatures. Many we know of but many we don't. They are just as mysterious as we are and seem to have their own agenda. When you are born among us, you may be born with the magic or you may not. You simply need to learn how to use it," said Darrien as he paused for breath. He glanced at the watch on his wrist and sighed. "It is late. We will continue this conversation tomorrow night."

"Yes, it is probably best that we retire for the night," said Jack as he pushed off the wall and uncrossed his arms.

"Aww. We just got started. How about we come back in the morning?" David asked eagerly.

"No, I am a working individual, as you are well aware, I hope. I must tend to my shop during the day," Darrien laughed at David's joy in the topic.

"So, who runs these kingdoms of yours?" Brooke asked as they stood up from their seats.

"That, my dear, we will discuss tomorrow night," said Darrien. He placed his ink-covered gloved hands on her back and began to lightly push her through the curtains that connected the room to the shop. "Until then, please rest."

Darrien pushed Brooke through the shop with Jack, Nicole, Mark, David, and Alex at their heels. When they reached the door, they exchanged their goodbyes before walking out.

"Oh, and Jack?" Darrien called.

"Yes?" Jack turned around to face him.

"Do me a favor and pick up a package from the carpenter for me?"

"Of course."

"Thank you, Jack. I will see you all again tomorrow night!"

With those final words, they departed into the night.

It was Monday evening. They had just left the carpenter's store and were on their way to meet with Darrien again. They were only two blocks away when they smelled something burning in the air, and spotted a tower of smoke looming over the buildings. Fear struck through all of their hearts as they realized where the smoke was coming from. They could only pray that they were wrong as they ran the rest of the way. Jack was the farthest in the lead.

Their fears were proved correct when they arrived at the cartographer's shop. The entire building was ablaze with fire. Multiple people in uniform and street clothes stood in the street, aiming their hands toward the burning building. Water sprayed from their hands and onto the flames, but they refused to go out. Jack burst into the building, fear and concern covering his face entirely. No one made a move to stop him.

Darrien was still in there! The fire was still too strong for anyone to go in. But that wasn't going to stop Jack. His overwhelming concern for his friend clouded all of his judgment. If he had been thinking, he may have thought of some other way to get inside. Something safer. But he wasn't thinking. And that's not what he did.

Jack aimed his glowing gloved hands in front of him and swept them to the side. The debris that had covered the door turned a black purple, the same as the glow around Jack's hands, as it was thrown to the side. Jack kicked the door furiously and the hinges splintered as the door flew inward. He dashed inside the burning building, desperate to find his friend and bring him to safety. He didn't seem to notice the beam that had fallen outside and the glowing letters etched into the wood.

David, Nicole, Mark, Alex, and Brooke ran after him. They all ran through the door, but Alex stopped before he could step inside. His friends disappeared through the door but he held back. Something out of the corner of his eye caught his attention. He jogged over to a beam and froze where he stood. In the wood, a message was carved out of fire, the letters still aflame. It read, *The bookworms are next.* If anyone else had found this particular beam and this particular message, they would have just been confused. They wouldn't understand what the message was implying.

But this message wasn't meant for them. It was meant for one person who would know exactly what it meant. Alex knew what it meant. He hoped that what he thought it meant wasn't what it actually did mean, but he had to know. He couldn't just shrug it off and hope it was just a coincidence. It could be, but what if it wasn't? Alex wasn't going to take that chance. He didn't want to leave Jack to deal with this alone but he had no choice. He knew Jack could handle himself. Alex took off running down the street, leaving the burning building behind him.

The five of them rushed into the building. The heat hit them immediately and sweat formed on their skin. The air was suffocating and they struggled to breathe. Tears dripped from the corners of their eyes from the heat. The room was an endless fire. The only colors were shades of orange and black. Bookshelves and maps were burned to a crisp but even their ashes continued to burn. Jack saw them follow him in but he didn't have time to argue with them. He scanned the room around them. Most of the shelves had fallen and few remained standing, but debris and pieces of the building's structure blocked their path. Jack thrust his hand above his head to form a shield around him and the teens in time for a beam to fall from the ceiling and break on the shield around them. Jack kept the shield above them as they rushed to the back of the room. They searched desperately but Darrien was nowhere to be found. If he wasn't there, they only had one more place to look. Jack tore down the burning curtain that separated the store from Darrien's study. They found him.

Darrien was sprawled across his desk, face down. Jack was unable to see the condition he was in, but he could tell that he was unconscious. A fallen beam crushed his back, pinning him to the desk. The fire around them sizzled and cracked. Jack used his powers to lift the beam off his friend and tossed it to the side. He rushed over, keeping the shield above all of them. He lifted Darrien and slung him over his shoulder. Jack could feel his friend's sweat from the heat drip onto his shoulder. He spun around to face the entrance, but as he did so the ceiling collapsed, blocking their way to freedom.

Alex skidded to a stop when he saw the bookstore engulfed in flames. His eyes widened when he saw the burning building. This can't have been happening. But it was, and his friends were still inside. The street was empty and not a soul was in sight. Where was everyone? Why wasn't anyone trying to put out the fire? The fire in this building was so much bigger compared to the one he just witnessed. He threw the doors open and flew into the library. He found Ethan and his mother on the ground. The long wooden check-out desk had fallen on top of them. They were struggling to push it off them, all the while coughing and hacking from the smoke. Alex swooped down and pulled the desk off them almost effortlessly.

He was amazed at how easily he removed the desk, but he didn't have time to wonder about that. He quickly made his way to Ethan's mother, but she held up a hand. Alex ignored the hand and continued to walk toward her. She struggled to get out words.

"NO!" She finally croaked. "Ethan…first." She pointed weakly to Ethan who was struggling to stand, his leg broken.

Alex nodded and swept Ethan up, flying him out of the door and onto the safety of the street. Ethan stared wide-eyed at Alex as he flew back into the building, only to return with his mother in his arms.

"I… I thought… you were human?" Ethan rasped as Alex set his mother down beside her son.

"I am human," Alex looked quizzically at Ethan before returning his attention to the situation at hand. "Where are your grandparents?"

Jack cursed and spun back around. He thrust his hand out toward the wall and it burst outward. A massive hole was all that was left. On the other side, they could see the night sky and people watering the enflamed building. They all rushed out, grateful for the cooler temperature.

Sadly, their excitement faded when they saw Darrien's condition. Jack had laid him on the ground, kneeling at his side. Some parts of Darrien's skin had burned raw, and he was covered in soot. His clothes were torn, and his eyes were seared shut. But that wasn't what scared them the most. A large, jagged knife protruded out of his chest. Blood pooled around it and onto the ground. Jack's cloak, shoulder, and shirt were soaked in his blood from when he carried him. The body before them was motionless.

Jack extended his hands to the knife but quickly pulled back. He slowly inhaled as he brought two fingers to Darrien's wrist. He waited a moment before pulling his hand up to his neck and doing the same thing. He stared at the dead man before him. He took in a deep breath before turning to face the shocked teenagers. He couldn't afford to feel sad now.

"Where is Alex?" Jack asked worriedly, finally noticing the boy's absence.

The four teens looked around them quickly.

"I didn't see him come in with us," Brooke noted.

Jack brought a small group of the uninformed citizens that were previously trying to put out the fire to take care of Darrien before making his way back to the front of the burning store. He searched the growing crowd but could not find the boy he was searching for. He turned back, catching sight of a burning beam that lay a few inches away from the building. He walked toward it to find the bright orange letters etched into it. He read the message over and over again, unsure of what it meant.

Brooke, Mark, David, and Nicole joined him, all reading the strange message over his shoulder. After a few minutes of confused silence, David spoke.

"Doesn't Alex have some friends at a bookstore?" David asked.

That was when it all clicked for Jack. He took off running and the teens followed.

"They're still in there," Ethan's mother choked.

"Do you know where?" Alex asked.

Ethan's mother shook her head.

"I'll just have to go find them then," Alex said. Before anyone could protest, Alex flew back inside, his image engulfed in flame. He flew around the large room, keeping to the wall. When he was at the back of the store, he found Ethan's grandmother. She was clutching onto a ladder against the wall. She was heaving, struggling to get air. The wood of the ladder below her broke and it began to fall backward. She screamed as she began to fall through the air.

Alex caught her in mid-air and flew her out. He barely sat her on the pavement before he was off again. He was just through the doorway when an explosion sent him flying across the street and into another building. His head spun and he could feel his vision clouding. The only sound was a constant ringing. He could hear nothing else. He couldn't pass out now. He still had to get Mr. Epoch to safety. Alex shook off the dizziness and flew into the building's broken windows.

He found Mr. Epoch on the ground. His arm hung limply at his side as he stood helplessly, trapped inside a fiery ring. The tall bookshelves began to fall one by one, like dominoes. The last one hit the shelf in front of him and it began to fall, books falling all around him. Alex took off as fast as he could. He flew beneath the falling bookshelf and thrust his hands above his head. The bookcase fell on top of him, and he cried out as the weight of eighty forty-foot-tall bookshelves fell on him. He felt himself begin to sag under the weight. If these cases fell, they would crush both him and Mr. Epoch.

Alex heaved as he gathered all of his strength and pushed the shelves upward. His muscles screamed out at him to stop but he pushed on. He gritted his teeth to keep from screaming. He tasted blood as it dripped out of the corner of his mouth. He ignored the pain and the blood as he flew upward. Once the shelf he was holding was standing up he thrust it backwards, sending it, and all the others leaning against it, falling the other way.

Alex flew unsteadily to the ground and picked Mr. Epoch up in his arms. His muscles ached and he struggled to keep consciousness. He flew Mr. Epoch out the door just in time for another explosion to send books, wood, and glass flying into the street. A crowd had gathered. Mr. Epoch ran to his wife and they hugged each other, both mindful of Mr. Epoch's bad arm. Ethan was cradled in his mother's arms as they both cried.

Alex fell onto his back and his chest heaved up and down as he caught his breath. Other than his aching body and bleeding tongue, he was unharmed. However, he wouldn't allow him to lose himself to the black just yet. It still wasn't over.

FORTY-SIX

Jack, Nicole, Brooke, David, and Mark ran onto the street to find another large crowd surrounding yet another burning building. This fire was bigger; flames reached higher than the towering bookstore and licked the night sky. The five teens wove their way through the crowd and found the owners of the store in the center of the crowd, along with Alex, who was on his back staring at the sky. He was breathing heavily, and blood trickled out of the corner of his mouth.

Alex sat up when he saw his friends, still unable to find the strength to stand. "Are you all right?" Mark asked, his voice full of concern.

"Yeah, I'm fine," Alex replied. "How about you guys?"

"We're fine. We're not hurt," Nicole said.

"Did you rescue Darrien?" Alex asked. Every head bowed; no one answered his question. He already knew the answer. "I'm so sorry," Alex said sadly.

Jack met Alex's eyes with a grim look of determination. Alex looked him over and at all the blood that was not his that soaked his clothes. Mark held out his arm and Alex grabbed it as Mark hoisted him off the ground and he turned to Jack.

"I'm sorry," Alex repeated.

A shrill scream pierced the air, causing them to cover their ears. They turned to find Mr. Epoch and his wife keel over in pain, clutching their chests. At first, Alex was unsure of what was wrong but he soon realized when he saw the fire emerging from their chests. Alex leapt forward to help, but he was pulled back by a strong arm. Alex looked up to see Jack holding him back.

"What are you doing?" Alex screamed. "Let me go! I need to help them!" Alex struggled to break free of Jack's grip, but Jack refused to let go. "Let me go!" Alex screamed.

"You can't help them! The fire eats them from the inside. Someone has placed it there deliberately! If you try to help, you will only begin to burn along with them!" Jack yelled.

Alex flinched at the volume of Jack's voice but refused to let up. Alex pulled but Jack kept his hold. Alex sagged in his arms as he looked on at the destruction taking place before him. Ethan was trying to run to Mr. and Mrs. Epoch too, but his mother held him back. They watched helplessly as Ethan's grandparents burned and crumpled to ash, held back by their guardians. Only when the last flicker of fire burned out in the ashes did Jack and Ethan's mother let go. Alex slumped to his knees. Ethan ran to the ashes, tears streaming down his face. His mother remained where she was, tears streaming down her face as well. She covered her face in her hands, and her shoulders shook with each sob.

The crowd was horrified. People cried. Others screamed. No one talked. They were all too astonished by the scene before them. Ethan scraped at the ashes and cradled them as they seeped through his fingers, tears dripping into them. A gust of wind whipped past them, sweeping up the ashes and carrying them away into the black sky.

Alex scanned the area around him. How could this have happened? Who could have done such a thing? That's when he saw it. A cloaked figure hidden in the shadow. Two eyes glowed beneath the hood. He felt a warm presence surround him. But it wasn't because of the fire. It was the same sinister presence he felt the night before. That was when he pieced it all together.

Alex stood up and took off running toward the figure, leaving Argent behind with Ethan. The figure leapt up into the sky and transformed into smoke. The smoke then drifted above the rooftops. The smoke re-formed into the same cloaked figure once it was on the roof.

"Where are you going?" Mark called in a shaking voice. He was still shocked by the previous events.

"After the one who caused this. You coming?" Alex called back. His voice was firm, steady, determined. Frightening.

The five of them exchanged quick glances. Jack was the first to take action, running to Alex. The others followed.

"Where did they go?" Nicole asked.

"Up there." Alex pointed toward the roof above them. "Let's go."

They leapt into the air and landed on the roof. They saw the hooded figure leaping from roof to roof four buildings away, the distance between them quickly growing. They ran after it, leaping over gaps between buildings. They were unaware of the passage of time as they tailed the figure. The figure suddenly stopped on the roof of a twenty-story building at the edge of the city and disappeared behind one of the many vents and chimneys that littered the roof.

"Show yourself!" David shouted angrily.

"I don't know if we should. Should we, Jenna?" a man's voice echoed.

"I'm not so sure. They are quite demanding," a woman's voice replied.

They were all thrown off. There were two people? They thought they were trailing one figure. Not two.

"How many of you are there?" Nicole called.

"Only two. Can't you do math?" the woman's voice taunted. A cloaked figure stepped out from behind an air vent. The figure's hands reached for the button around their neck and unbuttoned it. The cloak slid down their body, revealing the same woman they saw performing on stage during the festival in the last town. Another figure stepped out from behind her and did the same with their cloak, revealing the same man that performed by her side.

"My name is Jenna," the woman said. She pointed at the man. "That is my brother."

"My name is Jensen," the man replied. He pointed at the woman. "That is my sister."

"I don't care what your names are. Why did you hurt those people?" Brooke shouted.

"To get to you, of course," Jenna replied sweetly.

"Why would you want to do that?" Mark asked.

"That is for us to know and you to find out," Jensen declared.

Jensen and Jenna thrust their hands out at them and fire exploded from their hands.

"Scatter!" Alex shouted.

They all ducked and rolled out of the way as fire was thrown at them. As they ran, they were split into two groups. Jack, Brooke, and David were stuck with Jenna, while Mark, Nicole, and Alex were chased by Jensen. They all ran to the edge of the roof in an attempt to escape. Their plans were foiled when great walls of fire shot up from the edges, trapping them on the roof.

Jensen and Jenna took to the air, attacking them from above. Every time they tried to fly, they were struck with a ball of fire. The terrific duo was distracting them from being able to fly. They pushed their wrists together and aimed their palms toward the roof. Balls of fire formed below them and slowly began to spread, merging into one large sheet and forming a ceiling of fire. There was no way out for them now. They were trapped inside one large fiery box. The duo thrust their hands forward and slowly the fiery ceiling began to lower itself on the two groups.

Jack put a shield above the three of them for protection against the flames. Mark, Nicole, and Alex were forced underneath an air vent, but they knew the air vent would likely burn, too. Jack observed the two teenagers who leaned against him beneath the safety of the shield. He also saw the other teens cowering beneath an air vent on the other side of the roof. He knew they wouldn't survive the fire. And they didn't have time to run underneath his shield.

He leaned back to face the sky. Leaning against another vent in a kneeling position, Jack placed his wrists together and held his palms facing the fire that moved closer to them by the second. The shield above them expanded at his command until it covered the entire roof. He sent it upward, a purplish black version of the siblings' fiery force field. They scowled at this and sent the wall of fire down faster. Jack did the same. The two shields collided with each other, and there was a blinding light.

Both of the shields disintegrated, and the siblings cursed. They flew back down and continued to attack the young humans. Alex, Mark, and Nicole crawled beneath another vent before the one they were previously beneath burst into a ball of flames.

"We aren't going to survive this if we continue to run. We need to fight back," Alex screamed over the sound of fire crackling and burning around them.

"How do you plan on doing that exactly? They have magic! What do we have? Nothing!" shouted Nicole as she threw her hands in the air only to bring them back down to cover her head as the air vent burst into flame. They crawled beneath another vent to continue their conversation.

"Come out, come out, wherever you are, little mice! This cat wants to play!" Jensen shouted over the rooftop.

"We can fly, and we have fists. I have a sword and we also have Jack," Alex retorted as he counted on his fingers, bringing his attention back to them. "If we can't hurt them, we can at least distract them long enough for Jack to land the final blow on 'em."

"That might work, but how are we going to tell Jack the plan?" Mark asked. "He's on the other side of the roof!"

"He'll figure it out eventually," Alex called as he jumped out of their hiding spot. David and Nicole shared a quick glance before following his lead.

"Ah! My sweet little mice! About time you came out of hiding! This cat was just starting to get bored!" Jensen shouted, smirking when he saw them.

They all took to the air simultaneously, throwing Jensen off guard. But only for a second. When he recovered, he sent a shower of fireballs in their direction. Thankfully, they were able to dodge them all since he was aiming for one big target and not separate ones. The three of them flanked him on each side and shot forward to attack. Jensen didn't even bother moving. He shot a ball of fire at Mark before he could get within ten yards, hitting him head on. He fell backward and through the air, plummeting to the roof. Alex stopped the charge and dove for Mark. Nicole continued her advance.

Alex swiped Mark out of the air before he could hit the ground. He was knocked unconscious, and his clothes were burnt but otherwise he was unharmed. Alex settled him on the ground and looked back at Jensen and Nicole with dread. Jensen was holding Nicole by the throat at arm's length, choking her.

Jack saw Alex, Mark, and Nicole charge out from the air vent, prepared to fight. He knew what they were doing was dangerous but understood the purpose. He too was growing tired of this game. He grabbed David and Brooke and thrust them beneath the shield as fire was thrown at them.

"Do you think you can do what you did in the forest? Against the Clandestine Brobdingnagian?" Jack asked Brooke.

She looked up at him with a confused and surprised expression. "How did you…?" She stuttered.

"Forget how I know, can you do it?" Jack snapped.

"I… I don't know. I don't even know how I did it," she stuttered.

"What about you? Can you do what you did when Winona and Jaheim attacked?" Jack asked David.

"I don't think so," David replied.

Jack sighed. "Can you still fight?"

"Well, yeah! We can still fly, too. That's got to be an advantage!" David exclaimed.

"What he said," Brooke said.

"Good, because I'm going to drop this shield, and I'm going to need you to fight," Jack announced. As soon as he finished talking, the barrier dropped and they rolled out of the way of another fireball. Taking to the air just as the others did, they got themselves ready to fight.

They launched at Jenna full speed. She, like her brother, was also caught off guard at their sudden decision to fight. Before she could recover from shock, Jack created a charge Shadows and commanded them forward. The Shadows surrounded her in seconds, with more piling on. Soon, it was one large blackish purple ball floating in the sky. It was silent for a moment as Brooke and David flew to Jack's side.

"Is it over?" David asked.

"Not yet," Jack replied. He thrust his gloved hand toward the large floating ball and shot his hand to the ground. With impossible speed, the ball hit the roof of the building and shattered.

"Whoa! What was that for? We aren't trying to kill her!" Brooke shouted.

"We aren't murderers!" David added.

"Be ready," Jack countered. He refused to take his eyes off the spot where the ball shattered. They both looked down to see Jenna standing on the roof looking more than irritated. She slowly looked up at them with a snarling expression.

"You'll rue the day you met me!" she shouted. Both her arms shot up, and her palms faced them. A large stream of fire hurled toward them and forced them far back into the sky. Jenna continued to scream furiously as she pitched balls of fire at the trio.

Alex shot forward with amazing speed. He lunged at Jensen and gripped his arm that held Nicole. He squeezed until Jensen let go of Nicole's neck. She fell backward and flew away as fast as she could, coughing and gasping for breath. Jensen drew his attention to Alex. His eyes glowed slightly in excitement.

"You shouldn't have done that, little mouse," said Jensen, who then lunged at Alex. Alex brought his hands up. Their hands interlocked, and Alex fought to keep Jensen at bay. Jensen smiled wickedly, and his eyes glowed brighter. Alex's arms shook as Jensen pushed him further back. He gritted his teeth as he struggled to fight back. In a flash, his hands grew hot, and it took him a moment to realize what was happening.

Alex tried to pull back, but Jensen gripped Alex's hands harder. His hands grew hotter, and he could feel his flesh burning. Alex screamed in pain, and everyone's attention was diverted to the two. Jensen smiled at Alex's pain and leaned into his ear.

"Little mouse, you'll regret it," he whispered. The heat on Alex's palms intensified, and the heat traveled up his body. Smoke drifted up from his hands. Alex kicked forward, hitting him in a very painful place. Jensen shoved Alex forward and kicked him in the stomach, letting go of his hands. He smiled wickedly once again. Alex tumbled through the air and crashed against the roof. He was winded, and his hands burned.

Alex stared at his burned flesh. He felt light-headed and a memory flooded back to him. He fought back the memory, but it forced its way through his mind. Exhausted, he succumbed to the memory.

Alex's dream-memory transported him back three years. He saw and felt himself walk through the front door of his house. His family had moved to the city that weekend, and he had just come back from his first day of school there. His father was waiting for him at the door. Alex placed his weathered bookbag down on the floor. It was old and he would need a new one soon.

"Hello, father," Alex greeted his father, who was towering over him, blocking his path. He had changed out of his work uniform into blue jeans and a dirty white tank top. His black hair was still neat and slicked back. He was leaning against the doorway with a half-empty beer bottle dangling loosely from his fingertips. He must have just gotten home, Alex thought. His blue eyes glared at Alex threateningly.

"Don't 'hello' me. Where's my beer?" Mr. Shaffer demanded, his voice wobbly with drunkenness.

"Your... beer?" Alex asked, his eyebrows raising.

"Yes, my beer. Where is it? I had a rough day at work, and I'm down to my last few bottles. Now, where is it?" Mr. Shaffer nearly shouted.

"I don't know. Why don't you go buy some?" Alex asked, annoyed.

"Don't talk back to me. Go get me some beer!" Mr. Shaffer was shouting now.

"Father, I am too young to get alcohol. We already went over this. It's against the law," Alex explained, exasperated.

"Then break the law, I don't care. Just get it to me, ungrateful brat." Mr. Shaffer gulped down the last of the alcohol and slammed it against the wall. Bits of glass and droplets of the strong liquid scattered throughout the hallway. Alex flinched.

"Dad, you're drunk and you look exhausted. Why don't you go lie down?" Alex said fearfully.

Mr. Shaffer glared at him menacingly. "Fine then!" he shouted. "Disobey me. I'll show you where that gets you." Mr. Shaffer grabbed Alex's wrist and pulled him toward the fireplace. The burning coals cracked and sizzled from the heat. Alex squirmed when he realized what his father was going to do but couldn't escape his grip. Alex's eyes widened in horror as his father shoved him forward, hands first, into the fire.

Alex shook the memory away. He bolted upright and barreled toward Jensen. Jensen merely smiled at Alex's charge. He pointed his hand and sent a fireball at Alex. Jensen then turned to face Nicole again, thinking that he had dealt with the boy.

At the last second, Alex pulled his sword from its sheath, and flew above the fireball. He continued his path toward Jensen with his sword raised.

Jensen was surprised but not caught off guard. He grabbed Alex's shirt and tossed him against a vent on the roof.

"Alex!" Nicole shouted as Jensen threw him into the metal. The metal bent inward from the sudden impact, and Alex tumbled to the ground, dazed, winded, and unable to move. Nicole was done with all of this. She just wanted to go home. Why couldn't these idiots leave them alone? Without realizing what she was doing, she held her hand out toward the fiery man. Her palm faced the sky. A small ball of yellow light swirled in her hand until it began to take shape. When the light disappeared, in her hand lay a gun. She wasn't thinking about what she was doing when she pointed the barrel at Jensen. She wasn't aware of what she was about to do. It was as though her emotions had taken control.

Before anyone could react, she squeezed the trigger. A loud band rang out through the sky, followed by a quick bright light. Her hand opened again, and she let go of the gun. The gun hovered as it began to change back into a yellow ball of swirling light. The light disappeared into her palm, and only when her hand was back at her side and Jensen hit the ground did she realize what she had done.

Jensen lay sprawled on the ground. He clutched his leg as blood trickled down. Everyone had stopped fighting. All were staring at Jensen and Nicole. When Jenna recovered from the shock, she floated down and rushed to her brother's side. Jenna got down on her knees and ripped the bottom of her white shirt. She wrapped the cloth around her brother's leg as the fire on the roof around them disappeared.

Her brother groaned as she tightened the knot. She glared at Nicole, who was still astonished by her action. Jenna pointed a threatening finger at Nicole.

"You *will* pay for this!" Jenna growled as a tornado of fire spun up from their legs and slowly engulfed them. When the fire disappeared, the siblings had disappeared along with it. Evidence of their presence scattered across the roof.

Alex pushed himself off the ground after what seemed to be hours of silence. He walked to his gathered friends, his hands stinging with immense pain. He had seen it all, along with everyone else.

"How did you do that?" Alex asked.

"I...I have no idea," Nicole replied.

Jack appeared next to David, wiping perspiration that had gathered from the heat off his forehead.

"Did you see that?" Alex asked Jack.

"Indeed, I did," Jack replied.

"Do you know how she did that?"

"No, not yet. We shouldn't stay here for too long. I'm sure you would like to go check on your friend Ethan, correct?"

"Yeah, we should get going." Alex turned to Mark. "Can you walk, or do you need help?"

Mark's clothes were scorched black, and his hair was a mess, but otherwise he looked fine. His skin hadn't burned and other than his clothes he looked perfectly healthy.

"I'm fine. That fireball just took the wind out of me is all. I just want to get out of these clothes," Mark said as he touched the bottom of his shirt and some cracked pieces of brittle fell off. Jack looked at him with surprise but said nothing.

David's arm was slightly burnt but only on the very top layers of his skin and there was a large bruise around Nicole's neck. They were all too tired to fly and by now it was too dark to see where they were going anyway, so they all took the elevator down to the street.

The front door of the building led out onto the beach and the group walked along the sand in a sleepless daze, the exhaustion of the fight now catching up with them. Jack walked ahead of the group of teenagers with his gaze fixed on the sand. Alex ran ahead and slowed to a walk once he reached Jack's side.

"How are you holding up?" Alex asked.

"Holding up?" Jack turned to Alex questioningly.

"About Darrien," Alex replied softly.

"It's a part of life; death. It happens. No matter how much we don't want it to. My time to weep for his death has passed. He was an old man. He lived a long and full life. Now, we must focus on the present," Jack said somberly.

"Are we going to attend his funeral?"

"No. By the time they have it prepared we will have been long gone."

"What are they doing?" Brooke asked before Alex could inquire where they would be. She pointed a few hundred yards ahead of them toward the docks where people were loading crates, furniture, and other things onto ships.

"They are preparing. The barrier around this island will lift in five days," Jack answered.

After this they were all silent. The exhaustion that clouded their minds prevented them from seeing what that meant for them.

FORTY-SEVEN

When they arrived back at the bookstore, most of the crowd had dispersed. The people who had been extinguishing the fire at Darrien's place were cleaning up the burnt rubble that littered the streets. Ethan and his mother sat on the back of a floating boat painted white with a purple stripe. Ethan's mother had her arm around him; his head was leaning against her shoulder, his eyes closed. He was stroking Argent's fur, as the cat purred on his lap. A few men and women in dark purple jackets with a white cross on the back were attending to Ethan and his mother's wounds.

Alex walked over with the others close behind him. Argent saw him coming and leapt down from Ethan's lap and walked over to Alex.

"Let's see if we can heal those wounds of yours," said Jack who guided David and Alex to two women in jackets and explained to them what happened to Alex's hands and David's arm.

The women looked at the wounds and pulled a wrap of bandages out from behind the ambulance.

"Those are quite the burns there," one woman commented as she examined Alex's fingers. "What'd you do, throw your hands in the fire?"

"Something like that," Alex replied with a tired smile. The woman smiled back and held her hands a few inches above his. A white light emanated from them for a few minutes. As she did this, Alex could feel the pain in his hands fade away to a throb. Alex looked over and saw the other woman doing the same thing over David's arm. When she pulled away, Alex's hands looked clean, and any trace of the burns was gone.

"They may look healed, but you will have to wear some bandages around them for a while to keep them from getting infected and risk the chance of the burns coming back," the woman said as she wrapped the bandages around his hands. Once she finished and tied the bandages, a yellowish white light flashed off them as they shrunk to fit his hands perfectly, almost like a pair of gloves, before returning to their original color.

"Why'd it do that?" Alex asked as he flexed his hands.

"It makes it so they won't come off until you are fully healed, and the risk of infection no longer poses a threat."

"Thank you, ma'am," Alex said before she smiled and walked away.

David's arm was still being bandaged, so Alex looked around for the others. Mark, Brooke, and Nicole were sitting down on the curb, waiting to go back to the hotel. Jack was standing behind the floating boat talking to Ethan's mother. Alex walked over and pulled himself up next to Ethan. They sat there in silence, listening to Jack and his mother talk. Alex looked at Ethan's face, wondering if he could discern what he was thinking, but the light from the streetlamps didn't reach them.

"We're going to leave," Ethan finally said, shock evident in his voice.

"Leave where?" Alex asked.

"We're going to leave the island and move to the mainland. Mom is going to open up another bookstore somewhere in the U.S. She says she wants to go to the state of Washington. Apparently, I have an uncle up there. The only other family we've got."

"When are you leaving?"

"Next week, when the barrier lifts. Mom booked a hotel for us to stay in until then." Ethan's voice cracked at the end and he lapsed into silence.

"The stars are so bright tonight. I don't think I've ever seen that many in the city before."

Alex looked at Ethan only to find his neck craned upward, his gaze fixed on the sky. Alex looked up and was astonished to see so many stars, blinking through the black. Alex and Ethan sat there until Ethan's mom told him they had to go. Without another word, Ethan slid off the boat and walked beside his mother down the street.

"I think we should go as well," Jack said. Alex agreed and the two of them walked over to the curb where his friends were sitting. They were all leaning against one another, Nicole and David slowly dozing off. Jack and Alex shook them awake, and they all walked down the two blocks to the hotel.

When they woke up the next day, they had slept well through the morning and well into the afternoon. They each took turns in the bathroom to take a shower, if you could call that trickle of water a shower, then headed out to get some food in a numb, trance-like state. As they were walking through the lobby, the man behind the desk called Jack over.

"Are you Mr. Pandemonium?" the man asked.

"Yes," Jack replied.

"Yesterday morning a man asked me to give this to you. I meant to give it to you the other day, but I didn't see you come in." The man held out a large manila folder with Jack's name spread across it in fine black ink. Jack took the envelope and thanked the man before walking outside. The teens stood on the top steps and watched as Jack opened the folder.

"Who's it from?" Nicole asked.

"It doesn't say." Jack reached inside and pulled out a small slip of paper. It read; *Somehow, I have a feeling this will be the last time we will ever hear from one another. I do not understand why. It is only a feeling. Inside this envelope are six tickets to board* The Andrea *on the first day the barrier lifts. I hope you arrive at your destination safely and without much trouble. It has been a pleasure, my dear friend.*

Darrien

When Jack finished reading the letter, he looked at the five teens with a sad smile. "Thanks to Darrien, we will be on the first passenger ship out of here as soon as we can."

Jack reached inside the envelope and pulled out six white tickets with gold lettering and designs on the edges. "We all will."

Alex smiled as a spark of joy broke through the depressing haze brought on by last night's events. They were finally leaving this island, and his friends would be reunited with their families once again. But his life would never be the same. Alex's life wasn't something you would call normal, anymore. It was far from it.

ACKNOWLEDGEMENTS

First and foremost, I want to thank my mother and father. Mom, who listened to my never-ending rants and offered advice when I needed it, also helping to write countless emails. Jesan, who encouraged me to create this, and has given me invaluable advice on the creation of this story, and without whom I never would have thought to turn this idea into a book. Both helped me find and provide for services I needed to make this book real and have sacrificed so much of their time to help me. They have done so much for me, and none of this would be possible without them.

Thank you Paul Kocak, an amazing editor who made this book so much better and was patient with me the entire way; taking me in as his client despite my clear inexperience, encouraging me when I had my doubts.

Rachel Jenks, thank you for taking the time to meet with me and providing me much-needed and much-appreciated information about how to do all this when I had no idea what I was doing.

I want to thank my friends (you know who you are) for always being so excited about this creation of mine and giving me hope and support. It meant more to me than you know.

All of you played a part in the creation of this book, and I am so thankful for all that you have done!

Finally, I thank God for giving me the resources, the connections, and the ability to make this thing happen.